The Temple-goers

AATISH TASEER

VIKING

an imprint of

PENGUIN BOOKS

VIKING

Published by the Penguin Group

Penguin Books Ltd, 80 Strand, London WC2R 0RL, England

Penguin Group (USA) Inc., 375 Hudson Street, New York, New York 10014, USA

Penguin Group (Canada), 90 Eglinton Avenue East, Suite 700, Toronto, Ontario, Canada M4P 2Y3
(a division of Pearson Penguin Canada Inc.)

Penguin Ireland, 25 St Stephen's Green, Dublin 2, Ireland (a division of Penguin Books Ltd)

Penguin Group (Australia), 250 Camberwell Road, Camberwell, Victoria 3124, Australia
(a division of Pearson Australia Group Pty Ltd)

Penguin Books India Pvt Ltd, 11 Community Centre, Panchsheel Park, New Delhi – 110 017, India

Penguin Group (NZ), 67 Apollo Drive, Rosedale, North Shore 0632, New Zealand
(a division of Pearson New Zealand Ltd)

Penguin Books (South Africa) (Pty) Ltd, 24 Sturdee Avenue, Rosebank, Johannesburg 2196, South Africa

Penguin Books Ltd, Registered Offices: 80 Strand, London WC2R 0RL, England

www.penguin.com

First published 2010

1

Copyright © Aatish Taseer, 2010

An earlier version of the passage on pp. 38–42, beginning
'A few days later than the Ghalib Academy promised' and ending 'I didn't want to upset his calculations',
was first published in the author's Introduction to *Manto: Selected Stories* (Random House India, 2008).

The moral right of the author has been asserted

Set in Monotype Dante 12/14.75 pt
Typeset by Ellipsis Books Limited, Glasgow
Printed in Great Britain by Clays Ltd, St Ives plc

A CIP catalogue record for this book is available from the British Library

ISBN: 978-0-670-91850-8

www.greenpenguin.co.uk

'I will tell you a fact, gentlemen,' he went on in the same tone as before, that is, with extraordinary warmth, but at the same time he was virtually laughing, possibly even at his very words – 'a fact the observation and discovery of which I have the honor of ascribing to myself alone; at least, nothing has been said or written about it. The fact expresses the whole essence of Russian liberalism of the sort of which I am speaking. In the first place, what is liberalism, speaking generally, but an attack (whether justified or mistaken is another question) on the established order of things? That's so, isn't it? Well, my fact consists in this – that Russian liberalism is not an attack on the existing order of things, but is an attack on the very essence of our things, on the things themselves, not merely on the order; not on the Russian way, but on Russia itself . . . But at the same time, this is such a fact as has not existed or occurred anywhere at any time since the world began, not among any single people, and therefore this fact is incidental and may pass, I admit. There cannot be such a liberal anywhere else who would hate his very fatherland. How can we explain it among us? Why, by the same thing as before – that the Russian liberal is, as yet, not a Russian liberal; by nothing else, to my mind.'

The Idiot, Fyodor Dostoevsky

Prologue

It was just after dinner and on one of the news channels the murder was re-enacted. There was a clap of studio thunder on one side of the split screen, a flash of strobe lightning, the glint of a knife. A hooded figure, his clean-shaven face partly in shadow, pursues a fat girl through a keekar forest. Suspenseful music, punctuated by the crashing of cymbals, plays in the background. The darkened figure catches up with the girl; her eyes widen, her wet lips part in a scream. He plunges a knife into her body at various points. In the next scene, he cuts up her body with a kitchen knife, putting great handfuls of flesh into black bin bags, four in total. Then tying them together, he sets them afloat on a hyacinth-choked canal in whose dark water the red lights of a power station are reflected. On the other side of the split screen a passport-size picture of the girl flashes above the caption '1982–2008'. She's laughing, her milky, rounded teeth exposed. She seems so unsinkable. I could almost hear her saying, 'I'm twenty-six, running twenty-seven.'

I sat in my stepfather's study in Alibaug. It was a high, tree house-like room with ceiling-to-floor windows. Outside, the garden was still, the night punctured at even intervals by white path lights. Beyond the shadows cast by tall, fleshy plants was the sea. It came almost to the garden wall at night and its roar carried up to the room. I turned off the television and the various lamps in the room and made my way down a flight of modern wooden steps with no banister.

Downstairs, a sea breeze carrying cold currents made its way on to the tiled veranda. The Bombay winter. A deceptively mild wind for two weeks in the year, bringing clear skies and disease. The city was sometimes visible beyond the short stretch of water and its outline made Alibaug's mainland villages, with their pale yellow houses and red-tiled roofs, blackening in the sea air, seem like the island.

I sat down in a planters chair and called Sanyogita. There had been trouble between us in the past few days, but I thought the worst was over. Two days before she'd asked me not to call so much, then the following night she'd written, 'I am blessed to have you in my life but I need to fulfil the rest of it. You've been doing that for yourself for some time and you are an inspiration for having done it. I'm off to Mars now.' I had focused on her saying she was blessed to have me in her life and on the Mars reference, suggesting higher spirits. She only ever referred to interplanetary travel when she was in a good mood. But hearing her voice now, I realized I had misread her state of mind. She was in a taxi on her way somewhere, and frantic.

'It's not working, baby; it's not working.'

'Sanyogita, you can't end a two-year relationship on the telephone. And not in a cab.' It was an old technique: undercutting her good emotion with cold reason. She became quiet.

'I'll come,' I added.

I took her silence to mean consent, but she said, with uncharacteristic firmness, 'I won't call you for a while now. I'll need my time.'

I became agitated. 'Sanyogita, this is no way to end this. I'll come on the first flight tomorrow.'

She said something to the taxi driver. The interruption, though momentary, gave me my first intimation of life without her. Her voice returned, its timbre unstable, now strong, now sobbing faintly. Not so long ago, it would have irritated me. But wounded for the last time on my behalf, it felt like one more thing I had taken for granted.

'I'm going to hang up now,' she said abruptly.

'Sanyogita, listen . . .' I whispered, aware of a tremor in my own voice.

For a moment I held her attention.

'Why are you doing this?'

It was a foolish thing to say. Her reasons must have flooded back. She seemed to recall a formulation she had meant to use. 'My feelings have changed. I can't compete with the other intimacies in your life.'

When we hung up, my first thought was to cheat the panic that grew in me. It was not late; the night was bright; it would feel very long if I couldn't sleep. Like a man holding his breath, I went up to my room, got straight into bed and tried to sleep.

My mistake was to wonder what the date was. It was an unplanned admission of finality. No sooner had I plotted that point than my mind was prised open to other dates. Two years to the month nearly. A meeting in London. A year spent there, a happy year of work and study, of little-known restaurants, cinemas and bright international friends. Sanyogita was haunted by the happiness of that year. Then the year in Delhi, beginning in those hot months of flowers. The year when Aakash moved like a planet over our lives.

My sheets were warm, crushed; my bed was an alluvial mess.

I went downstairs. The lights of the Balinese fantasy house pierced me from every direction. They each had their barbs: the sharpness of the halogen spot; the sickly glare of the fluorescent path light; smoked glass and lizards on the wall. I poured myself a large whisky, lit a cigarette and sank into a planters chair on the veranda. But I was not a smoker and soon the fraudulence of the gesture defeated me. Then the phone calls began, to friends and family; repeated, abortive attempts at sleep; the hotness of the sheets; the impotence of air-conditioning; the sexual arousal of fear and panic; an orgasm before the glare of a computer at three a.m.

My last memory was of an orange moon, heavy and low, seeming not so much to sink as to slip over the water, fragment and float away.

★

3

I left the next morning. The road curled out from the coast to the jetty. We went past houses with open verandas and fairy lights; the foliage was bright and dense and encroaching.

At the jetty the sea was unseasonably rough. A row of pale clouds kept a purple, sepulchral sky in place. A ferry had trouble mooring. Its low white body crept up to the jetty's cement steps and was thrown back. Each time a chasm of greenish-brown water opened up. Women in pink and mauve saris wrapped twice about themselves shrieked. One man grabbed on to the ferry's second-storey railings, but then couldn't lift himself up and was nearly crushed against the jetty steps. At length he was rescued and the men watching laughed. Then again the wooden ferry and the barnacled jetty tried closing over the stretch of rough water. A column of nervous passengers crossed hurriedly. The jetty's cement pillars, showing exposed iron in places, cast gloomy shadows over the water racing between their legs.

On the ferry, Sanyogita's words sang in my head: 'I can't compete with the other intimacies in your life.' Their finality made what had felt like day-to-day life at the time now seem part of a chain of events. And many of the things I knew now, a feeling of waste, the destructiveness of the past few months, I hadn't known earlier. It was as if life had carried me along, anaesthetized up to a point, then channelled me out.

On the boat – the slowest there was – men in baggy trousers and polyester shirts clung to the railings, reading about the murder. Their soft, damp newspapers thrashed about in the wind, but they read on, in Marathi, in Hindi and English, stopping occasionally to consider the latest smudged images. And it was only now, with the perspective endings bring, that I could look beyond my particularity and see that I had been close to a story that had riveted a country.

The sea changed from green to brown; oily, rainbow patterns ran over its surface. Red-bottomed, rusting freighters, some with Russian and Arab names, came into view. Then tall white buildings and the pale red domes of the Taj Hotel. Bombay's mud-coloured water sloshed around us, bringing up plastic bottles and rose petals. We rocked in the brown water for a few minutes more, then gingerly disembarked. I was on the three p.m. flight to Delhi.

Part One

I

I had come to Delhi eleven months before to revise a novel. After college in America, I had lived for a couple of years in England, working as a reporter on an American news magazine. There I met an American journalist who read the novel I'd written in college and sent it along to an agent in New York. The agent wrote back a few days later, saying, 'Finished your novel this weekend and was mightily impressed. You are a wonderful writer – hyper-observant and able to convey real emotion . . . I was totally involved with the narrator's experience and the prose alone kept me riveted. Alas, the plot didn't develop enough and sort of veered off course for me when I least expected it . . . But a voice like yours comes along rarely and I would love to work with you on this, or any other book you are working on. It is worth fixing!' She also sent a separate editorial letter with a detailed list of suggested changes. I don't know if I really believed in the book; what I did know was that I wanted to leave Britain and return to India.

My mother had argued hard to make my stepfather pay for college in America, and more for her sake than his, I didn't want to return empty-handed. The agent was the ideal cover. My family in India didn't know much about the workings of publishing, but they knew about advances; everyone knew about advances. And just flashing the edge of this golden ticket before the eyes of my mother, who in any case wanted me back, was enough. A wider circle of friends and family was persuaded that my time abroad had not been misspent. I, in the meantime, signed a contract with the agent and told her I was leaving my job. This alarmed her. 'Go with your heart,' she wrote. 'Just remember there are no guarantees on advances (from passes, not interested to six-figure advances . . . everything is game), so take that out of the equation.' I did; and in less time than I thought possible, I found myself on one of the new Jet Airways flights from London to Delhi.

The reading lights in the cabin were icy white. In the darkness, they refreshed a childhood memory of playing with torches under blankets. The spotlit whiteness; the knobbed, dark blue headrest that could be adjusted into a gorge for the base of the neck; the personal screens in economy; and the staff – young, polite college graduates – drifting by in blue and yellow, offering red wine as if they'd stolen it from their parents' bar; these were the thrills of India's first private international airline.

I ordered some wine and watched a new film. It was about four college friends who lead an idle life, drinking beer, skateboarding, riding fast bikes in an old Delhi ruin called the 'classroom'. They are discovered by Sue, a young English girl trying to make a documentary about a group of Indian freedom fighters executed in the last days of the Raj by her grandfather, a British army officer. The grandfather had left behind a journal in which he had written of the courage the men showed and his own disenchantment with the colonial enterprise. The empire over, his granddaughter, six decades later, wants to use the group of young friends as actors in her documentary. But they resist her. And it turns out that their idle life and Western ways are more like a fear of life, a disillusionment with modern India. In a stolen, romantic moment, one of the boys says to Sue in Hinglish, 'It's been five years since I left university, but I'm here only. I just want to stay in university. On campus people know me; I have status. People say DJ will make something of himself. But out in the world, better DJs than me have been ground down in that crowd of millions.' Another says, 'What freedom, Sue? Have you seen the state of this country? No one believes this bullshit.' But Sue prevails; the documentary is made; the young men begin to rediscover their history. They travel around India; they shoot the documentary; they run through fields, tearing off their T-shirts; sepia sequences of the documentary, with them playing the historical parts, are spliced into the film.

It must have been the altitude, the wine, or maybe just home-sickness, but I suddenly found that I was crying. A kind of frightened euphoria at seeing India like this seized me. I muttered indistinct words to myself, tears ran down my face, my jaw hardened.

I reopened the screen and finished the film. It ended in carnage and nihilism. Just as the group of friends rediscover their country, a fighter-pilot friend of theirs dies when his MiG crashes. They watch it live on TVDelhi at a tea stall. The Minister of Defence, instead of taking responsibility for having bought bad parts, blames the pilot for the crash. This is too much for the group, so recently restored to idealism. They decide to assassinate the minister. One crime of passion and patriotism excites others and the film ends in further assassinations, patricides and the takeover of a radio station. In the closing scenes, commandos besiege the station where the friends are holed up, explaining their bloody deeds to the nation and welcoming callers. One by one – and on air – each of them is killed off; they bleed, laugh and sing as they die. Sue, in a taxi, listens to the broadcast.

I put away the screen and tried to sleep.

When I next opened my eyes, two flight attendants were walking past. They spoke in the dawn whispers that precede waking up the cabin for landing. Through a half-oval window, past dark sleeping figures, a thin fire burned precisely along the edge of a colourless sky. One of the attendants was a young woman with brown lipstick and hair held firmly in place by a wide clip. Her colleague was a tall man with darkening circles round his soft, attentive eyes. They were courteous, ambitious and bilingual. How different they were from the Indian Airlines ogres of my childhood. Those women with their boiled sweets and matronly tread, the stench of stove and state woven into their clothes, weary at serving men other than their husbands . . . were they the mothers of these bright, beautiful children?

Peering out of the white light at the two attendants, I attracted their attention.

'Sir, may I serve you with anything?' the man with dark, soft eyes asked.

The woman attendant smiled benignly, like a politician's wife.

The cabin lights came on.

'Lime water, please.'

'Sir, right away.'

The attendants went off.

I was flicking through the last of the channels when, a few seats down from me, I noticed a large woman with black, dimpled arms transfixed by what she saw on her screen. Thin clouds raced across the video display, then a patchwork of fields in changing shades of green appeared, dotted with cement roofs, swimming pools and corrugated-iron sheds. Pale quarries with green water and coppery edges came into view. The wandering eye of the camera caught slum roofs, a blue and pink polythene waste dump and brownish, algal rivers choked with hyacinth. A red earth road ran like a vein through the land. The widening bulge of train tracks, the yellow and black of taxis and, at last, the striped walls of Delhi airport.

The camera pulled the land closer and I saw what I loved most about Delhi: its trees. They managed a surprising unity, declaring themselves the first line to touch the city's white sky. Not so white today. As the land came close, I could see a dust storm rage, blurring the camera's vision. It stole through the trees like a spirit, ready to pounce on the city below.

Delhi vanished, the camera swung down and the runway's bumpy, oil-stained surface came into view. The large dark woman, watching peacefully until now, let out a cry.

At home, in my mother's study, Chamunda sat behind a silver tea set in a green chiffon sari. When she saw me, she extended a sharp, jewelled hand and clutched me to her breast; I tried to reach to touch her feet. 'Welcome home, baba, welcome home,' she said to the tune of may-you-have-a-long-life.

Then pulling away as if overcome with emotion, she poured

me a piped column of tea. In her other hand she held the silver strainer's handle. One wrist had green bangles on it, the other a Cartier watch and two inches of red religious threads, tight and damp from a shower.

'You're wearing so many,' I said, amazed at the thickness of the red threads.

She glanced at them as she finished pouring the tea. 'Politics, baba, all from politics.'

'Oh, of course. Congratulations. How long has it been now?'

'Nearly four years. Elections next year, baba. I want you to come and help me. Your mother will come too. It'll be hectic, but we'll have some fun. They're early in the year, so the weather will be lovely.'

Chamunda was my mother's best friend, and my girlfriend Sanyogita's aunt. She had been married into a small princely state, but her husband had deserted her just months after their marriage. She had joined politics as a young bride, defeated her husband in his own constituency and risen steadily. She was a member of the legislative assembly in the 1980s, an MP in the 1990s, a junior minister in 2000. Then four years ago, she had gone back to the state as its chief ministerial candidate and won. It had made her the Chief Minister of Jhaatkebaal, a small break-away state on the border of Delhi, important for its twin satellite cities, Sectorpur and Phasenagar. I had no idea what she was doing in my mother's flat.

'Chamunda massi, Ma is in Bombay, right?'

'Yes, in Bombay. She asked me to be here to welcome you home.'

This was doubtful. Chamunda was busy and selfish; I couldn't imagine her welcoming Sanyogita home, let alone me. And besides, I'd spoken to my mother on the way into town and she'd said nothing about Chamunda. I noticed that the edges of her hair were wet.

'Can you imagine,' she said, handing me a cup of tea, 'me in politics? Who would've thought it?'

13

'Is it difficult, being a woman and everything?'

'Yes, very,' she replied, pleased to be asked. 'But there are advantages.'

'Such as?'

'I like to take advantage of, exploit one might even say' – she smiled, showing little teeth and mischief – 'the very things that make it difficult to be a woman in politics. So for instance, I always dress the part. I always wear beautiful saris, never any ethnic crap. I always wear make-up and jewellery. I make a point to look like the Maharani of Ayatlochanapur. And if I'm talking to some bureaucrats or opposition leaders, or even treacherous elements in my own party, and my pallu accidentally falls . . .' She pushed the green chiffon end of her sari off her shoulder to demonstrate what she meant. Her cleavage showed soft and brown, dimpled in places. 'Then I may let it stay fallen for a few moments till I've finished my point and sweep it up when I'm done.' In one motion, she swung it back over her shoulder and the breasts were once again half-concealed behind a papery chiffon screen. 'And inevitably the response in these cases to what I've been saying is . . .' She paused, altering her accent to a strong Indian one and moving her head from side to side. '"Yes, yes, madam," or an emphatic "No, no, madam, of course not."' Chamunda chuckled wickedly, her pert comic-book lips arched. 'Or, I'll lean forward and let the pallu drop, very slightly.' She did; her breasts collected warmly, and though they remained hidden, the cleavage became long and dark. A gold chain with a Kali pendant dangled hypnotically in front of the tunnel.

Then suddenly, she was in a rush.

'Baba, I can't stay long. You might have heard, I'm having a small rebellion in my state. Bloody Jats. I have to go back and deal with it.'

'Jats?'

'It's a sub-caste. They want reservations in government jobs and schools. I tell you, the Congress Party has let a monster out of the bag with this reservations business. Women, dalits, scheduled castes, Muslims, now Jats . . . Soon the Brahmins and Kshattriyas will be saying, what about us? Then we can go ahead and carve up the country and no one will have to do a day's work again.

'I can't lose the election even before you and Sanyogita have come to stay with me. But enough about politics, tell me about your book.'

'No, nothing, massi. There's just interest in a revised version. Now I have to actually fix it.'

She smiled placidly.

'And your relationship with Sanyogita, all good there?'

'Yes, very good.'

'She's moved back too, you know.'

'I know.'

'Does she know what she wants to do?'

'She wants to write too.'

Chamunda looked serious. 'It's a racket, this writing business. You're writing a book, my friend Jamuni is writing a book, now Sanyogita wants to write a book . . .'

'What's Jamuni writing about? She hasn't written anything in years.'

'I don't really know. She wants to do a funny book, a rehash of her earlier book, but about Indian ostentation.'

'And Sanyogita?'

'She doesn't know yet.'

Chamunda bit at a cuticle.

'What's the matter?'

'No, nothing. Nothing.'

'Come on, Chamunda, tell me.'

'It's just that these girls, you know, these privileged girls, like I once was, I suppose, and like Sanyogita is – they feel that because these are modern times, the world owes them a job, a career. Your mother and I, we never thought this way. If our husbands hadn't both been such rotters, we would have been quite happy to settle down and produce a brood of children.

We worked because we had to work. You want to learn something about women in India? Learn this: India is a country where women work right from the top to the bottom, but they work because they have to work. And it's the best kind of work. Always be suspicious of these rich and middle-class girls who go off to college in the West and come back feeling that the world owes them a living just because they're modern women. I say this about my niece too and I'm saying it because you're a smart boy, you understand these things; I want you one day to marry her, but don't put up with too much of this silliness.'

'Come on, massi, she can't stay home and make me lunch and dinner.'

'Tch,' she spat with irritation. 'Is that what I'm saying? Do I look like a woman who would say something so stupid? No. All I'm saying is that you're setting out to be a writer, you've worked hard at being a journalist, you've secured a book deal –'

'An agent.'

'Whatever. All I'm saying is I don't like the sound of my darling niece Sanyogita, who is basically just following you back, also wanting to write.'

There was a knock on the door. Shakti, my mother's servant, came in with a cordless phone. She took it from him. 'Yes, yes, Raunak Singh. Yes. Tell them I'll be there very soon.' She punched the lime-green button and looked absently at me, as if for a moment forgetting where she was.

'Right, baba. I'm off. Come and see me soon with your mother, or with Sanyogita. Welcome back.' With this she was gone, leaving a trail of tuberose perfume behind her.

I wandered about my mother's flat for under an hour. Its familiarity, its inevitability, far from comforting me, oppressed me, seeming to force our old association. It made my few foreign possessions – a red Old Spice deodorant stick, an electric toothbrush, a Lush soap – appear out of place, as though I'd brought unwelcome friends to dinner. 'It *is* my mother. This flat is my mother,' I said, almost aloud. 'I'll have to scrape her off the walls if I'm to live here.' And so, just hours after I arrived, I escaped the flat for Sanyogita's.

2

The hot months before summer were months of flowering trees in Delhi. The silk cotton, a stony, shadeless tree, was among the first to bloom. I passed one on the way to Sanyogita's flat. Its fleshy coral flowers had appeared like women's brooches on its thorn-covered branches. Though I could have gone through Lodhi Gardens, I chose instead to take Amrita Shergill Marg, a laburnum-lined crescent that ran along one boundary of the park, connecting my flat with Sanyogita's.

The storm I thought I had seen from the plane turned out to be only a wind. It tore through the city that morning. Many of the trees were losing their leaves even as new ones grew. The wind swept away their old leaves, littering the streets with an autumnal scene. Bees and ladybirds crawled through the debris. The leaves that remained, though new, were in some trees brown before they were green. So it seemed like spring and autumn had come together in one afternoon.

The quiet on Amrita Shergill Marg was broken at even intervals by the tinkle of a cycle bell and the wail of a man in a lilac shirt collecting junk from house to house. At the end of Amrita Shergill Marg was a busy main road. Black and yellow taxis, now with green stripes across their flank that read CNG, rumbled past, their colours clashing with the black and yellow of the lane divider. Everything beyond was the post-independence Delhi of colonies; Jorbagh was among the first of these.

I entered through a tall iron gate and walked past low white houses with clean simple lines and small lawns. On my right, there was a narrow lane under a dense arbour. The cool and shadows of that lane had transfixed me as a child. I used to come here with my mother in our green Suzuki. Halfway down it was

Chocolate Wheel, where a jovial woman sold bread and fudge brownies. Ahead was the Jorbagh florist, still selling yellow gladioli. The pan shop. The Jorbagh colony market.

Sanyogita's flat was on one corner of a U-shaped garden with houses on three sides. Her building was white with a narrow plaster screen built into its façade. It ran down the building's entire length and a pink bougainvillea hung like a hive from its floral hollows. Outside there was a single dark mango tree with long twisting leaves and greenish-yellow flowers. I saw Sanyogita on her balcony watering plants. She hadn't grown up in Delhi; she was from Bombay. And to see her in so distinct a Delhi scene, I felt the special joy people feel for the migrant who masters their ways. Sanyogita, as if aware of her triumph, blushed when she realized that I was standing below.

The white marble stairs were dim and dirty. A green stone skirting followed them up to Sanyogita's flat; blue and red wires swelled out of an electricity box; the banister shuddered.

Sanyogita had planned a surprise. I saw her, with her back against the door, as soon as I reached the top of the stairs. She wore tattered tracksuit bottoms and a faded T-shirt. Her wavy black hair was twined into a rope and pulled forward.

'Baby,' she breathed.

She was large and shy and beautiful. That's not to say she was fat, she wasn't; but there was a prominence about her bones and joints, and a softness in her limbs and breasts. When she hugged you, you could feel her architecture. She had broken her thigh bone as a child, skiing in Kashmir. A man had crashed into her, leaving her crumpled in the snow. She had a scar from where they put pins into her leg. It was a great smooth-backed caterpillar crawling over her pelvic bone. Which itself was so prominent, and strong, that whenever I saw the scar I felt the force of the collision.

The flat inside, almost as if the squalor of the staircase were a deliberate part of the aesthetic, was a sanctuary. Its high ceilings, its rooms overlooking a secluded balcony, its shade and screens of twisted matting hanging like wet tobacco in front of the windows, faintly scented and cool, were like a preparation for summer. Though much of the flat was still empty, an entire wall of white shelves had been filled with colourful paperbacks. Seagrass carpets and runners with dark blue borders had taken their places in the bare rooms and corridors. So even empty, the flat seemed ready to be lived in.

Sanyogita led me by the hand down one of these shaded corridors. Past black metal grilles, I could see a small terrace with vine roses, potted frangipani and giant yellow and maroon dahlias. We came to a brightly polished double door with an old-fashioned bolt and a brass Godrej lock. Sanyogita took out a key she had kept pressed in her hand. It went loosely in and the lock fell open. We entered a long narrow room, the most furnished I had seen so far. It had a thin red rug, a black wood and cane chair and a maroon leather-topped desk with a green banker's lamp on the far end. A window on one side overlooked the garden terrace. Sanyogita, standing on the balls of her feet, watched me take in the room.

On a wall covered with bare white shelves, one shelf contained new books. There was a dictionary of Islam, something called *Infidels* by a Cambridge professor and bathroom books: Oscar Wilde's epigrams, a Second World War American soldier's pocket guide to France, *Elements of Style*. On the desk's maroon surface, marching along its gold border, was a family of blue and white porcelain elephants. I picked one up.

'Be careful, baby,' Sanyogita squealed on his behalf. 'He's the smallest!'

I sat down at the desk, slowly comprehending the surprise. Sanyogita watched with tense delight. At length I opened one of the desk's drawers. The lamplight obliquely struck a neat pile of letterheads and envelopes. They were held in place by a paper band that read: 'Alastair Lockhart. Fine writing papers, etc., Walton Street, London SW3'. And on the thick cream-coloured paper, under a faintly raised margin, it said Aatish Taseer in burnt red letters.

'Baby, a present for your book,' Sanyogita said, slipping her hand over my collarbone.

The room was the surprise.

She didn't have one to spare; she had writing ambitions of her own; and though her flat was barely ready, she had made me a present of a study. I was speechless; it was the nicest thing anyone had ever done for me.

Sanyogita's face shone with my delight. She became organizational: 'Vatsala could make you coffee. I've just bought her one of those Italian things.'

'Who's Vatsala?' I asked, trying to recover myself.

Sanyogita's eyes brightened. 'Vatsala, baby, the little goblin who brought me up?' She stuck out her teeth and flared her eyes.

Vatsala Bai! I did remember her: she was a devious little widow in white who had moved with Sanyogita to Delhi. Her family had been with Sanyogita's for centuries. She was devoted to her and suspicious of me, always taking every opportunity to remind me of how old and grand Sanyogita's family was. We stayed in the room a few minutes more, then Sanyogita locked it and pressed the brass key into my hand with a kiss.

The flat, but for one small terrace and drawing room, had its back to the park. The bedroom was still bare, but for a low bed. Cane blinds shut the room off from the terrace and a modern steel light, with a salon drier head, drooped over the bed like a flower.

Sanyogita sat on the white lace bedcover, her toes hanging off the edge. She was full of Delhi news. She told me of my old friends, her new friends, gay men she'd had lunch with, fashion parties and the agitation in Chamunda's state. It was Holi in a few days; she broke the sad news to me that my mother's sister was not having her party this year, as the metro had claimed her house. She'd organized instead for us to go to the *Times of India* party with Ra.

'Ra?'

'Ra. Rakesh. My friend the jewellery designer.'

She wiggled her head. Two earrings dangled happily. They were long, with a line of glassy, rectangular diamonds set around a many-faced greyish stone in a paisley shape. There was a single, prominent ruby at the ear. The effect of that colour, like a sudden red light on a misty day, was startling.

'He gave them to me as a present,' she said. 'You know, that way people see them around as well. He's just getting started, but he's good, I think.'

'Have I ever met him?'

'I think so. Short, squishy, like a pincushion? Adorable.'

'Maybe. And Delhi? What's been going on here? Any new things?'

'Delhi? Everything's new. New roads, new buses, new metro, new restaurants, new neighbourhoods, new money, everything except new people.'

Then I saw that she felt bad. This was not the arrival she had planned. Our stilted conversation seemed to trouble her. She began flipping through the pages of the *Times of India*. Her hair fell around her. I thought of the study, and then I felt bad; I saw that she might have wanted to make love.

I got up from where I lay at the head of the bed and crouched behind her. For a few minutes we sat like that, like two pods about to hatch; I read the paper over her shoulder. There was a picture of the new green buses. Their orange electronic displays transformed their destinations. Saket, Rajouri Gardens, Sector-pur and Phasenagar, running across a black screen in English letters, seeming suddenly like international places, places people ought to know of. The passengers, once just a crowd, became distinct in the bright modern buses, with their sunny yellow grab handles. In the background was a weary colossus from the old days containing distressed passengers. It was grey and yellow with deep scratches along its flank and an exhaust pumping out brown smoke.

Some bureaucrats had decided that the new buses should have bus lanes. They imported whole a model from Bogotá. It advised that bus lanes be driven through the middle of crowded arteries. And so blue lanes, with little brushed-steel bus stops appearing at even intervals down their length, had been threaded through long stretches of roaring traffic. But what had worked in Bogotá was not working in Delhi. The crowds that mob the bus when it approaches in Delhi blocked traffic. The cars, already squeezed for space, were further deprived of a lane. They refused to adhere to the new rules. Young boys with orange vests and flashing batons were hired to enforce the new system. There were delays into the night. The picture showed a late-evening scene in which a car owner was abusing a policeman. The car's headlights shone in his face. It was dark, haggard, on the verge of breakdown.

I was still looking at this scene of frustration when Sanyogita ran her fingertips along the edge of my face. I felt her body easily through her faded clothes. It was broad and soft, slightly damp. Her fig perfume mixed with Delhi smells of food and grime. I kissed her shoulder and came near something stronger.

'Baby's hard,' she said with laughter and surprise.

I hated it when she laughed in these moments.

'Why don't we go to the big room?' I said.

'You want to!'

'Yes.'

We walked to it through the corridors, reaching for each other in the afternoon gloom.

We made love simply and quickly in that outside room, overlooking the mango tree. She felt big and roomy. I longed to have her close around me, for there to be more friction on the edges. She was also dissatisfied. When I was finished, she climbed on top of my thigh. We did this often. I held her as she rocked up and down my thigh, moaning and muttering, 'Baby, it's so good,' as though I was somehow responsible for what was little more than masturbation. Finished myself and oversensitive, they were minutes of disgust for me. When it was over again, we lay there with our legs spread out, the sun

23

coming in. I felt fat. I squeezed my stomach into a mound with both hands.

'I'm going to lose all this.'

'Why, baby? You're not fat.'

'Perhaps, but now that I'm here, I'm going to join a gym and get a trainer.'

'Really? What else are you going to do now that you're here?'

'Get an Urdu teacher and learn to read my grandfather's poetry.'

'Baby! I didn't know your grandfather was a poet. The turbaned gentleman who was in the army?'

'No, not him. My father's father. He died when my father was six.'

'Oh.'

Sanyogita didn't like hearing about my father. She felt that his absence from my life was an unspoken source of pain whose emotional consequences she had inherited. To speak of it casually was almost to belittle the wrong she felt he had done my mother and me. She could be unforgiving in these matters.

I had thought I would return to my mother's flat that evening, but Sanyogita dissuaded me.

'Yes, stay here, baby,' she said. 'I don't know what you're doing staying in my aunt's sex pad anyway.'

'What?'

'OK, this is totally confidential, and comes from my mother, who you know hates my aunt, but she told me that Chamunda uses your mother's flat to meet lovers.'

'What lovers?'

'She has tons. There's one in particular whom everyone calls the "French lieutenant".'

'Does my mother know about this?'

'Of course, baby. Your mother's the fixer.'

'Fuck off.'

Sanyogita laughed out loud, then smiled thoughtfully as if she'd said something with more truth in it than she'd intended.

'I think it's great. If I was a high-profile politician, I'd like my close girlfriends to make sure I had some fun in later life, especially in this hypocritical society.'

'Well, it's settled, then.'

'What?'

'I'm never going back.'

'Don't! I'll tell Vatsala to send for your bags.'

3

'Junglee?'

'Yes, yaar,' the voice boomed down the telephone. 'It's a very sweet place. Not too expensive and the trainers are damn hot. I used to go myself in the promiscuous days.'

'And now?'

'Not so much now. Hubby doesn't like it. What to do?' She laughed uproariously. 'I was a big slut, but just a one-man woman now. So sad! No?'

Mandira was a Bombay friend of Sanyogita's now married in Delhi. Her father had died when she was a teenager and she'd had a difficult transition into adult life, namely a string of bad relationships through which Sanyogita had been a constant support. She was one of the people whom Chamunda had in mind when she sometimes said of Sanyogita, 'She likes birds with broken wings.' And it was Mandira who recommended Junglee when I was looking for gyms in the area.

In the days after I moved in with Sanyogita, I became anxious about routine. I had never worked as a writer before. I was back in the place where I grew up, supposedly writing about another place. I was worried that my ideas would slip away from me. I sometimes woke up with nightmares about having to call the agent in New York with the news that I had gone blank.

My imagined routine consisted of waking up at seven; being at my desk by eight; working till one, then having lunch. After that, I would sleep for half an hour, read in English till three, then from three to five read my grandfather's poetry in Urdu. (I still hadn't found a teacher but had spoken to someone at the Ghalib Academy, a crumbling, art-deco building with pink walls and smelly carpets, who promised me a teacher would call in the next few days.) At six, I would either do yoga with Sanyogita in the flat or go for a walk in Lodhi Gardens. I wanted to be in bed by ten or eleven. I refused to go out at night until I had made a start with the revisions.

But a few days into the routine, I realized there was a flaw. The exercise was too late and too little. By lunchtime I was longing for release. Sanyogita was doing errands and Vatsala buying vegetables when I stepped out from the study into the noon emptiness of the flat and decided to call Mandira about a gym.

Junglee was in Sundar Nagar, and like Jorbagh, an early post-independence colony. I had known it as a child for its antique shops where I had also come with my mother. I called Uttam, my mother's driver of many years, a gap-toothed Inspector Clouseau lookalike. He was downstairs a few minutes later.

We took a busy road past one edge of Lodhi Gardens, then another along the edge of the Delhi Golf Club, also with tombs dotting its putting greens and bunkers. We passed the Oberoi Hotel, the Blind School and a purple domed tomb marooned in traffic before Sundar Nagar appeared.

Its two- and three-storey houses were ranged, like Jorbagh's, round gardens with pale thin grass. A warm breeze made scraps of paper and heaps of dust race over the surface of the road. Uttam turned right and went down a grimy alley. Blackened cauldrons from a restaurant lay in the middle of the road along with groceries in white polythene bags. A man stacked cold Cobra beers into a fridge.

Uttam was staring longingly at them when I indicated to him to stop.

'Here?'

'Yes. I shouldn't be more than an hour. Have lunch and come back.'

I got out in front of a brushed-steel door. Painted on it was a pair of angry red eyes, scowling at the chaos of the little alley. A Nepalese security man in a light and dark blue uniform stood outside, holding open the door. Cold, incense-filled air tumbled out.

The light inside was dim but white. When my eyes adjusted, I saw dark plywood steps leading up. On the first landing a terracotta Ganesh basked in a fluorescent alcove. On my right, there were large framed pictures of shirtless movie stars.

At the next landing, a priest in white and gold prepared offerings in a steel tray. He stood between a line of red bulbs in clear plastic orbs and a temple on the reception desk with an orange porcelain Ganesh. There were fresh flowers and burning sticks of incense.

The priest rang a little bell and muttered prayers rapidly. He waved a brass lamp in a circular movement, its smoky yellow flame cowering in the blast from the air-conditioner, before the deity. Then he raced across the gym's rubber floor and tied a charm of chillies and lemons to a cross-trainer. He had returned to his silver tray and begun another cycle of chanting and tying when, on the way to a treadmill, a trainer in black stopped him. He gave the trainer a cautioning look. Loud music played in the background; the trainer, bobbing lightly, irreverently mouthed the words of a Jay-Z song.

My appearance at the top of the stairs gave the trainer his chance. He moved the priest aside and came up to greet me.

'Hello, sir. Welcome to Junglee. How may I help you?'

I assumed from his welcome that he spoke English. But when I asked him to show me the gym in English, his fluency vanished. A cold formality entered his manner. It was as if the English song and the greeting were part of a rehearsed role, creating the illusion of affability. In Hindi, he was intense and restless.

His skin was dark, dark to his gums. His colour was what Manto describes as blackish wheat. It meant that a paler second skin ran under a dark patina. The fineness of his bones, his large, mud-coloured eyes and small, slightly hooked nose, along with the fullness of his dark, faintly pinkish lips, gave me an intuitive sense of high caste.

He noticed me looking at him, but focusing at once on me, on the priest, on the other trainers, on a half-dozen people exercising in Junglee, he filed away the observation without a word.

The priest in the meantime made his way back to the reception desk. The trainer watched him as though about to strike a fly. And just as he was skittering towards the preacher curls machine, armed with a charm, the trainer grabbed him. The priest made a show of his arrest, contorting and shaking his fine-fingered hand. He ignored the trainer, appealing instead to the deity, then to the gym's ponytailed owner. The trainer draped his short, powerful arm over the priest's frail shoulders with mock affection.

'You see this?' he said, lifting up the thick rope of red and black religious threads, entwined with silver chains, round his neck. 'You see these?' he said, flashing a pearl, a meanly cut ruby and a diamanté band on his wrist. 'And you see this?' He took out a single white thread from deep within his black T-shirt. The priest looked at all of these things like a child shown treasure. 'So you understand then. I'm a Brahmin too. Now, go and do your dramas elsewhere and let those of us who are really working work.' The ponytailed owner had disappeared, and the priest, perhaps taking this as a sign of disfavour, began putting his devotional equipment away into a black and neon green bag.

The trainer gazed intently at a Hindi newspaper. A smile ran over his face. He seemed to arrange his thoughts. His dark, pinkish lips flowered with amusement.

'Pandit ji, there's a photo of one of my clients in today's paper. Would you like to see?'

The priest looked bitterly at him.

The trainer held up the paper for everyone to see. Below its red masthead was a painting of Shiva. It was a popular rendering of the god astride a white bull with matted hair and a trident, a tiger skin covering his loins. But in place of his once soft, gently protruding stomach, there was a blue six-pack. His sprawling chest showed firm but discrete pecs. And a bulging vein, like the trainer's, coiled down from his bicep over his forearm.

'And all without supplements.' The trainer laughed. 'Protein yes, but no anabolics.'

A few trainers guffawed, some clients laughed openly, the ponytailed owner reappeared on the stairs, smiling indulgently at the scene. The trainer, his joke successful, now warmed to the priest, putting his arm round him again. The priest smiled weakly. Junglee resounded with happy laughter.

Shiva's new body focused my attention more closely on the trainer's. Its proportions, the small of the back pulled up as if by a hook, the narrowness of the waist next to the prominence of the chest and thighs, the large arms but fashionable slimness, a shaped body and yet so clearly not one of a bodybuilder, seemed somehow to imply a knowledge of the world: of the Internet and TV serials; of protein milkshakes and supplements; of Shakira and Beyoncé; of drinking perhaps and sex before marriage. It set him apart, in the values it contained, from millions of thin-waisted figures in baggy polyester trousers and smoothly worn chappals who roamed Delhi's streets. It gave him a solidity and weight that could not easily be dismissed.

Lost in these thoughts, I heard his voice through a fog of white fluorescent light tinged red.

'Sir, sir,' he said, as if I had been holding things up, 'would you like to see the gym now?'

I nodded absent-mindedly and we began making our way through weight machines with their pink, yellow and orange plates. On the back of the trainer's T-shirt were Junglee's red glowering eyes. His tracksuit bottoms were of a slippery, black material with silver piping running down the side. Before going upstairs, the trainer looked at himself in the mirror. He had looked every few seconds so far. It was more than a look of vanity. He looked with such depth that he seemed really to be facing his reflection. It was hard not to look for what he looked for.

Junglee turned out to be a small gym with two floors, mirrored walls and dark plywood cornices, from which red light escaped. At this hour the main clientele were housewives and out-of-shape male models.

We saw the 'men's wet area': lockers, 'loos', a changing room and a small slimy steam room. We passed the women's. The trainer said with a short laugh that he couldn't show me that wet area.

The second floor was fuller than the first. Young women on treadmills held mobile phones in their jewelled fingers.

The trainer's arrival spread tension through the floor. The women trainers, small, slim girls in tracksuits, scattered to their stations, whispering cautiously.

'Cardio,' the trainer said, with a wave of his hand.

'What's got into all of them?' I asked.

'They don't like me,' he replied in English, almost with pity in his voice.

'Why?'

'I don't know,' he said, switching back to Hindi. 'They're always talking behind my back, carrying tales to the bosses. I've never said one word to them.'

Our tour over, we walked past a group of men in T-shirts like the trainer's, but grey to mark their being sous-trainers of some sort. They were small men, very dark, with bad teeth. To see them was to be made aware of what the trainer might have been without his good, clean teeth, his attentiveness to fashion, his rehabilitated body, and the confidence that came with these things. He spoke to them like an officer inspecting a regiment. They beamed as he went past and for some the thrill of being spoken to left them dumbstruck. I had a feeling the trainer wanted me to see his popularity among them.

Only Moses the Christian – Mojij, as I later discovered, to his friends – a tall, slim sub-trainer with longish hair, had the courage to make conversation. We were standing near the gym's tinted windows. Below were the antique shops round the pale grass square. A myna sat fatly, unmoving, on the tin ledge. Moses smiled at us and without a word pointed at the bird. The trainer looked puzzled, then smiled back. With great difficulty, he managed to say in English, 'She is pregnant.' Moses choked with laughter. The trainer, again in English, said, 'That is the labour room.' Moses bent double. He lacked the trainer's good looks but had a Christian's comfort with English. 'I'll inform the father,' he said. The trainer, now really feeling the pressure of so much English, said, 'Who is name is Praful.' The two exploded with laughter. They looked at a tall, reedy sub-trainer, who smiled frailly back as though used to being the butt of their jokes.

Then the trainer suddenly became serious.

'Sir, would you like to try out the gym before you make up your mind?'

I decided I would and thanked him for the tour.

'I'm downstairs if you need anything.'

This line, delivered in English like the first, sounded rehearsed.

I finished a short cardio warm-up and went down to the weights floor.

I watched the trainer with one eye and felt myself similarly watched. His jokes continued as if one of the duties of charisma. Two or three young men had come into the gym. The trainer moved rapidly between all three of them, muttering numbers to himself. As the sets advanced, inspiration seized him. His eyes seemed to fix on some distant goal. Like a painter reaching for new colours, he ordered the men who worked below him to bring him plates. When the clients' muscles failed under him, he threw off the coloured plates in levels, imploring them to continue, even if only with a bare iron bar. And with repetitions, he pushed them to the heights he had wished them to attain with weight. If left untended too long, the clients called to him, their voices filled with urgency. The trainer ran back with encouragement: 'Come on, man. You'll give me two more.' Then suddenly, he withdrew support. The clients, now feeling narcotic levels of fatigue, asked for more. But the trainer, by then aware of satisfactions beyond theirs, said, 'No. Done done-a-done done.'

After the sets, he rested on the edge of a red exercise bench, dropping his arms forward. It made his shoulders seem long and expansive. His eyes rolled back and his eyelashes sank under their own weight. The gym had a large flat-screen television. It played a loop of half-a-minute-long programmes, horoscopes and fashion shows. At present, two animated girls called Kitty and Witty were on. The trainer watched with half-closed eyes. Witty, a blonde in pink, said to Kitty, the brunette, 'What is the laziest mountain in the world?'

'I don't know,' Kitty replied.

The trainer watched with one eye.

'Mount Ever-rest!'

He was mystified, then a moment later his laughter rang through the gym.

I was doing some light weights on my own. I didn't really know anything about them, but someone had once taught me to do sets of fifteen, twelve and ten repetitions. I felt the trainer watch me as I walked over to the bench press. It was not the brief, suspicious look from before, but a frank, open gaze. It reminded me of the way he looked at himself in the mirror. Then the music changed. A Hindi pop song came on with a single English line: 'I will always love you, all my life.' The trainer, still looking at me, sang with great feeling, forming every word carefully. He seemed to take pleasure in the illusion of fluency, in the long first line and the rapid 'all my life'. He was totally absorbed in his role, but when the song ended, he was no longer a romantic hero; he was Shah Rukh Khan belting out the words of a super hit song. The trainer pressed his forearms between his legs, moved his upper body forward, bobbing on the balls of his feet. As the music quickened, he twisted his forearm in a downward movement, uncoiling a dark vein.

When I reached twelve repetitions, my arms began to fail. I looked up in time to see the trainer swing one leg over the bench and yell, 'Thirdeen, fordeen . . .' He had been counting through the songs. 'We'll do it slowly,' he ordered, adding with triumph, 'Fifdeen.'

I expressed my surprise that he had been counting my set.

'Man, whaddyou saying? I'm a professional person,' he said in English, and switching to Hindi, added, 'And anyway, us Brahmins, we look out for everyone. You see that man there?'

He pointed to a tall fair man, with a handlebar moustache and a white towel round his neck.

'That's Sparky Punj, one of the country's top lawyers. All the biggest industrialists and politicians turn to him for advice. But who does he turn to?'

'Who?'

'Who do you think?'

'You? Really? Why?'

The trainer smiled sadly at me, then said, 'Never mind. Come sit down.'

We sat at the desk from where the trainer had seen off the priest over an hour ago. In that short time, I had decided to become a member of Junglee. I now watched the trainer fill in the form in careful, rounded handwriting. He did it like a schoolboy with a fountain pen, waiting for every word to dry. Seeing the English letters appear, his large, athletic form poring incongruously over the page, a tongue flickering out in concentration, I felt about the trainer as I had with the Jet Airways attendants: he struck me as someone who couldn't have existed ten years ago. Not just that; his world, complete as it now seemed, could not have existed either.

'Three months or six months?' he asked, looking up.

I couldn't make up my mind; it was a question with deeper implications than he knew.

'Take three. Why should we bind ourselves to these fuckers? Right?'

I nodded unsurely. He gave me his small calloused hand, with its many religious rings, to shake.

'Name?'

'Aatish, A-A.'

He put down his pen and looked at me in amazement. 'Sir! Whaddyou saying? Double A like me!'

He slowly repeated, 'My name is Aakash, A-A-K-A-S-H. Aakash Sharma.'

4

At Junglee, the Hinglish-speaking trainers began referring to me as 'writer saab'. It was Aakash who coined the hybrid and it stuck. He quickly wanted to know what my likely advance would be. He put it to me as concern for my survival in the city. But really he wanted to know what to charge me for personal 'trainings'.

These trainings began without my knowledge. The day after becoming a member I arrived in the gym at noon. I was drifting about when he caught my eye and flashed ten short fingers at me. I went up to him in confusion. He was overseeing the recovery of an out-of-shape male model. 'Cardio,' he whispered, making the form of a running man, 'ten minutes.' I went upstairs and did as I was told. When I came down, he ignored me. He sat on the edge of his red bench, muttering numbers to himself like a Yemeni contractor. For some moments I stood over him, his face knitted up with concentration. Then theatrically, it cleared.

For the next hour he was in a fever. His mud-coloured eyes narrowed; his darkish pink lips tightened; his small, powerful body hovered over mine, the rope of black religious strings hanging down like a noose. 'No support, no support,' he began. 'Very good no support.' Then, 'Fix your balance, fix your balance, bring it all the way down. Don't worry, I'm here.' And at last, 'Thirdeen, fordeen, we'll do it slowly, fifdeen.' He sprang back with the end of the set. His face remained closed, lips moving, calloused fingers calculating, the eyes with their heavy lashes sometimes shooting around the room for inspiration.

And for that one hour of the day, Aakash's world became mine. Far from feeling that he was employed to help me attain something, I felt I was an accessory to whatever hunger was driving him. He would run his axioms for success by me. The most basic were: 'Whaddyou saying, man? I'm a professional' and 'I'm an *ad*-ucated person.' Then in Hinglish, 'Getting a person fit, what greater dharma could there be!' Sometimes the hard materialistic world would prevail. Then he would say, 'Man, I just need that one golden opportunity, then I'll put this idea I have in me into effect.'

'What idea?'

'Ash's! One place where a man can get his whole image set, his hair, his clothes, his body. Right now a person has to wander from place to place, getting this, getting that. He might trust one element, but how can he trust all? At Ash's, he'll get everything, a whole image.'

'What will you need to set it up?'

He looked at me as if we were about to do the set of a lifetime. 'Sixty lakhs!'

I nodded weakly, considering the enormity of the sum. The intensity of his gaze trailed away. Before I could say anything, he snapped, 'Come on. There'll be a gap. The whole workout will be ruined.'

And almost as if they were necessary to offset the brightness of his star, there were detractors: people who wished to see him fail.

He quickly drew me into the politics of Junglee. Everyone was his enemy. The ponytailed owners were drunks. They had made the gym with forty lakhs of their father's money. The female trainers were screwing the owners and were against him. The male trainers wanted his job. Montu especially, he muttered, was a chooda, and damning him for the highest form of amorality, said, 'Man, he is someone who will eat pork, beef, whatever you give him. That is the kind of chooda he is.' He looked irritated at my indifference to his food neurosis. 'Man,' he pressed me, making an allowance for the possibility that one of the two might be permitted me, 'would you eat both pork and beef?' 'No, never,' I lied. He nodded gravely. But his main rival, the Iceman to his

Maverick, was Pradeep, a fair, bulky, mild-mannered man and Junglee's only other full trainer. 'He looks like bouncer,' Aakash would say with disgust. 'He has bouncer's body.' Then switching to Hindi, he would add, 'They're all together against me.'

Pradeep supplied Junglee with its protein shakes. This was a long-standing arrangement. Aakash advised I buy the protein powder and told me to ask Pradeep. But when Pradeep approached me on the treadmill, Aakash glowered at us. As soon as Pradeep was gone, he trotted up.

'What was he saying?'

'Nothing. Just telling me that I should take two scoops . . .'

'One scoop.'

'OK. He said two scoops twice a day.'

'Once a day.'

'I'm just telling you what he told me. And to mix a banana in.'

'No banana.'

'Fine.'

'What else?'

'You know, just that he was married, used to live in Bombay, has two kids, that he liked Bombay.'

'Fucker,' Aakash spat, 'trying to cut my clients.'

I laughed. Aakash imitated my laugh, then laughed himself and walked away.

Soon I was paying him four thousand rupees a month on the side. Junglee itself for three months was twelve thousand. He justified it to me as a personal training hour. I justified it to myself as still less than what I paid in London. Besides, I wouldn't have gone without it. I felt that his passion for what he did strengthened mine. I had very few people like that in Delhi.

A few days later than the Ghalib Academy had promised, Zafar Moradabadi called.

Himself a poet, his name twice echoed the names of poets before him: Zafar, like the poet-king, Bahadur Shah Zafar;

Moradabadi, like Jigar Moradabadi, the other, more famous product of the brass-manufacturing town of Moradabad.

Zafar didn't like coming to me through the academy. I felt he was embarrassed at having to teach. Even on the telephone, he seemed to want to establish a reason other than financial need for teaching me.

'Aatish? Aatish Taseer?' he asked in his papery voice. 'But that's a poet's name.'

'Yes, sir. My grandfather was a poet. I want to learn to read his poetry.'

'Your grandfather was M. D. Taseer, the poet, and you don't know Urdu?'

'Yes.'

'Then it appears I have something of a duty to teach you.'

He came to see me a few days later in Jorbagh. He had a light, gliding step. He wore a safari suit, a white woollen cap and finely made spectacles. He was of medium height with a slight stoop. His eyes were yellow, his skin dark, he had a pencil-thin moustache and sores, black and bleeding, ate away at his scalp.

I saw them when I asked if he would like to take his cap off.

'I wear it because the wool from my head has come off,' he said, and laughed throatily. Then he folded away his cap and revealed his bald head.

'I can't take the heat,' he apologized when he saw me notice the sores. 'And in the conveyance I'm forced to use, auto-rickshaws, it's very bad.'

He sat there with his hands discreetly by his side. He didn't ask any prying Indian questions about how much money I earned and spent. He didn't look around the flat. I asked him if he would like tea.

'I don't normally. My constitution is quite sensitive.'

We started badly. I said I didn't want to learn to write, only to read.

'You can't take a language, break it into pieces, keep what you like and leave the rest for the Pakistanis. What if you find you need to write?'

'But I always write on my computer.'

'Yes, but what if you're in a poetry reading and you want to scribble down a couplet.'

'I can write it in Devanagari.'

His face filled with placid disgust.

'Then perhaps you should learn Hindi.'

'My grandfather's poetry . . .'

'I could have it transcribed for you in Devanagari. Problem solved.'

'Listen, please, I want to read Faiz, Manto, Chughtai . . .'

'All available in Devanagari.'

'I'll learn to write.'

His face bloomed with affection and concern. 'You know you have a responsibility. You're a poet's grandson; your great-uncle was Faiz; you have a tradition to uphold. I'm not saying that you should write poetry. I would never send you into poetry. It's finished. Look at how I've suffered. I tell my children all the time that poetry is finished. But what's been done is still there for you to read and know. You say you want just to read, but even that will only come easily when you can write.'

I offered tea again. He said he didn't normally, but he would.

When Vatsala came in with the tea a few minutes later, Zafar was saying that life had forced him to become an intellectual mercenary. Our first thrill as teacher and student were those two words, neither of which I knew in Urdu. We stumbled about for a bit, coming up with 'mental soldier', then I was sure I had it. 'Think tank!' We backtracked and gave up. It was only when he explained further that I understood what he had meant.

Referring obliquely to the dissertations he had written for money before he wrote his own, he said, 'I gave birth to nine PhDs before I was born, and after my birth I have given birth to three more. It's dishonest, I know. I take money to write people's

40

theses for them, undeserving people. It's wrong, I know. But I only ever did it from need. I feel that makes it less wrong.'

'How did you start doing it?'

'I used to work as an accountant,' he replied, 'but that slipped away from me. The accounts were computerized. I needed money badly. I even had a breakdown, you know?'

'What kind of breakdown?'

'A nervous breakdown. I was lucky. A south Indian doctor helped me. Only he knew what it was. Without him, I wouldn't be here today. There was a danger of brain haemorrhage.'

'Can that happen from a nervous breakdown?'

'Yes. My head used to become so hot my wife couldn't touch it.'

I began to think of his sores differently.

'He used to tell me, "You have to stop thinking." I said, "Doctor saab, it is my nature. Can you order a flower to stop giving off its scent? It is God-given."'

He shook lightly with inaudible laughter, finishing in a wheeze.

'At that point,' he said, 'a PhD candidate came to me. He had a famously strict adviser. A man who used to tear up theses if he didn't like them. He asked me to help him. I said, "Listen, I can't do this. I haven't done your research. I don't know what you wish to say." But he went away and came back with all his books, begging me. I said, "Let's just try it. If he likes it, then we'll continue." He agreed and I wrote the thesis.'

'Did the professor like it?'

'He said it was the best thing he'd read in twenty years of advising. After that,' he added bitterly, 'word spread. Would you like a cigarette?'

'Yes,' I replied, though I wasn't really a smoker, 'but outside.'

We smoked a Win cigarette on Sanyogita's front balcony. There, overlooking the single mango tree, he brought up money.

'I can't accept less than five thousand,' he said, taking back the blue and white packet.

'A month?'

'Yes.'

My face became hot with shame, but I said nothing. Neither his sores nor his haggard face could have expressed his poverty more extremely. He wanted five thousand rupees for two to three hours, five days a week. I didn't know how to say I wanted to give him more. I didn't want to upset his calculations.

Then there was a soundless disturbance in the air and a splatter. I turned to Zafar and saw that a moist indigo wound had appeared on his safari suit. I followed its dripping to the floor. A red rubber hoop lay among the drops. Zafar's face screwed up like a child's about to cry.

A white sedan with tinted windows drove by, leaving behind a trail of hiphop.

'Holi,' he spat, and dropped his cigarette into the colour. It fizzled and ran blue.

'A water balloon. Oh, God, I'm so sorry.'

'Why are you sorry?'

'I don't know, for bringing you out here.'

Just then the front door rattled and Sanyogita came in. She had been Holi shopping. The wooden ends of steel water guns stuck out from the bags she carried. I tried to signal to her to put them down. Zafar saw and looked irritated. I think he felt I was portraying him as a Holi curmudgeon.

'By all means play,' he said, ignoring me and addressing Sanyogita, 'I've played too. But these balloons are not nice. Spoiling people's work clothes when they're not prepared. Zafar Moradabadi.'

Sanyogita smiled, suppressing greater amusement. She held out her hand. He seemed unsure what to do with it. He dropped his head in greeting. Then he said he would call me after all the madness was over. It was Holi that weekend.

'Baby's found a creature!' Sanyogita said after he had left. 'He seems so sweet.' She made her eyes big and sorrowful and scrunched up her mouth in imitation. 'How old do you think he is?'

'He said he was born in '51.'

'But he's young, then!'

'That's what I said, that he was nearly a decade younger than our parents. But he said life had made him old.'

'Oh, you must keep him. Where will we put him?'

'Sanyogita, he has his own house. He's only coming for a few hours in the afternoon.'

'But it'll be so nice to have him here, in the evenings, when all the other creepy-crawlies come out.'

I suddenly felt very sad, thinking of him going home: the 'conveyance' he mentioned, an auto-rickshaw; through the smoke and roar of Connaught Place; past naked bulbs and into the evening congestion of the old city; his safari suit stained blue; his wife and her acknowledgement under dim fluctuating light that it couldn't be saved.

Sanyogita thought I'd taken her joke amiss. She pulled me towards her.

'Come here, baby. I'm only joking. I think he's the sweetest man I ever saw.'

5

Before the metro claimed her house, my aunt had a Holi party every year. The house was in the centre of Delhi with a large lawn and the party was famous. Hundreds of people came. And armies of children, of which I had been one, attacked them at the door, shooting jets of blue and pink paint on to their white clothes. They shrieked, shielding cold glasses of beer and Bloody Mary. Their starched muslin clothes caved in and clung to their bodies; paunches and lace bras appeared through the cloth. Then grown-ups who had already been coloured came with handfuls of green, yellow and pink powder. They smeared the faces of the newcomers, who put up token resistance but knew that there was no isolation greater than being left uncoloured. By noon the colours began to coalesce into a single rust red. As the sun climbed higher, the festival became more adult. Clay cups of bhang and small portions of food in leaf plates went through the crowd. Glasses of beer were traded in for full bottles. Musicians appeared with drums around their necks. By lunchtime, as the children wandered around vagrantly, the dance floor began to fill. The sun's blaze fell on the yellow bungalow and its pale reflection appeared in steel tubs of red water. These late-afternoon hours, a painted crowd with gleaming eyes and teeth, dancing on the lawn, were difficult for me as a child. I think, though I didn't know it then, that I felt their menace. My good memories of Holi were formed by those hours that came before.

But at the *Times of India*'s Holi party, there were no hours that came before; it began after lunch. In the years since the metro claimed my aunt's house, it had become the city's main party. It was also in an old bungalow with a lawn, but had an impersonal quality. At the door there were bouncers in black T-shirts with pre-splashed daubs of green and pink on them and 'It's Holi!' written in rubbery white letters below. One held a clip-board with a list. Sanyogita's friend, Ra, slid ahead of us, saying, 'Princess of Kusumapur and her boyfriend.' I didn't mind, but Sanyogita was embarrassed. She was not the Princess of Kusumapur, her mother was; and technically, even she wasn't any more. The bouncers looked blank but waved us in. Ra turned back, rolled his eyes bitterly and whispered, 'Happy Holi.'

We came into a large lawn protected by dark, heavy trees with strangler roots. On one side of it, a dance floor was full. A multi-headed sprinkler system spat clear water clockwise, then anticlockwise over the crowd below, making their colour run. A DJ with a goatee sat on a high stage, fortifying old film and Holi music with dull, electronic thuds. Beyond the dance floor was a wide makeshift bar crowded with people. It was the first time I had seen so many people since I arrived. My eyes played with the faces like with a hologram, but no one was recognizable. They were younger and more beautiful than I remembered them; many more Junglee-made bodies – and freer with each other. Couples kissed openly in the sun, the pink of their tongues showing like exposed flesh against their smooth, purple faces. Around us, forming a faintly threatening girdle, were additional security men in black, the splashes of pink and green on their T-shirts seeming to mock them.

Sanyogita knew many more people than I did. She had spent her teenage years in the city while I was in boarding school; she went out more often than I did; and her family, especially Chamunda, was well known. She liked to play the role of a protector when we went out together, making me seem unfriendly for her amusement. She now flashed me an urgent look as her friend Mandira came towards us. She had a strong, masculine face with prominent gums and small filed teeth. She carried silver paint, screeching 'Sanyo!' as she bounded up.

'Mandira, please, no. Not this chemical stuff. It makes my skin break out.'

'Don't be silly, yaar. It's Holi.'

Sanyogita dodged her and hid behind me.

'Fine, then,' Mandira said in her slow, booming voice. 'Maybe your boyfriend won't be so pricey.' She laughed loudly, showing her stubby teeth, and with a silver finger drew a cross on my face.

'No, not on his face,' Sanyogita yelled, pushing away her hand.

Mandira laughed, flared her eyes and threw her muscular arms around Sanyogita.

'So do you live in London?' she asked me abruptly.

'No, I'm here now.'

'London has the best food. I love London. We go every summer,' Mandira said. 'Nobu, Zuma, Santini's. So, yeah, I know London pretty well. Then I love this one place called Pucci Pizza. So sweet. You know, I just wish there were more restaurants in Delhi. Every time there's a new place, like the Chinese at the Hyatt, it's full because everyone has to go there. One doesn't even want to go because you have to say hello to so many people. So much kissy kissy. No time to eat. How d'you like Junglee, by the way?'

Sanyogita grabbed my hand before I could answer and took me in the direction of the bar. The sun fell sharply on a line of cane pavilions with people lazing on white mattresses inside. The party here was at a more advanced stage. At a buffet nearby stainless-steel dishes shone like helmets in the sunlight. We settled down in one of these pavilions and soon I was sipping Sanyogita's bhang from a clay cup and taking small bites of a potato cutlet.

The party affected each of us in different ways. It made Ra set off into the crowd with a pouch of coloured powder, which he patted lovingly on to the cheeks of people he knew. In Sanyogita it produced a kind of arousal. It was as if the sudden thrill of bhang and anonymity worked on her. She was normally fearful of Delhi's reputation for malicious gossip. But now, as if playing with the excitement of masks, she pressed her open palm against my leg and groin and said, 'Baby looks so good blue.'

Ra saw and laughed garishly. It made what was a frank but

affectionate advance seem somehow humiliating. I gently moved her hand away. But perhaps not gently enough; she seemed wounded.

The afternoon wore on. The sun blazed, making the colour feel like a second skin. I was hot under it. And this heat was like anxiety. The grass on the lawn was stained. Coloured water dried in the mud. Clay cups lay about in broken pieces and the sun's pale reflection slid into a puddle of muddy purple water.

Just as the sun was leaving the lawn, a flood of newcomers poured in. Among them was a fashion designer in a white suit. He was Kashmiri with red hair and blue eyes. He had slightly pointed, gapped teeth, which he displayed like fangs when he laughed. He was followed by three men of great beauty.

The first was tall with sharp features, high cheekbones and a prominent nose. He seemed vain and distant. The one next to him was shorter, darker and bare-chested. He had an open, friendly face and a horsiness that suited his solid figure. The third, the most beautiful of them all, was tall, with longish hair and a softness around the mouth and eyes. His features, like his physique, were strong and well defined, but covering the prominence of their lines, as if the work of their creator's thumb, was a gentle effacement. It carried over into the clothes he wore: low, loose jeans and a close-fitting, faded T-shirt, threadbare in places. His beauty seemed to embarrass him, and as if nervous of its effect on any one person, he kept moving about, distributing his attentions. The only person he looked frankly at, with his dark, doting eyes, was the designer. He seemed to need the little red-haired man like a circus animal its trainer. And the designer, though he passed like a ball between the men, laughing and bowing, at once an object of fun and their leader, exhibited something of the showman's coldness towards their beauty.

'Mateen Butt's models,' Ra, emerging from nowhere, whispered in my ear.

'The one with the long hair is pretty amazing-looking,' I said, finding it difficult to be open about male beauty.

47

'And guess where he was found?'

'I don't know.'

'In a village in Punjab. Not a poor boy, but straight from a village. Mateen literally drives through Punjab, pulling boys like this out of their homes.'

'And they come readily?'

'With their legs open,' Ra laughed, and seeing me recoil added, 'No, seriously, why wouldn't they? It's a golden opportunity. That one, for instance, was a full Sikh, bearded and turbaned. Mateen had him transformed overnight.'

The models now danced in a circle around Mateen. The sprinklers rained down on them. They taunted Mateen with their dancing, moving clockwise for a few steps and then, in time with the sprinklers, anticlockwise. The handsome model danced with his arms in the air, moving just his shoulders. It was a folk dance from Punjab. His faded T-shirt rose, the holes in it stretched and the pale inner portion of his arms showed. With every shoulder movement, he flicked his straight black hair off his face. Mateen laughed fearlessly as the model closed in on him and drew back. In his hand he carried a packet of light blue powder. He now took some out, and like a genie, blew it in the model's direction. The model closed his eyes and let the powder cover his face. When he opened his dark eyes, their sockets free of colour, he looked like a clown. He seemed to take a special pleasure in the desecration of his beauty. He smiled, then laughed at tasting the colour on his lips. But Mateen, as if he'd hurt him without intending to, pulled his neck under the sprinkler and the blue powder ran from his wheatish complexion.

It was difficult for any observer to look away or feel indifferent to their taunting. There was something equalizing in their physical beauty. It seemed to cut through the barriers of money and language. In Delhi, where these aspects of status had been encoded in people's looks, in their bad teeth and skin, their shabby clothes, their scrawny bodies, this flowering of physical beauty, people rehabilitated, and the licence that came with it, felt like avenues had been driven through the city's closed quarters.

A final arc of sunlight slipped away. The designer, his suit still mostly white, left the dance floor with a female model. She was in velvety tracksuit bottoms, and he drunkenly clutched her long, slim body. They staggered towards us, the designer speaking rapidly and the model responding with languid, filmy replies. I watched them vanish past the wall of our cane pavilion, their voices still audible.

'How do you do it, Mattu? Tell us your secret, no?' the model said.

'Nothing to it, Oozma,' the designer replied. 'I just keep my eyes open and when I see a hot little country boy, like this one here, I say, "Oh gawd, you have such a hard life. Why are you slogging! Come on, tell me, where is aunty? We're going to go and take her blessings. You are going to be the face of my new collection, Sher-e-Punjab."'

'And then,' Oozma asked, 'what do they say?'

'They come panting.' And I heard an imitation of a dog panting, followed by raucous laughter. 'Now, take this fellow,' the designer continued, 'short, pretty dark, hairy. But sexy eyes, great features and hot body. We give him a little stubble, mess up his hair, have it coming over the forehead, do up the eyes and wa-lah those black pink lips will . . .'

'No, Mattu, stop. He can hear everything.'

'Oozma, if he could understand, what use would he be to me?'

At this point I heard a third voice. 'Ey-ey,' it said in dialect, 'we'll see what aunty does when you bring this langur into my house.'

The voice made me sit up.

'Oh no,' the model moaned, 'I told you! He understood everything. Now he's going to bash you up.' Then laughing, she added, 'Dishoom, dishoom.'

49

'Yes, ma'am,' the third voice answered, now in English. 'Whad-dyou think? I am an *ad*-ucated person.'

'Oh gawd,' the designer said, 'and I thought you were a villager. Sorry. Ta-ta.'

I swung my head round. The designer was staggering away when a small, calloused hand pulled him back.

Through the cane lattice, I saw Aakash in a black T-shirt bedaubed pink and green. His lips were dry and his pointed tongue scraped over them as he spoke. He was standing close to the designer, his mud-coloured eyes burning with contempt.

They were in a grove of trees that had been wrapped in white satin. Where the Holi colour had stained the satin red, they looked like bandages. The shrill voice of a female playback singer broke through the afternoon.

The men in their pre-splashed T-shirts had stood out for their facelessness. It was what had struck me about them. Seeing Aakash reduced to this factory line jolted me. I hadn't thought of his world beyond Junglee. I hadn't thought it could include moonlighting at a security agency. The designer's assumption about the security had hardly been different from mine, but seeing it now misfire, I felt some shame at my blindness. The designer had been wrong, and though he could see his mistake, he wasn't willing to hear too much about it.

His little blue eyes flamed. 'I beg your pardon,' he screamed. 'How dare you, you two-bit little man?'

'Leave it, Mattu, no big deal,' the model said in her languid way.

A few people turned around and looked. A man carrying a tray of Bloody Marys stopped and watched. Aakash saw them, and though his face didn't show fear, a passivity crept into it. The designer yelled for the head of security; people were gathering round him, nodding obediently; and even as the head of security walked over, Aakash seemed to know he would be forsaken.

Outside Junglee he was bigger and his skin somehow darker. He seemed to be fighting to remain the person I knew. He had a hunted look in his heavy eyes. It was as if he needed to be reminded of who he was. And this was all that I did for him. I left the pavilion and appeared in the grove of bandaged trees.

In a few short moments, the situation had deteriorated. The fashion designer's anger had grown into a performance; the head of security listened sympathetically; Aakash, every line in his face inflamed, couldn't say a word. My appearance, but more importantly Sanyogita's behind me, shifted the balance and rescued him from the worst of all Delhi fates: being a man with no connections.

I slipped my hand through the tangle of people and prodded Aakash's pectoral. He fell back slightly and smiled with relief and fatigue. 'This, Sanyogita, is my trainer at Junglee. The man I wanted you to meet.'

She took some colour from her pouch and streaked his face yellow. 'Nice to meet you. Happy Holi.'

The intervention of two English-speaking guests broke the tension. Mateen and the model greeted and kissed Sanyogita. Ra had appeared among them. The head of security slipped off. Only Aakash stood where he was. He shuddered and came out of one of his trances, as if he'd just been planning my workout.

'Ash-man!'

'Yes, man,' he replied, pinching my sides as he did in the gym. 'Looking good, man. *Looking like me*, man.'

His confidence returned, but his face gleamed unnaturally.

We drove home through empty streets. Every now and then we encountered a car full of people like us, coloured, crowded, satiated. Only Aakash was in black clothes, with a single yellow streak. I had asked if we could give him a lift; Sanyogita pointed out that we ourselves were taking a lift with Ra; Ra happily agreed to have him dropped off.

'Where do you live?'

'Sectorpur,' Aakash replied.

Ra's face went blank. 'I'm sure my driver knows where it is.'

The car was quiet. The avenues swung past us like the spokes of a wheel. A kind of evening static, hushed and colourless, settled over the city. The trees acquired a violet tint. Weak outdoor lights came on in Doric-columned verandas.

'So quiet, no? Can't believe it's already over. I'll sing a song.'

Mandira sang a film song about Holi. It was spirited but sounded like a dirge for coming at the wrong time of the day. We were dropped off first.

'Ash-man.'

'Yes, man,' Aakash smiled, half-closing his eyes.

'See you, tomorrow.'

They drove off.

Sanyogita bathed me that night. I sat on her fifties marble-chipped bathroom floor under a naked yellow bulb. She sat on a red plastic stool, using a bucket and mug. The colour ran in stages from my body, leaving areas of uncoloured flesh ringed blue and pink. The bucket bath, the dim bulb, the colour running from my body to vanish in a vortex over a stainless-steel drain cover – these things, coming now at the end of festival in a new and altered city, each conspired in dredging up the Holis of my childhood. And it felt as though Sanyogita had put together this ritual knowing the effect it would have.

6

A few days later, Aakash was restless throughout our workout. We were exercising my legs, 'doing squats,' he said, rhyming it with bats. The exercise made me nervous. I didn't like the bar resting painfully on the back of my neck. I didn't like unhooking it and suddenly feeling the weight on my legs and lowering myself from the hips. The muscles in my thighs trembled and swelled. They had to fight to bring me up again. Thinking of them failing was terrifying: the bar with its pink and orange plates pushing me into the ground. Aakash, like a syce with a reluctant horse, belted a broad back support around my waist. Then pressing two corners of a white hand towel against the centre of the bar, he whipped it into a tube-shaped cushion. When it rested on the back of my neck, he gripped me under the arms, his short-fingered hands softening the surprise of the weight.

He remained quiet and intense throughout. There was no screaming, 'Come on, you'll give me two more,' no 'Done done-a-done done.' And when I was leaving the cold, incense-filled room, he said, almost threateningly, 'What are you doing later?'

'Nothing, I'm around,' I replied, surprised at the urgency in his voice.

'Good. I'm coming over. I'll call you to get the address.'

I went back to my mother's flat that afternoon. I was embarrassed to be meeting Aakash outside the gym. But the plan, coming so spontaneously and arousing my curiosity, felt part of the ease of Aakash's manners, his endearing overfamiliarity; to resist, I felt, would be to hold on to an imported idea of propriety. On the drive home the streets were filled with the forerunners of the May flowering: the silk cotton's coral corresponding to the gulmohar's burnt orange; kachnar's purple to the jarul's wispy mauve; and the oleander's yellow trumpet-shaped flowers, a deceptive but poor imitation of the laburnum. Just before South End Lane, a giant pilkhan towered over these slender flowering trees. Its dense canopy fanned black against the spring sky, now whitening with every degree of approaching heat.

I lied to Sanyogita about needing books in my mother's library, ate lunch on a trolley alone and sat down to wait for Aakash. At about three thirty, his name flashed on my phone. A few minutes later he was at my door.

I had only ever seen him in uniforms. Now in his own clothes, his attention to style was apparent. He wore low, loose jeans and a striped grey and black T-shirt. Its long sleeves were pulled up to the elbow. A small black backpack hung from his shoulders and a hands-free wire sprawled over their great expanse. Like at the Holi party, he seemed bigger and darker outside Junglee.

He was in a lighter mood than he'd been in at the gym, but watchful. A look of delight entered his eyes as they scanned the flat.

'You live here alone?' he asked.

'Yes.'

'Man, what peacefulness! I have never, not even for a minute, been alone in the place where we live. Not once, not for a minute. Do you get scared sleeping here at night?'

'No, I sleep at Sanyogita's. Do you live with your family?'

'Yes,' he answered. 'My father's an auditor in the defence ministry and so we have a flat in the Air Force Colony in Sectorpur.'

'Do you have any siblings?'

'Two brothers,' he replied, then seeming to read a question in my eyes, added, 'We're very close, but,' and now in English, 'they are very differ from me. My whole family are very differ from me.'

The kitchen door swung open and Shakti appeared with a glass of water on a tray. Once fresh from the village, the city and the job had turned him cynical. But though he'd never met Aakash before, his dull eyes brightened at seeing him. Aakash took the water and registered the interest in his face. Shakti watched him as he drank, the dull look returning to his eyes. Just as his gaze had drifted away, Aakash clamped Shakti's vast stomach between two fingers. Like a huge toy, Shakti exploded in laughter and surprise. Aakash smiled, holding on to his stomach while wiping his lips, then said, 'That wife of yours must treat you really well. What's this stomach hanging out? Too much rice?' Looking to me for approval, he added, 'Give me two months with this guy and I'll whip him into shape.'

'Shakti, Aakash,' I said, and for coming so late, the introduction made Aakash laugh out loud.

He was handing back the glass when his gaze landed on Shakti's feet. His face filled with concern. 'Why are you wearing those blue chappals?' he asked. 'They make you look bad, man, these cheap chappals.'

Shakti stared in amazement at his feet, as if the rubber chappals were the work of some conjuror. Bata's blue and white chappals were like a symbol of domestic servitude in India. I must have seen them smooth and worn on Shakti's feet all my life. But they never struck me as strange on him. I had not seen Shakti grow from being a slim man into a fat man. It had happened while I was away; and in a sense, no one was better placed than me to notice the change. But I had seen nothing. Aakash, without a trace of piety, looked as I couldn't. He didn't restore Shakti's dignity; he flung it at him as if forced to defend something that wasn't his. And Shakti was star-struck. He stood there, disturbed and intrigued, like an old woman who's just been whistled at in the street.

In his morose way, he said, 'Aakash bhai . . .' (He never referred to me that way; he called me sir.) 'How did you make such a good body?'

'With a lot of effort,' Aakash snapped, and sent him off to get him beer and sandwiches.

'Beer?' I asked.

'Yes, man, feeling thirsty. You'll have too, no?'

I looked at my watch, then outside. Afternoon sun poured into the flat.

'No. Not yet.'

Aakash was offended. 'Our first beer and you won't join me?'

'It's a little early.'

He said, 'I'm the kind of person who can wake up in the morning and brush my teeth with beer.'

A level of comfort entered his manner, as though, after surveying the flat, he had found it suitable and now wanted to settle down for a session. When Shakti returned with a cold Cobra and two glasses, I felt as if I were being drawn into an unfamiliar drinking culture: of hotel rooms, curtains drawn, a bottle on a plywood table with some nuts, an ashtray filling up quickly. Seeming to read my thoughts, Aakash asked if I had any cigarettes. I didn't but knew that there were some in the house. Chamunda insisted a packet of Dunhills be kept for her in the bar. I brought these out. Aakash looked at them admiringly, then pulled one out and lit it with cupped hands. He inhaled, inflating one cheek, then with the cigarette at arm's length, blew on to it, watching the end brighten through the smoke.

The Cobra was amber-coloured. Its pretty colour in the glass, catching the light in the room filling with smoke, made me want to have some. Aakash poured me one with great aplomb, exaggerating the tilt of the glass. I asked him how he'd come.

'Motorbike,' he said, letting out smoke from the corner of his mouth.

'What kind?'

'Hero Honda,' he replied, now inhaling strenuously, making a pained face as if it were difficult to talk.

'Nice.'

He smiled ironically, 'What to do, saab? I'm not a rich man. But this I can say, the bike was bought with my own hard-earned money.'

I feared some conversation about privilege when he surprised me. In English, he said, 'I've never sucking dick,' and laughed.

'What?'

'Yes, man. You know Sunil, he's the other trainer at the gym . . .'

'The big beefy guy?'

'No, no. Someone else; I think he comes after you leave. Anyway, *he* was called for a personal training to the house of a gay. They took him there blindfolded and brought him into the gay's office. The gay puts sixty thousand down on the table and says, "Sucking." Sunil ran out from there, but they had bodyguards and Alsatians and Dobermanns, and they say if you don't sucking, we'll let them out and they'll make keema out of you.'

'What did he do?' I said, now more horrified at the recounting of this wild story in the middle of the afternoon than at its bizarre, filmy details.

'He's sucking, man,' Aakash said matter of factly. 'He's sucking, sucking, for one hour, sucking . . .' He screwed up his dark lips so that their pink interior was more visible than ever.

'Aakash, come on, this is not true.'

'It's true, man,' Aakash insisted. 'It's true.'

'Did he take the money?'

'Why not, after he's sucking . . .'

'Yeah, yeah, please.'

Aakash laughed. 'He bought a Hero Honda.'

I was sure the story was a lie, but I couldn't gauge his motive in telling it. Was he trying to suss me out, see how appalled I would be? I was surprised at his own indifference; the story seemed hardly to make a dent in his notions of morality, as if all vice, no matter what its nature, was a luxury item.

He drank the beer quickly and yelled for Shakti, who appeared with another one. Aakash was enjoying this mid-afternoon revelry in the little-used flat. He poured me another glass without my asking for it. I had been under the impression that Aakash worked from five a.m. till late at night. I wondered how he'd found this block of free time in the middle of the day; I also didn't expect a trainer to have these habits. Most of all, I was surprised at how his earlier urgency had given way to such complete repose. I asked if drinking beer damaged his physique. After taking a large gulp, he put down his glass, stood up and walked to the middle of the room. Then he removed his grey and black striped T-shirt, and standing in a grey vest, flexed his chest and triceps. His skin now seemed lighter and his physique more proportionate. Where the muscles had been expanded near the chest and the arms, there were stretch marks, pale and hairless, like knife wounds. A fine layer of hair ran over his shoulders and back, culminating in a thick chasm between the pectorals. Red and black religious threads, entwined with a single silver chain, disappeared into the chest hair.

'I know,' he said, 'that if you were a businessman, you would take no interest in me.' He glazed his eyes and made a snooty face. 'You'd think this guy lives in Sectorpur, he drives a Hero Honda, he's not someone I can sit down with. But because you're a writer, you look at me and you want to dig inside, to discover what there is in this guy. Aren't I right?'

'Perhaps,' I replied, embarrassed.

'Don't worry. You don't have to tell me, I know. And in my lifetime itself, I've seen a lot of change. I've upgraded myself. When I was seventeen, eighteen, we were a group of three best friends. Our shoes were torn, soles coming off, we walked in the street in the heat, we took buses, we sometimes ate nothing more than a few toffees in a whole day. I remember you got two for fifty paise. The vest I worked out in had holes in it.'

He put his index finger to his thumb, indicating holes the size of one-rupee coins.

'I wanted to be a mechanical engineer,' he continued, 'I got the marks for it, but my father couldn't pay the bribe for the admission. You know, it was some seventy, eighty thousand. He said, "I'll borrow it from somewhere. You go, just go and get your degree." But I told him no; I'm going into fitness. I started working in one gym in Panchsheel Park, earning fifteen thousand. And slowly by slowly,' he said, 'I started picking up personal trainings, people liked my work, they liked that I got results, and so when Junglee opened I was hired there. I started on thirty thousand and in a year I doubled my income with personal trainings. I bought a bike, started buying good clothes. I upgraded myself. Man, and I know now for sure that if I get this one golden opportunity, I'll never look back. There's something in me, I know it. When I was born, our astrologer looked at my eyes and said to my mother, there's something in his eyes. He'll either soar or he'll destroy himself.'

It was strange to think of the eyes, which I had thought of only in terms of beauty, as signs of providence. His ambition had also blurred into an idea of religious duty and what I thought of as vanity seemed almost like a homage to the work of fate.

'But, you know,' he said, 'you might look at me and think, this guy, he's a trainer, his father's an auditor and that's all: they're low-grade people. But that's not all we are.'

He spoke in a mixture of Hindi and English. The speed with which he recounted his personal history was startling. It was ready on his lips. He carried it around like one of the dented and blackened silver amulets he wore round his neck. He changed lenses effortlessly. One moment he was himself, striving, feeling the heat of the day and the fear of failure, the next he imagined himself as me, considering his achievement, wondering if it was something I could write about. It was as if he wanted to show me his making, show me a measure of worth different from the one that had humiliated him at the Holi party a few days before.

When he said, 'That's not all we are,' I had thought he was referring to some intrinsic human worth, but he meant something entirely different.

'My great-grandfather was a famous priest in a village in Haryana,' he began. 'When he was very old, he was faced with a scandal. It led to him renouncing his life and drifting down a river.

He disappeared and wasn't heard of till years later, when some-one saw him in Kanyakumari.'

Kanyakumari, once Cape Comorin, was on the southernmost tip of India. It was some three thousand kilometres away.

Hoping to ground the story, I asked, 'What form did the scandal take?'

Aakash's eyes shone. 'There was an army officer's wife. She used to regard my great-grandfather very highly. She would work for him in the temple, help him with the prayers, clean the idols. Even before serving her husband, she would serve my great-grandfather. And so people in the village began talking.

'Then one day, her husband died. But despite this she went that morning to the temple. So you can imagine, the village went wild with talk. A crowd gathered outside the temple, chanting, "Abolish these corrupt priests." My great-grandfather heard their cries and appeared outside. Though he was heartbroken, he didn't say anything. He just told the woman to make sure that the following day her husband's funeral procession should pass by the temple before it went to the cremation grounds. Then he went back into the temple. The crowd was enraged, but they agreed to wait until the next day before acting.

'The following day, as he had asked, the dead army officer's funeral procession passed in front of the temple.'

'Aakash, when did all of this happen?'

He looked blank, as if I had asked him a childish question. 'Fifty to a hundred years, maybe two hundred,' he replied, 'maybe more.'

'More? But he's your great-grandfather, right? Your father's grandfather? Were the British here?'

'Yes, yes,' Aakash said, 'it was definitely the time of the British Raj. So anyway. When the procession comes by the temple, my great-grandfather appears outside, and addressing the corpse of the dead army officer, says, "Your death has disgraced your village and your community. And so I, as your priest, give you my remaining years. Rise now. I have renounced my life."'

The light in the flat had diminished. Aakash had smoked and drunk continuously. I stood up and turned on a few lamps. Aakash looked sombre, too moved by his own story to speak. I avoided his gaze, unsure of what to make of this afternoon visit. His conversation had included tales of forced blow jobs, social mobility and now magic. And though he himself had a hazy idea of time, his family's history in roughly three generations mapped perfectly on to the country's transitions: from its old religious life and priesthood, to socialism and his father's work as an auditor, to now and Aakash.

He lay back on the sofa, still in his grey vest, his wide arms sprawling behind him.

'Did he come back to life?' I said in the lamp-lit softness of the room.

'That evening!' Aakash replied. 'That evening he rose as if from a deep sleep, and when the people went to the temple, they found that my great-grandfather was gone.'

I wanted to ask any number of questions that would expose the story as untrue, but before I could he abruptly said, 'You know I'm telling you all this for a reason?'

'What reason?'

'I want you to come somewhere with me. My family go every year to the village where all this happened. We take food and offerings. People come from all over. I want you to come with us.'

'Why me?' I asked.

Aakash smiled, and draining his glass, said, 'Because I think it'll be good for you.'

And those words felt like reason enough. Aakash had broken into my afternoon with a gesture of friendship, made possible by its spontaneity; and from its success seemed to come this second invitation, now given rather than taken. Like the first, it was an acknowledgement of the mutual appeal our lives held for each other. But because it was instinctive, and inarticulate, and because behind that appeal I sensed some vague contest for

61

power, it had to be taken for now – like certain childhood friend-ships – on trust.

I accepted his invitation and he gave me a date a few weeks later on which to be ready. Then looking round for his T-shirt, he rose to leave.

He had put his arms in as far as the sleeves when he stopped. 'Thank you,' he said. 'It's been so peaceful here this afternoon. I really needed it.'

When he had gone, I felt that he had come with one intention and realized another. I went home smelling of beer and cigar-ettes. And that night, on Sanyogita's garden terrace, I noticed that the potted frangipani had died.

7

When I came back to Jorbagh, Sanyogita was in the drawing room. She wore her faded T-shirt and tattered tracksuit bottoms. Her legs were up on the sofa and the room was filled with pools of lamplight. They reached to the far corners of the high ceilings and emphasized the evening darkness. Sanyogita's small, squat toes gnawed the edge of the sofa. She had her computer in her lap and was tapping away thoughtfully.

'Baby!' she said when I came in. She observed me carefully and seemed to sense something strange in my manner, smelt something perhaps, but said nothing directly. 'Where have you been? I must have tried you half a dozen times.'

'I'm sorry, I ran into my grandmother. I must have left the phone upstairs. What are you doing?'

'Oh, nothing.' She smiled. '*Vanity Fair* has an annual world bazaar issue and I know this girl who's doing it. She wants me to handle India. I may get a byline.'

'That's great. Do you want to have a bath?'

'Yes! It's just what they need,' she said, wiggling her toes.

'They?'

'Baby, them!' She gestured to her toes; they wiggled happily.

We had an ongoing joke where we ascribed human characteristics to her toes.

'Oh, them!'

'Yes, they would hate to be left out!' They fanned from side to side as if they were about to get up and follow me into the bathroom.

'OK, but come quickly.'

'Baby, don't make it too hot.'

I walked towards Sanyogita's room, past my study with its red carpet and the garden terrace with its dahlias. There was no moon and the night filled the little terrace. I was about to enter Sanyogita's room when, from the light of a naked bulb, I made out the shape of a potted frangipani. From where I stood, its leaves seemed to droop and its trunk and branches had an unhealthy, pulpy texture. I pushed open the door to the terrace to take a better look.

Even before my eyes had fully adjusted to the darkness I could see that the tree was dead. Its trunk and branches had begun to soften and their ends were shrivelled. The large broad leaves hung on like the open eyes of a corpse. We hadn't planted the garden ourselves; we had inherited it. And the death of the slim-limbed frangipani only weeks before it was meant to flower gave me a terrible intimation of the whole garden dying on our watch.

In the time between leaving the terrace and opening the bath taps, I came to blame Sanyogita for the tree's death. It was not because she was in charge of the garden – I was – but because I had noticed and I knew she never would have. I worked myself into thinking that her not noticing was an aspect of a deeper complacency: how almost two years after finishing college she had no more idea of what she wanted to do than when she graduated; how she preferred cities like London and New York, with their cinemas, restaurants and Sunday papers, to all that India had to offer; how she was always late for everything; and how she now sat in her drawing room, wasting her time doing someone else's work.

I got into the bath, full of irrational rage. I knew that Sanyogita, in her mulish way, would carry on doing her work till the bath went cold. But I didn't want to call her because I enjoyed letting my anger grow. The water was hot and burned my skin. I sat there until it became tepid and seemed to cling to me. I felt a sick excitement when Sanyogita came in at last. I said nothing about the bath's temperature. I just lay there looking up at the saucer-shaped ceiling light.

When Sanyogita took off her clothes, I watched her. I saw her pale skin, her big bones, the caterpillar scar that ran across her hip from the skiing accident and her low-slung breasts. She saw me looking at them and became shy about the way her nipples had expanded. She dipped her hand into the bath so that she could harden them. It was then that her frank smile turned to confusion. Why was I lying in a bath that had gone cold? She could see that all wasn't well with me, but she was happy to get in the bath anyway, happy just to add some hot water and bear it for my sake, happy just to be in the bath with me. But as soon as she put one foot in and then the other, letting her large, smooth body sink into the few feet of soapy water, I got out of the bath and left the room without a word.

I saw her face as I left the bathroom, the smile, the confusion and at last the hurt.

When Sanyogita came out of the bathroom a few moments later, she was crying. She always cried silently, but her face was wet with tears, a different wetness from the glisten of her body. She lay down on the bed, just as she was, and wept.

I lay down next to her, noticing the things I found beautiful about her: the straight, strong bones of her shoulders and the paleness of the skin that collected over them now that her arms were raised; her smooth shiny black hair that dropped in steps down her back; the single skin-covered mole on her back which, if I ever touched, she asked me to be kind to as it was the only one.

Sanyogita, as if acknowledging the seriousness of the fight, didn't push me away when I lay down next to her. She seemed to be considering what the real problem might be. With the side of her face pressed against the bed, she said, 'Baby, is it necessary that you revise your novel here?'

'In Delhi or India?' I asked.

'Both,' she said, the conversation calming her down.

'No, I suppose not.'

'Because I'd like to go away for a while. And I want you to come with me.'

She seemed at once to warn me and to bring me in. The fact

that she had already read into the deeper vibrations of our fight, and felt no need to state them but had moved on to a solution, gave her an authority over me.

'How long?' I asked.

'The summer.'

'Where do you want to go?'

'Europe, America, anywhere. This place gets to me after a while, that's all. I need to be reminded that there's another world out there, a world where I feel better about myself.'

I didn't want to, but I gave in. I felt paralysed by the onset of the heat. I wanted to drink lime waters all summer, wear white salwar kameez and finish my revisions in my new study. My life in Delhi had acquired a serenity beyond all my expectations. The revised version of the novel was seeming much better to me. I wrote early in the mornings. Vatsala had learned to make coffee in the Italian percolator. It spat out a thick dark liquid. She mixed it with hot milk and brought me two mugs a morning. The effect of the coffee and the quiet work made me restless for Junglee. I'd spend an hour there and come back to a light vegetarian lunch with Sanyogita. Zafar came every afternoon. After he was gone, I'd walk three rounds of Lodhi Gardens. The park at that hour was filled with overweight women in salwar kameez and sneakers, slim-bodied young men hanging on each other, couples canoodling and old men in white shorts. There were also faces from the area: the Sikh gentleman who owned a bookshop called The Bookshop; the feuding brothers who owned The Music Shop in Khan Market; and an Australian woman who wore pink turbans and flowery dresses and bred beagles. After the walk, I'd read over my writing, drink a glass of wine and resist efforts to make me go out. I didn't want the slog of life in the West; I didn't want cosmopolitan life. I was tired of subtitled movies and Sunday supplements.

But almost as soon as I agreed to the time abroad, our relationship revived. The days that had seemed to run into each other now led up to a final date of departure. The heat that had seemed like a preparation for June's deathly white skies was now only enervating, somebody else's problem: Zafar's, who struggled under it every day, his elegant white umbrella providing hardly any protection from its exquisite blaze. It had made his dark red sores bloom and brighten so that he seemed to sweat blood. The heat was Aakash's problem, who left home even earlier now to avoid the worst of it. And though he was too vain to ever smell bad, his clothes now emitted the odour of cotton fibres baking in the sun.

Zafar took the news of my departure with gloomy resignation. He would feel the hole my five thousand rupees would leave in his monthly income. He feared that without practice, the Urdu I had learned would slip away from me. Aakash didn't even entertain the idea that I might be able to stay in shape without him. 'We'll have to start again,' he said, 'from scratch.' He was at first curious about my going off to the West and he liked telling the other trainers, but soon his supreme belief that anywhere he wasn't was of no interest took over. A look of pity entered his eyes every time the subject was brought up. He now spoke of our trip to his village, which was only days away, as if it were a send-off, a final celebration before my months of obscurity began.

I had told Sanyogita about the trip and feared she might react badly. But in her excitement about the summer away, she took it well and in fact became curious herself to meet Aakash again. He in turn said that I wasn't his client any more, I was his friend, and that it was wrong for me to keep him away from his bhabi. They both seemed in their own ways to be digging at an un-spoken desire in me for them not to know each other.

Then, one morning in May, the day before I was to go with Aakash to Haryana, Sanyogita rang while I was in Junglee. Aakash, who always held on to my phone while I worked out, answered it: 'Hello, bhabi. This is Aakash, sir's personal trainer . . .'

This was all I heard. I was unable to move and could only see Aakash drift off to the far end of the room. He stood under the dark plywood cornices, red light falling on him, chatting away happily. When he returned, he said, 'Plan is set. We're all going, you, me and bhabi, to Hookah. Man, you'll love this place. It's my favourite restaurant. It's just like in Ali Baba's time, with tents and platters and apple-flavoured tobacco.'

'But aren't we going to the village tomorrow?'

'Yes, so? We'll take bhabi's blessings before going, no?'

I knew the plaza where the restaurant was; I had come to the cinema there many times as a teenager. Fifteen years later, change had not so much come to the plaza as grown over it. It still had its same two- and three-storey pale yellow buildings, with their exposed drainpipes and black water tanks. There was still the cinema's original structure, low and wide. The plaza was still surfaced with uneven squares of red sandstone. At the centre was a large banyan with a circular cemented base; in the tree's shade, there were still food sellers, amidst mountains of leaf plates and sprinklings of flies; just near it, a 'Keep Delhi Green' dustbin still stained red with pan spittle. And still present among the groups of young men, apparently pulling off a miracle of inconspicuity, were a family of cows. But over this scene, over a portion of the pale yellow buildings, had grown the silver and red façade of a Puma shop with large glass windows. A new company, with gold-lettered branding and multiplexes all over the city, had taken over the old cinema. Its baggy shell had been carved up into smaller, more compact cinemas. The attendants all wore purple and gold uniforms. And where there were slim-limbed, moustached men in dull-coloured polyester trousers, eating from the leaf plates, there were now also groups of young boys, with headphones, gelled hair, black T-shirts and low jeans. It was this group, overweight and dull-eyed, that slipped into the apple-scented shade of Hookah.

The restaurant was arranged on two floors. The street level was virtually empty and the bright afternoon light disturbed its dim ambience. In the windowless basement, lit by spotlight, tents had been set up in alcoves by draping red satiny material over four-legged metal frames whose joints still showed their welding. The floors were of linoleum, the walls brushed gold, and in each alcove there was a gem-encrusted mirror. Boys sprawled on red and gold satin mattresses and bolsters, smoking water pipes and welcoming large brass platters of Middle Eastern food. The girls, their hair blow-dried and their faces made-up, sat primly on chairs. Some sipped bright-coloured drinks, others smoked joylessly. Only their handbags vibrating against their legs quickened their movements, causing them to reach hurriedly for their phones and make fresh plans.

Aakash sat alone at a table. His colour, his physique, his carefully picked clothes, his decorum, made him seem of a race apart from the people around him. And yet he was nothing like the moustached men under the banyan outside. Seeing him in this new environment, selected by him, I had a sense of how much more marginal he was than I had first realized. He had said the restaurant was his favourite, but I had a feeling he hadn't been there more than a few times.

His eyes brightened when he saw me, then became quiet and respectful at seeing Sanyogita. He seemed nervous, as if welcoming us to his own house. He asked if we'd like to sit in an alcove and yelled 'excuse me' in a loud voice; Sanyogita thought it would be better to stay at the table.

'I thinking the same thing,' he said in English.

I was worried our conversation would continue in English, but Sanyogita switched to her precise genteel Hindi and Aakash responded with characteristic fluency.

'Who wants to sit with that tribe of assholes anyway, right?'

Sanyogita laughed with surprise at the use of the word in the context and I sensed her relax. Aakash, as if the formality of the foreign word freed him from all other constraints, yelled for the waiter with another loud 'excuse me'. The man came over and Aakash ordered beers, hummus, salad, kibbeh. He treated the man with a rudeness that felt experimental, on its way to becoming habitual. The waiter was impervious; when he brought us only two glasses, Aakash said, 'And my bhabi here? Has she come all the way to look at your face?'

Sanyogita didn't like this, but tolerated it, as she did the restaurant, perhaps unsure of who should be the true beneficiary of her noblesse oblige.

As is so often the case when two people meet through a third, they inaugurate their new acquaintance by making light fun of the person who brought them together. It was in this vein that Aakash began to mock my gym clothes.

'Bhabi, I tell him to change those long-sleeved baggy shirts, you know those blue Lacoste or God knows which company's, but he says he can't because bhabi likes them.'

We had never had this conversation, but Aakash winked at me to play along. It turned out this was one of Sanyogita's favourite subjects and the two launched into a happy repartee about my sartorial missteps.

'I tell him keep them for the house then,' Aakash said, 'where bhabi can see them. Please don't wear them to the gym, where they conceal my hard work.'

'I hate those T-shirts,' Sanyogita said disloyally.

'But bhabi, you have to confess, he is looking better, no?'

'So much better, unrecognizably better. All this is gone,' Sanyogita added, pinching my sides.

Aakash noted the physical tenderness between us, and for an instant I saw a cold, unreadable expression on his face. When Sanyogita looked up he was smiling again.

Sanyogita was not a beer drinker and after the first glass she stopped. Aakash looked at me urgently.

'Bhabi's stopped,' he said, 'but that doesn't mean you will too, no? You'll drink with me tonight, won't you?'

Sanyogita laughed at his filmy language. Aakash glanced at her, then turned back to me, and as if making light of his own intensity, said, 'But what does it matter! Tomorrow you're going to see my village. No friend of mine from Delhi has ever come with me to my village. It makes you like my brother. You don't understand. We'll have so much fun – people will come from all over. Truck-loads of people will come, women with their dupattas down to here.' He held his hand to just below his chest. I looked over at Sanyogita, something I found myself doing less and less, and saw that her face had become small. Aakash's passion for the outing seemed designed to exclude her. But then, turning to her, he said, 'Bhabi, why don't you come as well?'

A smile brightened on her face. She had felt Aakash's subtle exclusion, then the excitement of unexpectedly being included. But his invitation – whether intended to do so or not – produced an ugly reaction in me. I didn't want Sanyogita to come. Whatever world Aakash was taking me into, I wanted my responses to it to come up spontaneously. I didn't want to have to think about how Sanyogita was responding. I said nothing at the time, but noticed Aakash watching me intently. Then his face cleared and he smiled. I thought he knew she wouldn't come.

I hadn't considered that Sanyogita, who knew me better than anyone else, would also have made something of my silence.

On the way back, a dirty orange sun slipped smoothly behind low sprawl and satellite dishes. A long straight road took us out of the city of colonies. Its small houses and patches of garden appeared in flashes. It seemed without centre and featureless. The bland stretch of road was interrupted by snarls of new flyover with orange railings. They dwarfed the city below, exposing the meanness of its proportions.

Uttam was driving. I leaned forward and said to him, 'We have to go very early to Haryana tomorrow. It's not far. Be ready by six. We'll go first to Aakash's and then they'll tell us where to go from there.'

He nodded and reconfirmed the time. From the corner of my eye, I was aware of Sanyogita listening carefully. Just before I sat back, she turned away.

A moment later, she said, her eyes dully focused on two boys with painted moustaches who, after doing cartwheels and bridges, had approached the car for money, 'I didn't know it was tomorrow. I can't come anyway. I'm having lunch with Ra.'

When we drove down Amrita Shergill Marg, the trees in the darkness seemed to burn with a strange, cold fire. At first I thought it was the effect of the yellow street light. But looking closer, I saw that the texture of their canopies had changed. They were featherlight and ablaze. Sanyogita's mood alchemized.

'Baby, look. The laburnum's out!'

8

Aakash's house! I knew he left it at four thirty a.m. after eating some 'brad butter'. Then from five till two thirty, he was in Junglee. From two thirty to eleven, he covered the city on his Hero Honda for his lucrative personal trainings. After eleven, he returned home, perhaps only to sleep. I knew he lived there with his father, mother, two brothers, sister-in-law and year-old nephew. I imagined him picking his way through the darkness so as not to wake anyone. It was where his steel tiffin wrapped in blue polythene came from. Most of all, it was where I imagined Aakash on Sundays, the day we didn't meet, the day he had an old-fashioned regard for: of curtains drawn, of not waking till noon and of eating unhealthy amounts of greasy food. And though I knew the points of this routine exactly, I couldn't imagine the kind of place he lived in or even what the streets looked like. And without an image of this other place, this counterpoint to Junglee, Aakash's existence seemed fictitious, a figment of the Delhi sprawl.

It was a city with a fragmented geography: a baggy centre of bungalows and tree-lined avenues, the British city; a walled and decaying slum to the north, the last Muslim city of both Zafar the emperor and Zafar my teacher; a post-independence city of gated colonies, with low houses and little gardens, stretching out in all directions; and beyond, new unseen cities, sometimes past city lines. But the sprawl was being slowly sewn together by new roads, buses and metros; the road to Sectorpur was part of a network of new, elevated roads, shooting out from a central stem, connecting city with airport and the construction sites and coloured glass of Gurgaon. These slab-like roads, with their orange railings, leaning white lights and marked, numbered exits, a concept until recently unknown to the Indian road system, performed infrastructural stunts, now splitting, now swooping down on unsuspecting neighbourhoods. Sectorpur was such a neighbourhood, a place to which the good road had brought life in the form of a property boom. And signs of this life, dull and bright, appeared close to its periphery: grey metal sheets concealing a metro station under construction; red highway tollbooths with newspaper still covering the windows; a city of concrete towers, dotted with the bright figures of Rajasthani women labourers.

The road swung right for Sectorpur, overshooting the turning for Aakash's house. It was necessary to get off the elevated section at a further exit, make a U-turn past families sleeping and cooking under the flyover and drive back at ground level. In this short drive, the city beneath the highway returned with force in the form of cattle, fenced-in plots of overgrown land and roadside fruit sellers behind bright walls of produce. 'Make a left just after the fruit sellers,' Aakash had said.

The road took on the distinct aspect of an army neighbourhood. High walls on both sides with rusty iron spikes held back pink bougainvillea; girls in navy-blue and white salwar kameez waited for the bus to the Air Force School; and blue and white signs with the colours of the Indian flag in concentric circles like a dartboard, read: '16 Base Repair Depot' and 'Photography Prohibited'. Where the high walls retreated, there were keekar trees with thorn-filled canopies and gnarled black branches. They reached out into the road like a sinister, vegetal extension of the dawn mist.

The thin, bumpy road ended abruptly at a sky-blue metal gate. Uttam turned the car right and drove into a colony of three- and four-storey government flats.

I had seen these blocks of flats, with their little balconies and drainpipes on the outside, all over Delhi. In a country which couldn't even standardize nuts and bolts, they were a rare achievement. Their squalor lay in their homogeneity and was not the Indian squalor, which was various and surprising. Small signs of that sunniness competed with the Sovietized scene. Coloured lights hung over the cemented verandas, a faded film poster could be seen through the iron bars of a window, and in the little patches of garden grew the Hindu sacred plants: banana, tulsi, a red hibiscus, its petals resting limply on the rusted points of a barbed-wire fence.

I stood outside for some moments, taking in the place. I noticed the yellow and black sign of a self-service convenience store, the clutter of motorbikes outside each little block of flats, the clothes drying on nylon ropes. I noticed these things because I thought this perhaps was where Aakash bought his 'brad butter', that one of these several bikes was possibly his and that on one of those nylon ropes I might see his fashionable clothes. It was this awareness of particularity, of feeling invested in Aakash, that broke the colony's drab uniformity.

I had thought I was alone, but Aakash's sudden appearance on the landing made me wonder whether he might have observed my arrival. Since we were visiting temples, I wore Indian clothes, an off-white kurta and a white pajama. Aakash now appeared in faded jeans and a striped beige and white knit T-shirt. My embarrassment was not easily explained. All I knew was that Aakash wore the Western clothes because he could. It was like so much else about him.

'Hi, man,' he said, reaching in to give me a hug. 'Looking fit.' Then, laughing and switching to Hindi, he added, 'Yaar, my house is very scattered. Please don't take it badly. I'm ashamed that you're seeing it like this.'

But I realized as we climbed the cement steps that the embarrassment would be all mine and none his. Aakash didn't know embarrassment; it was an aspect of his confidence. My embarrassment, which he would draw out, did not offend him as much as it aroused his curiosity. It was as if he wanted to know every detail of how his world would look once he'd left it behind.

The room we entered past a wire-mesh door and then a full metal door had powdery pink walls. Immediately in front of us was a large cloth hanging of Radha and Krishna and a blue sequined cow against a black background. The room was small and full of people. I couldn't take it in at once. There were some men, a large woman in a bright yellow and orange sari, someone held a baby. As soon as I entered, everyone quickly greeted me and dispersed. They did it with such alacrity that I had the feeling this was a standard courtesy extended to anyone who brought guests to the little flat.

These men were also in trousers and shirts, and seeing them, I began feeling unprotected in the loose, light clothes I wore. Once the room emptied, only Aakash and his father, a man with a youthful face and heavily dyed hair, white at the roots, remained. I looked for Aakash's face in his, but it lacked the fineness of his features, and though lighter in tone, was a flatter colour. For some moments no one spoke.

'Will you have tea and biscuits?' Mr Sharma asked.

'Sir, you'll have to ask my trainer,' I said, trying a joke. 'I never eat or drink anything without his permission.'

Aakash's father smiled proudly. Aakash swelled with laughter, which, at once self-deprecating and vain, filled the room.

The noise drew out a large toddler from behind a curtain, separating the sitting room from the rest of the flat. He came charging in, breaching the unspoken barrier between guest and family, and threw himself into Aakash's arms. His mother, the daughter-in-law, ran in after him, holding a bottle of milk. She was short and quite wide, with dark skin and silvery red lipstick. The gold jewellery she wore on her wrists, neck, nose and ears stood out against the colour of her skin. Dark blue flowers grew over her pale blue and white chiffon sari. Greeting me with an embarrassed smile, she tried to retrieve the child, who had already crawled on to his uncle's shoulders. Aakash reached behind him, and exactly as though performing a two-arm dumb-bell extension, lifted the child from his shoulders and swung him in front of the Krishna–Radha hanging. He pointed at the blue cow; the toddler's face shone with delight. It extended an unsteady finger in the direction of the animal and said, 'Tawoo'. Aakash guffawed, and turning to me, whispered, 'Cow,' the English word more magical to him than to the boy.

His mother reached again for him. Aakash ignored her, swinging the child back into his lap. Without looking up, he took the bottle from his sister-in-law's hand. She looked to me and said, 'He's very attached to his uncle.' Mr Sharma who was silent until now said, 'Yes, watch this.' He called to the child, who craned its neck to see him, then hit Aakash on the shoulder. An expression of fury came over the child's face. He did it again and the child jumped up, then held by Aakash, advanced on his grandfather, gnashing two tough little teeth and swinging his arms and legs. When Mr Sharma hit Aakash again, the child let out a piercing scream.

Aakash calmed him by rubbing the boy's face against his. Then lowering him on to his back, he put the bottle in his mouth. His ease with the child and the sight of it drinking contentedly from Aakash's heavy, dark arms riveted everyone in the room. Aakash, aware of the unsettling beauty of the scene, turned to me and said, 'I'm a trainer, but I can do these things as well.'

I watched in silence. This brief, physical scene in the small room, with the hidden flat beyond, made me feel that certain boundaries were being preserved on my account. A tension built on their edges, while the thought of their loosening unnerved me.

The child's mother, as if forever dismissed in this way, showed her guile as a daughter-in-law. She feigned a huff, making it seem that Aakash instead of showing her up before a guest was doing her a favour. 'Then you feed him, nah?' she said, and flounced off.

It was this child, who wore a neon-green T-shirt with a string of unconnected words on the back – 'Yo, yo graffiti' and 'Come out, let's play' – whose long curls, I discovered, were to be offered up that morning at a village temple.

Until now, my heightened awareness and inward concentration had made it difficult for me to take in the situation around me. But now I wondered what the delay was. Why were we sitting here in the first place? Some preparation seemed to be under way in the flat, but I couldn't tell what.

Aakash yelled at the curtain, 'Ma, come on, hurry up. We should leave quickly. Papa, please tell them to hurry.'

Mr Sharma nodded, rose and disappeared behind the curtain. I wanted to see the rest of the flat, but was somehow unable to ask to be shown it.

When we were alone, I said, 'Aakash, can I use the bathroom?'

A look of dismay ran over his face. He seemed caught between his host's willingness to satisfy any request of mine and an opposing desire to keep me in the visiting room. He said, 'Yes, yes, of course,' and then, as if submitting to the inevitable, added, 'I may as well show you the rest of the house.'

He flicked aside the curtain. I was faced suddenly with a short, dim length of corridor. It ended so abruptly that it was almost as if there was no flat behind the curtain. On my left, there was a tiny strip of kitchen crowded with three busy women in bright clothes. It had a purple fridge and a gas stove. A faint light came in from a frosted-glass transom over an exhaust fan caked in grime. A few steps further, there was a darkened bedroom with a single red bulb and a low bed.

'This is one room,' Aakash said. 'We've given it to my brother and his wife.'

The door of the other room was also open. A tube light with a black underbelly glowed brightly. Every inch of the room was covered in mattresses. It answered my questions: three in one room, four in the other.

Maybe feeling we'd come too quickly to the end of the flat, Aakash pushed open a further door to reveal a small terrace. It was cluttered with the skeletal remains of an old cooler and stacks of bedding, perhaps for when relations came to stay. Beyond a spiked wall, there was a large field of parched, uncultivated land, where a village of blue plastic tents had sprung up. The haze was burning away, the sky blanching fast.

We withdrew into the passage. Aakash pulled aside another curtain, revealing a sink and a cemented area with a tap, a plastic bucket and a metal door.

He opened the door for me. I stepped inside and slid the cold iron bolt into place. Only then, in the damp, dark confines of this cement strongroom, did the full force of my reaction break violently over me. I wished with all my heart that Aakash didn't have to live here. It was too ugly to think of someone with his charisma and ambition, and yes, physical beauty too, spending those treasured Sundays on a mattress on the floor. Was this where he crept in late at night to find a space among the sleeping bodies?

These thoughts had prevented me from focusing on the stained ceramic basin and the squalid circle of water I stood over. I wondered if, while holding my breath, I'd kept my eyes closed as well. I knew now that I stood at the source of the smell that pervaded – and always would, no matter what incense was lit or food cooked – the air in the flat. And just before I pulled the flush, a detail impressed itself on me. On a narrow cement windowsill below the paint-splattered glass, there was a thick accumulation of a hard yellow and red substance. Its colour and appearance made me curious enough to touch it. It was smooth and layered. When I dug my nail into it, a little flake came off easily. Wax! The remains of candles, red and yellow candles that had burned to their base. Their blackened wicks were embedded in the pat of wax. No sooner had I realized what the coloured substance was than a looming feature of life in the flat occurred to me: blackouts. It was to long hot nights dotted with red and yellow candles, burning into the morning, that Aakash returned.

I opened the door and found him waiting. He turned the tap in the little sink for me with one hand and held a towel in the other.

In the room outside, the family was ready to go. Five bags of food, offerings and water had been brought out. There were

79

three women, Aakash's mother, aunt and sister-in-law; and three men, his two brothers, one younger, one older, and his father. And there was the toddler, whose hair was to be offered up, sitting heavily in his father's arms. I waited for the room to empty. Besides the religious hanging, there was a painting of a Chinese scene, fluorescent green palms, pagodas and bridges on a black felt background. The only other decoration on the pink powdery walls was a narrow framed picture of a red rose, which for all its shabby sentimentality, was somehow affecting.

9

Aakash's father, as a testament to its importance, knew every stage of the fifty-kilometre journey from town to temple. He knew the last of the city's satellite towns with their single-storey constructions gathered close to the road and their multitude of chemists, automechanics and call booths. He knew when the land would become fields dotted for as far as anyone could see with the clay minarets of brick furnaces. He knew the Air Force base with its high walls of bougainvillea that came just before the Haryana border. He knew the flat green fields and pale blue sky of Haryana, once bare save for the odd red-brick construction, but now covered with uncooked bricks drying in the sun and chimneys evenly emitting black smoke. As if in homage to his destination, he spoke of magic on the way.

He spoke at Aakash's prompting. Since we'd left Delhi, Aakash had become protective of me. He put his elder brother, mother, aunt and sister-in-law in one car, and in my van-like car he put himself in the front next to Uttam, his little brother Anil far in the back and his father and me near each other in the middle row so we could talk. He would turn back every few moments, facilitating the easy flow of conversation and checking that I wasn't getting bored of the stories. When, occasionally, I looked ahead, I saw the side of his face pressed intently against the seat, his bright, arched eyes ready to wink.

The stories were not simply religious. At the heart of them was not just a reward or a moral intervention from the gods, but rather an emphasis on the powers of Brahmins, the Siddhis, continuing to this day despite the decay of modern times. They seemed designed to expand on what Aakash had said a few days before at Junglee: 'There's something in us.' The message, beyond proving the existence of these powers, was not always clear. In one story, Aakash's grandfather, killed in war, went to his father before leaving on his fatal mission. The father was old and perhaps sensed something. He asked his son to ask whatever he would of him. The man said, 'I have so many daughters and only one son. I am not rich. How can I be expected to marry them off?'

'Over the next six months,' Aakash's father said grimly, then chuckled, 'one of my sisters died every month.'

'My aunts?' Aakash asked not with horror but simple curiosity. 'I have an aunt in Rohtak . . .'

'The only one!' his father said, chuckling again. Then turning to me, he added in Hindi, and cryptically, 'Sometimes the truth of things has come out of my mouth as well.' He described the predictions he'd made of transfers in his office, of purses stolen and found where he said they'd be found, and of investments made at opportune times. 'The place we're going to today honours the memory of my grandfather, who renounced his remaining years for the sake of his family and community. It's a story from the last days of the faith. If it were not for him, people would have stopped believing.'

To hear Aakash's father recall the story made it even stranger than when Aakash had spoken of it in my mother's flat. Only two generations apart from him was this magical ending to a life.

Aakash knew all the stories. He prompted his father to tell more. Soon Anil, thinner and fairer than Aakash, with uneven teeth clambering over each other, was also prompting stories. I imagined them first told in the small bedroom covered in mattresses, the long nights of summer darkness, the smell of the bathroom, and yet the resilience of people to these things, the stories told anyway, the family life carrying on, the making of Aakash continuing unstopped.

He seemed to have an intimation that beyond the brief new friendship that had arisen between us, my interest in him had other depths. If ever he saw me watching him or I asked him a question about his personal life, his face would brighten as if from the amusement of a private joke between us. 'You're writing a book on me, aren't you?' he'd laugh, using the English word for book as if a book of that sort could only have been possible in English.

Before arriving at the village temple where the offering of hair was to be made, we stopped at a small town. While his family bought snacks, rearranged their offerings and went to the bathroom, Aakash pulled me into the shade of a teashop. The man, who always made a point of smoking Marlboro Lights, now asked the teashop owner for a single Gold Flake. He spoke in the Haryana dialect, with its threatening inflections, to make me laugh. His eyes blazed mockingly, his manner became at once aggressive and comic. The owner didn't catch the city joke and handed him the cigarette. Aakash lit it from the roaring blue flame that cradled the steel urn's blackened base, keeping its contents forever close to a boil. He put it in too far and half its short, cylindrical body blackened, with scattered orange points burning through. Its paper fell from it like dead skin. Aakash handed the cigarette to me after a few drags and slipped his arm around my shoulders. He seemed to take great pleasure in watching his family one by one load into the cars as he smoked with me in the gloom of the teashop. Then he bought one of the many silver packets of pan masala hanging in front of the shop, tore open a corner, and after blowing into it, emptied its contents into his palm. He gave half to me before slapping the rest into his mouth. After a short lull, the brown liquid in the urn seethed.

Our closeness in the teashop faded as the day wore on. It was replaced by a kind of aggression, as if a fault line formed between the recent fact of our friendship and the acknowledgement of difference. And though we forged the common ground on which a friendship might grow, neither of us yielded any easily.

The change in mood began on the way to the village temple,

or perhaps even some minutes before, when Aakash's nephew discovered us in the teashop. He ran in like a hound following a scent, then looked around in confusion, his eyes adjusting to the darkness. Aakash caught him and swung him into the light; the child let out a screech of delight; I winced, reminded of babies on planes and indulgent mothers. Aakash indulged the child too, letting him gnaw at the side of his face.

Sensing my discomfort, he archly said, 'With us, children are everything.'

The child now travelled in our blue van, being passed through all three sections of it depending on his fancy, his long, soon to be cut locks flying this way and that.

Before leaving the small town, we hit traffic. Orange-faced trucks with large loads crowded the narrow street. On the petrol tank of one, there was a drawing of a palm and dune. Below, white letters read: 'Iraqi water. Drink frugally, my queen.' For many minutes, the line of trucks didn't move. Aakash admired a new house: 'Look at the kind of houses people are building.' I had thought at first the remark was a sneer, but I was wrong; it was a compliment. The house was narrow, four storeys high, in beige sandstone, with red grilles, balconies and silvered windows.

When the traffic didn't move, Uttam tried to slip ahead of the queue. The minute the van nosed out of its lane, it was honked at angrily by oncoming traffic. The queue had closed behind us and Uttam was left with no choice but to take the car to the right, across the oncoming lane, as far off the road as he could. As soon as he did, the tyres caught in deep black mud. One by one, they confessed the futility of their revolutions.

Aakash jumped out to push, as did Anil; I hesitated, then got out too. At first they thought putting bricks under the tyres would be enough for them to catch, but soon it was clear that they would have to push the car on to the bricks. My position on the left was not ideal; the patch widened where I stood, I was wearing sandals. Despite my uncomfortable angle to the car, I pushed. The car broke its inertia, but just as the wheels left the deep grooves they had made, they splattered black mud on to my white pajama. My right leg was covered from my sandals to the hem of my kurta. Aakash roared with laughter, not now that self-deprecating laugh, but a harsh, instinctive cackle. Uttam appeared and began to wipe furiously at the mud, making things worse. I buried the anger I would normally have shown him for fear of being singled out as soft and privileged.

'You should have left it,' Aakash said, when his laughter subsided. 'There's a technique in pushing.'

I wanted to hit him. Uttam saw this and brought out a bottle of water from the back. Aakash took it from him and poured it down my leg, squeezing mud and water out of my pajama. Then he washed my feet, looking up at me the entire time. It was a difficult gesture to read. I couldn't tell if it was like the tenderness he'd shown me in the teashop or whether, by tending to me so thoroughly, he was further asserting his power as a man who could do anything.

After a short drive on a country road, past flat fields of ripened wheat, their arrows hard and golden like wasps, heralding better than any number of flowering trees the approach of summer, we arrived at a small open-air temple in the shade of a peepal tree. A pool of green water lay some metres below, surrounded by pale land.

'This first temple,' Aakash's father said as we got out of the car, 'honours an even older ancestor than the one I spoke of in the car. It is from him that we derive our caste.'

'How old?'

'Oh, I can't say!' Aakash's father said. 'Three, five, seven hundred years old. All I know is that it was even before the British time in India. It was during the Mughal time when Akbar was emperor.'

'So, in the sixteenth century?'

'Yes, maybe. Anyway, in that time, this ancestor did paltiyans from here to Jagannath Puri. When he arrived, the temple doors

85

were closed. So he says, "If I have shakti in me, these doors will open." The priest there said, "These doors will never open. Jagannath, Lord of the World, will not see you now." My ancestor said, "Move aside. You're just a priest; I speak directly to my god." And, phataak, the doors of the temple swung open, Jagannath himself appearing. He said, "Ask, if you ever meant to ask." My ancestor fell to his feet and asked the great Lord of the World that no one in his family or subsequent line should ever suffer from, how do you say, kodha . . .'

'Leprosy,' Anil inserted.

'Yes, no one should suffer from leprosy.'

After this explanation, Aakash and Anil disappeared, followed by their older brother, Amit.

Men and women of Aakash's caste had come from all over the area. Some arrived in open-backed trucks, the women's faces covered by the long fall of their saris; others arrived in low sedans. The temple was so small and basic that it was hard to imagine people coming from a distance to visit it. It was long and tiled and open on three sides, through which the tranquillity of the green pool and the heavy shade of the tree entered freely. Below a brass bell were Aakash's ancestor's feet in white marble. Directly in front of them, also in white marble, was a large pineapple-shaped structure, draped in lavender muslin. A wet temple clutter of rose petals, grain, coins, blue polythene and yellow laddus with smoking incense sticks lay at its base.

A mad toothless country cousin, with thick spectacles and a long white plait, ran towards the women in Aakash's family as soon as they entered the temple. The two women met and instantly began to dance around the pineapple. The daughter-in-law waited to be invited and when she wasn't, put a foot forward and joined in. Other women in pink, maroon and rose-coloured saris smashed cymbals.

I was watching the scene when from behind me the men in Aakash's family appeared, carrying between them a white and gold muslin cloth. The sight of them, dressed in nothing but long, ceremonial dhotis, produced a kind of panic in me. It was the culmination of weeks of anxiety that had been building since I stepped on to the Jet Airways flight to Delhi. Seeing Aakash now effortlessly assume his caste robes made me, in a mud-splattered kurta, feel all the horror of my removal. He hadn't meant to intimidate me, but he had terribly. He'd shed his wide jeans and close-fitting shirt and the effects of Junglee were on display. His sprawling shoulders and large arms were taut. The black religious strings entwined with red bounced lightly against his chest. They struck an unlikely harmony with Aakash's colour, the dark gums, the blackish-pink lips, the still-darker nipples and the fine coat of hair that covered his arms and shoulders. A beauty spot was faintly visible on his stomach muscles.

This darkness, like that of a charcoal sketch, made Aakash's body more than an object for aesthetic consideration; it seemed to have a kind of aboriginal power, as if issuing from the deepest origins of caste and class in India. But his brothers and father, with their paler, flabbier frames, did not unsettle. There was no regeneration visible in them: their gaze was placid; they were not gym Brahmins.

The men each held a corner of the white and gold muslin cloth, which they lowered over the marble pineapple, already draped in lavender muslin. It was filled in seconds with a shower of petals, money and garlands of rose, jasmine and marigold. Then the little boy was brought forward, and as a barber priest shaved a first inch with his blade, the boy began to wail. Soon long, dark hair was added to the moist mess of petals, polythene and money. The Brahmin men sat solemnly around the pineapple as the boy's large head was shorn. When his scalp was raw and cleanly shaved, cut dark red in places, the priest smeared it with sandalwood paste. It was only then that his mother appeared to ease the day's trauma.

I wanted to go back to Delhi, but there was lunch organized under the peepal tree and a second temple to visit.

'Eat as much as you like,' Aakash said warmly after returning from washing in the green pool with his entire family. 'Today

I'm not your trainer.' He had changed back into his jeans and T-shirt and had a fresh, turmeric mark on his forehead. He slipped his little finger into mine and led me to a place where a priest was putting these marks on other people's foreheads. He exchanged some words with the priest as if negotiating a special rate. The priest asked him a question I didn't catch, but Aakash replied, 'He's my brother.' The priest smiled, and slipping one hand behind my head, drew me closer, grinding the mark firmly into my forehead with his other hand. Under the tree, young and old men were coming around with metal buckets, serving warm puris and potatoes. I felt my exhaustion mirrored in the long afternoon light pouring on to the green pool and in my mud-splattered pajama, which had dried and become a dull brown colour.

That second temple, given to Aakash's family by the old Nawab of Jhajjar, was no more than a house. It faced a Jhajjar backstreet split down the middle by an open drain in which black bead-like bubbles rose in even intervals. Still, strong sunlight fell on an afternoon scene composed of a fly-covered dog, half in sun, half in shade, the street's blue doors and shutters, and a man on a stool, reading the paper behind half-filled toffee jars. The one sound was the jingling of a passing woman, in black, silver and red; the one smell, as powerful as the sunlight, as pervasive as the languor of the street, the stench of the drain. It eased its way past a PCO booth, through the blue grille gate and into the temple's cemented sanctum.

But no one held their nose, the ladies did not worry about their saris getting dirty, no one minded taking off their shoes some metres before the temple's freshly washed floors. We tumbled into its courtyard, fifteen of us, opening shutters and unlocking doors as if returning to a house that had been closed up for a season. Everyone headed straight for the sanctum and lay down, men, women and children, on an old carpet on the floor. Just ahead, half-buried in garlands of plastic flowers, were a black, beady-eyed Krishna and a white Radha in gold clothes.

Aakash took me aside and pointed to the painting of a sage in a glass case. In slow, broken English, he said, 'He is my great-grandfather.'

Mr Sharma already stood next to the glass case, leaning lightly against its orange frame. The statue inside was of a large man with a paunch showing through his saffron robes. There were three turmeric streaks across his pale forehead; and his fierce, jowly face, in permanent afternoon shadow, bore a distinct expression of irritation.

'I used to massage his legs,' Aakash's father said. 'He was a great man. If not for him, faith in this part of the country might have disappeared altogether.' Then an unexpressed sorrow, like that of the red rose against the black background in his flat, passed over his face.

I sat down on a low stool, despite the family's appeals to join them on the carpet. I realized now that it was not so much the smallness of the Sharma flat or the smell but its communal quality that had unsettled me. And Aakash, as if responding to that, as if reaffirming that he didn't want to live that way either, that he had meant what he had said about the peacefulness and privacy of my mother's flat, got up after a few minutes and came to sit next to me, his head resting against my knees. The undeclared power I had had over him until now, gained in part from his being my trainer and in part from Holi, dwindled. I felt that there had been a reversal.

The toothless country cousin was taking orders, hardly an hour after lunch, for tea and samosas.

'I don't have the courage for a samosa,' Aakash's sister-in-law said from the place where she sprawled on the floor.

Aakash looked at her, then up at me with a contemptuous smile.

'Kachori?' the old woman asked with a smack of her lips.

'No,' Aakash's sister-in-law moaned, rubbing her broad, dark stomach.

'Then khir?' the old woman shot back.

'Yes, khir would be lovely!' Aakash's sister-in-law smiled, feigning childlike mischief.

'Khir would be lovely,' Aakash imitated and guffawed, looking up again at me for approval.

'What?' the sister-in-law snapped. 'What's wrong with khir? I can't be like you, eating boiled food, boiled vegetables and protein milkshakes.'

'That's fine, but then don't come running to me: "Aakash, make me thin; Aakash, tell me what to eat; Aakash, your body . . ."'

'Let her eat, yaar. What is it to you?' Aakash's elder brother, her husband, intervened.

His remark made me wonder about the tensions between them.

Aakash said to me in English, 'See what I told you? She is very sharp.'

Then turning back to the family, he said, 'Why don't you stop thinking about eating for a second and pay attention to your son, who's become a sweeper?'

The entire family, as if in an abs class, rose six inches to see what the child was doing. He was at the far end of the little courtyard, brandishing a short broom made of fine sticks.

'Come here, you little jamadar,' Aakash yelled.

The word he used was a caste word no longer in politically correct usage for cleaners and sweepers. A ripple of laughter went through the family of reposing Brahmins. The child, seeing he had the attention of his family, began splashing water in a metal bucket no bigger than him.

'That water is dirty,' Aakash said pointedly to his sister-in-law and walked across the courtyard to recover the boy.

'Chee,' he said, as he picked him up, 'he's smelling.'

His mother, now clearly humiliated in front of the family, rose with irritation. 'It doesn't matter. He's wearing a nappy. We'll deal with it when we get back.'

Aakash shrugged his shoulders and handed her the child. But as soon as he did, the child slipped away and clung to Aakash's leg. He began touching his feet, saying, 'Tey,' every time he did. 'He's saying, "Jai",' Aakash said with delight.

Aakash's father looked up at me and said, 'See, unlike the Sikhs and the Muslims, we don't have to teach them the religion. They learn on their own. For instance, no one taught him to say Jai. He just heard us saying it when we pray and picked it up.'

The boy, now in Aakash's arms, was pointing unsteadily at the Nandi near the Shiva linga and saying, 'Tawoo. Tawoo.'

'He's calling Nandi "Tawoo",' Aakash laughed, then, addressing the boy, said, 'Not cow; "Nandi".'

Tea and samosas arrived, along with a bowl of khir. Aakash put the boy down and rejoined the others.

We had all barely had a few sips of tea, Aakash's sister-in-law had not touched her khir, when cries of 'Chee, chee', 'Look what's he's doing', 'The little sweeper' rose from the sanctum.

I had been facing the idols and turned round to see that the boy had removed his shorts, and now holding on to a tap as high as his arms could reach, was taking a happy pistachio-green shit in the courtyard.

'His T-shirt will be ruined!' Aakash yelled.

'Let it be ruined,' the boy's father said with hollow aggression.

Within seconds, the family's women, his mother and the old cousin, had pounced on him, while his grandmother looked on with a bitter smile. He eluded his mother and ran to Aakash, leaving a green trail behind him for his mother to clean up. Aakash grabbed him under the arms, swung him stomach down on to his lap and cleaned his bottom without any sign of squeamishness. Then along with his mother he inspected the child's bottom closely.

'Hai, look!' Aakash's mother said. 'He's got these big red dots there.'

'Not cleaning him properly,' her younger sister added slyly. 'Have to put Soframycin.'

'Have you seen the spots in his privates,' Aakash exploded at the child's mother, who was still sweeping up the mess.

She looked up, haggard. 'I'm just coming,' she managed.

Her husband, who had now taken the boy, was betraying her to the group. 'I've told her time and time again that she's not paying enough attention.'

Then Anil produced a wooden drum from within the sanctum. He started beating on it, and hearing this, the little bald child, who had been face down all this time, rose furiously and began to dance, shaking a small, angry foot unsteadily into the circle.

'Put your right foot in, put your left foot . . .' his grandmother sang, and the little boy danced as the group clapped and his mother swept away the last of the green trail.

We went home through flat land dotted with smoking minarets. The sky that had been pale in the morning was a pinkish brown on the way back. The thin, bumpy road that led past high, spiked walls, the '16 Base Repair Depot' and keekar trees, as malevolent in the evening haze as in the dawn mist, finished at a sky-blue metal gate.

'You know what's behind that gate?' Aakash said, putting his hand lightly on my shoulder.

'No.'

'The airport. We used to go there at night as children and see the planes and lights. It's better than take-off point. You're literally right there in the grass when the planes go by. Mind-blowing.'

I thought of my own arrival there a few months before on the Jet Airways flight. Then I thought of Aakash and his childhood memory of the airport. And even though a mood of inadequacy hung over the day's outing, with this thought my great tenderness for him flooded back.

10

Aakash insisted the day needed its 'super set'. I said, thinking
of his bald nephew in the temple, that I was sure it had already
had one. Then he wanted to know when and I had no answer
for him. He searched my face for a moment and turned back
to the task at hand. He was looking for a 'pardy' shirt. We stood
in his mattress-covered room with its pink walls and fetid air.
A green metal cupboard was open; many unsuitable options
lay strewn on the mattress below. Presently he found it, a black
shirt with silver pinstripes. Its thick shiny material glowed in
the white light.

A few minutes later, we were on his bike, driving through the
smoky Delhi night. It was my first time riding pillion on a motorbike and I felt exposed, embarrassed to be gripping on so tightly.
We drove through areas I didn't know existed. Broken, keekar-
lined roads, open fields and a hyacinth-choked canal, with the
red lights of a power station reflected in its dark water, appeared
on our way.

'Where are we?' I yelled.

'What?'

'Where are we?'

'In Sectorpur,' Aakash yelled back, 'just across the Jhaatkebaal
border.'

We came some minutes later to an arrangement of tall four-
square buildings surrounded by flat agricultural land. Though
the buildings were new, marks of decay had already begun to
appear on them. Pan spittle festooned their chalky-white walls,
metal slats along their side had begun to rust and sacks of cement,
plastic buckets and brooms cluttered their corridors. A white
wooden bathroom door was open and from the grey marble

interior toilet smells filled the lobby. We waited for the lift. Outside, a group of young boys chased a squirrel with an air gun. It ran up a tree and the boys stood below, firing aimlessly into the street-lit canopy.

'Fucking it,' Aakash said, when after many minutes the fat red number indicating which floor the lift was on didn't move. 'Let's take the stairs.'

'Listen, Aakash, are you going to tell me now who this friend of yours is?'

His eyes gleamed. 'What, man? Don't trust me, man? I told you, this is my very old friend. The Begum of Sectorpur. Now, come on.'

We ran up seven flights of stairs. The banister shook; there were broken panes on every landing, with sharp points of glass clinging on; below, rejoicing boys carried away the body of a squirrel; the land around was bare and dark, streaked with amber stretches of empty road. Halfway up, we were met by a thin young man with glassy eyes. He wore pedal pushers and a black vest. His small, dense armpits were exposed and emitted a wet, poisonous smell. He was overjoyed to see Aakash, and showing blackened teeth, kept monotonously asking how long it had been. Though Aakash paid him no attention, he jogged up alongside us, laughing and slurring. At every landing he looked back at me, his glassy eyes catching the light, and said, 'Any friend of Aakash's is a friend of mine.'

When we reached the eighth floor, Aakash slipped his arm around the man's wiry frame, and whispering purposefully, took him into the gloom at one end of the corridor. They were still talking when the front door nearest to me swung open. A woman in a pale green kaftan stood behind a black metal gate. She was a warm brown colour, with straight waxy hair and slightly jowly cheeks; her smooth hairless skin and raised eyes made me think she was north-eastern or Nepalese. The outline of her large, full body was visible through the fine cotton she was wearing. She clutched the gate with one hand and under the white tips of her French manicure she had tiger-print nails.

She smiled broadly at me and laughed girlishly when she saw Aakash.

'Suitors, Begum saab!' the thin man sneered before vanishing down the stairs.

She snapped abuse at him. When it was returned with a wayward cackle, lost in the darkness, she looked back at us and was gracious once again.

The gate opened and we entered a clean brightly lit flat with tiled floors. The begum shut and bolted an iron front door behind us. Apart from the main lock, there were some five or six other locks crudely welded on. A tile of Ganesh near the door read: 'May he bless every corner of this house.'

An Alsatian with cataract-clouded eyes bounded up to greet us.

'Stop it, stop it, Zabar,' the begum said, pushing aside the dog's snout and showing us into a drawing room, which contained a glass dining table, white leather chairs and sofas under plastic covers. A partially drunk bottle of Diet Coke and a glass-cleaning spray, half-full of blue liquid, stood on the dining table.

Within moments of our sitting down, the begum had rushed off into the kitchen and reappeared with glasses, ice and a bottle of Seagram's Indian whisky. Aakash looked at me and winked as she poured the whisky. The begum spoke rapidly, complaining about security, then about how Aakash never came to see her any more.

'At one point,' she said, looking over her shoulder at me, 'it was all, "Begum this", "Begum that" – "Begum, my friends will protect you", "Begum, can I give you a lift somewhere on my bike?" but now, since he's on his way to bigger things, since –'

'Ah, ah, ah,' Aakash said firmly.

The begum shut up, then a moment later looked mournfully back at me and said, 'Begum's been forgotten.'

When she brought us our whiskies Aakash took his, and quoting an Urdu poet, said, 'An age has passed, and your memory has not come to me, but that I have forgotten you – it is not that way either.'

The begum melted. 'Oh-ho-ho,' she said. 'Quoting back to me the couplets I taught you? How easily they come off your tongue.'

Aakash laughed and grabbed her through her cotton kaftan as she gave me my whisky, nearly causing her to fall over on to the sofa.

She moaned and recovered herself.

We drank two or three more whiskies. The begum spoke continuously. She made light flirtatious conversation; she complained about what a burden the Alsatian had become – 'A blind guard dog! That's all the begum's left with'; she lashed out at women more debased than herself but protected by the false sanctities of marriage; she complimented Aakash on his physique; she said her son, who was 'a carbon copy' of Aakash, was working as a chowkidar in some rich industrialist's house, couldn't Aakash help him get a job in fitness? This request caused friction between them. Aakash cautioned her with a cold stare and her tune changed. She became maternal even as she trailed her tiger nail down his cheek: 'How good and strong my little boy has grown up to be. I still remember when he was sixteen and –'

'Begum.'

'OK, OK, I won't say.'

Aakash affected a macho silence, the whisky and the begum's chatter seeming to relax him. But for the pinstripe 'pardy' shirt, he was like a man who'd just come home from a hard day at the office. To see him twice in the same day, and in such different ways, a hero among the people he grew up with, made me feel again the power of his position. His versatility was like a confirmation of how authentic and robust his world was. His Delhi was a city of temples and gyms, of rich and poor people, of Bentleys and bicycles, of government flats and mansions, of hookers and heiresses, and he asserted his nativity by moving freely between its varied lives. He made it seem like no less his right than taking one of the new green buses, riding the metro, seeing the sound and light show at the Red Fort or renting a pedal boat at India Gate and floating over the reflections of dark trees and pale sky in its sandstone water tanks.

He seemed to read my admiration, and perhaps helped by the whisky to see himself as I saw him, as many men to many people, here rubbing a baby's face against his to comfort it, there performing the ancient rites of his caste, he suddenly made a grab for the begum's breasts through her pale green kaftan, his mud-coloured eyes fixed on me. The begum wriggled joyfully, shrugging off her maternal instincts and becoming what she was. She had been sitting in his lap, but now she rose slightly and pushed her thighs and rear towards him. Her jowly face moved closer to mine while Aakash pulled hard at her breasts. She was inches from me, wiggling and gyrating, making a drama of her arousal. Aakash's eyes followed mine, his arched lips taut with amusement. My first reaction was anger, feeling this could only be some kind of sexual intimidation. But when he squeezed the begum's fat thighs and slapped her bottom, causing her to fall forward, her tiger nails clawing my thigh, a smile must have crept into my face. Aakash laughed loudly at seeing it. The begum tried looking behind her to see what was so funny, but Aakash turned her face back towards me, and taking her left hand from my thigh, pressed it into my crotch. It had no effect; I shrank with embarrassment.

Then Aakash lifted up the begum's kaftan and began to roll it back. He did it with mock assiduity, just as when he had prepared the towel as a neck rest during the squats. It formed a neat band just over her hips. I could see the outline of her exposed thighs and bottom. Aakash, making a face like a laboratory assistant or vet, raised two fingers in the air. When he was sure I had seen the gesture, he inserted them into her with the ease of a man sawing off a piece of wood. The begum groaned.

'Not here, not here. Come on, to the bedroom.'

Aakash pushed her head down roughly. The Alsatian, who

had been watching everything with its cataract-filled eyes, saw this action and jumped up, at once barking and wagging his tail. Aakash looked at the dog, then at me, and feigning confusion, offered the begum's exposed bottom to the dog with a sweep of his arm.

The begum saw and her face filled with anger. She lurched up, pushing out Aakash's fingers in the process and slapped her palm against his chest. Aakash nearly fell back.

'Motherfucker. Bastard. Wretch. Limp dick.'

Aakash folded his hands and begged forgiveness. The begum stormed round the room, sipping her whisky, staring at blank spaces, swinging round to glare at us. The back of her kaftan fell down and hung like a pleated blind. We sat unmoving next to each other on the sofa.

'Begum, please, forget it now, no? It was just a joke.'

'Just a joke? You dare humiliate me in front of your rich friends! Me? Who has known you since you were sixteen. I know everything about you. I could destroy you with a click of my fingers.'

Her tiger nails snapped in the air.

Her anger didn't seem real, but whatever threat she tormented him with had its effect. Aakash, prone to theatrical anger himself, looked around him for his phone and his bike keys, and rose to leave. He gestured to me to get up, and without looking at the begum, made for the door. The begum became hysterical. She clutched Aakash's arm, which he pulled away. She shook and pulled at her hair. She grabbed Zabar, the Alsatian, and dragged him along until she was at our feet, weeping, imploring Aakash not to go, holding up the dog's face, with its moonstone eyes, to hers.

I don't think I believed her exaggerated show of female emotions; I just didn't feel like leaving. I liked the flat's anonymity, the whiskies coming easily; I liked seeing Aakash play the role of the Sectorpur boy who'd grown up and gone away. I was also curious about what the begum had said about destroying Aakash with a click of her fingers. Destroy what? How? And for all these reasons, I tapped Aakash on the arm and said, 'Let's stay.'

He scanned my face, seemed quickly to make a decision, then turning to the begum, said, 'Ey, ey, listen, Begum. My friend here wants to stay. So out of respect to him we're going to stay. But you try anything crooked again . . .'

The begum sprang to her feet, kicking aside the dog. It was as if we were arriving for the first time. She straightened her hair as she slipped past us to pour two more whiskies.

Aakash chuckled at her good nature. 'Now she's set. Should we get down to it?'

'Down to what?'

He pressed what I thought was a packet of pan masala into my palm. When I felt its evasive hoop slide between my fingers I said, 'You're not serious? She's quite old and not very pretty.'

'She was my first.'

'Maybe, but . . .'

'It's for us, man. It's one of those things you have to do with your best friend.'

Before I could answer, he opened a bedroom door on our right and pushed me in. I was surprised at how domestic the room was, really like someone's home. It had glass, almond-shaped wall lights, a single plywood bed with a white lace bedcover and bedside tables. A stand in one corner contained what looked like broken ostrich eggs but were in fact the begum's foamy bras.

Aakash came in with her a few moments later. Her waxy hair was tied up with a pink scrunchy and instead of her kaftan she wore a satiny tiger-print slip. Aakash, seeing my alarm, began gently massaging the back of my neck. The begum walked towards the plywood bed, the dimples on her thighs forming new patterns with every step. There was something inoffensive to the point of attraction about her soft, hairless body. It seemed as though, once some original hesitation had been overcome, it would be possible to fuck her five times a night, in a way that would be less possible with more beautiful girls.

Aakash led me over to her by the neck, undoing his black pinstripe shirt as he walked. The begum had pulled out two pillows from under the lace bedcover. She rested her palms on one and her knees on the other. Her vagina was black, the hair around shaved clean, the thighs faintly powdered. As Aakash approached, she began to massage herself with her tiger-painted nails, and I noticed that on their yellowish-brown surface, interspersed between the black stripes, were also strands of red. I felt these details make too strong an impression. I knew that they would kill any possibility of sexual arousal.

Aakash at that moment had not only undone his own slate-grey jeans but was about to undo mine when I stopped him. I wasn't erect and the sight of his small, pencil-thin penis pushing sharply against his underwear intimidated me. His ease, his hedonistic ease, even as I had thought myself out of my body, intimidated me. I knew all along that this would be a problem. Seeming to read my mind, he pressed my crotch casually, and finding it soft, looked urgently at me, as if to say, 'Come on, man. Thirdeen, fordeen, we'll do it slowly . . .'

The begum sensed a disturbance behind her and looked back, perhaps thinking we were making fun of her again. Aakash was forced to act quickly. He pulled down his underwear, slipped his penis into the white latex he held in his fingers, and rising to the balls of his feet, pushed himself into the begum. Once he was inside her, he turned his attention back to me, draping one arm lightly over my shoulders for balance. He was no different from a man giving blood or urinating, and I stood next to him as though there for moral support. We made light conversation. I noticed a picture on the begum's bedside of a young man in a silver frame. He was dark-skinned and fine-featured, with amber Nepalese eyes and a cruel smile.

'Who's that?' I whispered to Aakash.

Aakash looked over, readjusting his balance.

'Her son,' he whispered, adding, 'my double,' with a smile.

But for the colour of his eyes, he looked nothing like Aakash. The begum must have heard us, must have felt Aakash move in her.

'What's all this khoospoos you're doing?' she snapped.

'Nothing, Begum,' Aakash yelled back. 'Just pointing out the photo of your son.'

'Oh,' the begum said, and lowered her head. 'Poor boy, working as a chowkidar.'

Aakash put both his thumbs to his temples and wiggled his fingers in a child's gesture of defiance.

When he was near climax, he rested his arm on my shoulder and began again to massage the back of my neck. His rough wrinkly fingers pressed painfully as he came nearer an orgasm. When at last he pulled out, in one movement tearing off the condom and thumbing out long strands of semen over the begum's back, I could hardly stand the pain. I pushed his hand away and he fell forward, dropping his body over the begum's for a moment and laughing euphorically.

'Slowly, slowly,' the begum cooed, as if glad to finally have some physical contact.

'Begum,' Aakash said in a broken voice, 'can I ask you something? You won't take it badly?'

'Tell me, baba.'

'I'm starving. Is there anything to eat? Brad, butter, a desi omelette?'

'Baba!' the begum said indulgently. 'Is this even something to ask for! Of course your begum will make you an omelette. You'll take green chillis in it, no?'

'Yes, Begum. You're the best.'

The begum rolled Aakash off her back, rose agilely and picked her way past me.

I sat down on the bed next to Aakash. He pulled his jeans back on and sat up. I thought that he spoke indirectly to me when he said, 'Don't mind what happened earlier. I have this problem routinely in my life. When I get involved with someone, I burrow into their mind. They can't get me out and they start behaving irrationally.'

'What was this deep, dark secret she kept going on about?'

'Nothing, man, nothing. She's mad. But let's leave all these serious things. We had fun, right?'

A few minutes later the begum appeared in the doorway with a plastic plate. As she handed it to him, Aakash looked up at her with adoring eyes. 'Food cooked by Begum's own hands,' he muttered, using Bollywood lines as he tore up the omelette with his fingers. She rested her palm on his shoulder. He sat crouched over the omelette, rolling up the long shreds he'd made before putting them into his mouth. Then lips glistening, chewing noisily, he looked up at us with the glazed contentment of cattle drinking. His self-absorption was that of a man who would have been truly amazed to learn that either of us had any plans other than to watch him wolf down a post-coital omelette.

My phone beeped. Sanyogita. 'Baby, off to bed. Will you be home soon?' I put it away, feeling an urgent longing for her bed and her warm, sleepy presence near me, washing clean the night's exposure. Aakash, licking his chops, looked resentfully over at the challenge to his centrality. The begum's nails drooped off his shoulder. The Alsatian had also now nosed its way in, and with its head edgewise, sniffed, and began licking clean Aakash's empty plate.

II

Delhi in that last week of May, despite the great heat, was filled with flowers. There were burnt orange blossoms on the gulmohar's fern-like leaves, mauve tendrils fountaining from the jarul's thatched canopy, and the blaze itself seeming to reside in the laburnum's yellow flowers.

On my last afternoon I sat with Zafar, reading the Urdu newspaper. The affection that had grown between us had softened his insistence on teaching me to write. I'd mastered the script's meaningful single and double dots and mysterious elisions, and had started reading well. But if I ever confused an 'n' with a 'b', he would croak irritably. If only I'd followed his advice and learned to write first, none of this would be a problem.

The newspaper was a thin, oily rag with splashes of bright colour and ink that blackened your fingers. The sessions with Zafar had reinforced my vocabulary in definite ways. I drank in ordinary words like 'often', 'perhaps', 'unintentionally' and 'complete'. Simple words; easy to take for granted till lost and regained in another language. The newspaper offered them up daily, and reading it also became a way for Zafar and me to discuss the week's events.

For months now the country had been seeing waves of new motiveless crime. In Bombay, there were the beer-can murders. A bearded jihadi wandered the city's streets, hunting down homosexuals. His calling card was a can of Kingfisher left by the bodies of his victims. Ra was hysterical about copycat murders in Delhi, now seeing its own incidents of brand-new crime in its satellite towns. In Sectorpur there was a flesh-eating serial killer in whose oven the skeletal remains of women and children had been found. And in Phasenagar there was a double homicide. A fourteen-year-old girl had been found with her throat slashed while her parents slept in the next room. When the police arrived, ready to arrest the servant, they found him face down in a pool of his own blood. The death of their natural suspect threw their investigation into disarray. A day later, the girl's father was arrested. He was said to have killed her for threatening to expose a wife-swapping arrangement with his best friend. The TV channels fed the public each detail in hourly intervals; the city was mesmerized. There was in the details an inexplicable . . .

'. . . vehshat,' Zafar offered.

'What?'

'Vehshat,' he repeated.

The sound that gave the word its ring was 'ehsh'. It had the same casual violence of words like lash and stash, but the 'eh' sound was less direct, less open, oblique somehow. It was a word that seemed to convey meaning before I knew what it meant; it rhymed with dehshat, terror, and began almost like vaishya, whore. But Zafar was stuck; he looked through three dictionaries without finding a synonym I could understand. The badly printed Urdu–English dictionary offered 'wild' and 'savage', but when I translated that back into Urdu for Zafar, he said that was wrong. We often ended up in these hopeless circles. I didn't understand his Urdu explanations and he didn't understand the dictionary enough to confirm or reject its synonym. So vehshat lingered, full of suggestiveness but without clear meaning. And yet it seemed so right, detonating from Zafar's lips as soon as he read the newspaper. The power of its effect on both him and me, and the lack of a synonym to describe that effect, made Zafar say more.

He seemed to measure me up before revealing what was on his mind. Then, as if resigned to the risk of being misunderstood, he said, 'There's a vehshat deep within this country. It comes, I think, from the religion. Or, perhaps, because the socially conscious religions, Christianity and Islam, never gained a firm enough footing. They could never close over the history of animalism and sacrifice. The land and people of this country retain this memory. And it gives them this capacity, a capacity for vehshat.'

Zafar treated me like a Muslim. The hunted-minority expression widened his eyes and stilled his lips. 'The land is stained,' he muttered. 'It has seen terrible things: girl children sacrificed, widows burned, the worship of idols. The people in their hearts do not fear God. Their law is not theirs, you see. It was first the Muslim law and then it was the English. And because the law is alien, they can always shrug it off and the vehshat returns.'

I turned absent-mindedly to the paper and was leafing through its greasy pages when I saw a picture of Chamunda. It was a grainy image of her in red and green astride a lion. If not for the distinctiveness of her features, her comic-book lips, her vast eyes, I might not have recognized her. She wore a gold crown and carried a trident. At her ankleted feet, a priest knelt over a Shiva linga, smearing it orange. Garlands of jasmine, roses and marigolds were tied tightly around its base. I couldn't read the caption and asked Zafar for help.

'They have made the BJP Chief Minister of Jhaatkebaal, Chamunda Devi, into the goddess Durga and are worshipping her in temples,' Zafar sneered.

I laughed, and before I could check myself I'd said, 'I know her. She's Sanyogita's aunt.'

Zafar looked sadly at me, as if I'd let him down by this admission of closeness to the Hindu nationalist party. Though it was well before the usual time, he asked that we take a cigarette break. I was suddenly aware of how frail he was. This awareness, alongside the fineness of his manners, the umbrella, the little cap, the pen always in place, the safari suit impeccable, made me feel that I hadn't so much offended him as manhandled him.

On the balcony, he took out his blue packet of Wins and offered me one. From inside the packet came a black windproof lighter with a near-invisible flame. He liked to tell me that the cigarettes were Italian and had travelled via the east, Burma in particular, to India. But today he just smoked quietly, looking out at the large trees shielding us from the sun.

Long black pods hung like many walking sticks from the branches of a laburnum. On the edge of the canopy, yellow blossoms pushed reluctantly through like paint squeezed from a sponge. Their bright colour against the black of the pods and the dull green of the canopy made them seem of a different material from the rest of the tree, more like points of sunlight than flowers.

'Amaltas,' Zafar said, 'the true beginning of the heat.'

And as if retreating from its glare, he put out his cigarette and went inside. I was studying his tufts of dyed black hair, dotted with maroon sores, when my eye trailed along his neck to a point between its base and the shoulder blade. There, off to the right, and seeming to catch a different light, was a small but distinct swelling. I reached forward and touched it. Zafar winced in pain. It was hard and knobby, somewhere between bone and cartilage.

'What's that?'

'I'm becoming a camel,' Zafar chuckled, his eyes betraying his fear.

'This isn't a joke. What is that? Have you shown it to a doctor?'

He took out a soiled and folded piece of paper from his pocket. It read:

Biopsy report: gross appearance, irregular greyish-white tissue along with dirty brown debris received, total measuring 1 x 1.5 cm

Histopathological report: microsection shows features of sebaceous cyst no e/o tb or malignancy seen

Diagnosis: sebaceous cyst

Dr Lipike Lipi, pathologist

'They say it's benign, but I'll need an operation. I'll have it while you're away.'

'Does it hurt?'

'Only when touched. The problem is it makes my reading and writing work, which I do on the floor, quite difficult. You can say that it's just part of old age.'

'You're not so old, Zafar. You're younger than my mother.'

'Yes, but life . . .'

'. . . has made you old,' I completed for him.

He laughed. Then as if wishing neither to alarm me nor to let me make light of what he had said, he added, 'The place I live has made me old.'

The place he lived! How embarrassing that I hadn't seen it. This attitude was a remnant of my childhood in Delhi, not so much a lack of curiosity as blindness. I resolved to go. Then a shudder went through me at the thought of this place that gave Zafar his sores, and now this new deformity. It was one other thing, like the heat, that he would bear while I was away.

The vehshat, the vehshat!

Sanyogita was part of a circle of creative-writing professionals called Emigrés at Home. Their weekly meeting coincided with our last night in Delhi. They met at a different group member's house each week, and as Sanyogita had not offered hers so far, she decided to host this last meeting in the Jorbagh flat. Her friends Mandira and Ra were part of the group and so the meeting was also a farewell party of sorts. When I went to have a shower after my lesson with Zafar, Vatsala and Sanyogita were preparing the flat. Lamps were coming on; aubergine dips were being laid out; some light Brazilian music had begun to play. I knew that this kind of activity, reminiscent of her London life, meant a lot to Sanyogita. We had been through a difficult period that hadn't been resolved as much as it had been presumed to end with our departure; I told myself in the shower that this would be the first active night of repair. It would start with my showing support for the creative writers. Her meetings with them were an assertion of her life in Delhi as separate from mine; but Sanyogita, who encouraged me in everything I did, would have liked nothing more than my endorsement for her 'thing'.

When I came out of the shower the heat was breaking in a dust storm. It had stopped the day's natural decline and cast a greenish-purple twilight hour over the city. After raging in the canopies of big Delhi trees, the storm entered the garden terrace, sweeping up fine dust off the floor, roughing up dahlias and denuding the dead frangipani of its last leaves.

In the lamp-lit room the meeting had begun. The people assembled were mostly older women in ethnic and tribal-print saris, with hair greying in buns for political reasons. There were also a handful of very tall, very thin young men with bad posture, as well as one or two older men in cotton kurtas and jeans. One dark, lightly bearded, young writer with sharp features sat at the feet of a woman with a red oversized bindi. She rested a wrist, heavy with silver bangles, on his shoulder as he stared morosely at the pages in his lap. His uncut toenails were visible in the blue rubber chappals he wore. The intensity of his stare, and a feeling that I knew him from somewhere, prevented me at first from listening to what the woman introducing him was saying.

In a far corner of the room, Sanyogita beamed at me, patting the empty space next to her. As I walked across the room, I heard the older woman, with her hand beating lightly against the young writer's collarbone, say that he had attended a creative-writing programme in America; he was among the group's most significant talents, best representing its theme, 'Children of a post-colonial god: Indians feeling foreign in India'.

He was to read his story 'The Assignation'.

The young man looked up at the room with dim, sad eyes. Prognathous, his smile, and later soft words, were almost lost in the cavity between his projecting lower jaw and face.

'"The Assignation",' he repeated in a south Delhi American accent.

'Where's your story?' I whispered to Sanyogita.

'I'm not reading today,' she said, clutching my hand. 'This is the last one.'

'There've already been a few?'

'Yes, a story and a poem. Now listen.'

Mandira and Ra, who were sitting next to each other, looked over. Mandira smiled; Ra clenched a fist into the air in a gesture of affection, then mouthed, 'Pay attention to this. It'll be really good. He's a new voice out of Sectorpur.'

'Has everyone read it already?' I said to Sanyogita. 'Shh, baby. No. Listen.'

The creative writer began: 'Winter in Delhi. The street was enveloped in a stagy mist, harbouring pink bougainvillea. Men outside the teashop acted their parts, wrapping scarves around their faces and rubbing their hands. The hard-bellied owner, looking down at them over a roaring blue flame, handed out cups of tea as though moving chess pieces. An astrologically auspicious window to marry had opened and in many houses fairy lights hung from the trees, white shamianas sprang up and tinny music tore out of concealed speakers. I had lived unseasonably since my return, forgetting what the winter meant. But as the city awoke inevitably to the season, these reminders of my own long history there pierced the haze of the past several months.

'I entered Lodhi Gardens through the park's old entrance. Its British name, Lady Willingdon Gardens, was engraved on stone pillars flanking the locked iron gate. An unsteady, bright green turnstile had been installed next to it. White cars belonging to politicians, with red sirens and black cat commandos, were parked boldly outside where some variety of municipal work was forever under way. To enter the park, I had to sidestep thin ladies in bright colours, carrying shallow dishes of cement to and from a mound of mud half-filled with water, and men, despite the cold, in fraying vests, digging soft earth out of the pavement.

'A path of concrete discs led down an avenue of white-trunked palms. On the left, the rough, red, crenellated walls of a tomb ran along a strip of clumpy grass. The tombs were bare, scarred and not beautiful, but faultless as ornaments for a park. One emerged now, with the remains of glazed turquoise tiles hanging like dead skin from its rough surface, evoking a Turkic memory deep within the Indian plain.

'There were new faces in Lodhi Gardens, less serious walkers whom the summer heat had kept away. Among the usual women in salwar kurtas and sneakers, couples canoodling under trees and idle youth walking hand in hand, there were tourists crossing the paths of fast walkers, social ladies in velvety tracksuits and Delhi queens.

'My walk was just beginning to gather pace, when passing one of the darker peripheries of the park, I noticed a slender young man watching me. I was struck by the fineness of his features and, despite his obvious poverty, his vanity and attention to style. He wore flared jeans and a close-fitting off-white shirt. He smiled first, not a bitter, gay smile, but a dark, malevolent smile. I returned it with a macho smirk saved only for bold advances from unlikely people. This seemed to register with the young man because he laughed out loud and approached in a dainty swagger. As he came out of the shadows, I marvelled at his physical beauty. His face had a Nepalese cast; he had dark smooth skin, a clean hairless neck and a small, precise mouth. His poverty though, was visible in his stained teeth and the murky whites of his light eyes.

'As soon as he came near, I felt acute social embarrassment. Lodhi Gardens was full of fashionable people whom I knew, or knew a little, and I didn't wish to be seen speaking to a man who was hardly better than a servant, especially a man as attractive as this one. He seemed to read my embarrassment and prolonged it. When I asked him for his telephone number, he responded with mock confusion: why would I want his telephone number?

'"Please, quickly," I said, as if speaking to a servant. "I have to finish my walk."

'"But first, tell me . . ."

'"Listen, I have to go. Do you have a mobile or not?"

'The mention of that magic status symbol stopped the man's playful delays. He whipped out his phone and held it insolently before me.

'"Give me your number," he said.

'I hurriedly gave him my number.

'"Name?"

'"Krishna," I answered.'

Krishna! The moment I heard the name, though he went by Kris and not Krishna, I remembered where I had seen the creative writer. He also worked out at Junglee, but with Pradeep, the other trainer. He was a friend of Aakash's top lawyer-client, Sparky Punj, and I had seen them many times, having a protein shake together after their workout. Aakash had taken an irrational dislike to him – linked no doubt to his choice of trainer – and called him Lul, literally dick, but more like limp dick.

'He's a gay!' he would say every time Kris walked past, oblivious to Aakash's hatred of him.

'So what, Aakash?'

'So what, Aakash?' he would imitate in a girly voice and fall back into a sullen silence.

The thought of Aakash gave me a pang. I had hardly seen him since the night with the Begum of Sectorpur. He had cancelled trainings without notice, didn't return missed calls and messages; he became moody at Junglee. His coldness, after the intimacy and excess of that day, affected me badly. I suspected that it was related to our episode with the begum. It was as if Aakash had rightly judged the unease it had left me with, but in a strange inversion, he pre-empted the possibility of my withdrawing by withdrawing himself. And in this way he had not only erased all discomfort I might have had from that day but also left me mourning his sudden absence in my life. I would find myself waiting for his text messages and phone calls. I'd reach for my phone first thing in the morning to see if something had come through. I thought up banal reasons to call him. If he didn't show up at the gym, I wouldn't work out, coming away feeling that not only had the hour been wasted but the day too. I cancelled plans made weeks in advance to see him, knowing full well that should something come up in his life, he would cancel me without a word. When I confronted him about his behaviour, he lied effortlessly. He had called, but my number was engaged; my text messages hadn't reached him; his brother had borrowed his phone. If I questioned him further, he became upset and conversation shut down. His lying was also an aspect of his confidence, a supreme belief that even if the details of what he was saying were wrong, he couldn't ever be wrong himself. His aloofness in that last week in Delhi put an added strain on my relationship with Sanyogita. She noticed that I was irritable and distracted and she sensed why. I couldn't explain my exact condition because I didn't fully understand it myself. I only knew that the euphoria I had felt on that Jet Airways flight back to Delhi, that cautious euphoria that reduced me to tears, had become tied up with Aakash and the world he opened up to me. But in the end, after many gestures of friendship, I'd stopped trying too; my last communication with him, to which I received no reply, had been a text message, reminding him of my departure and inviting him to Sanyogita's party.

Caught up in these considerations, I found I'd missed some of the conversation in the creative writer's story. The mention of his name drew me in again.

'"OK, Krishna," the man said doubtfully. "I'll give you a missed call."

'"OK, OK," I replied, in a voice that sounded as if I was instructing him to do some work for me, and moved on quickly. When

I looked back, I saw that the man stood where he was and a smile played on his dark lips as he finished entering my number into his phone. He must have seen me because he looked up and waved his arm at me. "OK, Krishna. Remember me. I'm Jai. I'll call you tonight."

'A few moments later, my phone vibrated in my pocket. I saved Jai's number and carried on with my walk.

'An assignation! I thought. I had made so many abroad, sometimes just walking past a man in the street: a suggestive look, a follow-up glance thrown over the shoulder a few paces later and an exchanged number. That was all. But now, despite being in my own country, exchanging numbers with another Indian, I felt on more unfamiliar ground than I had ever been on in the West, felt I couldn't judge the man's motives. This was what happened when everyone had a phone! It was amazing to think of the technology, available even to men like Jai, that brought us together and made possible the assignation, at once real but also indefinite and avoidable: the ingredients of anonymity.

'I finished my rounds of the park. The winter brought clearer days and the sky, still blue on my first round and barnacled with scaly clouds, burned with scattered orange fires on my second. The subsequent rounds of the park, the dimness of evening and the drama of the second sky erased my memory of the encounter with Jai. I arrived back at my flat to tea and heaters. By the time I came out of the shower, a mild dusk had submitted to the curfew of a smoky night.

'I ate dinner from a trolley in front of the television. The servants had gone to bed and I was checking my mail when Jai's name flashed on my phone. His beauty had faded from my mind; the night seemed deep and inaccessible; I answered the phone reluctantly.

'"Krishna?" the voice said.

'"Sorry?"

'"Is that Krishna speaking?"

'"Oh yes, yes."

"'Should we meet? Where do you live? I can come to you."

"'No," I said, asserting myself against the forcefulness of the voice on the other end. "We can't meet here."

"'Why?"

"'Because the servants are here."

"'So? You can't have guests in front of your servants?"

'I realized the offence I caused. It was true: Jai was too much like a servant himself for me to have him over at the house as a guest. I felt my Hindi fail me.

"'My mother's here too. It's better we meet outside."

"'Where?"

"'Can you come to the beginning of Tughlak Lane?"

"'You know I'll have to come by rickshaw. It's quite expensive and far."

"'I'll help."

"'What?"

"'I'll help you with the fare."

'A silence followed. "OK," the voice said at last. "I'll see you in fifteen minutes."

'Jai's desire to come to the house unnerved me. I removed my Breitling before leaving the house. I was aware as I entered the night of a pretence on my part: that this was like assignations I had known before, in other places.

'The depth of the night alarmed me. The haze compressed the yellow street light into tight orbs. The faces of the figures around the chai shop were wrapped up completely in their scarves, leaving only a little space for their eyes. They gathered around a shallow dish in which they'd started a fire. A bulb in the shop illuminated the grime in its windows. I could make out the owner's vast silhouette, over a blue flame and an eternally boiling kettle. Walking past the shop and its damp washing area, crowded with gas cylinders, crates and a young boy cleaning dishes in a metal sink, I felt I was leaving some final outpost. Though Tughlak Lane was hardly a hundred yards away, the short stretch of road ahead was deserted and badly lit. Occasionally, I passed other figures, all invisible men in their woollens; scrawny bitches, with udders flapping, crept along the edges of the road, scalloped with yellow pools of light.

'Between my street and Tughlak Lane, a single fluorescent lamp flickered in the darkness, interrupting the stretch of yellow lights. I waited under it for Jai's arrival. For the first time since I had arranged the assignation, I felt a pang of excitement twist in me, harden and settle among nerves and uncertainty.

'A few minutes later, the headlight of a rickshaw charted its way through the darkness like a submarine. Jai leaned out of it, alert and ready. As soon as he saw me, he swung out of the rickshaw and ran next to it for a few paces. His ease, his obvious street smartness, were intimidating. He seemed to take charge, and when I put my hand in my pocket, he signalled to me not to and paid the rickshaw himself.

'"He'd have given you a different rate," he said disparagingly as the rickshaw drove off. "So where do you live?"

'"Just around here."

'"Where?"

'"Will you stop asking so many questions?"

'Jai smiled. His manner seemed to change. "Come on, then. Let's go for a walk; it's a beautiful night."

'I had been on the verge of calling the whole thing off, but now felt a little calmer. I chose Tughlak Lane for its nearness to me, but also its beauty. The low, full boughs of the trees lining the lane formed a tunnel and the street lights buried in their canopies burnished parts of the tree with a metallic lustre. It seemed almost to plate the leaves, giving them a solidity they lacked in the daytime. Even the disease, covering the leaves of all the trees on Tughlak Lane with white blotches, now at night seemed part of the light's alchemic imagination. The Lutyens bungalows of Tughlak Lane were home to politicians, including the heir of the country's political first family, and the road we walked down was bounded by green sentry boxes, sandbags and high barbed-wire fences. Over the bungalows' low red walls were ochre houses with arched verandas and large lawns.

'Jai was impressed.

'"This is a VIP area," he said quietly.

'"Yes."

'"Are your family VIPs?"

'"No."

'"What does your father do?"

'My irritation returned, but this time Jai caught it. "Leave it," he said. "I don't want to know. I'll just say one thing. Today, when I met you, I felt I'd made a friend who could help me. You know I'm not a rich man or even middle class, but I have this desire to succeed that prevents me from sleeping. And I know that if I was given just a little assistance, that small lifting hand, I would make it."

'"What do you do?" I asked, annoyed at the mistake I felt I'd made. Only in India could you pick someone up and end up with a gulf this wide between their intentions and yours.

'Jai said he worked as a chowkidar; that his family in Nepal were high caste and had not always been poor; his mother lived alone in Sectorpur; he wanted to improve her life. I felt I'd heard all this before. I was wretched about my unreciprocated desire for Jai, which had grown with expectation. I noticed his dark smooth skin in the yellow light and experienced an angry sense of entitlement.

'We passed a house where a wedding was taking place. The blackish-orange heads of mushroom heaters, halogen floodlights and colourful satin cloth that skirted the tent's white roof were visible from the street. Indian bagpipers in kilts played over the din of voices and laughter. In the dark foliage on the edge of the party, fairy-lit in places, chauffeurs and uniformed banquet staff lurked among steel cauldrons and the light from naked bulbs. Jai wanted to go in. He guessed correctly that I knew whose party it was.

'We had come to a crossroads on Tughlak Lane. Ahead was a busy main road; on either side, dark service lanes; and behind us, the tunnel of twisted, gold-plated leaves. I looked up and

noticed sharp, razor-edged barbed wire coiled around the bent
necks of Tughlak Lane's street lights.

'I slipped my hand over Jai's shoulders and led him into a dark
service lane on the left. We entered those little streets of Lutyens's
Delhi, devoted entirely to servants' quarters and dhobis. In the
now much thicker darkness, I ran my hand over Jai's chest and
stomach, feeling its slim firmness through the cheap, synthetic
fabric of his shirt. Jai, who had spoken without stopping about
his aspirations, said, "You know, when I came here tonight, I
thought I would be spending the whole night with you."

'"I know, but we can't go to my house."

'"Why?"

'"Because of the servants . . ."

'"But . . ."

'"Because you're like a servant too," I snapped.'

Many different things – my familiarity with Tughlak Lane; the
need for respite from the story and its creative-writing theme;
the blunt violent line bursting from the author's dead lips; the
memory of Delhi in the winter – came together to make me
look up and around the room, like someone surfacing for air.
The others were captivated. The older woman's braceleted wrist
was rooted firmly on the author's shoulder; another tall, young
man, also in rubber chappals, took notes; Sanyogita listened
wide-eyed; only Ra noticed the disturbance near the door of the
lamp-lit room, and by following his eyes mine came to Aakash
in a red Puma T-shirt, leaning against his tricep in the doorway.

'Ash-man,' I breathed.

'Yes, man,' he replied, relishing my surprise, then puckering
up his blackish-pink lips as if about to blow bubbles, mouthed,
'Lul. Lul. Lul.'

I lowered my head, laughing silently, but Sanyogita saw me.

'Baby!' she hissed.

I pointed to Aakash. She looked up, smiled and gestured to

him to come over. He hesitated, then made his way swiftly through the crowded room. A few silver-haired women watched him keenly; the men looked gloomy and irritated. The creative writer stopped his story, perhaps from wonderment at Aakash's appearance so far from Junglee. As soon as he had sat down at our feet, the writer began again.

'Jai didn't mind. "I want you to know," he said, "that any time, I mean any time, night or day, you can call me and I'll come. If you have friends, whatever. See, the thing is, living in Delhi, I've developed a taste for money and I'm willing to do anything for it."

'"Do you want money now?"

'"Man, what are you saying? You're my friend."

'On our right, a village of washing lines appeared. The white clothes that hung limply from bamboo poles in the cold night had a morbid, ghostly aspect. Further on, a park with a thin grass cover and a sandy surface was coated in dew. Suddenly a pack of dogs leapt at the gate of the park, growling, barking, showing teeth and gums. I jumped back. But Jai, as assured as he had been with the rickshaw, raced forward, picking up a stone on the way. When the dogs didn't run from him, he flung the stone with a fast side throw and hit one of the dogs on the cheek. I heard the impact of the stone against skin and bone and the easy cruelty of it chilled me. The dog howled at so shrill a note that the others melted into the darkness of the park.

'Just ahead, there was a servants' colony. In the open doors and windows televisions flashed. A girl in a red sweater combed lice out of the hair of another girl and the smell of winter clothes in need of airing arose. The walls of the servants' colony were mildewed and blackish-green in places; some windows were bricked up; and in one the powerful, pythonic roots of a peepal tree slid into, and cracked, the front drain and wall.

'I pulled Jai back into the darkness.

'"How much?" I asked.

'"For what?" Jai said.

'I squirmed. I longed to be able to speak to him in English. I had no language in Hindi for what I wanted to say. At last, I said for a kiss, but it sounded absurd.

'"What a guy you are, you want to pay me for a kiss!"

'I leaned forward and kissed him. His lips didn't move; I tasted chewing tobacco on them.

'"Come on now," Jai said, "what do you really want to do?"

'"I want to suck your dick."'

At that moment Aakash looked up at me, his eyebrows dancing with amusement. I had hoped he wasn't following the story.

The creative writer's tone became urgent: 'Jai pulled me further into the darkness. We were near the washing village. He took me behind a grey electricity box; it had a rusting base, and a thick black wire, partly buried in the earth, spiralled out of it.

'"Then suck," he said.

'I was struck by his freedom; and opening Jai's flared jeans and pulling down his baggy villager's underwear, I felt I was dealing with a man who could always satisfy his appetites. And this was what had made me feel the limitations of being a Western-educated homosexual: in the love I had learned, there was a grammar, a language, living rules of conduct, all useless now.

'Jai's arousal grew; he undid my trousers and reached for my penis.

'"How come your dick is so much bigger than mine?" he said, holding it up from the base with his palm. "You must give your girlfriend a really good time. Does she suck you?"

'"Yes," I lied.

'"Where is she?"

'"At home."

'"Why? Doesn't she take care of you?"

'"Her parents don't allow her out late at night."

'"Where does she live?"

'"Greater Kailash."

'Though I lied, I felt it was somehow necessary, part of a social pretence. Jai, now obviously aroused, suddenly grabbed me and pressed himself against me, rubbing and shaking in a comic way. His movements became instinctive. With the same ease, the assuredness that had intimidated me, he turned me around and wanted to enter me.

'"No!" I said. "Are you crazy? Don't you think about protection or anything?"

'He misunderstood. "Fine, you come inside me, but then you'll have to give me something."

'"What?"

'"Just a little money, whatever you have."

'"This is not about money."

'"OK then, let me just seat my dick on you," he said, choosing a formal word used in relation to kings and thrones.

'I had never considered how important the vocabulary surrounding a sexual act was. I submitted to the new word, as if working under a new law. It was only when Jai's arousal grew further and he tried again to enter me that I fought him off.

'"Bas," Jai said, "I'm about to drop." I was also close to climax when Jai with some panic in his voice, said, "Don't drop any on me."

'It was then that I caught a glimpse of his Brahmin's thread, dangling from his shirt and vest. It tickled me to see this small notion of sexual cleanliness come out of him so late into everything. Somehow this unexplained barrier – a caste horror perhaps – had survived. Now, for the first time, I felt as though I had some power over this man who had flaunted his freedoms, whose strong sweat and polyester odour filled my nostrils and made me feel wretched. Close to climax, I slipped my right hand behind Jai's smooth Nepalese neck, pressing it lightly, and with my left, in a single wrenching motion, sprinkled watery drops of semen over the shaft and uncircumcised head of Jai's penis.

'He recoiled with disgust and began furiously wiping his penis. I squeezed out the last few drops on to his small closed fist and the dusty edge of the road.

'Then putting a hundred rupees in his shirt pocket, I began walking away. I wasn't envious of him now, but worried he might follow me to my house. I felt him grab my wrist and turn it over.

'"You don't wear a watch?"

'"No."

'He smiled bitterly. "A hundred rupees is very little."

'"Enough for a rickshaw," I replied, and turned away.

'After a pause, and once the protections of haze and street light had settled between us again, I heard yelled down Tughlak Lane the words: "OK, Krishna. Remember, call any time you like. Jai is there."'

The creative writer folded away the story's pages and rested his large veiny hands, with their fleshy, nail-bitten tips, on his kneecaps. There was no applause, but the room soon filled with praising remarks. 'Bold theme', 'exploitative values', 'neo-colonial alienation', 'Section 377 of the Indian Penal Code' were bandied about. Aakash listened with fascination; I read the gold letters on the back of his red T-shirt. They were the destination points of a Grand Prix: Sakhir, Hockenheim, Silverstone, Interlagos. A few minutes later, the creative writers disbanded for the summer. The Brazilian music picked up, dinner was laid out on the dining table – hummus, kibbeh, pomegranate salad – and vodka tonics in clear glasses sweated in dark hands.

Aakash drank purposefully, filling his glass two or three times. Whenever he'd catch my eye, he'd open his mouth wide and pour the remains of his drink down his throat. Sanyogita, drinking cold lethal vodkas straight, had slipped her arm into his and was taking him round the room, introducing him to Emigrés at Home. She could always include people, especially if she sensed they were important to me. The creative writers, especially the greying women, delighted in the attention Aakash paid them.

I heard one coo, 'No, now what is left for me? I'm no spring chicken. How can I get in shape so late in the day?'

'No! Whaddyou saying, ma'am? You're still a very young, beaudiful woman. Aakash is there, no?' I heard in reply.

Then Sanyogita: 'Come on, you big flirt. Stop charming the chappals off these old women.'

I was scanning the room for the author of 'The Assignation' when I heard whispered in my ear, 'Help, I'm Jai!'

I swung around and saw Ra.

'Hello, darling. So good of you to grace our creative writers' circle with your presence. So tell me, no? What's happening?'

'Not much. We're off tomorrow.'

'He's quite the little dish, your trainer?'

'Ash-man?'

'Hash-man. What did you think of the story?'

'You know, I know him a little, the author. He comes to Junglee as well.'

'Really? Poor Kris. Always so down in the dumps.'

'Why?'

'Tch, you know, these Hindi-speaking gay types have a very tough time, hiding from the parents, sneaking off with chowkidars, the self-loathing – it's all too squalid.'

'He can't be all that Hindi-speaking if he lives in Lutyens's Delhi and went abroad for university.'

'First generation. And he doesn't live in Lutyens's Delhi, he lives in Sectorpur.'

'I thought you didn't know where Sectorpur was.'

'I do now. In the kingdom of the divine Chamunda! He just writes about Lutyens's Delhi; it's his creative milieu. His father owns Jorbagh Taxis, you know?'

'How do you know so much about him?'

'It's not what you think; we're like two sisters.'

'Like three sisters,' Mandira said, hovering up with a Scotch and soda. 'Hi, Aatish, nice to see you out. Sanyogita tells me you've been being very pricey.'

'No, just work, Mandira,' I said, feeling a sudden dread at the mention of the word. 'It's not really coming.'

'I'm sorry to hear it,' she said thoughtfully. 'But come out and have some fun, yaar. You'll feel much better. How can you write anything if you stay cooped up in your flat the whole time?'

There was a lull. Ra looked nervously around the room, as if feeling the burden of keeping the conversation alive. Then his eyes glittered and he beckoned us closer.

'Got some goss?' Mandira giggled, taking a step forward.

Ra nodded his head vigorously. Then grabbing my head and Mandira's as if about to bang them together, he wetly whispered, 'Jai's not just any chowkidar; he's *his* chowkidar!' And letting go our heads, he shrieked with laughter.

His laughter coincided with a disturbance at the far end of the room. The double doors overlooking the park and mango tree flew open. A wall of wind and spray blew through the flat.

The creative writers gasped in one voice, 'Rain, unseasonal rain!'

The months before the monsoon were months of anticipation. The flowering trees, the glare, the blackness of shadows each played their part. The heat was to be endured and complained about, its dryness marvelled at; it was not meant to break like this, at the hands of a mutinous dust storm.

The older people, as if distancing themselves from an impropriety, said their goodbyes and began to leave. But for the young, rain was rain; what matter when it came. Sanyogita hitched up her long skirt and ran on to the little balcony. Of the four or five people who remained, only Aakash looked grimly on the scene, muttering, 'Not good, not good for the fields.'

But Sanyogita was in a spontaneous mood. She was often so guarded in her show of feelings that sometimes the need for release, working together with the effects of alcohol, would make her boisterous, impulsive, unaware of her own strength. She now wanted all her remaining guests to come downstairs and run with her in the rain. There was something inauspicious about the idea. It was a monsoon activity, a childhood activity; if resurrected, it needed its time; it couldn't be forced. But that night everyone felt the desire to please. After some token resistance the five of us, Sanyogita, Mandira, Ra, Aakash and I, ran down the darkened marble stairs into the rain.

It was warm rain, acidic and dusty. The earth was not parched enough to release the smells of the monsoon, the trees not thirsty enough to thrash about, blind worms not inconvenienced enough to appear from their holes on to Jorbagh's wet streets, shimmering with street light. And yet we ran through them alone, jumping in puddles and singing film songs. We ran past the flower shop, the pan wallah, the arboured street holding the Chocolate Wheel, until we came to the gates of Jorbagh. Beyond was the main road and the border of Lutyens's Delhi. A drenched guard in a canvas trench coat let us through before retreating to his green sentry box. The main road was empty but for the odd car hurtling home. We crossed it and walked along the periphery of Lodhi Gardens, its interior alive with white light and dark wet foliage.

Mandira and Aakash ran ahead. A sudden closeness formed between them, but Aakash seemed only to use it as a counterpoint to Sanyogita and me. He kept looking back, and if he saw Sanyogita with her hands draped about me, kissing me in the rain, he would find some way to hijack my attention. He was like a possessive best friend from the early years of puberty. His red T-shirt was soaked, and raindrops, each swollen with light, hung from his sharp features and bristly hair. Mandira was much more taken with him than he was with her, and with her hand curled about his face, kept yelling, 'So good to be promiscuous again,' into the night. Sanyogita, who had known her through her days of sexual promiscuity and only seen her find some stability after marriage, looked nervously at her regression. Ra, straggling behind, yelled, 'Shut up, you drunk bitch. Or I'll tell your husband.' His white designer shirt was soaked and his small hairy stomach showed through.

It was Aakash who first saw the mouth of Amrita Shergill Marg. It gave him an excuse to run back, take me from Sanyogita, and resting his heavy arm on my shoulders, pull me ahead to see what he'd seen. 'I want you to be with me when you first see this,' he said overexcitedly, pinching my face. 'I love you, man. I'm having so much fun.' His drunkenness, his intensity, his affection, all coming after the distance of the past few weeks, were overpowering. In withdrawing, he'd made me aware daily of his absence, and now filling the empty space he'd created, he filled it completely.

When we were just near the corner of the street, he pressed the palm of his hand over my eyes, and standing close behind me, marched me up the pavement. I felt us step down into the street, walk forward a few paces so that we would have been close to the middle. Then I was swivelled around and made to stand visionless, facing down the length of the street. Aakash held me there, and using my left arm, raised himself on to his tiptoes and asked in my ear if I was ready. Then he tore away his hand to reveal a tunnel of laburnum, its many millions of blossoms bleached in rain and street light. Under each little tree, distorting my sense of space, were spheres of petals, dropping like petticoats down the length of the crescent-shaped street. It was as if Aakash had broken open the trunk of an old tree to show me a sanctuary of moss and cool. 'I love you,' he said again, with that same desperation with which he'd once asked me to drink with him. 'I'm going to miss you, man.' I couldn't understand his urgency, but somehow it brought to this ordinary evening, but for the rain, an aspect of finality.

When the others caught up with us Aakash looked at me with such feeling that Mandira and Ra began teasing him. 'And I thought you were in love with me, you bloody cheat. Here I am ditching my poor husband for you!' Aakash was unaffected by their teasing; in fact, he was more fearless in showing his affection than before. But Sanyogita didn't joke or laugh; she'd seen something, perhaps not so much in his eyes as in mine. She came close to me and whispered, 'Baby . . .' in the softest voice. Aakash's eyes ran cold at the sight of her. He pulled me aside. I excused myself despite my embarrassment.

'What is it, man?' I asked when we were out of earshot of the others.

'Are we going to take them both or what?' Aakash said with fresh zeal.

I laughed out loud, then saw he was serious. 'Aakash, one of "them" is my girlfriend!'

'So what, man? I'm not saying –'

'No, Aakash. I know what you're saying and we're not doing it.'

I walked back to the others, leaving Aakash with some words still on his lips. He looked incredulous, then his face showed a hurt, dazed expression.

Ra pranced up to him. 'Come on, lover boy, stop being such a kebab me haddi.'

Aakash looked down at him, and his face clearing, he put one hand on Ra's stomach and said, 'I'm going to make you fit, man.' They began to walk up the street. Aakash spoke to Ra with the same energy and interest with which he had spoken to me. Ra shed his cynicism and was slowly seduced. His eyes turned from playful and flirtatious to hungry; I heard him invite Aakash to a party while we were away. He kept prodding his chest and stomach with a single finger, and saying, 'Hash-man, oh gawd, how disgusting, all veins and muscles.' They spoke about Delhi being quiet and peaceful in the summer and how it was possible to do things one didn't ordinarily do, like have breakfast in the old city. I heard all this and was jealous, miserably jealous. I knew now that Aakash wanted me to feel that way.

The rain, not being genuine monsoon rain, was sucked up by the atmosphere. An uneasy peace held between dry and humid heat, and the air, with its varying temperature, felt like a lake in spring. The drains clogged, and puddles heavy with dust and petals formed on the sides of the street. The double line of laburnums, prematurely stripped of their petals, the remainder discoloured, were like a regiment that had suffered a terrible defeat.

Ra's chauffeur-driven car, which had followed us, making our run in the rain seem even more of a pretence, now nosed its way down Amrita Shergill Marg. Mandira who had grown tired of Aakash's neglect jumped in.

'Ra, come on, no? Drop me home. Back to hubbie.'

He seemed reluctant to leave, offering to drop us all back.

'No, don't worry about it,' Sanyogita said. 'I want to walk back.'

I would have liked the ride home, but something in Sanyogita's mood made me feel it was better to stay. Aakash looked between the car and us, then specifically at me.

Sanyogita, with strange bloody-mindedness, intervened. 'Stay, Aakash. It'll be so nice. We'll walk back together.'

Aakash, not to be outdone in this perverse show of strength, agreed. The car drove away, leaving us alone on Amrita Shergill Marg.

Having been a different man to each of us that night, Aakash now became in those final moments a friend of the relationship. He walked between us, in his soaked red shirt, his heavy arms sprawling over both our shoulders. His smell, deodorant thinly holding back a damp stench from his armpits, lingered, now rising up when he rested his head on Sanyogita's shoulder, now meeting me as he leaned in to kiss my neck and tell me how much he loved both of us.

For those moments, he seemed to believe that even Sanyogita's and my relationship was only possible because of him. He spoke of trips we would take together in the hills; he said he would make every effort to come and see us in Europe in the summer, but wasn't sure he'd be able to get away this year. I knew he didn't have a passport, but he spoke as if he travelled all the time. He insinuated himself into our lives and we didn't stop him because it seemed harmless. But all the time, a mistaken idea of his import-ance was forming in his mind. When he slipped away a few moments later to take a pee, he went with the knowledge that the world turned on his axis. He peed brazenly, standing on the pavement, facing the street. Looking to see where he'd gone, we caught sight of him under a lamp post. He laughed joyfully, leaning back on his heels and pushing his black uncircumcised penis forward into the light. A smooth yellow sheen struck it and from its wrinkled nozzle, urine spirals fell to a puddle of spinning petals. His blackish-pink lips whistled the shrill tune of a film song.

His contentment was so deep and his exhibitionism so self-assured that the expression of fatigue it brought to Sanyogita's face would have come as a shock. And before I turned away, before he masked it with playful rowdiness, I saw in his eyes the rage of an Indian man insulted by a woman. His next action came so suddenly that later I thought I had seen it before it happened, the way one feels one might have saved a falling glass. I had barely looked forward again when I felt solid muscle smash against the back of my neck and a hand wrench my shoulder down. The street zoomed up in front of me as I was pulled to the floor, managing to squat just before I fell; Sanyogita crumpled.

The moment I saw her strong body thrown on to the tarmac, my mind flashed to the image of the skiing accident that had broken her thigh and given her the caterpillar scar. As she lifted herself from the street, I saw her pricked palms and a four-inch graze on her elbow. The long, colourful Rajasthani dress, with its mirrors and tinsel, was torn at the knees. Seeing her childlike face, mystified at the injury done to her, and Aakash retreating in horror, I did something for which Sanyogita never forgave me. Instead of attending to her, I jumped up and yelled at Aakash, telling him to apologize and help her up. I did it because I thought that if in that instant he begged her forgiveness, it might come; later it would be harder, much harder. But seeing her wounds and her eyes now full of tears, he hesitated; and in those seconds of hesitation, there was no one to help her up. By the time I gave up on him, it was too late. Sanyogita's pain had turned to anger. She slapped my hand away as I tried to help her up. Then she stood rooted in one place, the hem of her skirt hanging into the street, the crook of her arm exposed and softly bent where hurt. She stood perfectly still, breathing heavily, staring at me through her glistening eyes, wanting me to see what Aakash had done to her. Her head was cocked to one side and her long wavy hair glued in places to her face. She wiped it away furiously, looking still harder at me. There was an expression almost of curiosity in her eyes; it was as if she was trying to understand how I could have betrayed her. Then pushing me back, she turned around and ran. Despite her injuries and her flimsy slippers, she ran fast in the direction of Jorbagh. In seconds, she was swallowed up by the darkness and the steam now rising from the street. Aakash had gone too.

I left Delhi on a Virgin flight. The airport was in a state of great confusion. It had always had a makeshift quality: passages with tinted windows in peeling frames, grey stone floors coated in a fine layer of dust, idle men in olive-green uniforms. But now a private company, promising an airport of the future, had begun a renovation that left it barely standing. Cement and water dripped through the slats of a dented, white metal ceiling; a brown water stain crept across a wall hanging of a plump horseman; coloured wires grew out of their sockets. The warm, sweet Indian air infused here with government office damp, there with urine, now also smelt of chemicals.

On the flight, blonde air hostesses with jarring accents went past in red suits. Sanyogita sat next to me in a maroon velvet and white lace skirt. It hid the scabs that were forming on her knees. The grazes on her elbows were raw and visible. She made no display of them as she went about the small tasks of settling down for a long flight. She took down her magazines, rummaged in her handbag for lip balm, then reopened the overhead compartment and brought out an old toosh. Wrapping herself in it, she curled into her seat and slipped her long arms into mine. She had spent a miserable night, but she wasn't angry any more.

I had returned to see her bathed and in her nightdress. Vatsala had woken up and was tending to her, cleaning her wounds with Dettol, making her tea. Sanyogita was quiet, and even smiled when she saw me, but Vatsala looked fearfully up at me, like a dog who had just been beaten. Whenever I looked back at her, she'd hurriedly lower her head. But as soon as I turned away, I felt her eyes follow me. She packed Sanyogita's bag while I lay on the bed, making a point of taking down all her best suitcases, jewellery and shawls. She gave a short family history of each article, as if reminding me that Sanyogita was not alone, not without people. Just as we were about to go to bed, she tumbled in with her bedding, wanting to spend the night on the floor next to Sanyogita.

'Vatsala,' Sanyogita said, laughing, 'it wasn't him.'

'Bebi,' she said aghast, 'then who?'

'Just someone. But don't worry about it. You don't have to sleep here.'

Vatsala folded up her bed, smiled apologetically and crept away.

That night I received a number of text messages. At two a.m. in three instalments: 'What I've done tonight can never be forgiven or forgotten. I think of you as my brother. I've had an amazing time with you in these past few months. I wanted us to be friends for life, but destiny had other plans. Please from now on, don't call me, don't text for a long, long time. I can't be your trainer, but I will organize someone for you when you come back. I hope one day Sanyogita will find it in her heart to forgive me for what I have done. She will always be my bhabi. Ash-man.' I replied, 'Don't be so filmy, just send her some flowers in the morning.' At three a.m.: 'Man, not giving film lines. If she forgives me, I'm happiest man in the world. What are her favourite flowers?' 'Lilies,' I replied. At five a.m.: 'My dear Megha, tonight I have lost my best friend in the world. Now, you are all that I have in the world. Your boyf, Aakash.' 'Huh?' I replied. 'Who's Megha?' No reply.

And it was like this that I discovered what, if my mind had been clearer in those last days in Delhi, I would have seen anyway: Aakash had found a girl. The next morning, just as we were leaving, the chowkidar brought up a little cane basket containing a great deal of fern and foliage, six pink gladioli and a note of apology in neat, rounded writing.

12

Months went by though I don't know how.

The first two were spent in a village in the south of Spain. Sanyogita knew an English family who owned a hotel in the hills above Seville. They were of red earth, covered in orange, cork and olive trees. In the evenings, the long light and the silvery olive trees made the hills appear purple. The sky was cast in one pattern before evening fell. Then no matter how strong the wind in the hills became, it could never put the arrangement of clouds and clear sky out of true. Against the filters of this hung sky, the light distilled into darkness. From the semicircular window of the one-bedroom annexe we rented for 750 euros a month, we could see the white village of Cazalla. The red-tiled roofs on some of its houses were flat, smooth and new; and on others, rounded, mildewed, with browning stalks growing out of them. On all the bell towers and spires, great stork's nests had appeared. The chattering from them at night, mixed with the croaking of frogs in a field below, and that most Mediterranean of Mediterranean noises, the whirr of a Vespa, kept me awake for hours.

It seemed at first that we had salvaged our relationship. The quality of life and produce in the village was deceptive. It briefly made the small, borrowed idea of our stay in a European village ring true. In the mornings, we'd have breakfast in a shaded bar with high stools. A stern, leather-faced man brought us long pieces of bread with tomatoes, olive oil, garlic, salt and fresh orange juice. We posed as regulars, watching two inches of black coffee drip into clear glasses. The bartender assembled a saucer, a spoon and a large sachet of sugar as the milk heated. His self-assuredness stood out against our pretence; to him it was just another morning, café con leche just coffee with milk. And when the milk had heated, the saucers slid across the bar with a brief clatter. At lunch, in another place with tiles and a high wooden bar, there was fresh fish, salad and giant tomatoes with flakes of salt; all things that we hadn't tasted during the summer in India. They created the illusion of happiness, of the good life.

But it was also these things, and the settled world they spoke of, that made India recede. For as long as sensual pleasures lasted, it didn't matter. But when those satisfactions ran out, I realized I had no way into this kind of life. There was no context for Indians in Spain as there was for the English or Americans. The falsity of my situation overwhelmed me. Sometimes, late in the afternoon, I would look out of the semicircular window in disbelief at the cobbled streets and red-tiled roofs. The heat in the village dwarfed the heat of the subcontinent and this also added to my sense of futility. The streets were empty all day but for the occasional figure of an old veiled woman in black. The image might have been emblematic of the little village, perfect down to the late-afternoon blaze on the white houses and the bronze-faced lion spitting spring water into a mossy basin, but I wouldn't have known; I was on the outside, with too little knowledge, knowledge I took for granted in India, to enter that picture of village life.

I joined the village gym. It was a single room, with modern frosted-glass windows embedded in an old façade. A beefy, middle-aged man who taught spin cycling classes to the women in the village charged me thirty euros for the month. One half of the gym was taken up by old weights machines; the other by the spinners, spinning on through a haze of coloured disco lights and techno music. Teenage Spanish boys, with bad skin and short-sleeved T-shirts, worked out around me, eyeing me with suspicion. A metal wall fan circulated the warm, stale air in the room.

It was after one of these sessions, almost six weeks into my time in the village, that my mobile, now carrying Movistar, beeped with a voice message. I stepped out of the gym. It was seven p.m., but the blaze had not subsided. It was late at night in India; I could hear the beeping of scooters and the tinkle of bicycle bells in the background. 'How's you doing, man?' the voice began in English. 'I hopes you feeling good, man.' Then in Hindi, 'Yaar, I miss you a lot. What's this going and leaving your friend? Please, man, come back soon. There's so much fun still to be had. OK, well, call when you get a chance. Your friend, Ash-man. Oh, and please say my sorry one more time to Sanyogita bhabi.'

Walking back through these empty cobbled streets, with their narrow pavements and leather-faced men staring vacantly at me, I knew I had to leave. I just didn't know how I would tell Sanyogita. Money had become a problem as well. In India my mother had helped me with a small allowance and the few thousand I had left in sterling from my job in London had gone far. The village was cheap, but many times more expensive than India. Every meal was out; Sanyogita always ordered fish; we must have been spending fifty euros a day at an increasingly unfavourable exchange rate. The only hopeful news was that the revised version of my novel was complete. It was not an inspired revision, but I'd had detailed notes and had followed them closely. The manuscript was already with the agent in New York and I was awaiting a reply.

That night at the village casino, which was really just a restaurant with red velvet curtains, deep leather chairs and tiled walls, I tried telling Sanyogita that I needed to go home. But I framed my reasons around my confusion at being in a little village in Spain. Sanyogita seemed receptive. She listened quietly, sipping a small glass of sherry and occasionally wrapping a finger around a piece of acorn-fed ham. When I'd finished, she responded with a sweeping gesture which left me, like with the study, reaching in desperation for adequate feelings.

'Baby, listen, I've been thinking the same thing,' she said, 'and since this was all my idea in the first place, I feel I should do the cleaning up on my own. I wasn't going to tell you this till later in the month, it was going to be a surprise, but since you've brought it up, I'll tell you now. I have this friend, Nargis, who's a publisher in the East Village. She's like a big Buddhist and a Free Tibet person. And basically, she's decided to extend the privileges of her citizenship, especially since America has done so little for Tibet, by marrying a Tibetan in Delhi so that he can escape the tyranny of the Chinese and come and live in the States.'

I felt the frost round my glass of Cruzcampo start to melt.

'But if he's living in Delhi, hasn't he already escaped the tyranny of the Chinese?' I asked, feigning concern.

'Yes, yes, all right,' Sanyogita said, laughing, 'but Nargis doesn't know that. She's a big-hearted person, you know, a real do-gooder, so maybe she hasn't thought of that part. It all seems the same from America, anyway. But that's not the point.'

'What is the point?'

'That I've done a flat swap with her! She needed a place to stay in Delhi and so I've lent her Jorbagh for two months. In place of which, we have the most adorable little flat in the East Village with a cat called Kuku. You can work, I can do my thing. We'll have breakfast at the Clinton Street Bakery, we'll watch films, it'll be so nice.'

It wasn't that I didn't have a flat in Delhi where I could return to; I had my mother's. It wasn't that Sanyogita, in feeling she had to clean up this summer mess, had already bought our tickets to New York; I would gladly have reimbursed her, thinking of the money I would save by not having to live in New York for two months; it was that I knew Sanyogita, and I knew the place from where the gesture had come. This was no entrapment; it was a heartfelt and hopeful gesture, from the depths of Sanyogita's fairy-tale imagination, dreaming always of escape.

And so, despite great misgivings, I gave in.

After a summer of boredom and waiting, I left New York under these circumstances.

I had heard nothing from the agent. For two months, I waited, viewing every ending week with sinking hopes and every new one with fresh, but misplaced, anticipation. I checked my emails constantly, and if I was away from the computer for too long, I felt an ache at the thought of what news the little blue orb in my inbox might have brought. I tried to live my agent's life, thinking of when she would come into work, when she might be having lunch with a publisher, when – shaking off the effects of a bottle of red wine – she would write to me to tell me of what he had said. I thought of how she would have half-days on Fridays in the summer, and of where and for how long she would go on holiday. I thought obsessively of these things even as my agent sat in an office barely a few miles away. But I couldn't bring myself to contact her first. I felt certain that this action would turn good news to bad. I played games with myself. Every changing light – would I make it across the street while the little man was still white? – every arriving train – would the next train be an express train uptown? – every Sunday book review – would it contain any indication of what was popular these days? Indian writing still in? – became heavy with significance. I started to believe that the world around me, the minutiae of life in a big city, contained signs of whether I was to be a writer or not. If this feeling had come from a genuine wish to be a writer, it might have had a foundation in hard work and reading that would have given me solace. But it was an empty wish; it was like my novel, a wish for a lifeline.

One hot afternoon, when Sanyogita had gone to see an aunt in Long Island, leaving me to take care of Kuku, I stepped out to have an iced coffee. I felt in my pocket for the keys and let the door slam behind me. But even before its metal teeth had closed around the powerful cylindrical bolt, I knew that what I had thought were my keys was in fact loose change. I stood in an airless corridor, permanently lit by a yellowing fluorescent light, staring with aimless intensity at a floor of many tiny hexagons. I didn't have a phone; I had only enough money for an iced coffee. I didn't want to leave the building, as that would lock me out of the building as well as the flat. I could hear Kuku mewing, no doubt rubbing his scrawny body along the door, reminding me that I had to feed him. I felt an irrational hatred towards the cat for not being able to help me.

It was then that I had what I can only describe as a swarming of nerves. Already close to some kind of lip, they cascaded over. My body turned cold with sweat, I felt some kind of essential life-giving liquid drain from me and I had the desire to curl up on the floor by the door, with the strange belief that if I kept my face close to the centimetre gap of cold air between the door and the floor, I would be able to restart the flow of oxygen into my body. The city beyond terrified me. When I thought of it, I could think only of the crowds and commotion around Times Square. And it was like this, hardly able to walk, that I made my way down three flights of stairs, banging on every door in the hope that someone would be able to help me cope with the blackness rising around me.

On the ground floor, a girl in a summery dress opened the door. She had a garden flat, with an open window and a large white fan. I broke into the tranquillity of her room and collapsed on a purple futon, trying slowly to explain my situation. She listened, nodded, emitting a few comforting 'uh-huhs', then picked up a red telephone and called a locksmith. After a rapid conversation, she said he would be there in eight minutes.

The man who arrived was a Romanian, slim, blond, in a vest. He had been at a nearby café drinking an iced coffee, he said. He looked at the lock with dismay. He said that this was not the kind of lock his tools could open; he would have to drill it. Two hundred dollars. I had no choice. It was Friday and Sanyogita was not back until Monday. He took his drill to the brass lock and bore into a single point just above the keyhole. It was as violent a thing as I had ever seen; I could hear, as brass flakes flew, the lock's interlocking components break one by one. Then he took a wrench to the lock, and after many failed attempts pulled its little brass face from its place in the door, leaving an empty hole. But the door didn't open.

'It has a double-lock,' he said, 'but you didn't tell me.'

'I didn't know.'

'We'll have to drill that one too. It'll be expensive. It's a good lock. Yeah, yeah. Another two hundred at least.'

He bore into the second lock now. The brass flakes flew and the lock's components broke one by one; it was wrenched from its place in the door; a second empty hole appeared. The door fell open, the room reappeared, Kuku rubbed up against a sofa. But the door couldn't be left like that; the locks had to be replaced. Two hundred dollars each. I gave him the money in two-hundred-dollar instalments withdrawn from an electric-blue ATM outside a deli. It felt like cutting away parts of my body. He gave me two sets of brass keys in return.

I went back upstairs and wrote to the agent.

The following week, once Sanyogita had returned, the blue orb in my inbox brought this letter, a letter within a letter, of which painful snatches remained with me:

Aatish – Since I had to go off on a long weekend after your delivery of *An Internment*, I asked a colleague here – formerly a highly placed publisher and now with us part-time as a reader – to read your novel, and below you will find his report. For reasons you will appreciate (since the report does not pull its punches), I have debated whether to send this to you – but, on balance, feel it will be more helpful than otherwise to you to contemplate a neutral professional judgement. Of course, you are entitled to reject the judgement, but I hope you will find something of value in it.

Best wishes, Marie

AN INTERNMENT – BY AATISH TASEER

Although Tasser can write with fluency and intelligence at times, *An Internment* is a seriously flawed novel. It is far too early for him – or us – to be thinking about securing a publishing deal for his work . . .

The line-by-line style needs serious attention. There are so many awkward and over-elaborate sentences. I'd encourage Tasser to be as ruthless as possible with his own writing – to stop trying too hard – and to work on developing clarity and simplicity in his style . . .

All in all – I wouldn't recommend taking Tasser on as a client now – but it might be worth asking to see a substantially rewritten version of this novel.

As I finished the email, with its cruel misspellings of my name, I felt as though I had been set free. I realized that it was not so much the fraudulence of the literary effort but waiting for that fraudulence to bear fruit that had been the hardest part. I hadn't found a way to write about my situation. I had the disarray of my situation to show me why.

Stronger now for being stripped of my pretences, I boldly approached Sanyogita about wanting to go back to India. She was not angry. She only said, 'Baby, I hope you don't mind if I follow in a few days?'

Part Two

13

The season had changed. The moisture was gone from the air and the evenings were now a little smoky. The occasional cluster of yellow petals, the odd burnt-orange tendril, stubbornly hung on in the laburnum's branches and the gulmohar's stepped canopy. Their brilliance was unsuited to the new season and there was something of the gloom of streamers and confetti from a past celebration in their now rare occurrence. New pigments and scents flooded the leaves and branches of Delhi's trees and winter flowers began appearing on roundabouts. One tree particularly, the *Alstonia scholaris*, or the Indian devil tree, a weed-like cousin of the frangipani, marked the beginning of the festival season. Its nocturnal scent, when filtered through the smoky air, was sweet at first, then quickly cloying, filling the city's streets and avenues as evening fell. I sat in my mother's flat, awaiting Aakash and his girlfriend's arrival.

At Junglee, too, there had been changes. Pradeep, Aakash's pale, meatier rival, had moved back to Bombay, leaving the field open to him. The ponytailed owners, afraid to give him too much power, had promoted Montu, the pork- and beef-eating chooda, to the position of trainer, in the hope of putting up a counterbalance. This only inflamed the situation, and Aakash, with Mojij the Christian at his side, now spent a good part of the morning leaning against the cable crossover machine, ridiculing Montu. He would organize his clients' workouts based on what Montu was doing with his (most of whom were inherited from Pradeep, though even from these Aakash had pinched a few). Then, within earshot of Montu's client, he would point out his failings. 'See, wrists not straight. Weight is coming down behind shoulders so effect is falling on back, balance is off. Like that, anyone can do.

Now, follow this, wrist's straight, weight coming down here, yes, balance perfect, thirdeen, fordeen, we'll do it slowly . . .'

There were also changes in Aakash's physical appearance. His hair, once neat, short and bristly, was now long and uneven and fell jaggedly over his forehead. 'Messy look,' he answered briefly when I asked him about it. He had also, to go with the look, grown a short black dacoit's stubble with a vicious nap. If it grew too long, he would shave it off, leaving either the faint outline of a French beard or a triangle of stubble below his lower lip. He wore a diamond stud in one ear. His manner was also different, not colder, but harder somehow. It manifested itself in the smallest ways. We'd start a set; he'd correct me one or two repetitions into it; I'd ask that we start the count again; he'd tell me to continue, but then either repeat a number of his choice along the way or take the count past fifteen when I least expected it. He now spoke of Ash's, the one-stop total image clinic, as if it were up and running. He threatened to deny Junglee's sub-trainers their promised positions as masseurs and stylists if they spoke back to him; he had new phones, new ring tones; he was full of aggressive political opinions. The transformation was like a preparation. It was as if he was gearing up for some bigger fight, for which he could show no weakness, and I suspected somewhere in this the hand of the new girlfriend.

It had become a point of awkwardness between us that we hadn't discussed her. Aakash hinted at her existence, but said nothing openly. If she called while we were working out, he smiled knowingly at me, then slipped off into a corner. I came to recognize the ring tone – the Hindi pop song with the single English line – he had assigned to her. Once or twice I even saw her name flash on his phone. He hadn't saved it as Megha, but as chahat, longing. Then a few days after I came back to Delhi, we were in the final stages of an abs workout when, 'I will always love you, all my life,' rang out from Aakash's pocket. He hesitated, but then, continuing to lend me the support of his two fingers, answered it. 'Nothing, beev,' he said, looking down at me trying to lift myself a few inches from the floor, 'just finishing off sir's abs. Beev, you know I have no friend circle, only one best friend.' My abs gave way as Aakash became more engaged in his conversation. 'Because, beev, he is a very important person. He's just been two months in New York, and before two months in . . . where were you?' 'Spain,' I breathed. 'Spain, two months in Spain. Beev, he's very busy, he's a writer, his girlfriend, you know who she is? She's the Chief Minister of Jhaatkebaal's niece.' He let go of my hands and I fell to the floor. 'OK, OK, beev, I'll ask him.' Covering the receiver, he said, 'She wants to know why she hasn't met you, if you're my best friend?' My face, like my paralysed abs, was not able to express sufficient amazement at his nerve. 'Because her boyfriend's a sly Brahmin,' I managed. Aakash laughed uproariously, then said, 'He's inviting us for a beer party at his flat today, can you get away?' Looking down at me, he mouthed, 'Is OK?' 'Yes, fine,' I sighed. 'Good, then it's set,' he informed us both. When he'd put the phone down, I asked why he called his girlfriend beev.

'Short for beevi,' he said, grinning; wife. Then hysterically happy, he added, 'You're really going to get a surprise, sir!'

Aakash and his girlfriend were due at seven that evening. A few minutes before, Shakti came in with the news that there had been a series of bomb blasts in the city. 'So terrible what's happened,' he said with a morose smile. 'Who would do such a thing?' Then looking thoughtful for a moment, he added, 'Baba, it must be God's benevolence that I bought the samosas and beer for your guests before the blasts happened. He obviously does not wish me to go yet.'

'What? There was a blast in Khan Market?'

'Oh no, where would there be a blast in Khan Market? They were in Greater Kailash, in Gaffar Market, in Connaught Place and one little one in Sectorpur.'

'Then what benevolence?'

'Just,' he smiled contentedly and slipped away, knowing perhaps the simple pleasure of being alive when others were recently dead.

I turned the television on. The blasts were the third in a string of recent attacks on major Indian cities. A group called Indian Musthavbin was claiming responsibility. They had labelled the attack Operation BAD and had used plaster of Paris Ganeshs, now abounding in the city, as their method of delivery. The screen was split in three: on the far left, a large intact pink Ganesh, riding on the back of a scooter; in the middle, the scene of the crime, a hole blown through a green 'Keep Delhi Clean' dustbin and a bright pool of blood amid chappals, garlands and handbags; on the far right, an expert talking about the difference between a high-intensity blast and a low-intensity blast. 'In a high-intensity blast, the impact of the blast is high, in a low-intensity blast, the impact . . .'

I called Aakash.

'Have you heard?'

'Yes, man. I was there, beev and I were there. We were shopping in CP when it happened. I can't tell you, if it hadn't been for beev wanting Pizza Hut's garlic butter sticks, we wouldn't be here today. It's a matter of fate, no?' After a moment's silence, he said, 'Actually, no! Beev's appetite saved our lives.' At the cracking of this badly timed joke, I heard a howl of laughter in the background.

'Is that beev?' I asked.

'Yes, man.'

'Are you still coming?'

'Of course, man. Keep the beer ready. Who can tell how many life has to spare?'

It was nearly dark now. I could hear a siren wail in the distance. The bell rang. I opened the door to see Aakash in a red turban. He wandered in past me with no explanation for the turban or beev's absence. I followed him into the flat, where he flicked through the mail, picked a samosa off the tray Shakti brought in and drank half a glass of Cobra beer in one sip. Shakti looked adoringly at him, then shut the front door.

'Where's beev?'

The bell rang. Aakash bowed deeply and extended a hand. 'The beev at your service.'

I opened the door; then I almost couldn't look. In the light that fell from a single bulb, there stood a girl no taller than five feet in a red turban. She had one plump arm propped against the door-frame and was panting heavily. Beads of sweat glistened on her wet lips and pale face. She wore a baggy purple T-shirt which did nothing to conceal her vast breasts and stomach. The light, catching the grease on her face, shone dully on to the dark flesh that ringed her neck. Two diamond solitaires the size of boiled sweets gleamed in her ears. For some seconds, she didn't look up, making a show of her breathlessness. I felt Aakash's chin rest on my shoulder. 'Your new bhabi,' he whispered proudly, as if giving me the keys to a sports car.

She was quiet at first, smiling and watchful. She entered the flat timidly, brushing against the doorway and then the dining-room chairs. We walked in behind her, Aakash grinning and gaping at me, watching my every gesture for a reaction. When I showed none, he said, 'Beev's healthy, no?' She heard, and slowly turning around, gave him a cautioning look. He bit his tongue, but was encouraged by the reaction. 'And the funny thing is I'm her trainer. Beev, what an ad you are for me!' At this provocation, she swung around and made a short charge, yelling, 'Always making fun, twenty-four seven, seven eleven, making fun.' Aakash took her in his arms and kissed her tenderly on the head. The kitchen door swung open and Shakti emerged with more samosas and beer. His expression changed from morose to ribald delight at the sight of them, both in their red turbans. Aakash and Megha joined Shakti in his brazen laughter and I was left feeling somehow that the joke was on me.

When we came into the drawing room, Aakash dropped himself on the sofa, his arms sprawling behind him. Megha sat on the edge of a chair, looking only at him. He closed his eyes and said, 'Now, you guys talk. I'm going to sleep.' But when I asked how near they had been to the blasts, he sprang up. 'Man, you won't believe it. The silence. Can you imagine an area as big as Connaught Place silent? It was amazing. For two seconds, you could hear the wind, you could hear a brown-paper bag scraping along the road. You know how in the movies when they have mute slow-motion scenes, exactly like that. But I tell you, it's gone too far. Now something or the other has to be done. Bring back terrorist laws, have quick arrests, quick trials. I'm saying anyone there's a doubt about, that's it, straight in jail. It's gone too far.'

Megha listened carefully.

I wasn't in the mood for a political conversation. I said, 'Maybe. But until now there have never been any real arrests, no real evidence. Without that, terrorist laws just become a way to keep the wrong people in jail.'

Aakash's eyes hardened. 'Then each one of them will have to go.' He sighed. 'The lot of them.'

'Go where?'

'I don't know. Pakistan? Round them up in the Red Fort and blow them away? I don't care, but this can't go on.'

'Come on, Ash-man. You don't mean that. What about Zafar? Will he have to go?'

Aakash had met him once or twice and was fond of him. His face softened. 'In so large an operation, a few good people end up sacrificed too. And by the way, I'm not saying just Muhammadans, the bad Hindus should go too.'

For that one moment, Aakash seemed to lose his particularity. I saw in his anger and his hunger a greater Indian rage and appetite; and in his face, the face of a mob.

Megha spoke to me only in English, and to Aakash only in Hindi, no matter how much either of us tried switching to the other. It positioned her at the centre of conversation and brought up a wall between Aakash and me that had never existed before. As she became comfortable, she began poking fun at my Hindi, embarrassing me for speaking well rather than for speaking badly. 'Oh,' she teased, when I used the Hindi word for election, 'using such big words and all. Even I don't know words like that.'

I became curious about when they'd met. Megha beamed, and resting a small, fleshy hand cluttered with diamonds on Aakash's lime-green T-shirt, said, 'What now, it must be six, running seven months?'

'Seven months?' I gasped.

It was nearly exactly as long as I had known Aakash. I suddenly remembered, and now understood, what the Begum of Sectorpur had been referring to all those months before.

'Why didn't you tell me?' I said.

Aakash, seeming to enjoy the deception, said, 'I couldn't have, man. It's all been very secret. She came as a client. I was meant to make her lose weight so that her parents could find her a match, according to her caste, which, by the way, is much lower than mine.'

Megha nodded, apologetically adding, 'We're Aggarwals, the business caste.'

'And,' Aakash continued, 'according to her financial status, which is much higher than mine. Her father's not a lakhpati or crorepati, but an arabpati. He has three factories in Sectorpur, desi ghee, plastics, autoparts. Her brother went abroad for university; not that it did him any good.'

At this, the two of them eyed each other and laughed.

When their laughter died down, Megha explained, 'He's a homo.'

'A homo?'

'You know, homo?' she said, then rattled off, 'Homo, a gay, fajjot.'

'Anyway,' Aakash continued, 'her financial status is very differ from mine. No one in her family knows anything about us. In fact, I think I can honestly say that if they found out, they would probably try and kill me.'

'My brother suspects,' Megha inserted, 'maybe.'

'Why do you say that?'

'The homo saw us leaving Junglee together,' Aakash added

149

quickly. 'But what can he do? Zero.' Aakash stressed this by making the numeral with his finger and thumb.

Megha felt some explanation was needed. 'You know, money is status. That's a fact of life, but me, I don't believe in all of this. I can only marry a man whom I respect. Money comes and goes, but respect lasts. All the guys I meet in Delhi, they just want to work for their fathers and live off the family business. Only Aakash is someone I see who wants to make something of his own.'

Megha, as she became more energetic, had taken off her red turban and crumpled it in her lap. Her limp medium-length hair was streaked blonde in places; she had a nose ring. Without the turban, her features were thicker still, her head heavy and round.

The mention of marriage alarmed me; I felt a joke had been taken too far. At the same time I could see how a girl like this, rich, strong-willed and clearly in love with him, could be a great asset to Aakash. Though he enjoyed stressing her 'healthiness', deriving from it a kind of boisterous fun that Shakti also shared in, Aakash seemed to see a kind of virtue in her form. It was as if some notion of strong traditional values – of a woman who supports her man, and there were songs about this kind of thing in India – had become tied up with her substantial size. By choosing her, he expressed his contempt for the lithe modern girls he trained at Junglee. And I was not at all certain whether her weight was really so off-putting to him. His mother was fat; the begum had been fat. Certainly behind Shakti's laughter there had been a note of understanding, as if Shakti was congratulating him on making so robust a choice. In fact, the only person who was deeply uneasy was me. And Aakash, for whatever reason, whether pre-empting me or aware of my discomfort and hurt by it, or simply taking a kind of pleasure in offending my soft tastes, did all he could, after months of secrecy, to include me in his relationship with Megha.

Now smoking at will, sipping his beer, his turban still on, he read into my silence. As was so often the case with him, he had not introduced me to Megha without a purpose. He said, 'Our love match is not going to be easily accepted by this world. I'll need my friends. If things become difficult, you'll help me, no?'

'Me? How can I help you?'

'You can. You know people. Your mother's a journalist. The owner of TVDelhi just hangs out in your girlfriend's house.'

'The owner of TVDelhi, who do you mean?'

'You know that woman who was there that day at Sanyogita's when Lul was reading his homo story.' At this Megha's wet lips opened and her laughter rang out. I looked at Aakash in puzzlement. A private moment passed between them. Her eyes were full of some unexplained significance, which Aakash dismissed with a firm look. 'The woman,' he continued, 'with the red bindi and the grey hair, and those huge silver bangles, owns TVDelhi.'

'I had no idea,' I said, genuinely surprised.

'Please, man. You have to do this for me. In this country, we can't trust the police, we can't trust NGO workers, we can't trust government people, but we can trust the press. You have to speak to this woman about our situation. Just so we have help, if we need it.'

I couldn't understand his urgency. 'For what?'

'For nothing yet,' he said, draining his glass and sitting forward. 'But maybe later.' Removing his turban, his messy look pasted to his head, he added, 'Should things get ugly.'

14

The first pale sky of the winter was reflected in the tanks of dark water outside the National Museum. Pedal boats glided over its glassy surface, dark small-leaved jamun trees dotted the esplanade and bright ice-cream trucks crowded the edge of the grass. In the distance, a runway-sized road led up to the President's Palace, and Parliament, a low, punctured cylinder, brooded on the side. Nearer to the domed, sandstone museum, a black rubber hosepipe lay in the grass, choking out a wide puddle of smelly water.

A writer had come to town. My mother was a friend of his wife and was hosting a dinner in their honour. He was a writer I had come to admire. I had first met him in London when I was eighteen and on my way to college in America. He had advised me not to go: 'Indians go to these places and all they ever learn is the babble.' At the time the remark offended me, not because of what was said but because of his tone: cold, dismissive, uncaring that he had upset my plans. I went anyway.

The next time we met was in Delhi and I was in my last year of college. I was writing a thesis at the time on how the Mahatma, through a programme of celibacy and dietetics, had sought to overcome the body. In doing so, he negated the source of interests in Western society, interests such as property and self-preservation, making it possible for him to fight the British with a coin different from theirs. For all their threats to his body, they would never have any purchase over his soul. The writer listened for a while, sipping a martini he had been complaining about earlier, then said, 'But there's a great flaw in your theory. Because the British could have killed him; they could have destroyed his body. Then there would have been nothing to house his soul. What kind of victory is that?' The adviser in college who had fed me the idea for the thesis hadn't thought of that. When I went back to him with it, he confessed that the true rewards of the Mahatma's programme were not temporal but metaphysical. I did the thesis, but lost interest. I read the writer's books instead, all of them, carefully. He was the first writer I had read in this way. I felt a great feeling of release reading the books. He could take big ideas such as colonialism, defeat, occupation and show their effects in small human ways like lying and boasting, in hidden anger and resentments. I felt the writer release me from a sense of entitlement that I had about the West, a feeling that since they colonized us they owed us education, technology, duty-free goods. He released me by exposing the attitude as not post-colonial in any real way, but still very colonial; one that some in the West might happily endorse. It was an attitude that would forever leave us robbed of responsibility and the privilege of blaming oneself for one's failures.

My mother was hosting a dinner for the writer, but first he wanted to go to the National Museum to see the bronzes; he asked that I come along. I'd never been to the National Museum, though I'd been to many museums in many countries; I had never seen any bronzes. I was waiting in the porch of the museum when the writer's Ambassador drove in. His wife was with him, a handsome Punjabi woman with green eyes.

'Leave it, leave it in the car,' she said of the writer's green felt hat. She thought it would make him look English. It would mean us all paying the foreigners' entry fee, which was thirty times as much as the regular fee. I had already anticipated this and had sent Uttam in to buy three tickets in advance. The security was tight, both because of the blasts and because there was an exhibition in the museum of the Nizam of Hyderabad's jewels. Mobile phones had to be left outside, handbags were searched, a fuss was made over the writer's brown leather shooting stick. Then the security guard in his olive-green uniform wanted to know why we had bought the Indian ticket.

'Because we're Indians,' I answered in Hindi.

'Show me your passport or ration card,' he said.

We weren't carrying any identification, but neither were a group of young men in polyester shirts and baggy trousers.

'Why aren't you asking them for identification?' I said.

'Because they look like Indians,' the security guard replied.

'And why don't we look like Indians?' the writer's wife intervened.

The man was stumped; it was just a feeling, a class feeling.

'We're speaking Hindi, aren't we?' the writer's wife pressed him. 'Would we be speaking Hindi if we weren't Indians?'

The man smiled. 'Some foreigners have learned as well,' he said, shaking his head from side to side. 'But never mind, carry on.'

The writer had watched the whole scene. His eyes were dim and old, but intent somehow. They were set in a faintly Asian cast. They could make events occurring right in front of them seem far away. The writer had recently had back trouble and needed help up the stairs. He took my hand in his small, firm hand, and once he'd got going, he moved fast. When we went in, inhaling the musty smells that surround any organization linked to the government of India, he wanted to rest for a few minutes. We sat down in the lobby in front of an eleventh-century stone statue of a man and a woman; the woman was leaning into the man and gentle rolls of fat were visible on the sides of her waist. The writer caught his breath, then looked up and said, 'Why don't you sit down? You'll be able to consider it better that way.'

His wife, who was dressed in a green, black and yellow salwar kameez, continued to stand. I sat down; a few awkward moments of silence passed between us as I tried entering the world of the statue.

The writer started us off. He said that the statue was from Khajuraho and that he had a special feeling for the Chandela dynasty as he was named after one of its kings. 'The son in fact,' the writer said, 'of the man who was king when the invaders came. He had to move away. And that saved the Khajuraho temples. The bush grew over them. I fear that now they're admired for their erotic content, which is foolish.'

I looked harder at them, but I noticed only outside things: the spotlight and its loose wires; the roughly made pedestal on which they stood. They seemed closed to me; I still had nothing to say. I felt as I had with Aakash in the temple.

'What is nice,' the writer said, 'is the absolute confidence in the faces. These people are . . .'

'Complete,' his wife finished for him.

'Yes, yes.' Then rising, he said, 'We won't look at everything or we'll get tired; only at the fine things.'

We walked into the museum's main rooms past long pieces of carved stone.

'Lintels,' the writer said, pointing with his shooting stick. 'We didn't have the arch; we had lintels.'

We entered a circular passage with a grubby marble floor. On one side, past glass walls, was an open courtyard with a stone chariot in the middle. On our right was a red-painted sign for the bronzes. I was wondering when the building that housed the collection had been built and asked the writer about it.

He misunderstood my question or chose to answer it differently. 'I'll tell you, I'll tell you,' he said, as we entered a room with chalky-green walls. 'These bronzes used to be in the viceroy's house. They were collected by the Archaeological Survey of India. A British institution. It is safe to say that not a single Indian prince made a collection like the one we see displayed here, though he easily could have. The Maharaja of Patiala went to England, where he had his portrait painted, that was the thing to do, and he picked up a few nudes and brought them back. They gloried in their ignorance,' the writer said, 'gloried in their ignorance.'

The room we entered was in spotlight and shadow. And though in places a crucial light was fused, a pink bucket left in a corner, the glasses of the display cases fingerprinted and dusty, there was something entrancing about the green, dimly lit room with the bronzes and the shadows they cast.

The writer, as if wishing to give me the best of his energies, wanted to see the Natraj first. On our way to it, he stopped in front of an unfinished Chola Natraj. He looked for Shiva's drum, but it wasn't there. Next to the bronze was a black and white picture of an artisan working on the floor, illustrating how the object was made. The writer, as if anticipating a buried judgement in me, said, 'That man seeming to hammer out the image would have had all kinds of fine ideas going through his smooth head.'

Then following my eyes drift to the Natraj, he considered Shiva's dance of creation and destruction. He said it was very close to him; he described it as having entered his soul, this idea of the nearness of creation and decay. 'How did that idea, the twin forces of creation and decay,' he asked, as we approached the bronze Natraj, with its floating hair, and one leg filled with the tension of both rising and swinging, 'become enshrined in human form?'

'I don't know, I don't know,' he said, answering his own question. 'I don't think anyone knows. I think the thing just appeared like Venus rolling in from the sea in Cyprus in rock form. It was created wholly by the imagination of men.'

The Natraj had been turned into a national icon in India, appearing in airports and on HB pencils; the writer knew this.

'The image,' he said, 'is much debased. It's used everywhere, like some of the Leonardo da Vinci drawings.' Then looking at the little man, gasping for his life, on whom the dancing Shiva stood, the writer said, 'I will interpret it in my own way. He is standing on the monster of ignorance.' That monster the writer saw as representing 'the snare of life'. He didn't mean appetite, but irrationality, darkness and cruelty especially; the possibility men always have of being less than men.

Standing before this most Indian of Indian images, the writer could not have been oblivious to its context. He was a man who always knew where he was. He seemed to stand there considering the dark history that had landed the bronze image before him in a glass case, unseen, unthought of, in the country from where it came. He began to draw a historical thread. But even before he began, I had been thinking of Aakash. I don't know why; perhaps only because of his feeling for the gods, and my removal. The writer spoke directly to my thoughts.

'Many people don't know,' he said, 'that in the nineteenth century there was an anti-Brahmin movement and that the Brahmins were driven out of town. That was when there was a looting of their works of art and devotion. The people who were doing the looting didn't think what they would replace these images with. It was then that they began to appear in the salerooms of Europe and America.'

A nineteenth-century anti-Brahmin movement! Had that been the history behind the magical story of Aakash's ancestor? Had his run-in with the village, and his subsequent disappearance, 'the driving out of town', been part of a larger story, part of an anti-Brahmin movement that the writer, living thousands of miles away, could have read about? Was the statue I had seen of Aakash's ancestor, with his saffron robes and three streaks of turmeric across the forehead, a gesture of historical remembrance? It was amazing to consider.

The Natraj had been rubbed to shine in some places. The writer liked that. 'It's to me a nice idea, rubbing the parts they thought beautiful. No polish . . .' he began.

'Is as good as the human hand,' his wife finished for him.

We moved on from the Natraj and the writer's mood lightened. His earlier solemnity lifted, he spoke more generally about the figures. 'Someone asked me,' he said, 'why the figure had four hands. "It's not a human figure," I told him. "It's a human figure representing something. The arms are there to represent what is being honoured."' But when we came to a Shiva in a relaxed human posture with Parvati by his side, the writer chuckled. 'Here, when the figure has a consort and comes down from its pedestal, things become a little more complicated.'

In another glass case, there were Vijaynagar bronzes. The figures were squatter, thicker of limb. 'We were talking of security earlier,' the writer began, and speaking of the Muslim invaders and Vijaynagar respectively, said, 'They destroyed it and destroyed it completely. This destruction is made beautiful by the Left. You know, by the drawing-room intellectuals, the ladies with their fashionable grey hair and ethnic saris, ambassadors of the Caliph to the Republic of Letters. They say that it was destroyed by the Indians themselves. They are so completely degraded, they can't deal with their own defeat, but we mustn't let that spoil the beauty of what we're seeing.'

The writer began to get tired. We sat down, his wife and I on a bench, him on his shooting stick, with its Air India tag still hanging from it. He began advising me on books I might read about the bronzes. They were all by German and British writers. 'It's cause for shame,' he said, 'that Indians don't write these books themselves.

'You see, the English-speaking people of India don't come here. They think this is local stuff. They want to go to America and have their self-portrait painted and buy nudes, like the Maharaja of Patiala. And then they complain that the British looted them. These were in the viceroy's house. It was Nehru's idea to bring them here; it was a good idea, but no one wants to come.' He raised his hands, open-palmed, in despair.

The mood excited a story of Coomaraswamy, the Sri Lankan art critic. 'His dates are 1877–1947. He was half Sinhalese and rich,' the writer said. 'It was open to him to start up life as a Mayfair gentleman or in the country, but he decided to devote himself to Indian art. In 1917, when Coomaraswamy was forty,' the writer added, calculating fast, 'he heard that the Hindu University was being built in Benares. He offered them his, by then, vast collection of Indian art, which he was ready to give them free on the condition they started a chair of Indian art and made him the professor.' The writer paused.

'What did they say?' I asked.

'They told him to go away. They told him to go away. They told him to take his art collection and go away,' the writer said, laughing, his eyes widening. His repetition made simple and ordinary something shocking, in turn deepening its effect. His laughter rang out as if no calamity was great enough to smother its rumble.

'Where is it now?' I asked.

'It's in Boston.' He chortled. 'It's in Boston.'

A few Indians, middle-class-seeming people with cameras, sauntered in. The writer's wife took this as an opportunity to challenge her husband's earlier claim that English-speaking Indians were not interested in India's antiquities. 'Look, *they've* come,' she said.

'They've come for the jewels. Yes, yes, they've come for the Nizam's jewels. Their grandparents were taxed to death for the Nizam to have those jewels. And he didn't do a thing; he just handled his jewels. The Left adores the Nizam.'

Then suddenly, our visit seeming to wind down, the writer became urgent. 'You'll come back,' he said, 'and you'll look at these things. You'll look at what we've seen and then move on.'

Walking out, we passed a map of the places from where the antiquities had come. It annoyed the writer; it seemed to show nothing but the actual digs, with no historical or geographical points of reference. He saw one place somewhere near Calcutta; 'the Calcutta Museum,' he said, 'had a good collection, but kept badly. I think they would like to destroy them,' he added, 'but they can't. So they do the next best thing: they let the workers watch them. Yes, they let the workers watch them.'

Another group of Indians, in bold colours, were coming in just as we were leaving. They seemed from the south, with teekas on their foreheads and flowers in their hair. They were laughing and visibly excited by what they saw.

'You see my point,' the writer said. 'The people who come are the temple-goers and the ones who stay away are . . .'

'The anglicized . . .' his wife started.

'The green-card folk,' the writer offered, and laughed deeply.

15

Sanyogita didn't like the writer. She felt he wasn't kind; that was her word. She had begun many books of his. I think she read them for my sake rather than out of any real interest; and later I felt she left them unfinished for the same reason. One lay by her bedside now.

'I can't!' she said, standing in front of a dressing-table mirror, her head cocked to one side as she put in an earring, 'I just can't. I've tried, but they're so dry. And he's not kind to his subjects.'

'What do you mean "not kind"? What's kind got to do with it?'

'Well,' she said, 'I don't think he shows any compassion to the people he writes about.'

'Isn't just being plain honest a kind of compassion? Doesn't it give back to people a kind of dignity, just to judge them by your own good standards and not as people who've been colonized, defeated, oppressed or enslaved?'

She didn't answer; she was having trouble finding the hole. The earring slipped and clattered across the floor. Sanyogita, already in her heels, squatted down in one movement. But when she found it, it was broken. It was one of Ra's earrings, the one with the moonstone and the ruby. The moonstone was missing. It left a visible vacancy.

'Baby!' Sanyogita cried, and squatted down again, feeling around the floor for the stone. We found it under her dressing table, covered in wisps of dirt and dust. She handled the little paisley-shaped stone as though it were a chick that had fallen from its nest. She found these small, inauspicious tragedies very moving; they could almost reduce her to tears. Then she saw that I was squatting down next to her and she smiled. She reached a long arm up to my ear, rubbed its rim between her fingers and rose in one movement.

'No big deal, right? I'll get Ra to fix it. When are we meeting your mother?'

'Now.'

'OK, I'll hurry.'

My mother had flown in from Bombay for two nights. She was having dinner with Sanyogita and me tonight; the following night, she was having her dinner for the writer. We were meeting her at the new Italian restaurant in the Oberoi.

Outside on the garden terrace, the frangipani, its branches now completely bare, had shrivelled in its pot. But my premonition had been wrong. It was not the first casualty of a larger pestilence; the other plants were flourishing. From the shaft of light falling on the corridor, I could see the door to my study. Its brass Godrej lock hung heavily from the bolt; it hadn't been opened since my return.

Sanyogita herself had only come back the night before. She appeared in the corridor a few seconds later.

The Oberoi Hotel attracted a variety of people. Politicians in white waited for white cars with red lights. Young men in maroon shirts with black trousers and brushed-steel belt buckles wandered in. A woman in a pink salwar kameez stepped out of a blue Mercedes. The hotel's lobby was of black granite and heavily air-conditioned. There was a white marble fountain in the middle, with red rose petals circling on its glassy surface. On the way to the restaurant, we saw the hotel swimming pool through glass panels many metres below, brightly lit and blue in the darkness.

The restaurant had tall grey leather chairs. The tables were made of a faux-rustic stone and were very far apart. My mother, bejewelled and in a black and gold silk sari, tapped out a text message in front of a wavy, illuminated panel of frosted glass.

Because my mother had brought me up alone and our closeness was almost embarrassing since I was now technically a man,
we played at being offhand with each other. And so even after
not seeing me for months, she gave me a brief hug, said I was
looking skinny and fell into Sanyogita's arms. While they spoke
about jet lag and the summer, a young man in white brought a
bottle of Himalaya water to the table, then bowed in a deep
namaste and went away.

'That's new!' I said to my mother as we sat down.

'I know! Isn't it amazing? Biki has them all doing it.'

Biki was Biki Oberoi, the owner of the hotel.

'He must have picked it up in the East,' I said, remembering
the time when you couldn't even come into the hotel's restaurants in Indian clothes.

'Isn't that strange,' my mother said, 'that it should have gone
from here to there as a greeting, hundreds of years ago, and has
now returned via Biki Oberoi?'

We had barely sat down when I felt my phone vibrate for the
third time since we had arrived. I didn't answer it, but was curious as to who it was: Aakash, all three times. My mother and
Sanyogita were talking about Chamunda, about the dinner the
next day, about the blasts and demonstrations in the old city as
a result of a police encounter. I was sending a text message,
asking Aakash what the matter was, when my mother suddenly
said, 'Baba, have you called Zafar to see if he's OK?'

The question put my back up. Both because I hadn't spoken
to Zafar since I arrived and because Sanyogita, having seen me
check my phone for the third time, and guessing who it was,
compressed her lips. My mother, an observer of these currents,
badgered me for many minutes about how wrong it was. 'Your
poor old teacher,' she said, 'alone in the walled city at a time
like this. How uncaring can you be, Aatish! And to a man who
has given you so much, really.'

'Ma, he's not alone! He has a family. I'll call him.'

'It's the bad Pakistani blood,' my mother said, shaking her head, and withholding a smile, turned to Sanyogita. 'It's from the father. I've done what I can to improve it, but still it remains.'

A man in a dark jacket appeared to take our order. I ordered lamb, my mother a starter as a main course, and Sanyogita sea bass.

My mother, finding me more sensitive than she had expected, brought up the writer's treatment of his wife, taking pleasure perhaps, after not seeing me for so long, in winding me up.

'It can't be easy for her,' she said, 'married to a man like him. He's very demanding. It's a twenty-four-hour job. She can't go anywhere, you know? She's his wife of course, but that's it. And he can be savage to her. I've seen it. Stingy beyond words. She lives as he does, which is well, but I don't think she has five rupees of her own.'

'All right,' I said, 'but she *is* a writer's wife. The man has his vocation. That's the most important thing in his life; everything else is secondary. She married him knowing that.'

'She's given him her everything, given him her life,' my mother replied, no longer playful. 'He's the famous writer, but what does she get out of it?'

'To be his wife. Some men need that and some women are made to give that.'

No sooner had I made the remark than it seemed to crumble and change like one of those unstable compounds, returning to their baser elements with the slightest exposure. Defending something stupid can make the world feel beyond grasp. And that night, before my mother, the woman who'd raised me, and my girlfriend of many months, who might have considered spending the remainder of her life with me, I took a shred of a thought, this little idea that the life of vocation required the sacrifice of anyone who came within its circle, and ran with it. I poured my energy into qualifications and amendments, trying to pull out of a rhetorical train crash. My mother became grave. Sanyogita's face shrank, till it was like a pinpoint of pain and hurt. But she didn't say a word.

I said that certain people were touched with energies and talents that weren't theirs, and in acting on them, they weren't expected to meet normal standards of decency and good behaviour.

'What about love?' my mother said.

'What about it?'

'What about your responsibility to the people you love and who love you?'

Our food arrived. Sanyogita pushed behind her ear a lock of hair that had fallen forward and began quietly to pick at her fish. I thought I saw her eyes glisten. I took refuge in my lamb.

'The person who embarks on this kind of life,' I said at last, 'can't think of those things. He has to think of his vocation, whether it makes him happy or not, or those around him.'

'That's nonsense, Aatish. You really talk nonsense. What is life if not in the end to have been a good friend, a good wife or lover, or mother, to have a house by the sea that you love, and five beagles running about the place?'

'Not everyone has a house by the sea and five beagles.'

'Don't be cussed, you know that's not what I mean. I mean to have lived a full, balanced life, to be surrounded in the end by the things you love.'

'It's funny you mention that, the being surrounded in the end by *things* you love. Almost exactly the same conversation came up at the end of the museum visit the other day. And the writer said he wanted to die, like Van Gogh, "with hatred for no one and love for his art". Perhaps that's the difference, wanting in the end to be surrounded by art you love and which you have spent a lifetime creating, rather than by things you love.'

Sanyogita, who hadn't said a word so far, who had driven me to the depths of despair with her silence, said at last, 'What about the people who give their lives supporting you?'

I was about to speak when she anticipated me and stopped me.

'Who do it not from any sense of vocation, but out of love. Only out of love.'

At that moment, my phone vibrated for the tenth time.

I said, 'I don't know, baby. This is not personal or about me. Listen, I'm going to take this call because there seems to be some kind of serious problem. It's been ringing all evening. Will you excuse me for a second?'

And so, in this way I tried to put a rushed, modern ending to a conversation which, when I later tried to downplay to my mother, describing it as a slip of the tongue, she further described as, 'Yes, but a very revealing one.'

In the lobby outside, Aakash, using a Hinglish classic, said, 'Aatish, man, I'm taking a lot of tension.'

'Why, what's the matter?' I asked, beginning now to think of my own problems.

'Megha just called me. Her brother knows for sure.'

'How do you know?'

'He just confronted Megha.'

'Saying what?'

'"We sent you there,"' Aakash began, employing his distinctive ability to take on other personas, '"to get into shape so that you could make a good match, not so that you could run off with the gym trainer. Who is he? He is nothing. He doesn't know his station. If I wanted I could call Deepak . . ."'

'Who's Deepak, Aakash?'

'The owner, man. The fucker with the ponytail. "I could call Deepak," Aakash said, stepping back into character, '"and have him thrown into the street, his legs broken. The only reason I'm not doing it is because I don't want a public embarrassment. But end this relationship this minute, I warn you. Mummy has high blood pressure. If she gets to know her daughter has run off with such a low-grade person, it would kill her. You have one younger sister. Think of her. Do you realize you're compromising her marriage prospects as well?"'

'He said all this?'

'Yes, man! I think they're going to disappear her if we don't do something.'

'Maybe you should back off?'

'Whaddyou saying, man? We have once to live, once to die. We'll love once too.'

'Aakash, stop giving me these bullshit filmy lines.'

'They're not filmy. There's another reason; I'll explain later. What should I do, man? If her brother tells Junglee, I'm gone. Taking too much tension.'

'What kind of man is her brother? Big, small? Could he have you killed, your legs broken?'

'That homo, no chance! Aatish, man, he's a gay. And I have my people too, in Sectorpur. You've seen the guy. What can he do to me?'

'I've seen the guy? Where?'

'In Junglee only. A friend of Sparky Punj's? He even came that time to Sanyogita's house. Remember, when –'

'Who?'

'Lul! The guy we call Lul. Kris, Krishna. He is Megha's brother.'

'What? Lul is Megha's brother? Aakash, how could you not have told me?'

'I didn't tell you? I must have!'

It was a suppression of truth greater than a lie. It didn't just alter one reality but several that had come before. And it was the multiple deceptions contained in this one deception that gave it its particular sting, the sting of making me feel like a fool. It was also the reason it had been kept from me. It made Aakash seem like a man with secrets, a man playing for higher stakes, someone who didn't need to make confidences to friends. I wanted very much in that instant to turn away from him for good. How easy it would have been in this slippery-floored lobby, into which he'd never come, with my mother and girl-friend in the other room, to get a new trainer and never think again of Aakash. I could turn away and he would vanish.

There was also, beyond questions of truth and lies, my genuine amazement that Megha and the creative writer could be
brother and sister. Not only were they nothing like each other
physically, but they were so different in their concerns and values,
with almost nothing, save their taste for the rough side of Sectorpur, in common.

'Ash-man.'

'Yes, man.'

'Let's meet tomorrow and discuss this thing properly,' I said,
putting away the question of his deception.

'OK, man,' he said with disappointment. The time to tell
me about Megha's brother had no doubt been carefully chosen;
I thought he would have liked to have better relished the surprise it produced in me. 'I'll tell you,' he said, suddenly excited,
'tomorrow's Saturday, no?'

'Yes.'

'Why don't you come with me to the Shani temple? Megha
and I go every Saturday; after that, we'll talk as well.'

'Done.'

'Done-a-done done. Oh, and sir, one more thing, bring a brief-
case of money.'

'Why?'

'I'm going to take you shopping after the temple, and when I
shop I like to . . .' He made a sucking noise to indicate, I thought,
a credit card swiping.

I stood for a moment by the glass panels in the lobby, looking
down at the pool, still bright blue in the darkness, then went
back into the restaurant.

My mother and Sanyogita were talking like women do after
a man has behaved badly, conciliatory, making a show of having
a good time, but wounded somehow. I told them what had happened with Megha and her brother, but didn't mention who he
was.

'Well, that's no big deal,' my mother said. 'Even politicians
can't disappear a girl these days. Not with television the way it

is. One word to Shabby aunty and we'll have TVDelhi's cameras surround Sectorpur.'

'Shabby aunty?' I asked, uncertain where I had heard the name before.

'Don't you remember,' Sanyogita said, 'she's part of Emigrés at Home. She was there that night when . . .'

'Yes, yes.' I didn't want to be reminded of that night again. The scars, smooth and pink from her grazes, still remained on Sanyogita's elbows and knees, and if anything, the entire episode was more painful with time.

'She'll be there tomorrow night,' my mother said, 'Shabby. And Chamunda. You two have to sit between them. They can't stand each other.'

'Why?' Sanyogita asked.

'Your aunt thinks Shabby's channel is prejudiced against her because she's BJP. It's all that Hindu nationalist/liberal secular nonsense. Just don't let Chamunda get carried away.'

As we waited for our bill, the man in white returned with a silver brush and pan, sweeping away the crumbs from the table.

My mother looked irritated. 'You don't have to . . .' she began.

'Yes, I know, ma'am. I tell him, the manager, that in Europe people put their bread on the tablecloth, but he doesn't listen. He says, "Here is here."' Sweeping away the last of the crumbs, and leaving my mother struck dumb for once, the man said, 'Sorry if it was any inconvenience.'

16

When Aakash was 'taking tension', he liked either to go to the temple or to shop. As the day before he had taken tension in unusually high quantities, he wanted the next day to do both. He was astrologically under the influence of Shani or Saturn. Shani, lame and malevolent, could, once installed in your planetary house, move slowly through it for seven years, bringing luck that was not so much bad or good as it was patchy. And it was to lessen the effect of this roller coaster that Aakash, on Saturdays, went to Shani's temple on a main road in Sectorpur and stayed away from alcohol and 'non-veg'. He asked that we meet after the flyover. He had spoken separately to Uttam the night before, explaining where it was.

We set out the next morning at six fifteen. A cold, persistent drizzle, coming on the back of three days of rain, followed us the entire way. The traffic was terrible even at that hour and Uttam suggested we take 'the jungle route'. He swung off the main thoroughfare on to a thinly surfaced road overgrown with keekar. Their long, spiny branches reaching out to the car, like many frail arms, made a sound of nails on glass. On our left was a wide canal choked with hyacinth. And on our right, seeming almost desolate save for the bush that encroached on it, was a power station. Its iron men rose high above the foliage, their power lines slung wide between them, like a tug-of-war team. The foliage had grown so thick after the monsoon that it took me some minutes to realize that I had seen this canal once before. It was with Aakash, on the way to the Begum of Sectorpur, when I had glimpsed the power station's red lights reflected in the canal. Its dark water had seemed foreboding then; and now, too, for other reasons, there was a strange menace about it. It came in part from the thick clumps of hyacinth that grew on its edges and appeared like islands in its centre, so that they seemed not so much to be separate clumps as a single net of hyacinth strangling the canal. It came also from the factory drains, forming great mountains of white chemical foam where they deposited their refuse. And it was the plant life that grew so furiously from this poisoned river that unnerved me.

There had been a police encounter the day before in the old city in which one policeman and two alleged terrorists had been killed. The images that had flashed on everyone's screens for the past twenty-four hours had shown the dead policeman being carried away, but they had also shown a Muslim crowd enraged for being the target of the police encounter. There was talk of it having been staged. 'Just answer me one simple question, Aatish saab,' Uttam asked, full of political feeling that morning, 'if the encounter was fake, then how come one policeman is dead and another injured? Now, obviously they didn't shoot themselves, which must mean that the people they were having the encounter with had weapons too, no?'

'Yes.'

'So fine, even if they weren't the bombers, they would have been some kind of criminal. I tell you, saab, we suffer from the worst traitors in this country. And I don't mean Muslims; I mean Hindus. You put two Muslims next to ten Hindus and they will somehow subdue them. I hear it's written in their religion that if a man rapes my wife, she has to live with him and can only come back to me after she has divorced him.'

'I'm really not sure about that, Uttam.'

'And how is it that the Muslim guard in our building will say, "Namaste," but he'll never say, "Ram, ram"? I don't mind saying, "Allah." Sometimes I say, "Salaam alaikum," to him, then he's happy.' Uttam choked with wet, throaty laughter. 'And what about that driver that came around the other day? We gave him dinner, but he wouldn't touch the meat. I asked him what the matter was, and you know what he told me?'

'What?'

'He said he was vegetarian. A Muslim who doesn't eat meat? I said to myself, Can't be! That's one thing that couldn't have been written in their Book, because we know there were no vegetables in the desert. I thought, he's definitely hiding something. So I take the cook aside and ask him if he still has the receipt from the butcher. He did. I show it to the man; he sees that the butcher's a Muslim butcher and the bastard's face lights up. And he eats the meat! Now, why couldn't he have just said, "I don't eat meat that's not halal."?'

'Maybe he was being accommodating.'

'Yes, but why lie about being vegetarian? There's the slyness.'

Uttam's talk was making me think about Zafar, and perhaps misinterpreting my silence, he said, 'But I will say this, my father saved one once.'

'Saved what?'

'A Muslim. It was 1947 and the riots were going on. They were killing Muslims everywhere. My father hid one inside a barrel with holes in it and saved his life.'

'Good.'

'But,' Uttam said, already roaring with laughter at his own joke, 'we kept the barrel outside the house.'

The road widened and open fields came into view. They were dotted with dozens of tall apartment blocks. The land had barely been cleared. There were nothing but long, cracked streets lined with *Alstonia scholaris* and apartment building after apartment building decorated with geometric designs in dull colours. The foliage on the sides of the road was dense, and along with the fields, seemed to mock the new city that had sprung up. Long, grid-like streets with giant stooping street lights finished in fields. On some stretches of undeveloped road, headless lamp standards had rusted before ever being installed. I couldn't tell which building would have been the begum's.

The flyover that had brought life to Sectorpur had also swept away its older sections. A low city of half-painted buildings, black water tanks, orange and white mobile phone towers and the occasional gurdwara dome or temple steeple lay huddled under the flyover. Dotting the mismatched landscape were signs for medical centres, computer courses, cricket academies and foreign travel. And at the foot of the flyover was Aakash on his bike, indicator lights flashing, Megha riding pillion. Aakash wore a black faux-leather jacket; Megha, a now drenched purple T-shirt and a shawl. Uttam blew his horn. Aakash raised his arm without looking back and drove on.

We followed him for many minutes until we came on to a roaring street. I knew it well; not only was it the road to the airport, but a friend of mine lived not more than a hundred metres away. So when Aakash pulled over to the side of the road, I couldn't understand why he had stopped. Then stepping out on to the pavement in the rain, I saw, and for some moments stood wondering at how I had failed to see before, a large temple in pink stone with a tall steeple and a crowd at the entrance. Only a damaged eye could have missed it.

There were green and blue tarpaulins outside the temple, under which a man distributed steel platters containing a garland of marigolds, a clay lamp, a black cloth, a litre bottle of sunflower oil and a newspaper sachet of black lentils and asafoetida. Aakash bought one platter for himself and Megha and one for me. We lined up behind a frail old woman in a black and red sari. She was trying to garland the god's brass figure. Moustached and fierce in aspect, he was deep within a dark stone recess, covered in marigolds and black seeds. A steady stream of oil dripped from his foot. Around the feet of his brass elephant, several oil lamps cast their smoky light into the corners of the recess and over the god's dull metallic body. The combination of black offerings, the dim light from the lamps and the orange of the marigolds suggested a carefully worked-out harmony, playing on the idea of Shani as a dark god, a cousin of Yama, god of death.

The tiny old woman ahead of us missed the god with her garlands the first few times, then threw a garland clean over his head and was forced to retrieve it from between the elephant's legs. When at last she hit her mark, she brought down a small avalanche of marigolds on to the lamps below. As we waited, I asked Megha if only people suffering from the maleficence of Saturn needed to appease the god.

'No,' she said. 'He's good to me. I'm saying, "Good, you're good to me; now be very good to me."'

With this, she leaned forward, showing a long, pink band of Jockey underwear, and after dressing the deity in marigolds and black starched cotton she drenched him in half a litre of oil. Aakash, unshaven, his face intent, guided her hand in offering the lamp, then slipped an iron nail into the wire coiled around the god's ankle; iron was Shani's metal. With the enactment of each rite, which took us from Shani's brass form to offering clay lamps at the base of a peepal tree, to entering the main sanctum with its Shiva linga beneath a silver serpent, Aakash's mood softened. The sensual power of the rites, the feeling of oil, metal and pulses early in the morning, and their supposed relevance to the turmoil in his life, seemed to provide a reminder of enduring materials that would help him face the world beyond, all the more illusory that morning thanks to Shani's antics. And when at last we stood in the main sanctum, the linga in a bed of papaya leaves, surrounded by many little lingas in a white marble tank in the floor, and Aakash smashed the temple bell three times, I felt all the force of his restoration.

And then we shopped.

Aakash parked his bike outside the temple and he and Megha came in the car with me to Connaught Place. Uttam watched Megha intently as she got in. It was a high van, and when she put one foot on the step, her short, splayed fingers reaching into its cavernous interior for a grab handle, Uttam wheezed with laughter. Aakash saw, and as he had with Shakti, encouraged him by shooting up his eyebrows in quick succession. There was in this joking, this light humiliation of the woman in public, an element of Indian male pride and control. And Megha, as if it were a testament to their love for each other, increasing both their statures, only pretended to mind. She glowered at us all, then seated comfortably, smiled.

On the way, Aakash wanted to stop at Junglee. His mood had lightened. He hummed the tune of an advertisement jingle, adding a modified Hindi movie line to the ending. Where the hero says, 'Which sod drinks to stay in control? I drink to lose control,' he said, 'I drink because the cheetah drinks.' 'Do the dew, mountain dew!' he said vacantly to himself, as we drove into the grimy alley which housed Junglee.

He wanted me to come upstairs.

'Are you sure? Why?'

'Just trust me.'

The Nepali doorman pushed open the brushed-steel door and Junglee's incense-filled air tumbled out. Upstairs, the other trainers eyed Aakash come in, both in civilian clothes and with a member. Aakash ignored them, taking me straight to the locker room and the men's 'wet area'. He opened his dark green locker with a pair of tiny brass keys. Then, rummaging about among exercise clothes and a tiffin in blue polythene, he took out something thin and rectangular, wrapped in the *Delhi Times*'s social pages. I opened it and saw that it was a laminated certificate of sorts. My impressions of it were haphazard: I saw red and blue colours on the white board; the words 'Arya Samaj', Hanuman mandir; a picture of Aakash in a blazer and tie, looking like a schoolboy, against a sky-blue background; a picture of Megha, with a fat inky stamp over her face; their addresses, both Sectorpur addresses; and the word 'solemnized'.

How these scattered impressions came together to form a single, horrible realization of what had occurred, I can't say. Perhaps it was the pictures Aakash handed me of him and Megha, garlanded and in bright sunlight, that helped focus my swimming mind. Or it was his words, 'You see now why I can't back off?' reaching me from some distant place. But none of the finality of the deed lessened the dread it awoke in me. 'Ash-man, what have you done?' I wanted to say. 'What have you done?'

Scanning the certificate's smooth, laminated surface, my eye fell on the date.

'The 25th of July?' I gasped.

'Yes, man. You don't know what it was like. They were sending her to Bombay to meet a suitor. I was here on my own; you weren't here. I felt I had no one. I felt this was the only thing that would give me some protection. After that, they could do whatever they wanted to do, but at least we could say, "Look, here, we're married. Now do what you want to do."'

'Whose idea was it?'

'Hers. She came to me just before she was being sent to Bombay and said, "We have to do it now." She went straight to the airport from the temple. We even had to make the priest hurry up because otherwise she would have missed her flight.' He laughed. 'Can you imagine, some people go on honeymoon after their wedding, she went to meet a suitor!'

'What happened?'

'It didn't work. The guy thought she was too healthy. Can you imagine?' He smiled sadly. 'All these guys rejecting her because she's too healthy, then there's me who wants to marry her the way she is and they won't let me. You know, they're even considering sending her for lipo.'

'Lipo?'

'They suck out the fat . . .'

'Yes, yes, I know,' I said, looking up, then the thought of his marriage returned. 'Who else knows about this?'

'Nobody, man. Just you. You know, I don't have much of a friend circle. And I haven't told anyone in my family.'

I was caught between a feeling of tenderness at the confidence made only to me and deep irritation at Aakash's willingness to burden me with his problems. In just a few seconds, it had altered not only the way I saw his and Megha's relationship, but the way I saw ours. I felt it shed for the first time some of the strange intensity, as of a childhood friendship, that had defined it since its conception. And reckless though I felt he'd been, marriage made Aakash seem like a man.

Downstairs, the rain had gone and the sun was burning its way through. Whole sections of the street dried before our eyes. In the car, heading to Connaught Place, Megha knew of Aakash's disclosure. I thought she displayed something of the satisfaction of a daughter-in-law who's just won her first battle against her husband's family. She would have jangled the house keys in her palm if she had any. Aakash was visibly relieved. The weight of their dangerous secret had shifted for that moment on to me.

The car, picking its way from roundabout to roundabout, swung on to Janpath for the last time. The off-white colonnaded façades of the Eastern and Western courts, the Imperial Hotel and Delhi's few tall buildings lined the road, at the end of which the roar of Connaught Place could be heard. Its whitewashed façade was damp and streaked black. Its crumbling columns, poster-covered and pan-stained, seemed to revolve slowly around us that morning like a carousel.

'Van Hussein!' Megha said, pointing at the billboards that dotted the circular sweep of Connaught Place. Aakash and Megha knew them all – Nike, Reebok, Puma and Benetton. Though prime real estate, Connaught Place was still rent-controlled. And among the new showrooms there were ancient shops of my childhood: bookshops, coffee houses, sari centres, high-ceilinged games shops selling carom boards. In the gloom of their colonnaded passages, black wires ran like creepers along the high walls and fine heaps of dust collected under splashes of red pan spittle, rising so far up from the base of the white columns that the mind was forced to think of the chewer's technique. Fire extinguishers, thick coir doormats and plastic buckets cluttered the entrances of shops, and sleazy flights of stairs led up to the offices of reputable news magazines.

We hit every important shop with great precision. Aakash didn't shop for himself, but for me. He marched through each glass door, chest out, arms dangling at his side, like a man looking for a fight. He glowered at the doormen if he sensed even the slightest hesitation in their manner towards him. Once inside, he tore through the neatly folded displays, ruffling them up at will. He had me try on slinky black exercise shirts with many little holes, lime-green T-shirts with American road signs on them, and capris. Aakash and Megha were both wild about capris. I said I couldn't do it, but they insisted I try them on. Megha had a hunger for bold colours. But what might have been bold and still simple in Indian clothes got lost in the Western showrooms. It manifested itself in busyness and clutter, in pointless buttons, stripes and straps, in decorative pockets and zips that led nowhere.

Megha was very keen for Aakash to buy a pair of sports sandals. They were expensive and I could see Aakash recoil from them. He made excuses that were unrelated to money: that he had so many already, that they were better elsewhere. Seeing him in the showroom, unshaven and vulnerable about money, I felt again, as I had in Hookah, the fragility of his 'upgrading' of himself. It was possible to see him in the showroom, but it was also possible to see him in the street in blue rubber chappals and polyester shirts. And sometimes when he'd eaten pan masala and his skin was looking darker than usual, or his stubble too thick, he seemed even physically like a man about to slip. And how soundless that fall would be, muffled by millions below . . .

It was not a fear either Megha or I could have known. Even to imagine what constituted our security would have been strange. There were so many impermeable barriers unrelated to money, barriers of English and education and the people one knew. But now, thinking of them as married, their fortunes clubbed together so to speak, I felt I couldn't call the outcome. Could Megha, disowned by her family, fall with Aakash if he were to fall? Or was his upward momentum too great to be broken, so that she wouldn't fall far before he would take her fleshy hand in his and they would begin moving up again?

To witness some of this tension in the shape of the fat wife, still sure of her riches, gently taunting her husband over a pair of rubber sport sandals, was to imagine many future scenarios of this kind. And Aakash, giving an indication of how he might behave, became suddenly irritable. His heavy eyelashes sank, a look of boredom crept over his face; only the mud-coloured eyes, smouldering with contempt, revealed that he felt neither fatigue nor boredom, but irritation. Megha, who had pushed her way up to the shelves and shown another bit of pink panty as she took down the rubber sandals, now contained her talk about wanting to buy the sandals as a present for Aakash.

'What's wrong?' she said, seeing the expression on her husband's face darken.

'Nothing, appu,' he replied, using a term of endearment I had not heard so far. 'I'm just hungry.'

'Pizza Hut?' she offered.

'I'm sick of Pizza Hut,' he answered, and headed for the door.

When we were outside in the car park, waiting for Uttam, she produced a garlic stick from her handbag. At the sight of it, Aakash's eyes became two bitter slits of disgust.

'Mantra,' she announced urgently. 'Mantra. He gets very hungry on Saturdays,' she added apologetically to me. 'It's because of the fasting.'

On the way to Mantra, Aakash seemed really to wilt. His eyes, now yellow, receded into their sockets. Megha, like a nurse, turned back and forth between him and me. 'Let his hunger go,' she said optimistically in English, 'then he'll for sure want to pick up those sandals before going.' And tenderly to him, 'We'll get them, no?' He was too faint to reply. 'Do you want us to give you shoes for your birthday?' she said in Hindi, then laughingly added, 'Or do you want us to give you chappals?'

The car pulled up outside Mantra. It was a dimly lit restaurant with maroon leather seats, red chandeliers and gold-leaf walls and mirrors. It was owned by the same designer that Aakash had had his run-in with on Holi, the Holi that now seemed an age away. I mentioned this as we sat down.

'Really?' Aakash asked, mustering up some energy for the subject of wealth and fame, the only subject for which he always had time. He listened for a while, then spat, 'They're all creeps.'

Megha, who took in every word, said, 'No. I heard he only decorated it.' Her manner seemed to hide irritation that Aakash's restoration had happened before plan and by other means.

'He owns it,' I said. 'I've been here when he's had parties.'

Aakash liked this. He impressed upon her that I knew what I was talking about. But she was not to be put down; the two large diamonds in her ears gleamed like teeth. And when the waiter came around, the first thing she asked him, despite Aakash's hunger, was who owned the restaurant. Even when he had said, 'Mateen Butt,' she was undeterred. 'But I saw on Zoom,' she said, cross-questioning the man, 'that he only decorated it.'

Before he could answer, she ordered malai koftas, dal, paneer and butter naan, which she insisted on.

Because Aakash was not in the mood to talk, I began to ask Megha about her family's attitude. It turned out that, apart from her brother, her other siblings had also had their suspicions about Aakash. She said, 'The whole issue had died down. My siblings thought that I had given up Aakash because I'd stopped going to the gym. But twenty days back, when I started going again, they thought, ah, now she's started to go to the gym again. Aakash must be pressurizing her into marrying him so that he can get our money. That's when the trouble started again.'

'Surely their attitude would be different if they knew you were already married?'

She liked this, and as if tickled by the logic of it, laughed out loud.

The food arrived and Aakash revived further. Apart from his mood, there seemed to be a genuine physical change in his condition as if related to blood sugar. He said he was going to get a doctor to look at it. 'Ask Megha how much I ate yesterday,' he said. 'I ate some five-six times.'

This talk of Aakash's health and hunger, as it had with the Begum of Sectorpur, brought out affection in Megha and excited a story. 'One time, I went out with him,' she said, 'and he began to feel so hungry he couldn't walk. He drank a milkshake that if you drank one sip of . . . so *havy*, and even then he wasn't satisfied. He went home, and with his hands trembling, asked his mother for food. She brought out ghee on *brad*.'

At the mention of his mother Aakash took over the story in Hindi. 'Then I dug in and ate,' he said, 'and only then did I feel *behtar*. But before that, man, you won't believe. I was riding the bike and my hands were sliding off the handles.'

Seeing that Aakash was feeling stronger, I raised the subject of his marriage again. I said, more as joke, and because he had mentioned needing the help of the press before, that there should be a reality show on Indian TV in which couples that were in love, or secretly married, could confront their parents and in-laws on television.

Aakash looked scornfully at me. 'Are you serious, man?' he said mockingly.

'Half serious.'

'Half serious,' he spat. 'I know about television. I know what people will say. They'll say he could have done it quietly but he wanted the fame.' He slipped into role-playing, becoming many people at once. 'For months,' he said, transforming into the neighbours, 'they'll point to us and say, "Oh, there they go, the ones who went on TV to get the fame."' A second later, he was the TV journalist: '"Oh, you're marrying for love, are you? So many girls in the world, how come you found this one from a rich family? Oh, and a healthy girl too? And you're from a poor family? Could it be that you're just marrying her for the money?"' His tongue flickered, scraping over his lips as he spoke. We watched in fascination.

I said, 'Don't get so worked up. There's no reality show like this; it was just a joke.'

'I know there isn't,' he replied, his words bristling. 'That's why I just touched on it and quickly dismissed it.'

I said, 'TV should only be called in if there's a threat to your or Megha's life.'

'Yes, but if I go to meet Megha's family, there will be a threat to my life.'

'Were you planning to? This is the first I've heard of it. If you go alone, you really are mad.'

Megha nodded sadly in agreement.

'Take it from me now in writing,' Aakash said. 'The way it's going to happen is this: in a month, there'll be another suitor for Megha; her mother will try taking her to meet him; and then I will pressurize Megha to tell them and she will.'

Megha bit her lip nervously and looked at me. I shrugged my shoulders. Aakash looked viciously at us both.

'Is your stomach full?' Megha asked.

'Isn't it clear I'm full?' Aakash answered without a trace of humour. 'That's why I'm talking like this now. My energy has returned.'

'And aggression,' I said.

He smiled and became gentler.

'What can I do, man?' he confessed. 'Taking a lot of tension. This thing is constantly on my mind. I used to sleep till eleven on Sundays but now I wake up at five from worry. Thinking, thinking. I have many problems. It's not just this thing. I have to think of my career. How I'm going to upgrade myself. I have to think of how I'll take care of Megha. Fine, I can rent a flat in Sectorpur; she will stay there in the days when I'm work-ing or she could be with my mother so that she won't get bored on her own.'

Listening to this description, tender that it was, I felt sure that it would never become a reality. Something about Megha, her boisterousness, or perhaps her sheer size, defied any notion of her sitting alone at home in Sectorpur, or milling about Aakash's tiny flat with her mother-in-law. And this mention of boredom, linked somehow to the solitude of the modern apart-ment, seemed to bring alive Megha's resistance to any quiet sequestering in Sectorpur. As if also sensing the impossibility of living with Aakash's family, she said snidely of his brother Amit, 'And we know all about your brother and his wife.'

A tense moment passed between them.

'Everyone has faults,' Aakash snapped. 'You do, sir probably does too, and so does he.'

Turning to me, Aakash said in English, 'My sis-in-law is very sharp.'

'And very money-minded,' Megha added.

Aakash relaxed and said in English, 'My brother sometimes says me, "Why are you worried? You have Megha." Can you believe, man?' Aakash exploded, and switching to Hindi, said, '"And we count every little paisa, thinking, can we afford this, can we not? Let's not buy it now; we'll buy it next time."'

It was becoming afternoon when we left Mantra. The sun now shone on a different segment of Connaught Place. It showed me what I had not seen earlier: a single block, renovated, whitewashed, looking for the first time since independence how it was built to look. It was as hopeful a thing as I had ever seen, almost impossible to imagine, impossible to think of in the surrounding decay as the work of a brush and fresh paint. If it was so easy, why had it not been done before? Aakash explained that it was the first block to have been released from rent control. As soon as it had been, fresh life had poured into it.

We put Megha into a taxi headed for Sectorpur. Before waving her off, Aakash told her to be careful when driving into Sectorpur.

'Why for?' she asked.

'There's been an encounter,' Aakash said, 'with Muhammad-ans.'

'Not Muhammadans, Aakash, terrorists. Not all Muhammad-ans are terrorists,' I added prissily.

'Fine,' he replied, 'but all the terrorists are Muhammadans.'

'Same difference,' Megha said from within the taxi. 'Tell what happened, no?'

'The policeman killed was a Sectorpur man. All I'm saying is just be careful in case there's trouble.'

'Tch, that's nothing,' Megha said jauntily. 'Do I look like a Muhammadan to you?'

'No, appu! Now hurry up, you're causing a traffic jam.'

She was still laughing when the taxi drove away.

When she'd gone, Aakash asked me to drop him at Junglee. Driving back through the avenues, the canopies flaring and fading overhead, we passed the Human Rights Commission, the silver letters on its façade blazing in the light. Aakash pointed at it and smiled ironically. Then looking back into the boot of the car, he said with pride, 'We got things from all the brands. Puma, Nike, Reebok.'

As I was dropping him off, he asked for eleven hundred rupees.

'Why?'

'It's for a jagran we're organizing in my colony. I want you to come.'

'A jagran?'

'Tch, you really don't know anything,' Aakash said. Then looking at Uttam, he added, 'Tell him what a jagran is. I don't have the time right now.'

I took out eleven hundred rupees, including a red thousand-rupee note, and gave them to Aakash. He put them in his back pocket and vanished behind Junglee's brushed-steel door.

On the way home, Uttam explained that a jagran was an all-night wake of sorts, with devotional singing, pageants and prayers.

'It's all rubbish,' Uttam said bitterly, having seen Aakash extract a third of his monthly salary from me. 'Just a way for the Brahmins to make money.'

17

When that evening she was disappeared, the news came as a matter of course. Aakash especially, expecting it for so long, was the least surprised. He felt also that this was not the disappearance we had been waiting for: that she would return, and that then there would be some attempt at a forced marriage or a period of captivity designed to make her give up Aakash, for which we had to be prepared. He seemed almost irritated with me when I stressed that Shabby Singh was coming to dinner that night, and if there was a time to act, it was now. The drama with which he had opened the conversation, saying only, 'They've taken her,' drained from his voice. 'Tch! Take it easy. The ball is now in play,' he said. 'We have to think before we act. This is not the time when they'll find a boy for her.'

'How do you know?'

'They'll have to have the lipo done first, no? The recovery period from that itself takes a few weeks. Now, obviously they won't show her to a boy in that period when she has scars and bandages all over her.'

'They're going to forcibly lipo –' I grasped for the verb – 'liposuck her?'

'Yes, man.'

'Surely you can't do that.'

'Whaddyou saying, man? With money, in this country, you can do anything you like. The Aggarwals even have their own clinics. Who's going to stop them?' Then his cynicism vanished and some mixture of regret and self-absorption took its place. 'Man, I feel so bad. She kept saying, "Don't make me thin. Don't make me thin, otherwise they'll marry me off." If I had wanted, I could have shown results in a few weeks. I'm a professional person, you know? But I listened to her, and now look, because of me she is going to get lipo.'

'Get lipo': ah! I thought, that's the verb.

'So you want me to say anything tonight?'

'Nothing. Not a single word.'

Delhi drawing rooms. They were what I remembered of the city from my childhood. Perhaps it was Delhi's fragmented geography, or that it had no real restaurants the way Bombay had – restaurants that were not attached to five-star hotels – or just that it was an old city, closely bound, with people who all seemed to know each other, but there was no setting, no cityscape more evocative of the city I grew up in than a lamp-lit drawing room with a scattering of politicians, journalists, broken-down royals, and perhaps an old Etonian, lying fatly on a deep sofa. And it was a dinner like this, with two blue and red glass fanooses burning in a corner, jasmine floating in a porcelain dish on a dining table draped in a chikan tablecloth, ornamented with white-on-white flowers, that my mother gave for the writer.

He was annoyed even before we sat down. My mother had asked him for eight; he had arrived with his wife and shooting stick some ten or fifteen minutes past eight. Shabby Singh, in a black and red cotton sari, her large red bindi fiery that night, her politically grey hair in a tight bun, had come by eight thirty. She brought her husband, a small Sikh gentleman in a yellow kurta. Sanyogita and I were on time as well. But Chamunda was late, very late.

At nine, the writer, unaware that Chamunda was coming, but seeming to anticipate a general tendency on the subcontinent for late, drunken dinners, said, 'Udaya, we'll eat soon, won't we? We'll eat soon.'

'Yes, of course,' my mother said, covering his small, firm hand with her jewelled one.

'Good, good,' he said.

My mother, intercepting me on the way to the bar, sent me to take her place and dashed off into another room to call Chamunda. An urgent exchange was faintly overheard. She emerged a few minutes later, with a strange, nervous smile playing on her lips. She took the writer's wife aside, and, in Punjabi, rapidly recounted the outcome of her conversation. The writer, who had been talking to me a moment ago about the bronzes, now let the conversation between us die and turned his attention gravely to the women talking. His eyes seemed shut, and though he hardly understood the language they spoke, he drank in every word. His lower lip quivered and his expression became so dark that his wife could not continue listening to my mother. She turned to her husband with a large, prepared smile and said, 'Darling, Udaya is just telling me that Chamunda, her school friend whom you like so much, the Chief Minister of . . . Where is it?'

'Jhaatkebaal,' my mother offered.

'Jhaatkebaal! Is coming to dinner tonight.'

'Oh, good,' the writer said coldly. 'When?'

'Darling,' the writer's wife said, agitation thick in her voice, 'she's had some problem in her state, the discussion in the Assembly has gone on longer than she expected. Bas, she'll be here any minute.'

'Amrita, I'm not a child. If I get home past a certain point, if I am forced to drink too much, the following day is ruined. Ruined.' Then turning to me, he said, so everyone could hear, 'Amrita speaks to me as though I'm a child, as though I could be fooled into believing I haven't been waiting one hour.'

The room fell silent. The writer's wife was close to tears. She reached for some nuts. The writer saw this and smiled. 'Amrita eats nuts,' he said to me, but again for all to hear, nodding his head slightly. 'She eats nuts; she likes to eat nuts.' The Sikh gentleman in the yellow kurta, perhaps vicariously enjoying this bit of conjugal derision, of which he himself seemed incapable, laughed uproariously.

'Shut up, Tunnu,' his wife barked, fixing him with a stern look.

It was nearly nine thirty when the front door swung open and a mobile phone conversation, complete with bouts of wicked laughter, was brought leisurely to an end behind the stained-glass doors that separated our tiny hall from the drawing room. For a few seconds, everyone's eyes watched the double doors, the wicks of candles burning through their coloured panes. Then they flew open, coughing out Raunak Singh with his great moustaches, kohled eyes and gold earrings, and his boss, still, at this time of year, in chiffon. And what chiffon! The colour she wore was hardly different from her own, a chocolate brown, with tie-dyed diamonds of reddish-orange. She wore little bits of gold in and on her ears, nose and fingers, her straight black butt-length hair was open, her giant eyes wide over her face.

Chamunda, who moments ago had been late and rude, was now like a girl of sixteen, biting her lip from shyness at facing a room full of people. The writer had watched Chamunda's entrance carefully, seeming to record every detail, and now, as she went over to shake his hand and apologize for being late, deciding in the last instant to give him a brief hug, an amazing change came over him. The old writer began to laugh. A deep, asthmatic, rolling laugh rose from his depths, and like those whistles that only dogs can hear, diffused the tension in the room. 'Beautiful, beautiful, all beautiful,' he muttered to himself as Chamunda, after Sanyogita and I had risen to touch her feet, took my place next to him.

Dinner – shami kebabs, baby aubergine, cumin potatoes, lentils, raita, okra and chicken curry – was served very soon after. On the way to the table, Shabby pushed her way up to Chamunda. 'Where . . . where were you?' she said, prodding her. 'Not at a prayer service for yourself, I hope.' At this, her whole body shook with laughter. 'The divine Chamunda,' she sniggered, as though wishing for the writer, still finding his place on the table, to hear.

'Shabby, I don't know if TVDelhi considers this news, but there have been bombs in my state –'

'One bomb!' Shabby interjected. 'And that also a very small one.'

'There has been an encounter, a man from Sectorpur was killed, there are rumours of a backlash.'

'What about the two young boys who were killed?' Shabby demanded. 'What about that backlash?'

'They were terrorists, Shabby.'

'Terrorists, my foot. Show me the evidence. Where's the evidence? Just two poor Muslim boys framed by your police because they're too incompetent to catch the real guys.'

Chamunda gave my mother a look as if to say, 'Put this woman far away from me or I can't be held responsible for the consequences.' And, as my mother was in the process of seating everyone, it was easy to separate them. The writer went between my mother and Chamunda; the Sikh gentleman in the yellow kurta between the writer's wife and Sanyogita. With three men and four women, it was a difficult placement, and though Chamunda and Shabby could have been put further apart, any further and they would have been face to face. And so my mother, counting on me and the curvature of the dining table to ease the tension, put them on either side of me.

Shabby, perhaps sensing why the placement had been made the way it had, let drop her conversation with Chamunda and picked it up in a different tone with the writer.

'What do you think, Mr Vijaipal, of this dastardly situation we're in, here, in India?'

The writer, putting away small quantities of yellow dal with a teaspoon, wiped his lips. For a few moments, his mouth seemed softly to run over the words he was about to give Shabby. Then as if finding them too complicated, he began more simply. 'I think it's a difficult situation, a unique situation in fact. Unique, yes, unique. I'll tell you why. You don't have a Muslim-majority population, like Pakistan and the Arab countries, but neither is your

Muslim minority an immigrant population, like with the European countries and North America. This makes for a special tension . . .' He broke off, and as if articulating this tension directly was proving too hard, came at it from another angle. 'I was in England when they had their bombings. I felt then that the great shock was not the bombings themselves, but the headlines the following day.' Making the shape of a lengthening rectangle with his hands to indicate a headline, he said, 'They were all British!' The description had its impact and the table was silent. The writer, now only warming up, said, 'The shock of being attacked by one's own people, you know, the shock of being attacked by one's own. Very hard, you know, very hard.

'The English to some extent could distance themselves, knowing that the people who attacked them, though legally British citizens, were immigrants. That made it easier to bear. They had come to Britain no more than fifty years before. To undo that history would be no great thing. But in India we're talking about that same feeling, the feeling of being attacked by one's own, and the tension that arises from that, except in India we're talking about a non-immigrant population that constitutes nearly 15 per cent of the whole population. And of course a thousand years of history, bad history, most of it obscured or not dealt with. *That* cannot be so easily undone. Any serious eruption along those lines would tear the country apart.'

This last remark concerning the tearing apart of the country was understood on the table in very different ways. Somewhat elated, Shabby said, 'I know, I know. I keep telling these saffron-types that this was never a country; the British made it a country. It can never be ruled as one country. It must be ruled in small, manageable portions.'

'You want it to be partitioned again,' Chamunda flared, 'why don't you come out and say it? Do you see, Mr Vijaipal, what our so-called "intellectuals" want?'

The writer, seeming to filter many ideas at once, muttered, 'Yes, yes.'

'Yes, yes, what?' Shabby badgered him.

The writer answered her by ignoring her. Raising his old lion's face up to Chamunda's, a comic gleam entering his eyes, he said, 'I think they would like to make India destroyable. Isn't that right, Chamunda? That's what they're trying to do, yes?'

Chamunda clapped her hands like a little girl. She took the writer's huge face in her soft brown hands, with their reddish-orange nail polish matching, I could see now, the diamonds on her sari, and kissed it. 'Now this is a writer!' she exclaimed. 'Not a bit like our treacherous lot who feel that to be an intellectual means betraying your country.'

The writer purred contentedly. My mother laughed out loud, expressing the special delight one feels at characteristic behaviour from an old friend. I caught Sanyogita's eye and saw that she was embarrassed. In that instant, I wished for her not to be embarrassed and for her to be a little bit more like her aunt, not always so correct.

At the table, Shabby was far from defeated. 'What country, what country?' she was saying, now readily taking up Chamunda's challenge. 'That's what I'm asking. You tell us, Mr Vijaipal, what country? Was India ever a country until the British came along?'

The writer, who after his mischief-making had retired to the affections of Chamunda, now became interested in what Shabby was saying. 'I've always been intrigued,' he said, 'by how this bit of babble left behind by the British, and taken up by the Leftist historians, has survived in India till today. When people say India was not a country until the British arrived, what exactly do they mean? They could not really be saying that India wasn't a nation-state. That would be absurd. The idea of the nation-state, even in Europe, is a relatively recent idea, a nineteenth-century idea. So what they must mean, then, is that there was not even an idea of India, the way there was of Europe, or of ancient Greece; that there was never in the minds of its people the notion of belonging to a land called India.'

'There wasn't!' Shabby asserted. 'You ask the average Indian, not a princess or a goddess like Chamunda Devi here, but the common man, and he would not think of himself as an Indian. He would think of himself as a Gujarati, a Punjabi, a Tamilian, an Assamese. He wouldn't have the faintest idea of India, "the land".'

The writer seemed caught between the interruption and Shabby's raised voice, both of which he was unused to, and what he was going to say next. He lowered his head and muttered, 'Not the temple-going Indian, not the temple-going Indian.' Then raising his head and voice at once, he silenced Shabby. 'Not the temple-going Indian,' he said for the third time. 'People like you perhaps, but not him. He knows this country backwards. He forever carries an idea of it in his head. For him, it possesses a sacred topography. He knows it through its holy places. He knows it from the mountains in the north where the rivers begin, and from where the rudraksh he wears around his neck come, to the special place from where the right stones for the lingas come. He knows the rivers when they widen and the great temples and temple cities, with their stone steps, that have been set along their banks. He knows the points where those rivers meet other rivers, and their confluence becomes part of the long nationwide pilgrimages he will make several times in his lifetime. In fact, it could be said that there is almost no other country, certainly not one so vast, where the countrymen are as acquainted with the distant reaches of the land through their pilgrimages as they are in India; perhaps no country where poor people travel more. They think nothing of jumping on a bus or train, for two or three days, to journey to Tirupathi in the south or Jagannath in the east. And in this way, the religion itself is like a form of patriotism.'

Shabby was nodding her head vigorously even before he had finished. She took a chopstick out from her grey bun and began playing with it in her fingers. An arch smile rose to her lips.

'Ah!' she said. 'So you have a communal agenda. I get it now.'

'Communal?' the writer said, with genuine confusion in his eyes.

'"Communal" in India,' my mother explained, 'means advancing the interests of a particular community or religious group; to be divisive.'

The writer chuckled happily.

But then, as if thinking still of what he had said, his thoughts turned inward. I had the feeling he was not quite finished. It had been very affecting to hear him speak, very affecting to watch his distant observations coincide with smaller, more particular observations of my own. I had thought only of Aakash as he spoke and was feeling some relief that the appeal he held for me was not mere obsession, that there was something more abstract, more general, behind it. But it was an unstable feeling, edging on euphoria and hysteria, and what the writer said next broke my composure.

'You know,' he began, looking deeply into the room, where illuminated foliage could be seen beyond darkened windows and the orange coils of an electric heater burned steadily, 'they say that Benares is a microcosm of India. Today, most people take that to mean that it contains all the horror and filth of India, and also, loath as I am to use these words, the charm, the beauty, the magic, whatever you want to call it. But Benares was once a very different kind of microcosm; it was a very self-conscious microcosm. The streams that watered the groves in its Forest of Bliss were named after all the rivers of India, not unlike the avenues in Washington, DC, being named after the American states. All the princes from around the country had their palaces along the river. And they would come and retire there after they had forsaken the cares of the world. The Indian holy points, the places of the larger pilgrimage, were all represented symbolically in Benares. It was said you could do the whole pilgrimage in miniature in Kashi. And Kashi, too, was recreated symbolically across the country. It wasn't a microcosm; it was a kind of cosmic capital.

'And on certain days the moon would appear in the afternoon

and the water from those symbolic Indian rivers would run through the groves and flood the Ganga, which, at one point, curls around the city. The ancient Hindus, with their special feeling for these cosmic changes, would gather at high points in the city to watch, like people seeing a fireworks display. Now consider this: it is mid-afternoon, the sun is out, but probably obscured by clouds, appearing now and then like a silver disc, the moon is low over the river and there is a kind of daytime darkness. The sound of water can be heard in the silence. It is the sound of streams gushing through the Forest of Bliss and emptying into the Ganga. And then suddenly, at the exact point where the river bends, the Ganga, flowing smoothly in one direction, stops and begins, as if part of the magic of that darkened afternoon, to flow in the opposite direction. That was how people, common people,' he added pointedly, 'were brought in touch with the wholeness of the place, in just the same way as someone crossing a street in Manhattan might feel when, looking to one side and seeing the sweep of the avenue, he says, "I'm in New York!" It's my dream to see that wholeness restored in India.'

There was an interruption from an unexpected quarter. 'This thing you describe,' Shabby's husband asked urgently, receiving a dirty look from his wife, 'can one still see it in Benares?'

'No. What is there to see now?' the writer replied sadly. 'No one has seen it since the thirteenth century, since . . . They destroyed it six times, you know, the invaders. Six times, over hundreds of years, they smashed its temples and carried away its stones until they had broken its orientation. The river no longer performed its tricks, the Forest of Bliss was bricked over, its pools and ponds drained, and the lingas, once placed ingeniously across the island city, uprooted. I think they even tried to call it Muhammadabad.'

The writer's descriptions had perturbed everyone at the table; Chamunda had tears in her eyes. 'No one knows any of this. No, Udaya?' She reached past the writer and held my mother's hand. 'That's our problem in India, no one knows any of these things.'

Shabby had also fallen silent and played thoughtfully with a large silver ring on her finger.

'Chalo,' my mother said suddenly, alarmed perhaps at the mood that had descended over her dinner party, 'let's sit soft.'

I had meant to keep many things to myself, but the vision of completeness that the writer's descriptions had inspired, as well as a thought about the city beyond, smouldering from some of the tensions that had arisen that evening, forced me to ask, 'How do Indians who aren't "temple-going" participate in this Indian idea?' I was thinking in part of myself, but also of non-Hindus, men like Zafar, whom I had arranged to see in the old city some time over the next few days. He had had his operation while I was away and was still convalescing.

The writer, perhaps thinking I was being political, coldly dismissed me. 'It's more difficult for them,' he said. 'If you mean Muslims, perhaps they should begin by thinking of themselves as converts to Islam and not invest themselves so emotionally with the invader. If you mean the green-card folk . . .'

It was too much for me. I burst out with the story of Aakash. I spoke in disjointed sentences of this Brahmin trainer I had become friends with, and how he was many men to many people, now a trainer, excited about brands and malls, now a Brahmin, performing the ancient rites of his caste. I spoke of his hunger, his ambition, of the disappearance of his ancestor down a river and how he had taken me to see the place where he had lived. I told them of my discovery in the National Museum, and how I had seen first hand, but cast in a magical way, the history of the nineteenth-century anti-Brahmin movement that the writer had spoken of. And in my excitement, I also let slip the story of Aakash's affair with an industrialist's 'healthy' daughter who that very afternoon had been whisked away so that she might make a better match. And of Kris, her creative-writer brother, who was determined to break her love for Aakash. I said that I understood her love for him very well, understood how she might want to take a chance on him, how she might have come to believe in his star. I said all this, without thinking of the consequences, without thinking of who might be listening, and there was some agitation in my voice. The writer listened enthralled; he seemed to see that I was trying to get something off my chest. And when I had finished, when I had told him how Delhi for Aakash was a city with temples to Saturn, how the weeks now for him were jam-packed with religious observances, fasts, shopping for new kitchen vessels, a great jagran that he and his friends had put together in their colony . . .

'A jagran?' the writer asked.

'It's a kind of wake,' I said. 'I've never been to one, but people sit up all night listening to religious stories, watching pageants, singing devotional songs, I don't know.'

When I had said all this, the writer stopped me, and with great sympathy in his voice, asked, 'Do you envy him? Do you envy this trainer?'

'Envy?' I laughed.

The whole room – my mother, my girlfriend, Chamunda and Shabby – was watching me.

'Do you envy how simple it will be for him?'

The writer had seen with an astrologer's vision to my depths; to lie now would have been an act of self-destruction too great. 'Yes,' I said bitterly. 'I envy that terribly. I envy the fact that when the world becomes his, which it will have to, or none of what we're saying has any meaning, he will be able to put his hand straight in the fire, with his language, his religion, his idea of who he is, intact and close around him. And people like me, who never played any part in rejecting these things, who inherited this rejection from the generations before us, will have no place in that world. What I feel when I see him is something like a nostalgia for a childhood I never lived. But it's not really childhood I'm craving; I didn't realize that until now. It's the cultural wholeness you spoke earlier of, the security of which I have, in my mind, substituted with the security of childhood.'

'I see, I see,' the writer said, now very gently. 'I see very well what you feel you lack when you see this trainer . . . Aakash, you said his name was?'

'Yes.'

'How difficult it must be for you,' the writer said, his tone so full of sympathy that I thought he mocked me.

The women had begun to smoke Dunhills. More whisky sodas arrived. Chamunda put her legs up on a footstool and hitched up her sari to her knees, revealing two gold anklets dropping from her dark legs. Her toes, also with fine gold rings on them, fanned forward and back like Sanyogita's, suggesting deep relaxation.

'Now stop being so serious, all of you,' Shabby said.'Let's have some goss.'

Soon the room was alive again with laughter and chatter, and together with the cheerful gaping face of the electric heater, an atmosphere of such congeniality settled over it that someone entering the room at that moment would never have guessed the seed of fresh discord that had been sown between Chamunda and Shabby, nor the effects that my disclosures would have on its fruit; nobody would have noticed Shabby, who knew Megha's brother and had once seen Aakash, putting two and two together; no one would have known, once they retired quietly, that the writer and his wife had been there at all; no one would have imagined how in Delhi, a city of fifteen million plus, small, mean motives, and unsettled scores, governed what seemed like large outcomes. No, perhaps all anyone entering the room at that stage of the evening, bringing with them the winter smokiness and the faint, sweet smell of the *Alstonia scholaris*, might have seen was how Sanyogita's large, smiling face had shrunk, and the painful, sidelong glances with which she now looked at me from time to time.

18

A few days later I found myself at dawn on the edge of the old city. Zafar and I had spoken the night before, and to avoid the congestion and crowds of the old city, he had suggested I come very early. He told me to call him for directions when I was near. Once we'd left the Delhi of roundabouts and white bungalows and were on Bahadur Shah Zafar Marg, which, named for the city's poet-king, connected the old and new cities of Delhi, I tried Zafar's number. It was dead. And just yesterday his name had flashed on my phone. The city I knew, the familiar city, receded, and in the one we entered the buses in their depot were still of the old type, grey and yellow, torn and rusted at the edges; the split ends of rail tracks were visible under a bridge; and the cold, white haze that hung over the street brought to it the aspect of a tunnel.

Off-duty traffic lights flashed aimlessly through the fog. Our car dived under a red and yellow railway bridge, circled an old city gate with a high-pointed stone arch and came on to a crumbling, colonnaded street. Shuttered shopfronts ate up the covered walkway that ran on either side of the street; the square panes on the second-storey windows were grey and broken; sunken columns showed iron and plaster insides; and an even layer of dust and litter lay strewn over the street. In a peepal's flat-leaved canopy, like some straggling bird from another season, was a single purple kite.

Normally, we would have had to park and either walk or take a cycle rickshaw. But in these few hours between night and morning, we could drive deep into the old city. The streets closed around us. Nests of black wire hung overhead, buildings leaned and tottered, and the sky became a jagged strip of grey. I was surprised Uttam was still willing to drive. On every surface, dark sleeping bodies wrapped in woollens sprawled with their arms outstretched. A newspaper seller set up shop over an open drain with grey rippling water running in it, a bent sweeper made figures of eight with a tiny, brambly broom and a teashop served its first customers. Now without the crowds and traffic, it was possible to see the full ugliness of the old city. All the old façades had been covered over with cement and bricks, the old doors had been replaced with dust-encrusted metal shutters, and a glimpse every now and then of a slim wooden balcony or a high-pointed arch only increased the sense of irrecoverable ruin.

'This is Ballimaran,' Uttam said.

It was a historic quarter; the poet Ghalib had lived a few streets away. It was also all I knew of Zafar's whereabouts. Uttam became anxious to leave as I tried the number again. The occasional sound of locks opening, shutters going up, water splashing meant the city was waking up; and he had minutes to get out. I let him go and we agreed to meet on the colonnaded street in case I was unable to find Zafar.

I was drawn towards the green doors of the teashop, the smell of its stove filling the street. Rickety wooden benches, smooth with wear, were ranged outside, and nearly half a dozen street cats crouched under them in anticipation of something. I sat down on the bench and considered my options. On the open green doors ahead of me, like an inscription in a book, red Urdu letters instructed: 'Say not to your prayers that you have work to do, say to your work that you have prayers to read.' As a final hope, I scanned my mobile's call register and found Zafar in calls received: Zafar Moradabadi, 19.45. I pressed the green button, the white screen glowed, but this time, instead of failing, the little dots ran across the screen and the number rang. A sleepy girl's voice answered.

'Is Zafar Moradabadi there?' I said excitedly.

'No, he's at the office. He sleeps there,' the voice replied.

'Office? What office?'

'The office of *Peshraft* magazine, on the little baradari, off Ballimaran.'

'But I'm there now!'

'Well, so is he. Wake him up. Tell him his daughter gave you permission.'

Clearly blessed with her father's wit and timing, the girl hung up the phone. I realized now that Zafar had given me two numbers, office and home, of which only the latter worked. I looked up from my bench at the pot-bellied man framed against the white tiles and tube light of the teashop. He was pouring hot, brown liquid between a ladle and a glass. I asked him if he knew where *Peshraft*'s offices were.

Without looking up, the teashop owner gestured to a dark, smooth-skinned adolescent who, despite the cold, was in a vest and a blue checked dhoti. 'Show this man *Peshraft*'s offices.' Then, as an afterthought, he asked, 'Who are you looking for?'

'Zafar Moradabadi.'

'The poet?'

'Yes,' I answered, thrilled at the recognition of his name.

The slim boy put on his blue and white rubber chappals, stepped gracefully into the street and led the way without a word. A few paces ahead, past a family of goats moving unsteadily in our direction, he vanished into a pitch-black, medieval passage. The air was stale and musty and a high-pointed arch showed further light ahead. On a wooden table next to us, two men were asleep, their limbs dropping into the darkness. At the end of the passage, the boy followed the curve of the road right. I became aware, now that a strip of sky was visible above, of rainclouds. We came to a raised, pan-stained doorway and a flight of steep whitewashed stairs.

'*Peshraft*,' the boy said, his dark, chiselled face and murky eyes holding me.

I gave him ten rupees and he vanished. Climbing the steep stairs of the airless passage, I had little conviction that it would lead to Zafar. There was no landing; the stairs stopped abruptly in front of an old wooden door closed with a hook. I beat against it, and it shook from the hinges. After a moment's silence, Zafar's papery voice asked who it was.

'It's me!' I said with delight at having found him in so old-fashioned a way.

The hook fell; the door swung open; Zafar's gaunt figure greeted me with a wry smile.

'You've come,' he said.

Then very quickly he was embarrassed. The room I entered had no bed. It was bare except for some light matting, a green metal filing cabinet and shelves in the wall crammed with old editions of the Urdu magazine. The smell of decaying paper filled the little room, with its hanging tube lights and dusty windowpanes; it was hard to believe that the day could ever break here. The telephone lay in one corner on the floor, its wire neatly wrapped many times around it.

Zafar had grown much frailer since the operation. His entire figure was slumped to one side as though it were paralysed. He was thin, unshaven, and the bullet-size sores on his head, still bloody at their hub despite the milder weather, seemed now to hint at a deeper malaise, like mould suggesting damp.

He was also afraid. 'You shouldn't have come,' he muttered as if to himself, and looked blankly at the room.

'What do you mean? We spoke last night. You told me to come.'

'I know, I know,' he said, lowering himself painfully on to a cushion in front of a very small, sloping desk on the floor, 'but I've had news since that there's going to be a demonstration here today. It might become difficult to get out.'

'Why didn't you call?'

'I only heard once I'd left my house. And the phone here,' he said, pointing to the green instrument wrapped up in its wire, 'has been disconnected.' How he had expected me to call him at all was a mystery; this side of him, his scattiness, was like an aspect of his distress. 'I know!' he said with fresh energy. 'I'll take you to where I live. We'll be safe there; it'll be calm there. We'll be able to have breakfast in peace. Why don't you sit down here for a few minutes? I don't have anything to offer you,' he said, looking desolately again round the room. 'Sit, sit, sit,' he added, hurriedly rising, then wincing with pain. 'I'll get dressed and then we'll go.'

His nervous energy, now subdued, now excited, unsettled me. Zafar gathered a bar of green soap and a towel from a shelf and went quickly down the stairs. I sat with a cushion behind my back and looked through the papers on his desk. They were colourful sketches of geometric shapes, a circle, a right-angle triangle, a rhombus. From where I sat, I could see the street below and a few minutes later I saw Zafar squatting next to a blue bucket in an open cemented area, pouring water over himself. He wore baggy white underwear of sorts, and in his present posture, his long, stringy body seemed like a child's. Then standing in a towel, he chewed on a neem twig as he shaved, facing a red plastic mirror. It was cracked in the corner and a bit of brown board showed through. When I looked again, an elegant figure in a black, knee-length coat and tight, white trousers swept across the street and climbed the stairs.

'You're looking very stylish,' I said when he appeared in the doorway.

He laughed throatily. 'I'm wearing it because you've come,' he added, running the back of his hand down the length of the black coat, 'otherwise, what need is there?'

'And what are these?'

'Now that I'm no longer a camel, I've become a children's entertainer. They're going to use my sketches of shapes in a children's geometry textbook.'

'Really?'

'Really,' he said, lighting a Win cigarette. 'One has to do many things. But come on, it's getting late.'

I was in the street, waiting for Zafar, when a bicycle cart covered in a blue tarpaulin came down the narrow street, leaving a trail of red liquid behind it. Its appearance made the cats spring out from their hiding places under the teashop's benches. Like little detectives, they inspected the red liquid and began delicately to lick it. The bicycle cart stopped and the driver threw off his tarpaulin to reveal a cart-load of bleeding buffalo parts. There were shanks, thighs with the hoofs and coat still on, and whole horned heads, with blank, skyward-turned eyes. Their black coat against the pink flesh, the rainy sky reflected in their glassy eyes, made a strong and gruesome impression. In the meantime, a butcher in a glass-fronted shop, which said 'Halal' in red letters, had begun, bare-chested, to chop up the fresh meat. A dozen riveted cats watched him and in seconds it became apparent why. He appeared in the shop's raised doorway, wearing only a checked loincloth, and threw handfuls of neatly chopped blackish-pink liver into the street. The cats, with their long, sharp teeth exposed, tore at the small, square pieces. What had earlier been feline poise quickly became a watchful vigilance for competing predators.

Zafar appeared at my side; and as if this dawn carnage was the very thing he had wished to protect me from, he put his arm in mine and we withdrew. We walked to the periphery of the old city, literally to beyond its walls, as though re-enacting some medieval flight from a besieged city.

Half the old city lay between the colonnaded street and the art-deco cinema near where Zafar lived. We started out in a cycle rickshaw, but no sooner had the driver wiped its red leather seat, wet from the light drizzle that fell softly around us, than cries from the demonstration began. They reached us like an echo from within the city. The rickshaw driver looked unsurely back at us. 'Come on, come on,' Zafar yelled, in a voice I would not have thought him capable of. The driver put all his weight on the raised pedal and the rickshaw began to move.

Although its rhythmic footfall, its gathering momentum, the faint music of its chanting and slogans condemning police encounters and the killing of innocent Muslims stayed with us the whole time, we never saw the demonstration. It felt as though we circled a stadium or a bullring from which every now and then a column of terrified spectators came rushing out, followed by policemen in olive-green uniforms, beating them with batons. After the bestial display of cats devouring the liver, squatting on the ground, eating of it, with a furtive air about them, almost mistakable for guilt, there was something hollow and airy in these casual acts of violence.

But the rickshaw driver was unnerved; he kept telling Zafar that we couldn't go any further. It seemed like a strange thing to say, as the streets and wide main roads surrounding the old city were relatively empty, and except for a police presence, there was little preventing us from going on. But the ease of our progress, free of the old city's daily commotion, with no other rickshaws around, was exactly what worried the driver. When we came at last to yellow metal barricades, an expression of relief passed over his small, dark face.

'Now it's clear,' he said, 'we can't go any further.' As long as we had been in the rickshaw, above the ground and in motion, we had felt secure. To now suddenly be deposited on the empty stretch of road, with the option neither to go forward nor to go back, was to feel that we had fallen into a trap. It was as if this sudden exposure, where a singing bullet might fly out of some unseen sandbag, was to be feared more than angry mobs and baton-wielding policemen.

One policeman, seeing a perhaps unlikely pair huddled near the barricade, approached with long strides. He was tall and attractive with pale, wheat-coloured skin, a thick dark moustache and a prominent mole on his cheek. He swung a stick in one hand as he walked, while the other, in his pocket, dug conspicuously at his balls. He had perfected an expression of bored cruelty; his eyes seemed to search only for prurient excitement. They glazed over when Zafar made his simple request to be allowed past the barricade so that he could go home.

'Who's this?' he said, pointing at me with his stick, but addressing Zafar.

'Why, my student!' Zafar replied.

'Go on,' the policeman yawned.

We slipped through a foot-wide space between two barricades. We had walked only a few paces when the policeman said, 'Ah, ah, through there.'

He rapped the wooden frame of a metal detector, which not only was not switched on but had its black wire coiled up in a heap next to it. We did as we were told. The young policeman smiled, then sniffed his fingers.

The enclosed area within the barricade was deserted. On our right was a covered arcade of sorts with shuttered shopfronts. The curving line of simple, cylindrical columns was covered in pink, white and blue bills. Their thin paper had turned soft in the rain and seemed about to slide off. Zafar, in his long black coat and white trousers, moved at a fast pace ahead of me, like a man running to catch a train. Everything was still and silent, muffled by the rain. Only the dull cries from within the city could still be heard. So deep and cinematic was this silence that neither Zafar nor I heard the sudden approach of a dark blue van with a red siren light and white letters painted on it. Even when we saw it, it seemed to be just another prop in the theatre of the morning. It screeched to a stop in front of Zafar and a small, stout police-man in olive green fell out, with a string of abuse ready on his lips. All of it was aimed at Zafar; he didn't address one word to me; it was as if I wasn't there. Zafar's response was to assume a stance of high refinement. Speaking to him in his educated Urdu, he tried gently to reason with him, as though hoping to prevent a standard of decency from breaking down. 'But listen, brother, we were permitted to cross the barrier by your colleague over there.' We all turned around at the same time, but the man who had let us through had vanished and the barricade was unmanned. This failure at so crucial a moment gave the fat policeman his chance. His shiny face gleamed with satisfaction. 'Now move, bastard,' he said, reaching for the back of Zafar's neck.

'He's had an operation!' I screamed.

Zafar winced, then smiled.

The policeman now turned to me and said courteously, 'I'm sorry, sir, but you can come and pick him up in a few hours at the station.'

'But why are you arresting him?'

'He's crossed the police line, sir. It's a routine arrest.'

'But why . . .'

The policeman anticipated my question. 'Sir, I'm very busy. Here is my card.' He produced a visiting card with a gold police emblem on it. 'T. N. Vohra. It has mobile too. Now, please go home. It's not safe at this time.'

With this, he pushed his hand into Zafar's, locking fingers with him, and led him into the blue van with its caged windows. Zafar stepped elegantly on to the footboard and sat down on a bench next to a young demonstrator with a sweaty, bloodied face. Just before the door closed, he said apologetically, 'I shouldn't have worn this.' He ran his hand down the length of his black coat again. 'It made me a target. This mistake won't happen again. Please excuse the trouble I've caused.'

The van sped away, leaving me to walk back to the barricade. When I approached, the young policeman had reappeared to let me through.

Zafar was released at seven that evening. The fat policeman was right: it had been a routine arrest. The place to which they had taken him was a squat building with screened balconies, each level painted in two shades of orange. There were neem and peepal trees outside, motorbikes parked in the shade and a roaring street beyond. From a makeshift porch of white metal and green fibreglass, there hung a large blue and red sign which read: 'Police Station, Lahori Gate'.

I'd never been in a police station before. I was surprised by the congenial, government office atmosphere, the fluorescent lighting, the potted plants, the simple sign that read: 'Lock-up'. Releasing Zafar was no great task either. After my initial panic, and yes, a few wiped-away tears, Uttam came to pick me up. We drove to the station, and on the way I called my mother and Sanyogita, who both called Chamunda. At some point around mid-morning, after tea and breakfast in the car, a fixer of sorts showed up. He was not from Chamunda's office – she couldn't interfere with these things – but worked for a businessman. He was a man who 'knew how to talk to the police'. He carried three mobile phones, had a Bluetooth piece in his ear and a weak handshake. Within minutes, he was joking with T. N. Vohra, and setting in motion the process by which Zafar would be released.

The day went by languidly and was spent mostly in the car, with occasional forays into the station. A mild winter sun burned away the rain. There was a fresh warm afternoon, then a fat orange sunset, and later the street hung in wisps of fog and bright kerosene lamps. In fact, Zafar's arrest might have had something of the mood of a picnic or a long drive had it not been for one thing: Zafar, in the lock-up with some twenty other men, refused to sit down.

At first this gentle protest went unnoticed. Vohra's sub-inspector tore around the room, prodding men with his stick, roughing up the ones he thought more guilty, but he didn't touch Zafar. It was only after his second incursion into the room, some time around noon, when our arrivals at Vohra's desk coincided, that the sub-inspector remarked that the old poet fellow had been standing in the same spot for nearly five hours. Vohra laughed at the genteel manners of people like this. I was concerned because of Zafar's operation. Vohra nodded, promising to send in a chair for him. But at two p.m., Zafar had still refused to sit down. I was sent in to talk to him. I saw him leaning lightly against the wall, an empty chair next to him and dozens on the floor around, like nursery school children. He glided up to the lock-up's bars when he saw me, reassuring me that he was fine. When I implored him to sit down, told him it would be a long wait, he smiled mysteriously and said he was fine standing.

By mid-afternoon, Zafar's protest had become something of a

religious event in the station, and everyone was perturbed. Vohra said he could not release him until the demonstration in the old city was over, but begged me, seeing now that I was someone of clout, to make my old teacher see reason. I, more than anyone, wanted Zafar to sit down. The whole episode would be no more than a harmless brush with Indian officialdom, if only Zafar would sit down. But when, at five p.m., the sub-inspector tried to push him down by the shoulders, Zafar pressed his back against the wall and locked his knees.

It was the sub-inspector who told me this as I waited outside for the last of the paperwork to be finished, and for smudged purple stamps and little signatures to complete the formalities. 'Bloody Gandhian,' he said, visibly upset. He had chosen his words well, because in this country, with its special feeling for victories of the mind over the body, Zafar's protest, the refusal of an old frail man, wrongly arrested, to sit with the others on the prison floor, or even on a chair, acquired all the force of a spoken curse.

And when at last Zafar walked out, moving his legs with difficulty after standing for nearly twelve hours, the applause he was met with in the station sounded like a plea for forgiveness, like young, superstitious men with families asking to be spared the anger of a miracle man.

Zafar's protest had not spared me either. Of course India worked on influence, everyone knew that. But I had used that influence – which to some extent was so innate that it had prevented me from being arrested – for a good cause. It could have allowed me to go home with an easy conscience that evening. But because Zafar's protest was to some extent aimed against the casual violence of the system that sought to diminish him, I, acting even more casually than the police officers, felt the more implicated. In the end, its sting had nothing to do with 'communal' issues or even class ones; it was just a poet speaking to an aspirant, asking him to think hard, to really consider, as someone concerned with beauty and not with politics, whether what was at stake was worth defending or not.

He was a stubborn man, of this there is no doubt. But there was nothing he had been more stubborn about than his determination to be a poet against terrible odds. In the car home, as if remembering who he was, he told me the story of how he got his pen name. 'I was called Muhammad Shafiq,' he said, 'but when I was about seven or eight, I became enchanted with the word aashiyan; I didn't know what it meant, but I liked the ring of it. So I kept it as my pen name, Muhammad Shafiq Aashiyan. And I began to use it in my schoolwork. A few weeks later, the teacher was calling out our names and she said, "Come here, Muhammad Shafiq Nest." My face became red with shame. Aashiyan means "nest", like bird's nest!' Zafar's rasping laugh broke from his blackened lips. 'It was then that she said to me, "If you want to be a poet call yourself Jigar or Kamar or Zafar." And since there was already a Jigar and Kamar Moradabadi, I called myself Zafar.'

Uttam stopped the car in front of the art-deco cinema. The area had now returned to life and was teeming with rickshaws, pedestrians and naked bulbs in shop windows. There was nothing to suggest the morning's disturbance except a column of yellow metal barricades, gathered neatly at the side of the road.

Zafar stepped out of the car, with some relief I thought, perhaps at being his own man for the first time all day. After a hurried goodbye, he vanished around a gloomy corner, illuminated by a single street light, heading home to the house and family which had once again eluded me.

19

Sanyogita had begun to see a therapist. She said that there were many things she needed to sort through, related to her mother and aunt. Things that might explain her inactivity in adult life. They were both, in different ways, strong women; she felt they might have stifled her. The therapist was fast to confirm these doubts. He had Sanyogita write a letter to both women, a letter Chamunda later described to me as 'four pages of pure vitriol', with accusations that she abused her. 'She accuses me of calling her a "stupid child" when she was little,' Chamunda ranted down the phone. 'One says that! It's like saying, "Stupid boy". It doesn't mean "you are a stupid boy".' I could imagine her wagging a jewelled finger as she spoke. 'Aatish, please speak to her. She's left a lot of hurt in this house. I'm told by a friend who's had years in psychoanalysis that they blame the family as the source of all troubles. But, Aatish, I know if she would only get married and pop out a child or two, all of this would go away. And guess who introduced her to this psychoanalyst?'

'Who?'

'That fat cow Shabby.'

Chamunda, as Sanyogita's guardian in Delhi, was forever asking me to make her understand some particular point of view or to get her to agree to come to some event she was hosting. Most of the time I was happy to make her case, but lately my own position with Sanyogita was not what it had once been. While I had been distracted with Aakash and then Zafar, I had moved slowly from being one of the people Sanyogita considered on her side, to one of the people she viewed with suspicion.

It had begun the night Aakash pushed her over; the summer of boredom and flight had not helped; the two dinners, at the

Oberoi and at my mother's, had made things still worse; and my general state of preoccupation prevented me from seeing many opportunities for repair. She was someone in whom these emotions percolated slowly, but once a definite shift had occurred, a reversal would have required the full use of my emotional energies.

And these were divided. In the period when Megha had been abducted to the lipo clinic, and Aakash was organizing the jagran in his colony, he made great emotional demands on me. I saw him nearly every day, Junglee aside, spoke to him two or three times and received countless text messages. He had become a master of the text message. In his bad, broken English, he always succeeded in expressing some forceful emotion or plan that would change the course of my day. There was also a powerful sexual tone to these messages. I might be sitting with Sanyogita, the heater yawning in front of us, and my phone would beep. Sanyogita, now wise to the fact that 90 per cent of these messages were from Aakash, would get up or look away. The moment would be spoiled for her. Still worse was the suppressed expression of amusement on my face.

Going against all her high notions of privacy, she would ask, though feigning boredom, 'What does he say now?'

'Nothing, nothing,' I would reply, still smiling.

She would press me; I would try and laugh it off; she would become agitated and we would have a fight. 'If it's nothing, why can't you tell me what it is?' she'd ask.

'Because it's just the principle of it,' I would reply half-heartedly. 'I don't ask you what Ra says in his text messages.'

'Yes, but the point is that we don't have these fights about Ra, do we?'

'We might if I was to start hounding you in this way.'

An acid silence would fall over the room. I would think back to the message, seeking solace in the playful mood in which it was sent. The message might say: 'Arse bandit.' How Aakash had learned that expression, or come to find it amusing enough to put it in a message, without any provocation, and send it to me, I don't know. But it was part of a string of messages of this kind. The first, literally the first, after I told him I had a new Nokia, was, 'It's lost its virginity to me, that phone will never be the same.' A few days later he wanted me to have lunch with him. When I said that I would have loved to but couldn't, as I was meant to be having lunch with Sanyogita, he wrote at 21.39: 'That is going to be your problem, for you have to be with Sanyogita. All I can suggest is that we make a concoction like you wouldn't believe for her which knocks her out for a couple of days.' The next day he told me he'd spoken to Megha and that, though they could only speak for a few minutes, she was fine and would be back soon; the lipo had made a great difference. He also said that when she was back, he was going to make her have lunch with Sanyogita on the days when he wanted to have lunch or a drink with me alone. I replied, referring to Megha's condition, 'Good to hear it,' to which he, at 14.49, while I was still at lunch with Sanyogita, replied, 'I thought you might like that. I told her that she'd better start making friends with Sanyogita if she wanted our relationship to progress.' Then at 14.53, four minutes later, 'What if they end up fucking each other?'

And it was in this way that Aakash began to excite a fresh tension in our friendship. I knew from the start that it was only his vanity declaring itself in new and corrosive ways. He liked now to speak of bisexuals and metrosexuals, sometimes confusing the two, but like his 'messy look', it was really just a part he was trying out. It gave him an illusion of privilege and indulgence. And he always needed his audience. We would come back after an afternoon of drinking – we drank a lot in those days – and he would stand behind me, as Sanyogita lay on a sofa reading, and begin massaging my shoulders. In the mirror in front of me, I could see a large potted fern, the white sofa on which Sanyogita lay and Aakash in a small, tight T-shirt, the afternoon light striking the vein-like muscles in his arms, making golden their pale inner portion. If Sanyogita ignored the tension of the three-way scene, he would say, 'Bhabi, do you massage him? Do you treat him well? You know, he needs it.' Sanyogita then either played along or laughed it off, but I could see that her eyes shone painfully. I would shrug off Aakash's attentions, and he would drift around the room, lightly fingering the bookshelves or picking up and closely inspecting an objet. Till just the other day, any mention of homosexuality had appalled him. He had once said to me, like with the Muslims, that they must be killed off. But now again, like a preparation for a future life, he tried out a new self.

It was in this period, walking one day in Lodhi Gardens, that I ran into Megha's brother, Kris, the creative writer. The park was full of early-evening mists and bougainvillea. The number of walkers had multiplied with the cool weather, and the hurried fall of evening seemed to correspond with their eagerness to go home and dress for the endless engagements, weddings and card parties whose fairy lights filled the trees.

I had come around a shaded corner of the park when I saw him, pulled along by a basset sniffing the cold, moist earth. His thin figure, and the round hardness of his collarbones and wrists, were visible through the T-shirt and light, V-neck sweater he wore. Because I knew him through his short story, and saw him now almost magically in the story's setting, I had no trouble recognizing him. It was as if he had always been there. But then what I knew of him beyond the fiction, here from Megha and Aakash, there from Ra, returned to me. I remembered that he was Megha's brother, that he didn't live in this part of town, and thought it strange that he would have brought his basset from Sectorpur, nearly an hour away, to walk him here.

These thoughts rose so fast in my mind that their very momentum made me blurt out his name as he passed. He looked up; his eyes, set deep in their dark sockets, were wide and expressionless. A faint smile rose to his lips.

'Aatish?'

'Yes.'

He held out a large dark hand.

'How are you?' I said, taking it in mine; it was slightly damp. 'I haven't seen you around for a while. Do you still go to Junglee?'

He replied, 'Me? Yes, I'm fine. Junglee, you said?' Then laughing awkwardly, he added, 'Yeah, I still go to Junglee, but at a different time, and so that's why you haven't probably seen me around. And you? All well there?'

His speech, though still American, had more Indian rhythms than I remembered.

'Yes. Fine, fine.'

'Good, good.' He smiled.

An uncomfortable silence settled round us.

'Well then, chalo, I'll see you around.'

'Yes, Kris, definitely.'

We were about to part. His basset, after panting patiently at our feet, had stood back up on his heavy paws when I said, 'Kris, actually, do you have a moment?'

'Yes, yes, why not?' he said, with some satisfaction. 'Why don't you walk with me? Beyoncé here won't let us stand in one place and talk.'

'Beyoncé?'

He laughed. 'My sister named her.'

Beyoncé had now picked up a scent, and nose down, waddled forward, her ears dancing about her.

'Kris, actually . . . it's your sister,' I began, 'that I'd like to talk to you about. You know I'm a friend of Aakash's.'

'I know,' he replied.

Then I wasn't sure what to say.

'I hear your family's very upset about their relationship.'

'Well, thank God my parents don't know anything about it. But yes, us brothers and sisters are naturally very upset. She's compromising all our futures over this low-grade person who's only after our money.'

I began to see now for the first time how Megha and Kris were brother and sister. His entire language, even his facial expressions, changed as he spoke about Aakash. The creative-writing language of the short story fell away. He made grammatical errors in his speech, almost as if a different language was needed for the different values expressed.

'Do you think that's what he's after?'

'What else? Aatish, have you seen my sister?'

'Yes.'

'Do you honestly believe a guy like Aakash would go for her for any other reason except that she's loaded? Let's see, she's a dwarf –' he tapped his fleshy, nail-bitten digits – 'she's healthy as hell, she has a face like a chapati, she's of a lower caste than him . . . I can't think of anything else, except that she's also very annoying, but probably he isn't too concerned about that.'

'What about that she loves him? Maybe that's what he sees?'

'Everyone loves Aakash! Find me a person that doesn't love Aakash. The trainers at Junglee love Aakash, the clients love Aakash, my friend Sparky Punj loves Aakash, you love Aakash, even my fucking chowkidar loves Aakash. So many people love Aakash that I don't think he even notices until he comes across someone who doesn't love him.'

His mention of his chowkidar brought to my mind the description of the man from the story. How real he had seemed, with his smooth skin, stained teeth and murky, amber eyes; it was as if I had seen him myself.

'Yes,' I said, forcing my mind back to what was being said, 'but people like that, people who please, can be very insecure.'

'Aakash is not insecure; he's ambitious. There's a difference. He doesn't doubt himself for a minute; he just sometimes doubts whether the world will deliver.'

I laughed; Kris's face was still. 'But don't you like that? Don't you think his ambition is an impressive thing?'

'Not when it's aimed at my family's wealth,' he replied.

'And what about your sister? What about her happiness?'

'Aakash will not make her happy, believe me. She's happy now because she's getting some Brahmin cock. And we all have this thing, us baniyas, this love of Brahmins. We're like the untouchables of the upper castes, you see, so nothing excites us more than Brahmin love. But believe me, when Aakash has her in the bag, she won't be getting Brahmin cock no more.'

I had forgotten Kris was a 'Western-educated homosexual'; I had forgotten how freely he had learned to speak of these things. And his language, now discussing the subtleties of caste, now of cock, was unpredictable in tone and in content. Its fluctuations, going so easily from mellow to harsh, gave me an intimation of his disturbance.

'Where's your sister now?' I asked, concealing in the airiness of my tone knowledge of her disappearance.

Kris seemed to search my face for any sign of previous knowledge.

Seeming either to make a decision to trust me or just acting out of indifference, he said, 'She's getting that gross body of hers . . .' He put his large hands, with their fleshy fingertips, to his mouth, making the shape of a nozzle, and emitted a long and graphic sucking noise, like a child blowing into his hands to make a fart sound. Then he laughed garishly and was once again of a piece with his sister.

'And then?'

'Marriage, I suppose. She's holding up the queue, you know. I have two younger sisters, less fat, who are both eager to get married.'

He seemed so pleased with himself that I experienced a feeling of triumph on Aakash's behalf. I wanted almost to say, 'Well, you're too late. He's already married her and there's nothing you can do about it.' My face perhaps gave away some of my distaste, because he became conciliatory. 'You know,' he said, 'don't think I don't share your values. I've been to college in America too. I'm all for the little guy rising. But you know, don't mind my saying this, I understand this country a little better than you and Ra and people.'

'Who is me and Ra and people?'

'You know, English-speaking people.'

'You're English-speaking.'

'Yes, but only first generation. We're still very much part of the Hindu way of life; we're still very traditional. To you, Aakash is someone exotic and fascinating; to me, he's very close. He knows that he can fool you, but he can't fool me. He knows that when he does his poor boy from Sectorpur number around you, he's got you where he wants you. The filmy dialogue, the temple visits, the red teeka on the head, all that works on you, but not on me. I have neither any caste fascination nor any love of Bollywood heroes. And in India, aside from film and religion, what else is there? Aakash knows this and that's why he hates me. He knows that I know what neither you nor my sister knows.'

His information impressed me. How did he know of the temple visits? Clearly not from Megha. Then another possible route took shape in my mind and gave me a fresh sense of Sanyogita's unhappiness: she must have spoken to Ra, Ra to Kris. Seeming to enjoy the effect of his knowledge on me, he added, 'And are you going to this jagran?'

I nodded, wishing to give him no extra pleasure.

'When is it?' he blandly asked.

'In a couple of days.'

'When exactly?'

'Saturday.'

'Hmmm, around the time my sister gets back. She better not try to go.'

'Why?' I asked.

'Because we'll kill her,' Kris blandly replied.

We had come to the park's tall iron gates, which were never open.

'Well, I better be going,' Kris said, stepping through the green turnstile. A Jorbagh taxi was waiting for him and the uniformed chauffeur had opened the back door for Beyoncé, who showed not the slightest willingness to jump in on her own.

'Kris,' I asked, as the chauffeur helped Beyoncé into the car, 'how's the writing going?'

'Pretty good, buddy. Thanks for asking. Should have a story out soon in a US mag.'

'The one you read?'

'No, no, are you crazy? My poor mother's blood pressure would blow her head off. No, a much gentler story. And you? I hear you're writing too.'

'No. Yes. I mean nothing; it's all gone cold on me. A complete blockage. I'm beginning to feel I have no material.'

'Sorry to hear it, man. But keep at it. There's always a break-through round the corner.'

With this, he got into the car, Beyoncé panting on the seat next to him, and drove away.

20

On the morning of the jagran, Aakash had a different hairstyle. It was no longer 'messy', but parted in the middle and combed back in the style of an eighties hero. He had a little orange mark at the centre of his forehead from the inaugural puja that morning. We finished early at Junglee and he asked if I would drop him off at the nearest metro station. He had to go back to Sectorpur and help with the preparations. Sixty kilos of wheat had to be turned into puris before eight p.m.

Factoring in a standard one-hour unit of delay, and that we would be awake all night, I left the house at eight fifteen. But by eight forty-five, just as Sectorpur's flyovers and cramped sprawl came into view, Aakash began calling to see where I was.

'Five minutes away.'

'Good. Come fast.'

We drove past the 16 Base Repair Depot and took a left after the fruit seller's. It was a clear mild night, hardly cold for November. Uttam entered the Air Force Colony, and even before we'd come as far as Aakash's street, we could see the preparations. On one side there was a blue water truck and a park bounded by banana, neem, ashok, *Alstonia scholaris* and gulmohar trees. At the centre of it, a large white tent, with scalloped satin skirting, flapped lightly in the wind. On the right was the community centre, a single-storey, pale yellow building. In an open cemented area in front of it, a few hundred people, many of whom were children, sat on the floor on long strips of green carpeting. They ate from leaf thalis coated in a silver laminate, which glistened in the bright light falling on the diners from halogen lamps overhead. Young men and boys walked with bent backs down the line, serving great spoonfuls of chickpeas, vegetable curry and spongy puris from buckets.

Aakash stood among the diners, in his black capris and beige and white knit T-shirt. He came to meet me outside when he saw the car drive in with a look of tired exhilaration. There was a little piece of puri stuck to his cheek. 'Hi, man. What's you doing, man?' There were others from the gym around him: Mojij in a pink shirt, almost with cuffs, and Montu in a tight T-shirt that made him look even fatter than he was.

After his initial pleasure at seeing me, Aakash's manner changed to that of a child interrupted in the middle of a game. Having observed the formality of asking if I'd like some tea, he passed me on to his little brother.

When I failed to recognize him, he said irritably, 'It's Anil. You met him in Haryana, remember? When we went to the temples?'

I did remember; it was just that then, as now, my perceptions were overwhelmed.

As Aakash walked away, he yelled, 'Give him a stiff cup of tea.' Anil nodded and we began to walk towards the flat. But we had barely taken a few steps when the power failed. A red city sky suddenly fell over the jagran. A few stray invertor-run lights glowed, the odd naked bulb, but the colony was in darkness.

The air became filled with voices, men in Aakash's family and colony calling the electricity people, appealing to them to turn the electricity back on as there was going to be a jagran that night. The friendly responses they seemed to be receiving, the exchange of first names, some stray laughter, gave me an intimation of how the religious occasion would have served as common ground, how it might have made human the usually clinical communication between citizens and government servants. The man on the other end might also have lived in a colony with a jagran and was perhaps happy to see what he could do.

We walked towards Aakash's apartment block, which even in the mixture of moon and tube light seemed to have received a fresh coat of peach and beige paint.

'It has!' Anil said. 'They did it in the summer.' He worked at a travel agency and was telling me that, despite the recent terrorist attacks, tourists, especially Spanish tourists, were still coming in large numbers. He had just been in Pushkar, leading a group, and was thrilled at how many temples there were in a small area. 'We handle inbound and outbound tourism, but inbound is naturally more interesting.'

'Why?' I asked as we made our way into the candle-lit flat.

'Just because it's more interesting,' he replied, 'to show people what there is in your country than to promote another. I doubt there's another country in the world with as much to see as India.'

Everybody loved India; everybody worked hard. Mojij, who'd followed us in said he was at Junglee every day until two, then at college till six, doing a BA in media studies. Anil, whose English was good, much better than Aakash's, said he'd been learning French as well, but had never found the time to immerse himself in the language. We sat in the pink front room, in the light of a few slim red and yellow candles. Their glow expanded and shrank, sometimes throwing light as far as the lime-green pagodas, the red rose and the sequined Radha and Krishna, sometimes leaving them in darkness. I noticed that the cushion covers of the brown wooden sofas had embroidered scenes of chalets with fences and gardens. A few moments later, Ma Sharma, in a purple salwar kurta, came in with sweet, strong cups of tea. The little sweeper ran around half naked in a red and white Hawaii T-shirt. The power cut had scattered the mosquitoes into the general darkness, but occasionally one of the women in the house could be heard slapping a fleshy arm or thigh, and loudly exclaiming, 'Machchar!' I was beginning to wonder what I had come for when the sound of an exhaust fan and the dim sputtering of lights announced the end of the power cut. A slight feeling of embarrassment ran through the room at the sudden exposure.

Just then, Amit, Aakash's elder brother, appeared in the metal doorway and ushered us downstairs, insisting we eat. Before being led into the cemented area, I stopped at the durbar.

I knew that the word literally meant court, but also had the connotation of a viewing or an audience, of being in the presence of the deity. Amit explained that the boys in the colony had begun the jagran five years before. This came as a surprise; I thought it would have been going on for many years. To think of so large a religious occasion as recent – and put on by young people – was to be aware instantly of new prosperity – and the gods to which people felt it was owed. Amit said that the boys of the colony had just been sitting around one day when they thought, the other colonies have jagrans, why don't we? They put together a committee, gathered funds and that year put on the first jagran. It was an instant success and the numbers grew each year, with people's relations coming from out of town for the event. They were very proud this year of the size of the durbar. And they had reason to be; it was vast. Giant papier-mâché mountains, like the mountains of Ladakh, rust, yellow, purple, blue, towered over the tented enclosure, recreating Kailash, Shiva and Parvati's alpine dwelling. On every summit of every peak there were gods, Shiva, Krishna, orange-tongued and orange-palmed Kali, and at the highest summit, Santoshi Ma, the mother of contentment. Below her, 108 brass lamps were arranged like a champagne pyramid, representing the goddess's 108 forms. The tent was still empty and a group of colony children were playing on its thick floral carpets. In one corner, a small band warmed up on a podium with Roland equipment, keyboards, brown wooden drums and powerful black speakers. Halogen lamps and free-standing heaters, filled with blackish-orange coals, heated the empty tent.

We ate dinner in the community centre. There was little conversation, but Anil pointed out that the pumpkin sabzi would aid digestion. I threw my tray away and saw irritatingly that I had made a little yellow stain on my kurta. I had hardly spoken to Aakash so far and thought I might lure him away for an after-dinner cigarette. But he was not in the mood. He passed me on to Amit, who was only too happy to take me to the neighbour-hood convenience store, provided he could borrow Uttam to pick up some friends of his. When I said he couldn't, he became sullen.

The convenience store was the front room of a ground-floor flat in another block. It had a single grille window overlooking the park and contained sacks of grain, bottles of tomato ketchup and some tinned food. We entered it furtively, almost with the air of people entering a back room for a line of cocaine. The barrel-stomached owner sat in his vest in the window, and like a card dealer, fanned out two Gold Flakes as we came in. We took one each and sat down on a charpoy. The owner threw us a box of matches without interrupting his vigil at the window. The harsh tobacco had begun to compress the food in my stom-ach when the second power cut happened. Again, voices filled the darkness; the boulder-shaped owner lit a match. People scur-ried in and out of the convenience store, now asking him for candles, now for five more kilos of flour. This last request was handled by Amit, who dashed out of the room, leaving me alone in the convenience store, with the orange end of a Gold Flake burning steadily to the butt. I was beginning to feel completely bereft of company and purpose when Aakash's face became vis-ible through the candle-lit bars of the grille window.

'My friend in here?' he said quickly.

The shop owner didn't reply.

'Yes,' I said frantically, like a castaway calling out to a ship.

'Come on. We have to go,' he hissed into the darkness.

'What's the matter?'

'I'll tell you on the way. Hurry up.'

Outside, people shuffled urgently about as Aakash searched for his bike among dozens of others.

'Let's take Uttam.'

'We can't,' he said distractedly.

'Why?'

'He's not here.'

'What do you mean? Where did he go?'

'My brother sent him to pick up some people from the airport. He said he asked you.'

'Yes, and I said no.'

'Fucker,' Aakash said. 'He's always doing this. Anyway, don't worry. He'll be back soon.'

Aakash, having found his bike, was wheeling it out into the street.

'Come on. Get on,' he said.

'Where are we going?'

Aakash stopped wheeling back his bike, swung one leg over the seat, and trying to locate me in the darkness, said quietly, 'To pick up Megha.'

'She's back!'

'Yes, man. She's run away.'

'Fuck. When did you find out?'

'Just a few hours ago. Can't you see I've been taking so much tension? I couldn't even greet you properly.'

'What'll happen now?'

'I don't know, man. We'll find out.'

We couldn't continue the conversation because, at that precise moment, a large, moustached man, seeing Aakash on his bike, approached, asking if he could have a ride.

'Sure,' Aakash said, 'let my friend get on, then you get on.'

'How can three go?' the man asked, eyeing me morosely.

'They can.'

I got on and, a moment later, felt the fat man's stomach pin me in place. The bike sank, then rose and rolled out of the colony gates. Aakash steered it unsteadily, speaking to Megha on his mobile as he drove.

We headed down the dark, keekar-lined road that ran from Aakash's colony to the main intersection. At the fruit stall the fat man got off. A little further on there was a line of yellow lights gathered under a flyover, and a restaurant with a sign saying 'Sher-e-Punjab' in red letters on a white background. Aakash ordered a few bottles of Thums-up, which arrived with straws on metal trays, and we sat down to wait. I made a few attempts at conversation, but Aakash seemed too tense to talk. The only question that aroused his interest, and that had been circulating in my mind from the moment I heard of Megha's return, was how changed she would be after the lipo.

'I don't know,' Aakash said, with some wonder in his voice. 'We have to be prepared for any eventuality. She told me on the phone that they gave her lipo in eight places and removed nearly five litres of fat. Five litres!' he repeated, flaring his eyes. 'Apparently, she still has her bruises and her skin has become very dry.'

With this, we sank again into a solemn silence, like two children newly aware of the hard realities of adult life. But neither the silence nor this mood lasted long, as a few minutes later Megha's grey Hyundai pulled up in front of Sher-e-Punjab.

'Oh my God-d,' Aakash said, and chuckled with delight at seeing Megha step out of the little car in a pink silken kurta and beige capris. 'Loddof difference.'

Megha stood timidly in one spot, smiling up at us, her nose ring catching the light from the restaurant. Aakash trotted down the two steps that stood between them and took her in his arms.

'Come here, and look at my brand-new wife, thin and all,' Aakash yelled back to me. As I made my way down to them, Aakash was saying, 'Appu, these lipo people are for real! They've pulled off a miracle, no? Sir, whaddyou say?'

I was dumbstruck.

'Yes, yes,' I managed. But it was a transparent lie. And Aakash and Megha must have seen it was, because she said angrily, 'Five litres, they took out, you know!'

Looking at her, you wouldn't have known it. There wasn't an ounce of visible difference. The greasy rolls below her neck were intact; her breasts were still vast; and above the hem of her pink kurta, her stomach still sprawled. I was also puzzled by how, if she had run away from home, she was able to pick up her car. These questions, swarming in my mind, were put temporarily to rest by the appearance of the fat man Aakash had given a ride to. He wanted a ride back. Aakash handed him the bike keys and told him to drive it back to the colony. We would go with Megha.

In the little Hyundai, with plastic still covering the seats, Megha, perhaps thinking of the experience of the past few days, looked back at me and sighed. 'Look what trouble your friend causes me. I think he's going to cause me a lifetime of troubles only.'

'This is just the beginning, my darling,' Aakash replied stylishly, and leaned in to kiss her.

In the car, it emerged that although Megha had run away from the lipo clinic, she had not actually run away from home. She had taken advantage of a journey from the lipo clinic to the house of a suitor to give her uncle in Bombay the slip and escape to Delhi.

'I went straight to the airport,' she said. 'Thanks God, my father hadn't cancelled my credit card. So I bought a ticket and came back.'

She had even gone home, met her family and picked up her car. Her father was angry at first, but then pleased to see his little girl. He had said to her, 'The problem is you're too healthy. We've tried our best, but I suggest now that even when you go to the market, you try and look nice. You never know where an offer might come from.' She also added that among the Aggarwals, there had recently been five or six love marriages. 'Then there is the age factor and that I have had lipo. The doctor told my parents that I should wait six months before getting married. I'm twenty-six, running twenty-seven. So if I wait three months, twenty-seven will be complete. All this makes me feel that my parents will now be willing to hear my choice.'

Hearing this, Aakash leaned over and kissed her, softly whispering, 'Appu.' Then abruptly: 'What did you tell them before coming here?'

'Nothing,' Megha replied jauntily. 'Just that I was sleeping the night at my friend's house.'

As we drove into the colony, past the community centre, Megha asked me how the food had been.

'Very good,' I replied.

'You would say that. But it must not have been "very good" because not many are eating.'

'What are you talking,' Aakash exploded, 'we've fed some six hundred.'

'Oh, so you're counting,' Megha said, and laughed.

We returned to find that the power was back and the jagran was beginning. Bejewelled women, clutching their saris, rushed towards the tent. Aakash ran upstairs to try on the kurta Megha had designed and stitched for him in the lipo clinic. As the two of us waited downstairs, Megha explained her family's position. 'Now, if my father is going to spend two crore on the wedding, then at least the husband should be making fifty lakhs monthly. No?' Aakash, I knew – though still a huge amount for a trainer – made only sixty thousand a month: a tenth of that amount.

'I know!' Megha cried. 'Now what to do? Every day my mother comes to me and says, "Such and such person has had a son. And her husband went out and came back with a tempo full of stuffs. Refrigerator, microwave, laptop, jewellery, saris – you name it, he bought it." Imagine how I feel, thinking when I have a son, who will go out and buy a tempo full of stuffs?' She spoke with such feeling, her eyes beginning to glisten, that it was hard to believe she was talking about electronics and home appliances.

During this sharing of intimacies, I came out with something that had first occurred to me in the car. I had wanted to tell Megha and Aakash then, but had been prevented by some inexplicable feeling of loyalty. But now, fully won over by the cause of their marriage, I told Megha about my accidental meeting with her brother in Lodhi Gardens.

'That bloody homo,' she whispered viciously, 'let him try. Kill me? I'll make keema out of him and each of his little yellow-fingered friends.'

And though it had seemed a real threat at the time, returning now as an echo from Megha's lips, it seemed absurd. Of the two, she was without a doubt the more unsinkable. She muttered angrily to herself for a few moments, and then, as if it were too much for her to contain, started yelling, 'Aakash! Aakash! Listen to what Aatish is telling me my fajjot brother has been saying.'

'Megha, no, listen,' I said quickly, 'don't tell Aakash.'

'Why?'

'He'll just get worked up over it. And there's no knowing what he might do.'

I wasn't sure myself why I didn't want him to know. I think, bizarre as it might sound, that I had a superstitious fear of his dormant Brahmin's powers.

And perhaps some of my nervousness was felt by Megha too, because when Aakash appeared, bare-chested on his balcony, having heard her voice but not what was actually said, she didn't repeat herself.

'Bas, nothing,' she said, 'we're coming up.' She gestured to me to follow her and marched up the stairs. At the first landing, in part perhaps from fatigue, she swung around and said, 'And by the way, one other thing. My father, he doesn't know that that brother of mine is a chakka.' She used the Hindi word for hitting a six in cricket, which also meant eunuch, and flicked her wrist effeminately. 'But he's got a pretty good idea. If he finds out, he'll not just cut him out of the will, he will also kill that half-starved gandu.' With this, she swung back around and climbed the remaining steps.

In the now empty flat, Aakash walked around in his towel, his hair wet and messy. His nipples were small and high, and his body, expansive and well made. We followed him to the end of the flat, past cluttered sideboards where a telephone table, tooth mug and bedclothes were stacked close together. The kurta, a

VIP kurta with a gold and white collar, lay on his bed. Aakash vanished, only to reappear a moment later in just a pajama, the drawstring hanging out.

'Tie it, no?' he said to Megha, seeming to enjoy the execution of this intimate gesture in my presence. Then he put on the kurta over the grey vest he always wore and experimented with hairstyles, messy, the eighties, which Megha vetoed instantly, settling in the end for something in between.

Megha looked adoringly at him and said, 'Aakash, you're looking very black today.'

Aakash looked hard at himself and replied, 'Appu! Why do you say such things! It's because I haven't slept. You know, whenever my sleep is incomplete, I look blacker.' Then scrutinizing his reflection, he added, 'Actually, I'm not looking black. It's your imagination. Sir, am I looking black?'

'No,' I replied.

Megha glowered at me, then smiled and produced some of the other things she had made for him from the green metal cupboard.

'Pure linen,' she said, showing me a short-sleeved shirt with many little pockets and straps, 'and all for rupees five hundred. If you went to Giovanni, the same thing would be two thousand. No point spending too much on a kurta because he never wears it.'

'I never wear it,' Aakash confirmed, still fixing his hair and applying deodorant.

'Then why to waste money?' Megha said. 'This way even if he wears it five times, it's only rupees hundred each time.'

Downstairs, the tent was almost full. We made our way towards the stage, passing armies of children sitting cross-legged on the floor beside women in bright, hot synthetics. There was a smell of warmth in the tent, but it was not unpleasant. Aakash went to the front of the crowd and began ushering people backwards to make room. He was like a hero among the children, whom he would pick up and swing back, or run at, stamping his feet, causing them to shriek, laugh and retreat. The rest of his family sat solemnly on a white podium – Amit's wife, the 'sharp one', had a pink mobile phone tucked between her legs – where a young boy had begun chanting in Sanskrit into a mike. He was identifying where the ceremony was being performed, beginning with Jambudvip, India, Isle of the Jambul tree, and zooming in on Bharatvarsh, Delhi, and finally, the little colony where we were.

'What's the name of this place?' he asked, hardly taking a breath.

'Chitrakut,' the others answered in one voice.

'Chitrakut,' he repeated, working it into his incantations.

He was dark-skinned, with a pubescent moustache and pinkish lips. There was a confidence, bordering on a glint in the eye, about him. I thought it came from an awareness of his own fluency, the knowledge that, despite his youth, he uttered powerful things effortlessly, filling the people around him with admiration. As the prayers continued, the senior priest took over and his apprentice began going through the crowd, tying orange threads to our wrists.

At that moment, the master of ceremonies for the evening appeared. He was a great fat man in an off-white shirt with gold rings on his fingers and a gold medallion of Kali around his neck. His teeth were bright orange from eating pan, and like a cross between an Elvis impersonator and an evangelist, he reminded me of medieval friars in Europe, rotund and jovial, with a hint of corruption about him. As people stood close to the durbar, all holding their hands over the pyramid of lamps, a knotted red thread covered in butter and oil was set aflame. Ghee and fire dripped from it. And it was with this oily fire-dropping thread that the MC lit the central lamp. From its flame, men who had been crouched round the podium began lighting the other 107 lamps. Soon they were all flickering contentedly in the light breeze that came through the tent. The MC, who hadn't said a word so far, now yelled into the mike, 'Victory to the true durbar!'

'Victory to the true durbar!' the congregation yelled back.

The MC's orange teeth gleamed and he began taking dona-tions, speaking the donor's name into the mike and blessing him in public.

Aakash and Megha were in line to receive the blessing. Directly behind them stood Amit and his 'sharp' wife. Everything was going smoothly until the MC leaned forward and seemed to ask Megha something. Megha took a moment to answer, but when she did, Amit's wife, now sharper than ever, gasped aloud, 'How can one lie in the presence of the goddess?' Aakash's face went pale even as Megha's burned with anger. She swung around and there was a loud exchange between the two women, which spilled over into a fight between Aakash and Megha. Aakash seemed to be trying to cool the situation, but soon there was an opening in the crowd and Megha charged out, tears of rage streaming down her face. Aakash dived out behind her and the crowd closed again.

In the meantime, the MC, who had a powerful singing voice, launched into a devotional song, raising his hands over his head and clapping. The pyramid of lamps burned brightly behind him, the colourful mountains shone in the halogen light, and soon the tent-full of people were clapping along and joining him in the song, stopping only to say, 'Victory to the true durbar.' It was eleven thirty.

I always knew that I wouldn't have lasted the night. Within an hour of the singing beginning, my bottom began to hurt and my feet fell asleep. I tried wiggling my toes, but it made no dif-ference. The feeling would subside, only to return with greater force. My restlessness was heightened by Aakash, now with a red and gold Om scarf around his neck, coming in and out of the tent with an expression of deep worry darkening his face. So after another ten minutes of song and hand-raising, I slipped out into the cool night with its spokes of yellow street light. Uttam sat on a chair with his shirt open in the dark. I went up to him and said that we should leave. Aakash was standing near the tent. When I told him I was taking a break but would come back, he said, 'You're going now? Fine, go. Looks like everyone is letting me down tonight.'

'What's the matter?'

'What's the point of telling you? You're leaving, what help can you be to me?'

'Where's Megha?'

'Does it look as though I know?'

He was like a man who had been struck at by his superior and was now striking down at the man below him. But I had been too low on this food chain for too long and I was beginning to tire of it. I had only myself to blame; I had allowed, I had welcomed my own diminishing. My belief that Aakash could rescue me from being an outsider in India had led me into a kind of self-effacement. The place had been so strong and yet out of reach that now that it felt nearer I wished it to wash over me, even as Aakash wished to define himself against it. But that night I felt my own particularity acutely, and tired of the crowds, and of Aakash's antics, I questioned him no further. I promised to return, but he didn't seem interested. It was from his father that I learned that I should return at three thirty a.m., when the story would begin. With this, I left.

21

When I returned at four a.m., Megha had returned too and the night was entering its second phase. Aakash still stood at the wings where part of the tent flapped open. The anger he had shown me earlier had gone and tiredness like that of a child, joined with some feeling of satisfaction, had taken its place. The red in his eyes brought out their mud colour. Seeing me walk up, his father, standing near Aakash, said, 'He's come at just the right moment.' Aakash seemed pleased to see me and rested his elbow on my shoulder. Megha sat at the other end of the tent with the women of Aakash's family. Their fight, Aakash explained, had been caused by the MC asking Megha and Aakash whether they had come as a married couple. Megha, feeling she could not lie in the presence of the goddess, had replied, 'Yes,' and Aakash's sister-in-law had overheard. Aakash said that he had tried to cool the situation, but Megha felt he was letting her down. She had apparently got back into her car and driven home. Aakash had had to bring her back in person; and he was now worried that members of her family had discovered where she was. 'Tonight's final,' he kept saying in English. An uneasy peace prevailed between Aakash and Megha, and its mood was mirrored on stage by two children, in liver-coloured satin, playing Krishna and Radha in a pageant of sorts.

The boy wore a black matted wig with painted sideburns and heavy make-up. There was something dark and tantalizing about his exposed armpit hair, seeming to emphasize his adolescence. The girl was plump and well formed, with a reddish-brown dupatta falling from a bun at the top of her head. They had a confrontational relationship, now dancing, now sulking, sometimes they were making up, sometimes she was attacking him with a rolling pin. His favourite expression was an appeal to the crowd, a stunned wide-eyed expression seeming to say, 'Isn't she mad?' before retaliating himself. She never looked at the crowd, more like a soap opera wife than Krishna's consort. There was a lot of Bollywood-style dancing, which ended with a freeze in godly postures. It was at this point that Sudama appeared.

A group of colony boys had collected at one side of the stage, slouched on chairs, laughing and hanging on to one another. One of them said, as though he'd seen it many times before, 'This is really something to watch.' Aakash suddenly became protective of me, and taking me by the hand, led me to one side of the tent, away from the blaring speaker. He gestured to me to sit down, then sat next to me. I felt, as I had many times with him, that in his moments of self-doubt and trouble, he rehabilitated himself through his friendship with me. In these moments he was tender, giving, eager to please, as if my approval could restore him to his normal levels of self-confidence.

A boy with a broken tooth and a thin, expressive face appeared on stage. He wore simple white clothes and his hair was tied with red rubber bands in a long cone. He was Sudama, Krishna's childhood friend who falls into poverty. Barely able to feed his family, he goes looking for Krishna, who has by then become the King of Dwarka. But when he arrives at his doorstep, the guards prevent this near beggar from going in.

Standing outside a make-believe door, the teenage Sudama began singing a moving song, which at times had the audience in tears. Calling Krishna by all his different names, he sang, 'Murli vala, your memory would trouble me, my faith in you must not break.' In the end, he seemed to have succeeded in informing Krishna that he was standing outside his door, because Krishna, having dropped his godly freeze, now rushed out, and taking the broken Sudama in his arms, fell to the ground and began washing his feet. At this moment, Aakash, with tears in his eyes, put his hand behind my neck, massaging it as he once had at the Begum of Sectorpur's. Forever able to see himself in exalted scenarios, whether it be Bollywood or Dwarka, he said, 'Remember?'

'Remember what?' I said, not wishing to let him down.

'Remember the time when I washed your feet?'

On stage, Krishna had brought Sudama into his palace and had seated him on his wooden throne with its red felt fabric. Radha had seen this and was enraged. But Krishna by this point had had enough of her and pushed her aside. Some great tension was expressed here, but it wasn't clear what. The colony boys were both riveted, and judging by their scornful howling, repelled by Sudama's story. It was easy to imagine how these Indian stories glorifying poverty were not always pleasing to them, easy to see how they were at once familiar and something young people, especially, were a little tired of.

I could hardly believe, given the hour, that the tent was full, and at least half full with children. They sat mesmerized, watching the re-enactment of these ancient stories. And for a moment it felt as if we were all children, with our tired, gaping expressions. The pageants in their medieval and ribald way brought out instinctive emotions – tears, laughter, sadness and joy. And this also deepened my feeling of childhood.

In his second act Sudama became a comedian. He had a mobile phone, which rang incessantly. He would answer it, saying, 'Oh, hello, you're such and such person from Madras. Funny, you should call right now, you know who I'm sitting with? Yes, Krishna, Krishna Kanhaiya, right here in Dwarka. Oh yes, he has a very nice palace. The wife's a demon, but the palace is beautiful. What? You want to speak to him? Hold on one second.' Then he would run among the crowd, handing them the phone. Each skit ended with him hugging and kissing the person he gave the phone to. He came over to us and gave Aakash the phone, and from the applause and hooting that came from the colony boys, it was clear how much they admired him.

When he had gone, Aakash, perhaps feeling better, began to tell me some of what had occurred between Megha and him.

'She showed me her scars, you know?' he said. 'Her skin is bruised and dried up in many places. I can't tell you, I felt such anger. She was saying, "Take me away from here. What kind of people are these, who don't love me the way I am, but make me have lipo so they can marry me off?" I felt so bad. I could have made her lose the weight, but she said, "No, if you had, they would have married me off. You were right to leave the weight on. And anyway, anyone who marries me won't marry me for my figure, but for me." You know what her mother said to her?'

'Her mother?' I said, fighting my way out of this sudden out-pouring. 'What, does her mother know?'

'Yes, man. Lul told her. Not about the marriage of course, but about the relationship. I told you before, tonight is final. Every-one's finding out.'

'What did the mother say?'

'She said, "Pack your things and go. He's eyed your money and that's all. In a few days, when the money doesn't come, he'll start saying, 'Come pick up your daughter, she's waiting.'" She was ready to come then and there. I'd spoken to my father and he also agreed. He said, "Bring her. We'll give her the full respect of a daughter-in-law." But I consulted with some people and they thought it wasn't wise. The family could have slapped a kidnap-ping case on me.'

'But you're legally married.'

'Still, they can,' Aakash said gravely. 'You know, I'm not worried about myself. I think nothing of my safety. It's my family I'm wor-ried about. I don't want them to endure anything on my account. I worship my father, you know? He's done so much for me.' Then his tone changed. 'But if they lay a finger on me,' he said, 'I have some pretty good connections too. I've lived many lives. I know people who even make thugs shit in their pants, believe me. And they'll never find me. I'll quit Junglee; my address, they don't know; my credit card is not linked to my home address; they'll never find me.' It was the first time I had heard fear and resignation in his voice. And it drew animal instincts like self-preservation from him.

He said, 'I love Megha. I would do anything for her happiness. But you know, I've come a long way too. I can't throw it all away for love. I have to think of my family, their reputation in the colony . . .'

He was unable to say more because the MC, now full of fresh energy, had retaken the stage.

Though it was nearly five a.m., he said, 'The second phase of the night is about to begin. All that has occurred so far has only been to awaken the night.'

The tent rang with cheers and applause. The MC smiled, showing bright orange teeth. 'The most important segment of the night is the telling of the story of Tara and Rukmani, the two daughters of Raja Patras. I am inclined, as I tell this story, set over three lifetimes, to sometimes forget what I'm saying in the middle. Should this happen, you must come to my assistance.'

The tent thundered in approval, then a deep quiet fell over the crowd and the story began. But a few seconds into it, someone was heard speaking in the back. 'Go home and sleep,' the MC snapped. 'Really, go home and sleep. This story is the jewel of the night. I will tell it even if there are only five people listening. If you're going to utter even a single word, then please go home and sleep. This story is not for you.' A shamed silence prevailed. A few people turned their head to see who had spoken. The MC, calm once again, restarted the story.

'Raja Patras, content in his kingdom, had all that he ever wanted – money, power, the love of his people. The only thing he lacked was a child. He prayed to the goddess, performing the appropriate ceremonies, and soon he won her favour. He was told that within a fixed period he would be blessed with two daughters. And he was.'

At this, a stray cry from one of the colony boys went up: 'Victory to the true durbar.'

The MC's expression darkened. He held up his hand, with its many gold rings, threateningly, like a mother about to beat a child. The tent shook with laughter.

'But when the daughters had their astrological charts sent to be read, the royal priests returned with grim news. They said that while Tara, the eldest daughter, was born with a great future and would make the kingdom proud by marrying another powerful king, Rukmani, her sister, was twice accursed and would live among fishermen, among scales, among boats and black water.' The MC, with his special Hindu horror of the sea, dragged his words. The crowd howled with dismay.

'The king was shocked to hear this news. But the Rishis consoled him, telling him that the girl was no ordinary accursed girl, but Bhargavi, the sister of Suraya.

'"Who is Suraya?" the king asked timidly.

'"Suraya," the pundits began, "was a very pious princess who, about to make a ritual offering one morning, saw that there was no food in the house for the offering. So she asked her sister Bhargavi to go out and buy some. But when Bhargavi arrived at the market, she found that there was nothing available except for raw meat. Seeing no other option, she returned with the raw flesh, and putting a cover over it, left it in the kitchen. When, a few moments later, Suraya resumed her prayers, asking her sister for the offering, Bhargavi handed her the covered vessel. But it was only once Suraya had made the offering that she discovered her sister's deception."'

The people in the tent, each with food anxieties of their own, emitted a collective gasp of horror. The MC, answering their consternation, picked up the pace: 'Discovering her deception, Suraya was filled with fury. And in that instant she cursed her sister. It was a vicious curse: "In your next life," she said, "you will be born a creature that eats flesh its entire life and scavenges after tiny, many-legged creatures."

'And in her next life,' the MC said with some resignation, leaving a pause for the crowd to wonder what creature Bhargavi would be born as, 'Bhargavi was born a lizard, clinging to walls and eating spiders, insects and other many-legged creatures her entire life.'

Toning down the horror in his voice, and seeming almost to begin a new story, the MC then said, 'Now, just at that very time, etasminn eva kaale, as they say in Sanskrit, the Pandavas were performing their great ceremonial sacrifice, their mahayagya. And our little lizard, by some happy chance, finds that she is a lizard on the wall just as the mahayagya is about to begin. Not only this; she is an eyewitness to the revenge of a sage whom the Pandavas had forgotten to invite to the sacrifice. The sage, blessed with the ability to take other forms, in his revenge adopts the form of a small animal, a mongoose, and sabotages the Pandavas' sacrifice by polluting the offerings with the body of a dead snake. As it happens, our little lizard sees him do this. But what can she do? She can't speak; she has no way to let the priest know that the offerings are polluted. All she can do is sacrifice herself and save the ceremony. So just as the priests and sages are beginning their incantations, she lets herself drop from the wall and lands in the offerings. The priests see this and are enraged. The ceremony is brought to a halt and they curse our little lizard, telling her that in her next life she will live among fishermen, among scales, among boats and black water.'

The tent roared with delight, being brought, two lives later, to where the story had begun.

'When the priests,' the MC said, begging the tent's patience, 'when the priests tell the servants to throw out the offerings, or rather bury them, so that no other creature should eat them, they discover the dead snake at the bottom. The men come running back to the priests, saying, "But this lizard has saved us: the offerings were polluted anyway!" The sages and the priests sadly confess that a curse once given cannot be taken back, but they offer an amendment: in her lifetime, the accursed girl will see the curse broken.'

The crowd in the tent murmured at the excitement of this fixed outcome, with the respectable depth of two lifetimes behind it.

Taking the voice of Raja Patras's advisers, the MC picked up the story's original thread: '"This girl born to you,"' he said, '"is that very same girl!"

'But Raja Patras was disconsolate. "What can I do?" he asked. "I can't abandon her. She is my daughter, and a royal princess." The priests thought hard about what might be done and at last advised that she be placed in a gem-encrusted vessel, half-filled with jewels, and set adrift in the river to find her own fortune. And this was exactly what was done.

'On the morning the vessel was set afloat,' the MC said, 'a Brahmin performing his ablutions on the banks of the river saw something glitter in the water and his heart was filled with greed. He asked a nearby fisherman if he would help retrieve the vessel. The fisherman said, "Why would I do that? With the time I waste retrieving your vessel, I could catch so many fish and feed my entire family." The Brahmin answered, "All right, whatever is in the top half of that vessel is yours, whatever is in the bottom is mine." The fisherman agreed and the vessel was retrieved. When the two men looked inside, they found the girl in the top half and the jewels in the bottom half. The fisherman was delighted. He said, "All that was missing in my life was a child and now I have one!" The Brahmin, also now cured of his greed, said that the fisherman should take the jewels, sell them and spend the money they would bring in on the girl's marriage. And,' the MC added pointedly, 'her education.'

At that moment one of the colony boys yelled, 'Sure. Did the "Save the girl child" commission make you put that in?'

The MC bristled. 'Who said that?' he shouted.

The colony boys offered up a thin-limbed, bespectacled candidate, who grinned sheepishly at the congregation.

Seeing him rise, the MC bellowed, 'Come here, you little wise ass. I'll show you "Save the girl child" commission . . .' As the boy approached, the MC took hold of him, and shaking him up like an old rug, said, 'Who will save your girly little neck?'

The boy, with his faint pubescent moustache, feigned fear. 'Please, sir, forgive me, sir. I didn't know what I said.'

'Shame on you,' the MC said, and becoming serious, added, 'You know what a remark like yours is saying to those around you?'

'What?' the boy whined, as the MC clenched his ear.

'That our great religion, that our great forefathers, who produced these marvellous texts and stories, were not wise enough to protect our lovely damsels. That we need the government of India to tell us what to do with our girl children.'

An expression of fear crossed the face of the young boy as he realized the gravity of the offence he was being charged with. 'No, no,' he said, squirming, 'I would never say that.'

'But you did,' the MC said, laughing, 'you did. And now, for the rest of the story, my little girl child, you will sit at my feet.'

The congregation made known its approval of this punishment through loud applause and laughter, then the MC resumed the story: 'And so, gradually, both girls grow up. Tara, a prize catch, is married to the king of a neighbouring kingdom and lives the life of a queen in palaces. Rukmani, coincidentally married to someone who works in the same palace, lives the life of a maidservant.

'One day Rukmani's husband falls sick and she goes in his place to the palace. There she sees the palace temple and falls to her feet outside it, asking for a child. For some reason, perhaps being very tired from nursing her husband the night before, she falls asleep in this posture. And this is how Tara finds her. Waking her, Tara asks her why she is outside the temple. "I am of the fisherman caste," Rukmani replies, "and forbidden entry into the temple." "But this is nonsense," Tara says. "Don't you know that in front of the goddess there is no big or small, all are one?" Rukmani, moved by Tara's compassion, tells her of her longing to have a child. Tara advises that Rukmani perform a jagran.

'Victory to . . .' the MC prompted.

'Victory to the true durbar!' the tent thundered.

The MC smiled and returned to his story: 'And to help her, she gives Rukmani a pouch of money. Rukmani takes it and wanders from temple to temple in the vain hope of trying, as a low caste, to organize a jagran in her house. Who will come to her house? One priest says, "You can give me the money and I'll have it for you in the temple." But she refuses: "It must be in my house." At last, in tears, she bumps into a holy man who tells her that she must give her pouch back to Tara and ask her to host the jagran at Rukmani's house on her behalf. If she accepts, then everyone will come. Rukmani follows this advice and Tara accepts.

'In the meantime,' the MC said, his tone becoming conspiratorial, 'in the meantime, a barber has overheard the entire exchange. And when the king comes for his haircut, the barber accidentally cuts the king's finger. The king starts yelling at the barber, but the barber, low as he is, says, "This is nothing. What is a slight cut on the finger of a man whose wife is going to the house of a low caste tonight for a jagran?"

'The king is mortified,' the MC breathed, 'and asks the barber what he should do. The barber tells him to tie a salt bandage around the wounded finger. This way he'll run a fever and he can ask his wife to be at his side. She won't be able to refuse him. And this is just what he does. He returns to the palace moaning and complaining. The wife is bound by his request and rests his head in her lap.

'In those days,' the MC said, changing his tone, 'the dutiful Hindu wife considered it her religion to obey her husband. Not like today, where the woman is walking ahead with her handbag.' The MC did an imitation of a woman stomping ahead. He looked quickly down at the colony boy whom he was still holding captive, then raising his eyebrows at the audience, he said, 'And the man is running behind, with the money, buying her things.' He trotted down one side of the stage, his hands hanging limply by his large chest. The colony boy saw his chance and fled. The late-night crowd howled with delight at this spontaneous entertainment. The MC walked mournfully back, returning with a sigh to his story.

'Tara puts her husband's head in her lap and settles down into one position for many hours. But when it becomes dark, Tara, true to her vow, replaces her leg with a pillow and sets out into the night for Rukmani's house. On the way, she encounters two bandits who try and rob her. She falls to her feet and prays to the goddess. Immediately one of the men is mauled by a wild animal; the other loses the light of his eyes. When finally Tara arrives at Rukmani's, the two of them, within closed doors, perform the animal sacrifice to Kali.'

The tent was silent. A new urgency entered the MC's tone. The open sky above the tent had become pale. The MC looked up and was alarmed.

'I must hurry,' he said. 'The morning is on its way.' Then looking back at the crowd, he began, 'In the meantime, Tara's husband has woken up to find that Tara has gone. He instantly saddles his horse and sets out in search of her. On the way, he, too, encounters the same bandits who had tried to rob Tara. They manage somehow to tell him where she went and he gallops on, arriving at Rukmani's hut just as the sacrifice is about to begin. From a window he watches the two women perform the rites to Kali. When they are complete, Rukmani offers the raw meat to Tara, urging her to eat it. Tara balks and tries to resist, making the excuse that she can't until her husband does. But Rukmani implores her, saying she knows that Tara intends to return to the palace and distribute the meat without eating it herself. She must at least take one bite to show that she has honoured the sacrifice.'

The crowd watched in horrified silence as the MC raised two fingers to his mouth, holding an imagined morsel of flesh.

'Tara is about to eat the meat,' he says, 'when her husband, now no longer able to restrain himself, barges in. Tara quickly hides the meat in the end of her sari. "What are you hiding there, Tara?" the king demands. "Nothing, nothing," she says. "I'll tell you when we're back at the palace." "No, tell me now," he says, and pulls at her sari. It comes away in his hand, but instead of meat and blood, honey and butter fall to the floor.

'Raise your hands,' the MC roared, 'and say, "Victory to the true durbar!"'

'Victory to the true durbar!' the tent thundered back.

The MC, adopting his best sarcastic voice, and imitating Tara's husband, said, '"Oh, Tara, you've learned magic in one night, have you?" She says, "No, this is the goddess's work." "Is that so?" the king replies. "Then let's see if your goddess can fix this." He pulls out his sword and in one stroke slices clean through the neck of his favourite horse. At that very moment Tara is herself transformed into the goddess. "What harm did this animal ever do you?" she asks the king. "You think this is a test of my powers? Go home and sacrifice your son, then you'll see my powers."'

The MC was speeding along, fighting the break of day: 'Tara returns to her original form and the two rush back to the palace.'

'But their horse?' one of the colony boys yelled.

'What?' the MC snapped.

'How can they go back if their horse has no head,' the boy asserted firmly.

The MC's face soured. 'Tch, bloody fool. He's a king, you think someone won't lend him a horse? It's a bloody honour to lend a king a horse. He could get land and money.' He chuckled. 'Made me lose my thread. Stupid boy.'

'They go back to the palace,' someone yelled.

'Yes,' the MC said, his momentum returning, 'they go back to the palace on a *borrowed* horse. And there the king, on seeing his son, severs his head from his body and cuts him into small, small pieces. You must have heard of the killings in Sectorpur. Just the same, but even smaller pieces and not with a knife from a mall, but with a sword. Can you imagine, a father cutting his own son, cutting, cutting . . .'

The crowd let out a cry of dismay. 'And then he offers it to the goddess. There they sit, Tara and him, performing the greatest of all sacrifices to the goddess. But the meat stays meat; it doesn't become the boy.' The MC looked with relish at his audience; they looked back expectantly, knowing that in India stories didn't end this way. 'The king turns to Tara and says, "Look what you've done. You've sacrificed my heir for your bloody goddess." Tara falls to her feet and raises up her hands in supplication. And once again she becomes the goddess. "Divide the offering into five portions," she orders. "Feed the first portion to your horse . . ."'

'What horse?' a colony boy yelled.

'Bloody fool,' the MC yelled back, 'wait for it. The king is amazed, but he takes the meat of his son to the stable where he finds his horse restored to perfect health. What's more, the meat has turned to apples, oats and sugar cubes. Victory . . .'

'Victory to the true durbar!' the crowd screamed, and threw up their hands.

The MC smiled. 'Then the goddess says, "Feed the second portion to your son." Again the king is amazed, but at just that moment the boy appears, saying he was woken from a gentle sleep where sweet lullabies were sung to him, and as he says this, the human flesh in the king's hands turns to sweets and soft things. Because this is what children like . . . ,' the MC said. 'Victory . . .'

'Victory to the true durbar!'

At this point, the MC's saffron-clad helpers had appeared in the crowd and were handing out tea and sweets. As the MC detailed where the remaining portions of the human sacrifice were to go, the ending of his story became the end of our jagran. The sky was now full of light and 108 lamps fluttered in the morning breeze.

'The king was told,' the MC said, 'that Rukmani was none other than his own sister-in-law. And in this way,' he added, now tired himself and hastily wrapping up the tale that had reached its conclusion with the break of day, 'the curse of two lifetimes was broken.' With this, the MC announced a final opportunity to donate, a closing ceremony, the ritual washing of feet and the distribution of food and offerings, 'Then you to your houses and me to mine.'

The presence of daylight on the all-night gathering was at once jarring and beautiful. Everyone was recovering from the strange effect of the story and its ending timed to meet the morning.

Megha rose, pushing her way to the front of the closing ceremony. She told me firmly to stand next to her. Soon I could see why. The family, Amit and others, were all pushing close to the front so that they could be part of this final ceremony. Hands clutched at hands. Food that had been left at the front as offerings was distributed. Amit made sure that I got a small leaf plate with a blessed one-rupee coin.

'What about me?' Megha asked.

He ignored her.

'Amit?'

'Don't speak too much out of turn,' he snapped.

She pulled a banana off the plate and marched out of the tent, gesturing to me to come along.

Outside, in the clear morning light, fat black ants crawled over the sandy ground and carpet; wires hung limply from the halogen lamps; a man lay sleeping on a cemented surface; a concrete water tank loomed; cows appeared, looking for things to eat. Little girls were assembled at the front of the tent and Aakash's family symbolically washed their feet. On one side, Aakash was distributing puris and a mountain of sweet, pulpy food. Megha called to him from time to time: 'Aakash, kaka, Aakash, kaka.'

He looked grimly up at her, then told her for no apparent reason to be quiet. In the meantime, the little sweeper had appeared and was digging with his small, strong nails at a piece of offering. Around us, the durbar was being taken down, gods undressed and carried away, their torsos separated from their legs. Kali's lion was being stripped of its mane.

Megha picked up the little sweeper and pointed at the now shorn animal.

'Loin!' she said. 'Loin! What does a loin do?'

The little sweeper roared, raising his short, tough arms over his head and gnashing his teeth.

I had managed to escape unnoticed and was standing apart, scanning the street for Uttam, undoubtedly asleep in the front seat of the car, when I felt Aakash's hand on my shoulder. 'Hey, man? What's you doing, man? Dude?'

Around us, cows having found what they wanted, walked away with orange rinds in their teeth.

'Go and sleep, my friend,' Aakash said. 'We'll see what tomorrow has in store for us.'

'Tomorrow?'

'Today,' he said, and laughed.

He leaned in to give me a hug as Uttam drove up. Then pressing the side of his face against mine, he held it there. Its bones were hard and its stubble rough, but it was also tremulous and wet with tears.

22

The atmosphere of fable that the jagran awakened carried over into the next day. The city awoke to television images of policemen in olive green wading through a hyacinth-choked canal in Sectorpur, its banks thick with keekar. In the background were the power station's iron men with electric cables slung between them. In the foreground, four black bin bags. They were marooned among the hyacinths, bobbing, rolling over on to their side, suddenly straightening up with the policemen's touch, like four happy ducklings in the misty sunshine.

The policemen took cautious steps into the canal's poisonous water. The bin bags playfully resisted their capture, slithering away just as one of the men was about to get hold of the rope that tied them to each other. Only the stillness of the camera's eye brought some gravity to the scene. The country's three main news channels all claimed to have been tipped off but were vague on details. TVDelhi's red scrolling banner said no more than 'Scare at Power Station'.

I had woken late at Sanyogita's and watched in my pyjamas. Sanyogita had gone out, and Vatsala brought me some toast and orange juice. My head was still soft with sleep and the winter sunshine pouring into the room made me want to prolong the feeling of morning. The light in Delhi had changed; it came now from another angle, and far from striking the surface of buildings, seemed to lose its footing on rooftops and columns. And though it was warm, you could sit in it for hours without breaking into a sweat. Hazy and scented with smoke, it rose like a glow from the city, heightening the sensory power of the Delhi winter. The bougainvillea, the occasional smell of kebabs, the wail of a garbage collector created so acute an impression that it was as if some part of an old photograph, having shed the inertia of years, had gently begun to move.

I watched the news unthinkingly for many minutes, but when the channels gave up on the bin bags, I did too and switched to a feature film. I had begun to doze again when I roused myself purposefully and went to have a shower. The puzzling effect of staying up late, sleeping for a few hours, getting up in the early hours of the morning, then sleeping again, and now entering my third morning in a single day, brought on a kind of reverie. The glass doors of the shower had steamed up and yet, through their foggy walls, I could see the orange bars of a bathroom heater. And it was through this pleasant blur of heat and water that Sanyogita's cry broke, not a piercing cry, but a haggard groan, with many dying falls.

It was followed by the slamming of a door, a charge through our bedroom and the bathroom door being wrenched open. As she entered, I think she must have tripped over the heater, kicked it aside, straightened it, and then perhaps known the unreasonable, synaesthetic confusion of feeling you can't be heard in a steamy room. But I heard her. I heard her cry, 'Baby, oh God, baby, they killed that girl,' then bitterly, 'Your friend killed that girl.'

I let a second pass, in which I felt a strong desire for privacy. I turned the tap slowly, feeling in the abrupt cessation of hot water the mood beyond the cubicle.

'Baby, can you give me a towel?'

Sanyogita stared bleakly at me, then found me a towel. I wiped myself thoroughly, and wrapping the towel about my waist, took her hand and walked back, past my locked study, into the room with the television.

TVDelhi's red scrolling banner had changed from 'Scare at Power Station' to 'Another Grisly Murder in Sectorpur'. The screen, when it wasn't showing a small photograph of Megha laughing, her rounded, milky teeth visible over wet lips, a caption below reading '1982–2008', showed Aakash, arm in arm with two policemen, his eyes half-open and burning, as they became when he was tired and hungry. He was still in his capris and beige and white knit T-shirt; his shoulders, sandwiched between the thin, forceful limbs of the policemen, appeared larger than usual. The colony, with its peach-coloured buildings, was visible behind him, as was the white tent with its scalloped red skirting. I was finding it difficult to stave off the confusion of having recently been present at a place that was now on television when the phone rang. This, at least, was something to hold on to.

'Hello, Aatish?' said an unfamiliar voice from an unfamiliar number.

'Yes.'

'Sparky Punj here.'

'Sorry?'

'We've met in Junglee. I'm one of Aakash's clients.'

Of course I remembered him: tall, lanky man with a handlebar moustache, a white towel perpetually around his neck. Sparky Punj, the lawyer and Aakash's prized client. Among the very few in Junglee to whom he gave preferential treatment over me.

'Yes, yes, of course,' I said, walking away, Sanyogita's eyes desolately trailing me. 'Have you spoken to him? I was just going to try calling, but –'

'His phone's off, buddy,' Sparky inserted quickly. 'Do you have a minute?'

A few minutes later, I was hurriedly getting dressed as Sanyogita fired questions at me.

Did he kill her?

I don't know.

But is she dead?

Yes.

Who was that?

A lawyer called Sparky Punj.

What does he want?

He wants me to come and see him.

What for?

I don't know. He wants to help Aakash.

Oh, so you think Aakash is innocent?

I don't know. I'm just going to hear him out.

You're on his side, aren't you? It could have been me and you would be on his side. Yes?

No, I'm not on anyone's side, but what is the harm in seeing what the deal is?

Silence.

So where are you going?

Just down the road, in fact. He lives in Jorbagh.

Silence. A softening of tone.

Do you want me to come?

No, baby. I think you'd better not. I'll be back very soon.

Sparky Punj was not home when I arrived at his single-storey bungalow. A servant in white showed me past darkened sliding doors into a wood-panelled study with black leather sofas, a glass coffee table and a brightly coloured Souza on the wall. A dim picture light fell over the painting. A few rays escaping from its brass tubular frame entered the crystal boat and dagger objets on the coffee table. I was fingering the line of prominent brass studs that ran along the sofa's arm when nearly an hour and a half later Sparky entered. He was all in white, down to the socks in his black leather shoes. He wore collapsible spectacles, connected at the bridge with the help of a magnet, behind which the eyes, darkened around the sockets, were afflicted with a tic, causing him to blink rapidly when he spoke.

'Aatish. Good, buddy. Glad you made it. Here, take a look at this,' he said, tossing me the afternoon paper. It was folded in four to Shabby Singh's column, 'The long arm of the divine Chamunda'. At the centre was a picture of the canal from which the four bin bags containing Megha's body had been retrieved. There was a police line encircling the crime scene and a crowd around it. The column detailed, with some relish, the problems a small breakaway state like Jhaatkebaal could face when, by virtue of being on the border of Delhi, it experienced sophisticated urban crime in its jurisdiction. But Sparky didn't wish me to read the column at all.

'Look at that picture, buddy,' he said, crouching next to me. 'You know who that guy is?' He picked out a balding man with a moustache from the crowd scene in the main photo. He stood outside the police line, wearing khaki trousers and a black leather jacket.

I shook my head.

'You see that he's hiding his face in the picture.'

He did have his arm raised over his head, but I said I thought he might have been shielding himself from the glare of the sun.

'No, buddy,' Sparky said, 'he's concealing his identity, you see. Because he's operating outside his jurisdiction.'

'How do you mean?'

'He's a Delhi officer,' he exclaimed, 'operating illegally in Sectorpur. The best man Delhi has. Now, let me show you something else.'

He took the paper from me, flipped to another page, and again folding it in four handed it back to me. This article was about him. It showed a picture of Sparky next to a picture of Aakash. The headline read: 'Sparky Punj Takes up Trainer's Cause'.

'So you're acting on his behalf?' I asked, hoping now perhaps to get some real information.

'No, buddy, that's the funny thing. Well, at least not when this article was published. Basically what happened was that I was in my office in Sectorpur when I heard the terrible news from one of my contacts in the police. It hit me damn hard, buddy, double-hard: it's not just because of Aakash, you know; the girl's brother is a pal of mine. Very sweet guy, wants to be a writer and things. No, this was close to home, I assure you. I could hardly think straight when I heard. And the crazy thing was I had a time set for a training with Aakash literally a couple of hours later. The standard practice on Sundays was that I'd pick him up from his place, we'd drive into town and work out there. I sometimes use Junglee, but my main gym is at the Ashoka Hotel. I think Junglee's a little grimy. Anyway, when I get this call, telling me Aakash's girl is the victim, I decide, despite all that had happened, to drop what I was doing and head over to Aakash's. You know, to offer my condolences and basically be around in case he needs any help – no formalities. I like the guy; damn good trainer if you ask me.'

'Yes, yes, of course . . .'

'I arrive to find the family all sitting round. Devastated; I mean, you've never seen people in greater shock. They've just had some religious occasion, a jagran or some such jazz. The girl was with them till the morning; on the sly, mind you. She goes home, no problem. Six hours later she's dead and they have the police and press wallahs at their front door. I'd met the girl too – sweet, bubbly, polite. Great shame, you know? They made an adorable couple. Her family wasn't happy of course, but this sort of thing resolves itself with time.

'Aakash's father's a long-time government servant, you know? He's from a decent Brahmin family; they're not used to handling this crap. TV cameras, broadcast vans, Shabby going at them great guns.'

'She was there?'

'Oh yes. In full fettle. Anyway, I figure there's not much for me to do at that point. So I pay my condolences and am slipping off when a reporter from one of the city papers catches me. She asks if I'm representing Aakash; I say no and leave it at that. But her photographer takes a picture of me anyway and they run a small item in the afternoon edition. Now, one result of this article is that the police wallahs become damn suspicious. "Why is a lawyer coming here? If he's innocent, why will he be needing a lawyer?" The other is that a few hours later I receive a call from – I won't name any names, but from a very senior police officer who's seen the report in the paper. He knows me a little, our girls are in school together, and so he calls me up and immediately says, "Sparky, are you representing this trainer chappy?" I said, "Sir, no. I mean, I know the guy, but the story in the paper is groundless. He's just my trainer. I went to pay my condolences, nothing more." Now, at this stage, I can see that suspicion is beginning to fall on Aakash. And no wonder. Poor boyfriend of rich girl, you know? She leads him on for a while, but then doesn't want to marry him; jilted lover, you know the score. Motive's there, opportunity too, and it's not as if I *know* that he's innocent.'

'No.'

'I like the guy, but nobody can tell what another man is capable of. I don't know if my own chappy here won't cut my throat for a little extra dosh; you get the picture. Anyhow, this guy says to me, "If you're not his lawyer, I damn well hope you will be, because he'll need a good one." Literally, his exact words were, "We hang our heads in shame, because they're going to pin the whole damn thing on him." He said the whole business is shit-high with politics. There's a lot of pressure on Chamunda Devi to act. The case is technically in her jurisdiction, it's the third of this kind this year in Jhaatkebaal and she has an election next year. And Delhi, he said, won't get in her face over it; they'd prefer she destroy herself. So they'll stand back and let her goons in the Jhaatkebaal police force do as they wish.'

I tried at this point to say something, but Sparky stopped me with a raised hand, and urgently bringing this circular torrent back to where it had begun, said, 'And that's when he tells me about the top cop in the picture – you know, the one I just pointed out to you. He says that since the murder had happened so close to Delhi, he'd taken the liberty of sending one of his men under cover to the scene of the crime. This guy's literally seen hundreds of cases like this. And he comes back and reports to his superior that there's no way on God's earth that the trainer could have done this.'

'Why was he so sure?' I said, a little subdued by Sparky's energy. 'Who does he think did it?'

'Nepali job. Hundred and one per cent a Nep job. You've seen some of the crime they're responsible for. I tell you, these guys are fucking crazy. It takes nothing for them to flip. Ninety-nine per cent of this kind of crime, at least in Delhi, is done by Neps. And they just slip back across the border when things get too hot. Would you like some tea or coffee or anything, by the way?'

'No, thanks.'

'Water?'

'No, no, nothing. Thanks.'

'Anyway,' Sparky began again, running his fingers over his moustache and blinking rapidly, 'just after I hang up with this guy, Aakash calls me to say that they're thinking of detaining him for a narco test.'

'A narco test?'

'It's a kind of free run through the subconscious. They do it when they don't have a better idea. It doesn't stand up in court, but it can at best shed some light on an obscured aspect of the case. If you ask me, it's bullshit. It can be fudged and in some countries it's actually labelled as torture.'

'Have they arrested Aakash?'

'No,' Sparky replied, 'they've only detained him. But they could arrest him.'

'Is there any way to speak to him?'

'No, buddy, not at present. Only his lawyer can and that too with permission.'

'So what now?'

'Well, this is where you, or rather your girlfriend, comes in.'

Sparky smiled and blinked fast. He enjoyed the surprise his remark brought to my face.

'How?'

'Well, what my advice to Aakash is going to be is the following: that before the Jhaatkebaal police file a charge sheet, we make an appeal saying we question the judgement of the Jhaatkebaal police and want a full CBI inquiry. I've already warned him that the CBI will do a far more thorough investigation. And if they find him guilty, they'll file a watertight charge sheet, on the back of which alone he could spend the rest of his life in jail. So if there's even 1 per cent guilt on his part, he'd best be warned.'

'Did he agree?'

'Yes.' Sparky smiled. 'He's a good boy. Said there wasn't a shred of guilt on his part and he was ready for any kind of inquiry.'

I nodded, then it occurred to me that I hadn't understood where I came in.

'Well,' Sparky said, as if delivering a closing statement, 'if we go straight to the centre, this will reflect very badly indeed on the Jhaatkebaal police, and by association on the state's chief minister.'

'Yes, yes, of course,' I said, wishing to cut short his excitement.

'So much the better that, since you have a link to Madam CM, you communicate our position to her directly and that way she will avoid a potentially embarrassing situation. We, in turn, can avoid the headache of taking the matter to the CBI. That'll also rescue her from Shabby Singh, who, if you ask me, is baying for blood. Am I right?'

'Yes,' I answered, and said I would talk it over with my girl-friend.

While we were sitting there, Sparky's mobile phone rang. He flashed me an urgent look and took the call on his Vertu.

'Hermann, hi, Hermann. Buddy.'

He listened briefly, then said, 'Hermann, listen, there's no point in my speaking to you at this stage because everything I say will be misconstrued. I've turned down CNN-IBN too. If I support the CBI, it will be seen as my wanting them to give my client a clean chit. If —'

He was cut off.

'The police have announced a reward for the murder weapon,' he said absent-mindedly and blinked his eyes.

'What does that mean?'

'That they're groping around in the dark,' he said smugly, detaching his spectacles at the bridge.

'Tell me something,' I asked, a little irritated by his tone, 'what's in it for you?'

He smiled patronizingly, then answered, 'It's a big case. Don't get me wrong: I want to see justice done. The girl's brother's a pal of mine and so is Aakash. But if I took cases for those reasons, I'd be nowhere today. No, honestly, I believe this'll be a very important case. A watershed moment.'

'Have you spoken to Kris?' I interrupted.

Sparky looked blankly at me, then his face clearing, he said, 'Well, obviously now's not a good time. But later, I'm sure.'

We shook hands and I rose to leave. Sparky followed me to the house's tinted sliding doors. As I was walking out, he said, suddenly grabbing a few inches of fat round his waist, 'Listen, buddy. You don't happen to know a good trainer, do you?'

I thought he was joking and laughed.

'No, seriously, buddy. Aakash and I were just about getting rid of this belly, and though I'm a decent lawyer, I doubt I'll be able to get him off in the next week.'

I said I would ask around and turned to leave. Sparky stood on his veranda, watching me until I had closed the gate behind me. Then he turned around and went in.

Outside, it was still early evening, but not mild like the night before. This would be a real north Indian winter night, thick, cold and smoky.

I arrived back at Sanyogita's to find her more distressed than before. Her eyes were swollen. They glistened from the light of a computer and she kept rushing back to the television every hour. The news channels had run out of material and the racier ones now showed images of a girl, healthy like Megha, running through a keekar forest at night. Her pursuer was clearly modelled on Aakash, and every now and then the glint of a knife was visible in his hands. Then the screen would darken and in the next scene

257

Megha's killer was stuffing bin bags and setting them afloat in the still, black water.

'I don't get you,' Sanyogita would say, at the end of each cycle. 'How can you see this and not feel anything?'

'I do feel something, something much worse. I just don't feel what they're showing me.'

'What is between you and Aakash?' Sanyogita snapped. 'Are you fags or something?'

'No, Sanyogita, we're not fags or something.'

'So what did the lawyer say?' she asked.

I began to report in full detail what Sparky had told me. Sanyogita listened to every word and I could see that the very act of my making the confidence eased the tension between us. Her face brightened when she heard of Aakash's willingness to pass through the CBI's trial by fire. He became for a moment the beneficiary of her vast reserves of compassion. But when, re-enacting Sparky's line of reason as I had heard it, I came to Chamunda's intervention, Sanyogita's expression changed. The colour drained from her face and a contorted smile began to play on her lips. She seemed on the one hand elated by some marvellous realization, but on the other hardly able to stand the bitterness it brought up in her.

'What is it?' I said, unable to continue under the scrutiny of her gaze.

'You must think I'm a fool,' she said, shaking her head in disbelief.

'What are you talking about?'

'Well, either you're blinded by your love for this guy,' she said, rising and beginning to pace around the room,'or . . . or you really think I'm an idiot.'

'Sanyogita, what is it? Tell me.'

'No, you tell me,' she said. 'If they have, as they say, this watertight plan to bring in the CBI, why tell my aunt?'

'It's obvious. They'd prefer not to have to deal with the CBI, but will if they have to. This saves everyone the hassle.'

'*Why* would they *prefer* not to?'

'It complicates things, it's a gamble, it takes more time . . . I don't know.'

'So they'd rather go the easy route by exploiting my aunt's political fears to clear Aakash's name. And then no one ever finds who really killed the girl . . .'

'Sanyogita!'

'What! Am I saying anything that isn't true? You know as well as I do that if Chamunda hears of this plan, she'll make sure your friend's found innocent whether he is or not.'

'But this just saves her the embarrassment . . .'

'I don't care. Let her be embarrassed. If her police are so incompetent, she ought to be embarrassed. And,' she added, trying to mitigate the effect of her words, 'don't worry about Chamunda. She's a political animal; she can look after herself.'

I reached forward to hold Sanyogita, and surprisingly she let herself be held.

'I know we've had a difficult time in the past few months, but . . . this is not a trial on us, you know? It's very serious . . .'

'That's exactly why we can't get involved,' she said, pulling away and becoming forceful once again. 'Not you for your friend; not me for my aunt. I haven't asked for much recently, but I'm asking you now to promise you won't interfere.'

'What if Chamunda calls us?'

'Then we'll see. But you won't call her.'

'Sanyogita . . .'

'Promise.'

I wanted desperately to act on Sparky's advice, but Sanyogita was so full of high-sentence, so eager now finally to test our relationship, that in the face of her anguish I gave my word not to interfere.

The hours rolled by one after another; the heater stared up at us, open-mouthed; the television became more gruesome as night fell. Vatsala brought us Rajasthani blankets and hot-water bottles. Sanyogita fell asleep in front of the television.

From that moment to when I removed my arm from under her, seeking the cold night air, I felt myself at the centre of an emotional exchange: Sanyogita, asleep and childlike, grew distant, her reactions less immediate, her concerns less important; and Aakash, returning cycle after cycle on every channel, grew nearer, his predicament more urgent, his personality more forceful. Sparky's rationale sang in my head. I began imagining that Chamunda was waiting for my call. I felt my insides ache from inaction. The chaste logic of betrayal took shape in my mind: of course Sparky was right, the Jhaatkebaal police force had nothing on Aakash; if they had, they would have arrested him; he would now suffer needlessly, losing time and money, Chamunda would be politically harmed, and all so that Sanyogita could settle personal scores . . . The dilemma ceased to be moral, my mental energies becoming focused instead on the undetected removal of my arm. And it was with something of the elation of a jail-break that, around eleven thirty, I stepped on to the terrace and rang Chamunda.

Minutes later I picked my way past Sanyogita, asleep still on the sofa. Downstairs, the chowkidar, wrapped up in a woollen cap and scarf, had lit a fire in a shallow cement dish outside his bunk. It burned steadily in the circular hollows of his bifocal spectacles. We were both standing over it, warming our hands, when Chamunda's white Ambassador and escort turned into the U-shaped lane that ran in front of the house. The car door opened and she gestured to me to get in. She had been at dinner when I called and the Ambassador's roomy interior smelt of tuberose perfume and cigarettes.

'Where's Sanyogita?' she asked.

'Upstairs. Asleep.'

She looked deeply at me through the gloom in the car, reading into my short reply.

'Does she know you called me?'

'No.'

'Good,' she said. 'She can get a little emotional in these situations.' Then her soft hand covering mine, she leaned forward slightly and said, 'Driver, take a little round. We want to chat for a bit.'

The car drove out of the lane and into the dark streets of Jorbagh.

The information that I had given Chamunda on the phone – that Aakash was my friend and trainer and Sparky his lawyer – the information that had been enough for her to want to see me immediately, now, in its extended form, complete with details of Sparky's plan, irritated Chamunda. She wanted, with the pride of someone used to having special information, to assert herself over me.

'Nothing new there,' she said. 'It's all very standard what he's saying. Baba, I didn't come here tonight out of any fear of what Sparky Punj or Shabby can do to me. I came because this chappy's your friend. That's what concerns me. And I'm willing to do everything in my power to help him. What I need to know from you, though, is how well you know the guy. I mean, is he just the trainer or is he a pal of yours too?'

'A pal too, I suppose. Why do you ask?'

I felt she was indirectly asking me to vouch for his innocence. But I was wrong.

'Can we trust him?' she presently said.

'Sure . . . But what for?'

'Well, see. The idea that came to me the moment I heard he was your friend was that if we could trust this fellow, then we should remove him from the sort of detention he's in – he was never arrested so that's not an issue – and move him into a more informal detention.'

'Like a safe house?'

'Something like that. Let's say guest house. I know the place. It's just across the Delhi border, in Sectorpur itself. You know, just till this media frenzy dies down and we have a better idea of who really did this thing. We can give the press some vague line: he's being interrogated but isn't under arrest etc. . . . . What I want to know from you, though, is how dependable he is. Will he stay quiet, away from Shabby and people like that? Will he give up this crazy plan of Sparky's?'

'I'm not sure, I suppose,' I said, unable to gauge her logic completely and also unable to articulate what I was missing. Chamunda pre-empted me.

'In return,' she said, 'he has my personal assurance that no one will touch him. I've already spoken to my SSP in Sectorpur. He's willing to let the scent go cold as long as this trainer fellow of yours doesn't give us any trouble while the investigation is under way.'

Jorbagh was a gated colony. The driver had not left its confines, but had driven us around its residential parks, circled the market, entered a nether region with fewer street lights and was heading back in Sanyogita's direction. I could see now what Chamunda was asking me to stand as a guarantor for. And it was harder to gauge than the question of Aakash's innocence. What she wanted to know was – innocent or not – would Aakash remain loyal despite the power he would hold over her? It was of course the one thing about Aakash that I had never been able to determine myself. But I took my chances, knowing Chamunda wouldn't be taking hers without some greater precaution in hand than my word.

'I think so, yes,' I answered.

'Good,' she said, then added a second later, 'I'll need you to go, you know?'

'To the safe house?'

'To keep him on side.' Smiling, she added, 'Informed regularly of the advantages of doing so.' Then adjusting her tone from business to business with a personal touch, she said, 'I'm glad you came to me, baba. You know I know how sound your judgement is. If your man runs into trouble in my state, you must tell me. It's your duty as my nephew.'

Just as we were about to turn into the U-shaped lane my phone rang.

'Baby, hi. I was just –'

'You're with Chamunda,' Sanyogita said, her voice thick with agitation.

'I was –'

'Please don't fucking lie to me. The chowkidar told me she picked you up.'

'I'm not lying. I just –'

'You *are* fucking lying!' Sanyogita screamed loudly enough for Chamunda to hear. 'Saving your friend,' she sobbed.

Chamunda looked gravely at me. I could hear her mind change gear, and that feminine genius that could power many intelligences at the same time understood what was happening. 'Take another round,' she said to the driver, then sternly to me, 'Give me the phone.'

Already on the other end the voice had broken down. Cries of anger and despair containing the build-up of months – 'Saving my aunt, saving your friend, saving everyone?' yelled again and again – filled the car. Chamunda held the phone in her lap, its blue light seeming to blaze in the gloom of the car. Only when the voice had tired did she begin.

They spoke for only a few minutes. Chamunda repeated Sparky's rationale, then added to it her own plan, plus an offer that surprised me: 'I think you both should go . . . Yes, yes . . . Yes, go and stay. It's a very nice place, very comfortable; Ra decorated it. There's even a gym. I want you to go. You'll be helping me by going.'

I looked at Chamunda in confusion; she patted the air with her hand as if to say, 'I know what I'm doing.'

'I agree with you, darling. You want to see justice done; so do I. But if we keep him in prison, he'll slip out of our hands. So I'm saying go there . . .'

'No,' Chamunda said firmly, as if having encountered fresh

263

dissent. 'Aatish will go no matter what. Now it's up to you whether you want to join him or not.'

I looked nervously up at Chamunda, but she seemed to have forced her way through. 'Absolutely,' she said now. 'You know I've always wanted you to fill my shoes. I'll stop by myself tomorrow and we'll work out a plan. Now stop crying, darling. We're two seconds away. Go and pack a bag.'

Chamunda's preparations had been so complete that even the car I had thought was her escort turned out to be our escort to the safe house. Now, as we waited outside Sanyogita's, Chamunda asked as if in an afterthought, 'Your friend, how long had he been with this girl?'

'Chamunda massi,' I said, weighing up my options, 'he married her almost six months ago.'

A deep silence followed.

'That's very good,' she murmured cautiously, 'very good. Baba, it's all going to be fine. I want you to leave right away. Your friend will be there before you arrive. And,' she added, looking up, 'take care of Sanyogita. She's very emotional right now.'

Sanyogita was walking down the drive in tracksuit bottoms and rabbit-faced slippers. Her head was cocked to one side; she held a small bag in one hand. Her distress was such that for a second she didn't even realize that we had pulled up in front of the house. She was cold but polite to Chamunda. To me she said bitterly, 'I'll never forget this. Never. No one has ever made me feel so worthless before.'

A few minutes later we were both in the car on our way to Sectorpur. Keekar trees raced alongside the tunnel our headlights made; veils of white fog were cast aside; and the backs of trucks, with signs saying, 'Use Dipper Please', zoomed close and fell away. Sanyogita fought tears in the darkness of the car, her face turned away.

Taking refuge in banalities, I said aloud, 'Shit, I didn't bring anything.'

'Like what?' I was surprised to hear quietly asked a moment later.

'You know, clothes, a toothbrush, my phone charger.'

'I've packed them,' Sanyogita replied sadly, leaving me more wretched than ever.

23

My suspicion that Chamunda was more nervous about Aakash's botched detention than she was letting on was confirmed when I saw the 'safe house'. The driver had been on the phone throughout the drive with someone at the house and just as the road became more residential he turned the car left and stopped in front of a large black gate. Two or three security men waved us through with a quick glance at the licence plate. We drove down a long private drive lined with bunkers, sandbags and pre-fab government offices, each, despite the hour, with white lights flickering in aluminium windows. At the end of the drive was a double-storey bungalow with a curved, colonnaded veranda overlooking a large lawn. From the porch and garden lights, it was possible to see that it was painted in the local Jhaatkebaal style, rust, with chalky-white borders running along its pediments, arches and balustrades. Fountains of bougainvillea hung from its many terraces. And Indian blinds, marble floors and screened doors brought a colonial aspect to the bungalow.

Aakash, arch-Brahmin that he was, was not unaware of the significance of his accommodation. He sat like a dacoit on a planters chair in front of a coal fire on the veranda, wrapped in a shawl. He didn't get up when he saw the car approach, but instead leaned forward and stoked the coals, causing sparks to leap up. Then sitting back, he took a long drag on a cigarette held in a fist and rested his drink on the chair's long arms. He would have been expecting me, but the appearance of Sanyogita from the car must have come as a surprise, because he rose suddenly.

'Bhabi,' he said as she jogged up the veranda's shallow steps, 'welcome. I mean, welcome to your house. I must say, your aunty knows how to take care of her guests.'

Sanyogita ignored him, saying only, 'It's freezing. Let's go inside.'

'Of course, of course, bhabi, let's go inside.'

Sanyogita opened the screened door and hurried in. Aakash put his arm round me, then pinched my waist as he always did, and said with some sarcasm in his voice, 'Looking good, man. *Looking like me*, man.'

The front of the house was in darkness and seemed to have an administrative function of sorts. A servant with a dishcloth over his shoulder had appeared from nowhere and led us in, unlocking and relocking doors behind us. There seemed to be a sharp division between its public and private sections. We passed through dim corridors and a large room with picture lights over portraits of moustached men in turbans and pearls.

We came up to a final locked double door, through which shafts of bright light escaped. Aakash, who must already have seen beyond it, grinned broadly.

The room we entered had high ceilings, large carpets and a burnt-red recess containing a bar, and along its mouldings and fireplace there were blue-painted parakeets with gold necks and feet. It was not the splendour of the room but its familiarity that left Sanyogita and me in silent wonder. That familiarity was to be found in its white sofas, its chandeliers and crystal coffee tables, and especially in the black and white pictures of thirties beauties in silver frames. It could be seen in the large number of Nepalese maids, in bright, traditional Jhaatkebaal saris, now setting the dinner table; it was there in the brood of pugs that came running in on our arrival; and traces of it were even visible in the large moustache, gold earrings and kohled eyes of a uniformed butler carrying a crested silver tray. It was the familiarity of Chamunda's palace at Ayatlochanapur and Sanyogita recognized it immediately. 'She's brought the whole place here!' she gasped. It was then that I realized that this was no guest house. Jhaatkebaal's official capital was a remote, desert town with a lively handicrafts industry. The state's real centres were its satellite towns,

Sectorpur and Phasenagar, and the house we had arrived in was already seeming like Chamunda's own base in Sectorpur, the place where she could be at once in Delhi and in her state.

Aakash, never slow to settle in, was eager to show us the rest of the house.

'You see it,' Sanyogita said, addressing me. Then more gently, 'I'll settle in and join you.'

When she'd left us, Aakash stared at me in amazement. 'Don't tell me . . .'

'No, nothing like that. She's just upset by everything that's happened. And trust me, more with me than anyone else.'

Aakash nodded his head slowly, then his face clearing, said with a lambent smile, 'How's you doing, man?'

'How am I? How are you?'

'Fine. Just my head is confused after the test.'

'Test?'

'Narco test.'

'I'm so sorry . . . About everything. I can't even imagine . . .'

'Don't say anything. This is what life is after all. All our scriptures, our plays, our stories . . . What, it's for a moment like this that they prepare us, no? Let's not get lost in these things now; let's see the house, your girlfriend's house.'

Aakash began to lead me through room upon room, in whose coloured walls, each coated in a silver hue and Tanjore glass paintings, I recognized Ra's distinctive hand. He showed me a moonlit courtyard with a rectangular fountain, containing flat, fish-eaten lotus pads and pink flowers. He threw open the door of a modern gym with a rubber floor, dumb-bells, a power plate and treadmill. Finally, he led me down a long corridor, at the end of which, visible through a cloud of incense, was a brightly lit temple room. It was dedicated to a black and silver Kali with a red tongue. Her shadows filled the little room and she had under her – just where she wanted him – a demon, into whose throat she plunged a trident. From somewhere behind her fierce form, a hidden music system played 'Om', chanted in a steady drone, again and again.

And past a mesh door, off from the temple room, was a garden containing holy plants.

'This,' Aakash said, as if completing an estate agent's tour, 'is what I would like my house to be.'

We were still staring into the room, with its lesser gods and silver vessels huddled under Chamunda, when the servant who had showed us in reappeared, followed by Sanyogita.

Confused that she was behind him, he began by addressing us. Then perhaps aware of her rank in the house, he turned around and told her that dinner was served. At the sight of Sanyogita a sudden solemnity entered Aakash's manner. He said we should carry on; he wasn't eating.

'Why?' Sanyogita asked blandly.

'I'm keeping a fast,' he replied, 'for my wife.'

'Well, we're inside,' I said.

'I'll join you in a few minutes,' Aakash answered, and using the same tone in which he had once said to me, 'With us, children are everything,' added, 'I want to be alone with her memory.'

Sanyogita turned around and walked out without a word. I followed her into the dining room, where a feast of lamb shank cooked with ginger and green chillies, lentils, pickled white radish and okra was being served. Aakash appeared a few minutes later, was seen lingering by the bar, then came and sat down.

That night, despite everyone's best efforts, a lightness prevailed. We were like people arriving at a house in the country for a weekend, children at a sleepover, three unlikely friends holed up after a blackout or a terrorist attack. The house, combining an unfriendly exterior with familiarity within, seemed at least to Sanyogita and me like houses from our childhood. Sanyogita, though still quiet and fierce, was temporarily consoled by her surroundings. And I, taking my lead from her, too guilty to do otherwise, sought shelter in this brief peace. Aakash's mood fluctuated: he was restless, one moment grieving and cast down, the next alert and attentive. Though there was not much conversation between us, we spoke at cross-purposes. An idea of

Aakash's new fame had settled in his mind, and in between whisky sodas, he would stop to ask me how he had looked that day on television. 'Not too black, I hope?' Then he remembered that it was Megha who used to say that of him and a moment of sadness returned.

'She did it for our love,' he said, 'gave her life for our love.'

'She didn't give her life,' Sanyogita snapped. 'She was murdered.'

'Yes,' Aakash mumbled unsurely, and then animated again, said, 'Did you see, on the television, they showed the colony and the jagran tent? They interviewed Mama, Papa, Amit. Anil too, I think. Strange, no? One minute you're there; the next minute it's on TV.'

Sanyogita's face soured. Aakash saw and became serious.

'How's the investigation going?' she asked.

Once again he mistook her meaning. 'Fine,' he replied. 'Sparky, sir, says that it shouldn't be too long now.'

'For what?' Sanyogita asked pointedly.

But Aakash, now wise to her, mechanically replied, 'For justice to be done.'

'And do you have any idea –'

He cut her short: 'Can't say, bhabi, just can't say, but maybe Sparky, sir, is right. Maybe it is Nepalis.' Then after a solemn pause, he said, as he once had of Muslims, 'I think they'll all have to go,' and looked around the table for confirmation. 'No?'

The next morning, after showers and breakfasts eaten separately, Sanyogita, Aakash and I gathered in a study upstairs in front of a flat-screen television. It was a windowless room with green walls, slim glass bookshelves, lit from below, and an orange and yellow chandelier. We sat in a row on a deep Oliver Musker sofa, white with large white woollen flowers. Chamunda was on the screen.

She wore a dark blue printed Kashmiri silk sari and an uncoloured pashmina decorated with tiny pink flowers. She had just come out from addressing the Chamber of Indian Builders and the old socialist building, with its generous use of patterned concrete screens, hung in the background. A journalist had stopped her on the way out to ask about the Megha case.

Chamunda looked sternly at the camera, then out at the misty winter day, and said, 'I have already suspended two officers. Let it be an assurance of my commitment to solving this case that I will suspend the SSP Sectorpur if we don't see satisfactory results in the very near future. That is all I have to say.' With this, Raunak Singh swept her away in a white Ambassador.

I thought it wasn't much, but Aakash, who knew more about these things than both Sanyogita and I, was impressed. Nodding his head, he cryptically repeated, 'No empty threat, no empty threat.'

'What do you mean?' I said finally. 'What's the big deal if she suspends the SSP Sectorpur?'

'The Senior Superintendent of Police, Sectorpur,' Aakash said with sudden fluency, 'is the most important police post in Jhaat-kebaal. This man oversees every extortion and kidnapping case there is, taking his cut and where necessary even acting as a guarantor so that money actually changes hands under his supervision. He would have paid five crores of rupees just to get the post, which he is probably still paying back. To lose his position at this stage would ruin him. It's a lot of pressure. Something's going to burst very soon.'

By mid-morning, Chamunda's office had leaked the information of Aakash's secret marriage to the press. We sat together in front of the television when one of the Hindi channels began running pictures of the red and blue Arya Samaj certificate, with its pictures of Aakash in a blazer and tie and Megha with an inky stamp over her face. They had even got hold of a picture of the newly married couple, garlanded and in bright sunlight. I was worried about a bad reaction from Aakash, but it never came. He smiled at me knowingly and continued to watch. It was as if he was seeing a bigger game come into play, and far from being nervous of riding its currents, he was riveted, keen to know where to get on. And though it was not said, I sensed that, as the wronged man in the right position, Aakash felt the nearness of a golden opportunity.

As Chamunda would have predicted, the complexion of the story began to change with the revelation about the marriage. The re-enactments of the murder, or at least the ones in which an actor modelled on Aakash chased Megha through a midnight keekar forest, stopped running. Apart from Shabby's channel, all the other channels began portraying Aakash and Megha as being on one side, co-victims, with the forces of the world against them. The murderer once again became someone in the world beyond, and no longer a specific man against whom the right evidence had only to be found.

But Chamunda had miscalculated. In putting pressure on her police force as well as shifting the focus of the case away from Aakash, she had opened the way for the police to hastily turn their attention elsewhere. And it showed that she didn't know the men who made up her police force; that she thought them no different from Delhi police. It was an easy mistake to make, easy to think of the border between Sectorpur and Delhi as only administrative. But it had a significance deeper than she knew. It was the border between town and country, between old ways and new, city ways, between rural poor and urban middle class, between the mall-goers and the wild men of Jhaatkebaal. And across that border on all sides, where women in brightly coloured clothes worked in fields and men lazed on charpoys drinking tea, young girls did not wear capris, or send text messages, or have boyfriends; and they certainly did not marry out of turn. Just miles into that country of truck drivers and dangerous moustaches, with Delhi still visible, people thought nothing of killing a girl who had dishonoured their name. It was from this world that the bulk of Jhaatkebaal's police force was recruited.

And so when revelations broke about Aakash and Megha's secret marriage, and romantic text messages sent through the night saying 'Appu this' and 'Aakash that' came to light, and

Airtel's call register revealed late-night phone calls made from Megha's phone, not only to Aakash but to 'other strange persons', it was with some sympathy for a brother, understandably forced to silence so loose a sister, that the police arrested Kris, the creative writer. They would just as happily have arrested his father, but Mr Aggarwal was over seventy and out of town at the time of the murder.

Chamunda's SSP, a dark-skinned Sikh gentleman with a face as fierce as a grease wrestler and a purple police band across his olive-green turban, addressed the press conference himself. Facing a room full of Delhi journalists, he managed in broken English, a little pleased with himself at the formulation, to say, 'Krishna found Megha and Aakash in an objectionable but not compromising position. Incensed, enraged, infuriated, he took matters into hand.' The room fired back angry questions. 'Did he have any real evidence against the boy or was this all conjecture? How could he offer this as a motive for murder? Did he not know that Kris had been to USA – to Hampshire College, Massachusetts – for his university, that he didn't possess these backward values?' At first the SSP came out fighting. He pointed to Megha's frequent communications with strange men; he gave the room an idea of the clothes she liked to wear; he said that she sometimes drank; and on the night in question she had left her house, without her parents' permission, to meet her secret husband; she had even driven herself. But gradually, as the distaste in the room grew, and cries of 'character assassination' rose from the press corps, the SSP became sadly subdued. He realized that he was among a strange lot, modern and valueless.

Even before the press conference was over, the city was on the boil. Megha's mother, also a large woman, was shown standing among a crowd of people. Her daughter's face was visible in hers; she wore a brown printed kurta. 'Would a brother kill his own sister?' she said, weeping and on the verge of breaking her bangles. 'Today I have lost not only a daughter but a son as well. And Megha's murderer is still roaming free. The police are lying through their teeth.' Kris was shown next, being silently led away by the Sectorpur police, his protruding lower jaw hanging open. Within hours, vigils of university students, with flowers and posters of Megha, had formed in the street, standing up against 'character assassination'. Bloggers went like flesh-eating fish through the SSP's remarks.

By the time Chamunda's convoy of white Ambassadors and Jeeps had driven into the safe house, Shabby had already interviewed Megha's mother in her newsroom and, via satellite, some of Kris's American friends, who spoke of how gentle and artistic he had been in university. She had also launched a full investigation into the political pressure police officers were forced to operate under in Sectorpur. In our own small group in the upstairs TV room, deep tensions had arisen. Sanyogita's eyes, so recently dry, had begun to flow again at the sight of her friend Kris being led away. And when Aakash whispered, 'Lul,' to me, causing me to laugh out loud, she rose and left the room.

Chamunda's arrival brought the house together for a late lunch. It was Aakash who saw her first. He had gone to the bathroom, leaving the door of the television room half-open. A few moments later I saw him on the balcony, looking at the courtyard below. He didn't hear me come up behind him. Downstairs, Chamunda in her dark blue sari and shawl, her sunglasses on her head, was standing by the lily pond instructing a servant on how to lay the table for lunch. When he put a clear globe-like vase of violet dahlias on the edge of the table, she rushed ahead and moved it to the centre. Aakash watched mesmerized as she told the servant where to put the wine glasses, corrected the arrangement of cutlery, then stood back and looked from a distance at the table that was now nearly ready. Watching Aakash watch Chamunda, I felt I knew what held his attention. I was willing to bet that until that moment the privileged women Aakash had met were too good for housework; they would have worn black Western clothes, led idle lives and required Aakash to keep them slim so that their husbands didn't stray. That kind of woman would have had her attractions, but Aakash could not really have respected someone like that. In Chamunda, however, he would have seen traces of the traditional Indian woman that he could never have done without, as well as new and seductive things, like money, independence and power. The combination would have been beguiling.

Chamunda, aware of us watching her, shielded her eyes from the sun and looked up. For a moment she giggled with girlish embarrassment, then firmed up her voice and said, 'Come on, boys. Come down for lunch.'

We followed an internal staircase, with old movie posters on the walls, and came out through a bright blue door into the courtyard. The sunlight went right through the pond's green water, where orange fish flashed from time to time. The foliage round the pond was thick with palms and ferns. Behind the lunch table a tall forest-green bamboo fence protected the little court-yard from the view of those working in the house. Chamunda now sat at the table sipping a glass of pomegranate juice, a brood of pugs yapping at her feet.

'Hi, baba,' she said, with some distress in her voice, as I reached down to touch her feet. But with Aakash following my example, it melted quickly into embarrassed laughter, and, 'Oh no, you don't have to. It's only because I'm like his aunt. I've known him since he was this high.' Then, 'May you have a long life, my son,' she said at last, with resignation in her voice. But when he rose and she saw his face, seeing perhaps even more clearly than me the marks of his caste, I thought I saw a different light in her eyes. It was as if her various screens – of being chief minister, Sanyo-gita's aunt, politician, older woman, princess – fell away and those vast eyes were now for a moment limpid. There was nothing innocent or unguarded about this gaze; if anything it was blacker despite its heat. And as quickly as it came it was gone.

A moment later, Sanyogita appeared from a corner of the house and we sat down to lunch. It was a grim meal during which everyone seemed to be negotiating their way out of some private mood. I had served myself meat curry and rice when I saw that Chamunda wasn't eating.

'You aren't having anything?'

'I've eaten, baba,' she said. Then perhaps to deflect attention from herself, she added, 'Here, have some wine,' and filled both mine and Aakash's glasses. Sanyogita looked sourly across at her. 'Can I have some too, Chamunda massi?'

'Tch! Yes, of course,' Chamunda said, and passed the wine.

Silence fell over the table. Only Aakash, though still watchful, had a surprising calm about him. He ate and drank wholeheartedly, like a man celebrating a victory. He looked up occasionally at Chamunda with sidelong glances, seeming to finesse his study of her. At length we began talking about the case.

'It's a stain,' Chamunda said bitterly. 'It'll blow over, I know, but it's a stain and that bloody Shabby will do everything to draw attention to it in the run-up to the election.'

'How can she not?' Sanyogita said. 'You've got the wrong . . .'

Her words were lost in her throat. Chamunda, though having gauged their meaning, made her repeat them. 'What?'

'Guy!' Sanyogita said. 'You have the wrong guy.'

Chamunda's face darkened, but she didn't say anything.

'Isn't there any way to save face?' I asked.

'No, not at this stage,' Chamunda replied. 'We've made one mistake already.'

Aakash looked up from his food and smiled, his lips glistening.

'This other one's more serious. It's galvanized the whole city. Now if we come out and say, "It wasn't him either, we just arrested him because my SSP got it into his head that the girl was of loose morals," we're going to look really bad. We need to keep the case going with this brother of hers as a valid suspect for at least some time. Till we can find an out.'

The remark seemed aimed at Aakash, but he said nothing.

'Keep it going,' Sanyogita said, 'i.e. keep my friend in jail until then?'

'You think I bloody want to?' Chamunda exploded. 'I have to!'

'Why do you have to?'

'Because your fat friend Shabby will crucify me if I don't. This is politics, all right? It's not fun, it's not creative writing, but it has to be done.'

'I don't understand, if people like you don't stand for justice and the rule of law, how is it –'

'I can't listen to this shit,' Chamunda snapped. 'I'm not Gandhi. I'm working with an imperfect system. Yes, I don't want an innocent boy to go to jail, but I'm not losing my job over it.'

Sanyogita put a last mouthful of rice and lentils in her mouth, coldly moved the fork a little right of centre on her plate and rose. She looked at me, but I pretended not to notice. Then after kneeling down and stroking one of the pugs, she slipped away.

Chamunda had upset herself so much that she reached for a plate. She was about to serve herself some food when Aakash stopped her.

'Ma'am, don't. I have a solution. Everything will be fine.'

Chamunda looked stunned, perhaps both at what was said and the tone with which it was said. Recovering her poise, she asked, a smile playing on her comic-book lips, 'Well, can I at least have some lunch?'

'Better not, ma'am,' Aakash replied quickly. 'I was hoping to repay your hospitality by giving you a session after lunch.'

'A gym session?' Chamunda said with wonder, then looked at me as if I'd brought a lunatic into her house.

'Yes, ma'am. I'm a professional person,' Aakash said in English, and let out a short laugh.

Chamunda fell silent, her eyes wandered and for a moment it seemed as though she didn't approve of this over-familiarity. Then looking up, she breathed, 'Why not!'

Aakash laughed at the success of his overture and looked to me for approval.

Chamunda in the meantime had stood up. 'All right, then,' she said, as if convincing herself that she was truly about to work out in the middle of the afternoon on a day when her government was close to falling. 'I'll get dressed. Raunak Singh! Raunak Singh! Get my exercise things ready.'

'Very good, ma'am,' a voice returned from some hollow section of the house.

'Aakash, in the gym in five minutes?'

'Yes, ma'am.'

With this, Chamunda gave me a little kiss on the head and disappeared behind one of the rust-painted courtyard's many blue doors. I turned in amazement to Aakash, who at that moment had submerged his entire hand into a silver finger bowl.

'What now?'

'Nothing now. We'll see.'

'Well, what's the solution?'

I thought he relished saying that he couldn't tell me; that he wanted to but couldn't; that his future was at stake.

Chamunda appeared a moment later in her exercise clothes. She wore denim shorts, exposing her brown, faintly dimpled legs, New Balance trainers and a T-shirt. It was a simple white T-shirt, with a cartoon image of a Hollywood blonde in grey sunglasses, the lenses each mapping perfectly on to Chamunda's large breasts. Hanging from the cartoon blonde's neck, and stretching over our chief minister's soft, slightly protruding midriff, was a pair of binoculars. Giving me a little wave, she trotted up the couple of steps that led from the courtyard into the gym.

Aakash followed her a moment later, leaving me in the courtyard alone.

Oppressed by the solitude, I went upstairs to get a book. Sanyogita was checking her emails in an involved, distancing way. The house, which had been driven since the morning by a jolting, uneven energy, was at last quiet.

★

It would have been an hour, an hour and a half later, once the late-afternoon light had almost left the courtyard, that Chamunda emerged from the gym, sweating heavily, her long hair in a bun, visibly exhilarated.

'He's very good, your friend,' she said, 'much better than my fellow. I think I might get him to come and give me trainings. He had me do ten to fifteen minutes inclined walking, then very light weights and finished me off on floor exercises. My body is breaking.' She rested a hand heavy with rings on my shoulder, and becoming quieter, said, 'Baba, he'll probably tell you what we spoke of. Please, not a word to Sanyogita. Not till tomorrow.'

At that moment a band of fairy lights coiled around one of the trees in the courtyard came on. They followed a cycle: one strip at a time, they worked their way up the trunk, then all the lights glowed at once and burst into rhythmic flashes. Chamunda wiped her hands and lit a Dunhill cigarette. She offered me one, but I declined. We sat in silence for some minutes. The rising smoke moved sideways over a ruled page of fine, slatted light coming in past the green bamboo fence.

'So listen, baba,' Chamunda said, 'it looks like no one will have to stay here after tomorrow. I mean, you can stay on, of course, if you want to, this is your house. But what I mean to say is that you don't have to stay here. You don't know how grateful I am that you came, though. These have been trying times, really. But you watch, we'll win the election and then we'll have some fun. We'll get your mother here as well. You know, I love her like a sister. Much more than a sister.' Chamunda laughed wickedly, thinking perhaps of Sanyogita's mother, with whom she had strained relations. Then as an extension of that thought, she added, beetling her eyebrows, 'Try and make Sanyogita understand that her aunt is not such an evil person. You don't know how she wounds me. I have no children, so she's like my own, but she's always edgy around me. I want her to get in touch with India. We'll need someone from the family at some point. Already there's no one to contest the parliamentary seat from Ayatlochanapur. Get her to sort herself out. Creative writing! Emigrés at Home! What is this nonsense!'

At the time, it didn't occur to me to ask how Chamunda would have known the name of Sanyogita's creative writing group. Nor did I think she was purging her guilt as she spoke. I thought she was acting with her niece's best interests at heart.

Raunak Singh appeared a moment later with a cordless telephone.

'Right, baba. I must go. I'll see you in Delhi.'

I sat in the courtyard a while longer, looking at the flashing tree, and got up only when I saw Chamunda, now in a turquoise sari adorned with reflective, gold-rimmed flowers, go out of the house for the last time, followed by a small entourage.

Aakash had not emerged from the gym. When I went in a few minutes later, he was working out himself, barefooted, barechested, in just his jeans.

'Hi, man. How's you doing, man?' he said, swinging his arms up in bicep curls.

'Fine,' I said, and sat down on a workout bench.

'It feels so good. I can't tell you. It feels like I haven't worked out in weeks. Everything's gone. Look, look,' he said, flexing a tricep, which emerged obediently like a great vein in his arm.

'Aakash, it's fine, really.'

'And chest,' he said, shrinking his face and pushing out his pectorals.

'Also fine.'

'But abs are really gone, no?' He pulled down the skin from his stomach and the faint outline of a six-pack emerged, the beauty spot on it, reminding me that I had seen it before.

Then he looked hard at my reflection, and seeing perhaps some fatigue, some sorrow in my face, he stopped and turned round. 'You're all right? No?' he asked with concern. 'Not angry with me, I hope. Chamunda Devi told you what happened between us?'

'No.'

His face cleared.

'You're upset this is our last night.' He laughed. 'You were getting comfortable. Come on, I'm going to cheer you up. We're going to do something I used to do with my brother when we were children.'

'Aakash, I'm fine.'

'No, no, no. I can see there's a problem. Come on.'

With this, he pulled me out of the gym. The house was in half-light. It was caught in that special Indian hour when the day has gone and the servants are still to turn on the lights. Under the cover of this dusk hour, Aakash stole into the dimly lit pantry, past a few Nepalese maids, and hunted round for something. Not finding what he wanted, he stuck his head out and said, 'Sister, where is the wine kept?' She pointed him to another area of the kitchen, and not wishing to break momentum, he rushed over there. The sight of many bottles of wine of varying quality confused him.

'Aatish, help me out,' he whispered.

'Choose something from the top.'

He stood on his tiptoes and pulled out a bottle of wine. It looked Californian and expensive. It had a single red drop falling against an off-white label. Around the drop, as if it had broken the surface of the label, were faint ripples, also in off-white.

'Mod . . . mod . . .'

'Modicum.'

'Good?' Aakash asked.

'Probably.'

'Great. Let's go,' he said, taking two glasses from a shelf.

We made our way up the internal staircase to the first floor. When we reached the landing, Aakash whispered, 'Now, really quiet.'

We tiptoed past an open doorway, in which Sanyogita, now in darkness, could be seen still in front of the computer. Two or three doors down, Aakash gently slid back the bolt of a room I hadn't seen so far. The light outside had become so dim that

I could barely make it out. A kind of purple gloom spread through the room and only the silver of a mirror at the far end was visible.

'Fuck,' Aakash said, a moment after we entered, 'I forgot the screw thing. I'll go back. You wait here.'

Before I could protest, he had slipped out, leaving me in the empty room. As my eyes slowly adjusted, I could make out a crystal dressing table in one corner, a dark wooden cupboard from the fifties and an old four-poster Calcutta bed with a white bedspread. I wandered ahead absent-mindedly, opened a wide, heavy door with a long brass handle, and found myself in a dressing room. Past a further door, there was a high-ceilinged bathroom, with an art-deco floor of black, white and beige stone arranged in a large rhombus shape. Great panels of mirror, screwed into the wall, whose silver had rusted and fallen away, stood over a black bathtub, and steel capsule-shaped lights threw low-voltage shadows over the room.

I was still taking in the bathroom when I heard Aakash enter behind me.

'So you've found it,' he said. 'Good boy.'

He pushed me into the room and locked the door. The bottle of wine was open. He poured me a glass and sat me down on a cane chair against the wall. Then, still only in his jeans, he leaned across the vast bathtub and opened the taps. There were some bath salts on the edge, which he smelt suspiciously before scattering them in large handfuls into the bath, turning the few inches of water cloudy.

As the bath began to fill, he sat down on the edge of it and took a large sip of wine.

'It's good, man!' he said.

It was very good – heavy and smooth.

The moment overcame him, and as if wondering how it was that life had brought him into such varied situations, had shown him both poverty and luxury, he said, always with that special ability to explain complicated problems in simple material terms, 'Now Chamunda Devi, she smokes Dunhills, right?'

'Right.'

He nodded. 'On Marlboro packets the price is shown, on Benson the price is shown, but on Dunhill there is no price.' He took out a packet from his pocket, and twirling it in his hand, showed me it had no price. 'What does that mean?'

I thought it was a rhetorical question and didn't answer, but he pressed me for a response.

'I don't know.'

'That it's imported! Now people might say,' he said, taking on the voice of an impressed observer, '"Right, so she smokes Dunhills, she must be very rich." They don't stop to think, why does this person smoke Dunhills?'

Again, I thought I was not meant to give an answer, but Aakash waited for one.

'Because of the length, the quality of the tobacco?' I offered.

'Right,' he replied, a little disappointed. 'But those people will say, "Such and such person smokes Marlboro, that's all right, not bad." My brother smokes Benson, but Benson you can buy loose. Dunhill, you have to buy a whole packet at a time. "So, good, this person must be pretty rich." What they don't see,' Aakash said, seeing perhaps some confusion in my face, 'is that the person who smokes Dunhills might also smoke Gold Flake should the need arise.'

At this point the bath was more than half-full and the clouded water was steaming up the mirror.

'Let's get in,' Aakash said abruptly. 'I'll explain in a minute.'

I didn't question him, but undressed to my underwear. Aakash watched me the entire time. When I took a step towards the bath, he said, 'Come on, man. You insulting me? I'm not a fucking gay. Take your underwear off. This is like something I would do with my brother.'

I took my underwear off and put one foot into the bath. It was still very hot and I could keep only one foot in at a time, even as they began to tingle from the heat. I was able slowly to manage both, then to lower myself in. Aakash watched, smiled with satisfaction, then seeing I had left my wine by the chair, went over and brought it to me. When I was up to my neck, he took off his jeans and stood for a minute on the edge of the bath, looking at himself in the browning mirror. He watched himself take a sip of wine, rubbed his body with his other hand, pulled at his foreskin, which had become small and shrunken, then let himself sink into the bath.

'So I was saying,' he said, once we were both in the cloudy water, our knees sometimes touching, our bodies mostly sub-merged but occasionally floating to the top like refuse, 'that everyone is in their correct place and working accordingly.'

In the suspense of the filling bath, I had missed the importance of his words. I hadn't seen that behind the rambling about tobacco and brands was a philosophical, almost Hindu, way of dealing with the problem of inequality. The world to Aakash was not illusion; it was real and material, and he was hungry for it. But it was impossible to live in India, especially the new and shaken-up India, without having a way of coping with its inequalities. Zafar had his idea of the poet, and though Aakash had a corres-ponding idea, a new idea, of himself as a trainer, to which he was willing to ascribe Hindu notions of duty, he also had some-thing else. He had his high idea of himself as a Brahmin. With it came an innate acceptance of fate and the inequality of men. And even though, in the new scheme, Aakash's caste was not on top, he saw this more as a practical problem than a philosophical one. He said, 'So now what am I to do, if I don't have money? Perhaps the day won't be far off when I'll have more money than the people who were to be my in-laws, perhaps even more than you. And what will they say then? "Fine, you can marry my daughter"?'

Interrupting him, I said, 'You loved her a lot, didn't you, Ash-man?'

'Yes, man,' he said warmly. 'She would have been a great wife. You know, when you're upgrading yourself, many people try to make you feel small, make you feel you're nothing. But with her by my side, I would have felt strong.'

I was won over. His calm, the preternatural strength of his nerve didn't seem out of place. It was as if it flowed from his unshakeable belief in the preordained. And his own gritty modern story, with its amorality and sudden reversals, didn't seem so far away from the stories I had heard around him, like those of his ancestor and of Tara and Rukmani. In fact those stories were like a fount for his own. And when things were at their worst, I felt sure they gave him his power to switch off, taking consolation on the one hand in the disinterested work of fate and on the other in the always auspicious light of his star.

We had made our way through half the red wine; we were both drained from the heat, lying back in the vast bath, our penises bobbing limply to the surface.

That was where I should have left things. But in that deep moment of relaxation it suddenly occurred to me to ask, 'So then what was the solution you gave Chamunda?'

Aakash half raised his head, his dark face flushed, and said, 'It was simple, really. I told Chamunda about the threat Megha's brother made a few nights before. Yes, she told me about it in the end,' he added seeing the surprise form in my face. 'Oh, and also I drew her attention to a certain short story – what was it called? – "The Ass –". . . "The Ass –" . . . you know the one?' he said, and laughed.

Seconds later, there was a great banging on the door outside.

Epilogue

The sea changed from green to brown; oily, rainbow patterns ran over its surface. Red-bottomed, rusting freighters, some with Russian and Arab names, came into view. Then tall white buildings and the pale red domes of the Taj Hotel. A terrorist attack had left its façade blackened, its windows boarded up. There was now heavy security outside. Bombay's mud-coloured water sloshed around us, bringing up plastic bottles and rose petals. A businessman's yacht prevented us from docking. The passengers on the ferry stared in wonder at its white body, darkened windows and European crew. We rocked in the brown water for a few minutes more, then gingerly disembarked. I was on the three p.m. flight to Delhi.

Uttam was there to pick me up at the other end. There was new weather in Delhi. The winter had dried out, and though the silk cotton's fleshy flowers were yet to fill with their coral colour, the months of flowering trees yet to come, there was an unruly wind blowing, carrying in its wilfulness, rather than in its temperature, hints of summer. Delhi was my city. I knew its every mood, its every colour; it could only surprise me now on hidden levels when, like a spy agency, it would unseal from some shade-filled crescent, dark as a forest, a new memory.

But I couldn't think of that Delhi. It was another casualty of the ending romance. And Sanyogita, as if claiming it as part of her settlement, chose to meet in Lodhi Gardens. We came to it now from different directions: I, from the Lutyens's Delhi end; she, from the Jorbagh end. I had walked there every day when I lived in Delhi. Her suggesting we meet there felt like an appropriation. Trying to gauge the fine meanings in these messages – her new assertiveness, her calm – I became aware before entering the park that our relationship was over.

In the days that followed the night at the safe house, I took my mother up on a long-standing offer to visit her in Alibaug, at my stepfather's and her house by the sea. I wanted both to be in India but to hold it at bay. I found myself wishing for the oblivion of my childhood, for the inevitability of my surroundings.

I might have stayed indefinitely at that house by the sea, with its dim view of Bombay and its blackened beach, on to which the carcasses of turtles and dolphins occasionally washed up, had Sanyogita, some eight weeks after my arrival, not called. All that had happened over the past year must have clarified for her too. And released from a cycle with me, she decided to be released for good.

She always wore a fig-scented perfume. But not that day. And other small things were different too. She dressed warmly, and for comfort, though it was not cold. Normally she would have worn her light, pretty clothes as soon as it was warm. Her long-ish black hair was twisted into a single plait and pulled over her left shoulder. Her smile with its tinge of sadness seemed now in sadness to be cheerful. It also had a humorous or ironic colour, as if projecting some fairy-tale notion that this inversion was the greatest sadness of all. It was as if she had dismantled the person she had been before. And it felt both like a defence and a renewal. I thought I saw in her face relief that it was over.

It prevented me from making any kind of case. It felt too much to overturn the serenity of the evening. We met as we'd met many times before; the only difference was that we wouldn't meet again. It was a small park, but intricate, and we walked many times around it. We walked past the bare tombs with their line of glazed turquoise tiles hanging on over the centuries. There was bougainvillea, the avenue of white-trunked palms and an old bridge of high pointed arches. We stood there over a mossy pond.

Thinking only of her words from the night before, obsessed with them now, I said at last, 'Is it because of what you said last night, about not being able to compete with the other intimacies in my life?'

'Not only,' she replied, 'not only,' making me feel that the passion from the night before had gone out of her. 'My feelings have changed,' she said again.

'Overnight?'

'No, not overnight. Over many months.'

'Why didn't you tell me before?'

'I didn't want to believe that they had.'

It was so beguiling an answer. I felt our emotional equivalency evaporate.

'Have you heard from Aakash?' she asked with no rancour.

'Come on. I hope this is not about –'

'No, no, really, no. I'm just curious.'

I could see she was not lying.

After Aakash revealed the secret of Kris's homosexuality to Chamunda, and Chamunda, with his short story in hand, revealed it to the press, a new motive had arisen for the murder. 'Brother kills sister,' the *Hindustan Times* said, 'after she discovered he was a gay.' Another paper wrote, 'Sister dies for threatening to expose homosexual ring'. Lurid extracts from the story had appeared in all the papers. And though this was not enough to incriminate Kris, it was enough to check the public support that had grown after his arrest. Shabby still fought on, but the energy behind the cause drained away. Aakash, who understood the sensibilities of the newly prying society better than anyone else – knew its values had not caught up with its new degree of self-knowledge – would also have known the contempt such a revelation would arouse in people's hearts.

'He always lands on his feet,' Sanyogita said, smiling. 'Look what I saw today, driving through Sectorpur.'

She took out a folded piece of paper from her pocket and handed it to me. It was thin, crinkly and glue-stained. I opened it and saw that it was an election poster. On a green background were, as in a family tree, oval-shaped pictures of the party leaders. Chamunda, once again in saffron chiffon, towered in the foreground. And at her feet, a lotus seeming to form a mane round his head, was a picture of Aakash, looking blacker than usual. It made me think of Megha and the little sweeper. 'Loin! loin! What does a loin do?' Poor Megha. Her jovial memory seemed so distant now.

'Did you know he was contesting?'

'Yes,' I lied. 'What as?'

'Oh, just as an MLA, but still. Chamunda gave him a ticket as repayment for what he did for her.'

'Didn't the press hassle her about that, giving a ticket to a man who was almost charged with murder?'

'Are you joking? It's virtually a credential.'

We had come to the green turnstile leading out of the park.

'And Kris?' I asked.

'Kris is free,' Sanyogita replied. 'The CBI got him out. After Aakash no longer needed him, Sparky Punj became Kris's lawyer; they were friends anyway. But the case will go on. I doubt they'll ever find the real guy. It's easier that way.'

'But won't it hurt Chamunda in the election?'

'It could. And so maybe they will find someone to pin it on.'

Politicians' white cars were parked outside the garden's gates. Thin ladies in bright colours carried shallow dishes of cement to and from a mound of mud half-filled with water. Sanyogita, picking her way past a column of men in fraying vests digging up the pavement, walked towards a chauffeur-driven car.

'Sanyogita?' I called out.

She turned round.

'How's the garden?'

'Oh!' she said, stopping herself from saying 'baby', 'it's fine. Flourishing.'

'And my study?'

She smiled sadly at me, seeing now where this line of conversation was headed.

'It's fine too,' she said quickly, as if worried I was going to ask next about her toes or the family of porcelain elephants.

Through the tinted window of the chauffer-driven car I could make out the profiles of Ra and Mandira. They had come to pick her up. They saw me and waved, but didn't get out. Nothing like one's girlfriend's friends to bring home the pain of a break-up. Sanyogita turned round once more, smiled apologetically, then got into the car and drove way.

It was Eid that night and I finally made it to Zafar's house. I was glad not to have seen it before. It would have destabilized me. Zafar lived in the Sui Valan section of the old city of Delhi. He picked me up outside Delite cinema, admonishing me for bringing him flowers and sweets. As we entered the old city, some men from the abattoir were unloading a truck of meat. Our rickshaw splashed through a pale brownish-red puddle, its smell and the frenzy of flies giving it away as blood. Narrow streets, crowded that night with bright kerosene lights and people in their new clothes, led us to Zafar's house. We arrived in front of a darkened entrance. Near an open drain, a bitch tended to her family of fluffy grey puppies. A flight of steep stone stairs, chipped at the edges, led up to a pale green door and a landing lit by a single light.

Zafar had warned me many times on the way how small his house was. 'But the hearts of the people in it are big,' he now added. I had imagined his house as a small flat with a kitchen, a bathroom, two rooms perhaps, with at least room enough to stand up and walk around. But Zafar's house was just a single room, no bigger than a carpet, covered with sheets of checked cloth. Its greasy blue walls were high and there were shelves all around, stacked to the ceiling with hard suitcases and trunks, so that it felt almost like a godown. Everything was neatly in its place: a sewing machine with a pink satin cover; a little shelf with holy Zam Zam water, oils and a pair of scissors; green-covered copies of Zafar's new book. Zafar's family of five couldn't physically fit in the room. That was why he slept on the floor of the magazine office where I had visited him on the day of the demonstration.

'I once had enough money to buy a better place,' he said as we sat down, 'but in 1997, the year when the accounts became computerized, my wife fell from the stairs and all my savings were spent on her treatment.'

She was there now, a fat woman with curly hair and pale skin. She got on her haunches and tried rolling out an oilcloth with roses on it, matching the large red flowers on her black kameez. Then wincing, she stopped and sat back down.

'My back,' she said to her husband, who watched her closely. She was smiling, her face was made up, but her eyes suggested damage, almost as if unused to emotions other than distress.

Zafar looked over at his wife, around the room and then at me. 'I'm thinking of a complete renovation,' he said with his wheezing laugh, 'thinking of replacing everything.'

'We'll replace you before we replace ammi,' an offended daughter said from the kitchen area, which was a three-foot ledge with pulses and grains stacked high on one side. Its stone surface was used for washing, the water disappearing through an opening in the floor.

Zafar laughed again. The daughter crawled over and finished unrolling the oilcloth. Another brought out warm bread and meat curry. Zafar gestured to his young son, Atif, who sat slumped in one corner watching cartoons on a twelve-inch television, to come over.

'All he does is watch these cartoons,' Zafar said to me as he joined us in our circle. The boy had a thin face, a squint and thick glasses. 'Speak to him in English; he's got to learn. He's meant to be learning in school, but the teachers are very bad. They can hardly speak it themselves. I don't want another generation to grow up without English. Look at how I've lost out.'

I tried speaking to him in English, but he became quiet and ashamed. He replied softly a few seconds later in perfect Urdu.

The men ate, the women watched. I felt embarrassed and asked them why they weren't eating; they said they already had. Zafar turned gently to me and said, 'Between Aatish and Atif, I make no difference, you're both like my sons. Where have you been all these days? You could have at least called your old teacher to say you were OK.'

I used the only excuse I knew would work with him. 'I've been trying to write.'

His face brightened. 'Writing something modern, I hope,' he said, 'something fresh and original. Don't hark back to the past. Look forward.' Then using the English words 'fiction' and 'non-fiction' in both instances to mean fiction, good and bad, he said, 'In the way men live today, the pressures upon them – and there are great strains and injustices – you'll find fiction. The past is all non-fiction.'

'And write in English?'

'In English,' he answered firmly. 'The Indian languages are finished; or, at least, literature in them is finished. When I began there were magazines, poetry meetings, the progressive writers were still around, poets could write for the screen, there were readers, libraries, critics – all gone, swept away in one generation. It's a very fragile thing, you know, literature; it needs an infrastructure. You can't spend your life writing into the dark like me.' The thought of his own writing evoked a memory. 'I once wrote a string of couplets,' he said, 'that all ended in "turned to water". Very hard to do, you can imagine, to make each couplet finish that way. "In the end I stayed loyal, my friends, to the ways of the age. But in this effort my blood turned to water." One more,' he said eagerly, feeling perhaps that I had not gauged his meaning, '"In the toil of a lifetime, each strand flowed away, all moorings were lost, Zafar, when the road turned to water."'

He had finished eating and was sitting back against the wall, smoking a Win cigarette. One daughter was clearing away our steel plates and wrapping up the oilcloth; another was making tea on a tiny stove. I asked to wash my hands. Atif rose and opened what I thought was a cupboard door. The bathroom was a single metal sheet, three feet by three feet, leading to a drain. Its fetid air filled the room. Everything was hanging – towels, toothbrushes, clothes, including a green bra, all heaped over a nylon rope. Atif poured out the water from a red plastic urn, then handed me a rag to dry my hands. Its strange colour made me look more closely at it: it was grey, but in a frayed bottom corner, where a button and a pleat still remained, there was a deep indigo stain.

Back in the little room porcelain cups of frothy tea were being passed around. Zafar looked at me expectantly, as if hoping to have generated a response of some sort.

'So,' he said finally, 'is it coming along well?'

'No, not really,' I replied. 'I keep coming up against barriers.'

'What kind of barriers?'

'Of language, of class, of having my material in one place, my readership in another. I can't seem to string it all together.'

Zafar nodded, and putting out the Win in a wooden ashtray, said, 'Can I offer you a suggestion?'

'Please.'

'Write in the first person.'

'Really? Why?' I asked, surprised at his specificity.

'When the terrain is unfamiliar,' he said, 'the world new and freshly uncovered, which at this present moment in India it has to be, the first-person narrator plays the guide. He eases the reader's journey through this uncharted territory; his development becomes part of the narrative. Look at Manto; he even had a narrator called Manto.

'This, at least,' he said, shaking with laughter, 'is the humble opinion of a man who's never written a line of prose in his life.' Then serious once more, he added, 'And lastly there's the secret ingredient for which no one, no matter how experienced, can help you.'

'What's that?'

'Luck.' He smiled and offered me a Win.

★

It was ten p.m. when I came back to my mother's flat. I had left it and returned to it so many times that I felt like a stranger there now. Still, there was something about seeing the lights on in my mother's study, the room unchanged from my childhood, that gave me the special pleasure of anonymity in a familiar place, something like what a late-night traveller might feel at entering a service flat he has used before. It was quiet but for the occasional swinging of the kitchen door: Shakti closing up for the night, switching off the drawing-room lights, leaving water at my bed-side.

My senses, in part from the emotions of the day, in part from being assailed in the old city, still smarted. I was at the end of a cycle, but full of the energy of beginnings. It felt suffocating to suddenly be home early, with no outlet, with no plans, with no one to call. After pacing around the flat, feeling cramped by Shakti's nocturnal rituals, I settled down in the study and mirth-lessly re-read old emails.

I had had one that day from the writer and his wife. I had written to him regularly since our meeting five months before. He never wrote back, but his wife often did, communicating his responses to my emails, and even something of his style, using words like decay and debase. That morning she had written, 'We are laughing so hard that we will write after we digest your FABULOUS emails slowly by reading them again. Vijaipal says you have a flair for the comic! He thinks you should write comedy; India has no real comedians.'

This, I must confess, came as something of a shock. I hadn't meant for the emails to be comic. The emails they had found so funny were weekly supplements of the Aakash story, told to them complete, with details of his secret marriage to Megha, the jagran, the murder and his now steady rise.

In the year I had been back, I had barely got used to seeing India on TV. I don't mean the state-run channels of my childhood, but real India and real TV. Drunken mobs of shiny-faced men in saffron, like men after festival, at once satiated and hungry. Fires, black smoke, garbage in the streets, meanly built houses, cement and pale land. All known to be there before, but for the first time on twenty-four-hour networks with handsome presenters and millennial music.

And now, my dark friend, in a striped T-shirt and faded jeans, as TVDelhi's red and gold fires burned below him. Watching him, his ease, his instinctive gestures, his raised pectorals, his language, I felt once again the removal that had made me want to be near him in the first place. He spoke in his local Haryana dialect with which he had so often made me laugh. He judged perfectly how his eloquence in this rough dialect would sound. Behind him, a littered maidan showed the end of an election rally. I felt burdened by the secret that I had known him when he was just a trainer in Junglee gym.

Soon after, he rang. I hadn't heard from him in weeks. He must have guessed I'd be watching.

'Did you see it?' he said, his voice full of adrenalin.

'Yes.'

'You'll come, no?'

'Come to what?'

'To help, to see it, to give me support.'

'No,' I answered, mustering up all my courage.

'Man, whaddyou saying?' Then switching to Hindi, he said, 'Whatever problems we've had recently, it doesn't mean that you won't come now.' He switched back and said, laughing, 'This is the golden opportunity.'

I asserted myself again, said goodbye and hung up the phone. I was sure I wouldn't hear from him for a while now, not unless he thought he could weaken me again. I continued to flick joylessly through the hundreds of channels in dozens of languages that Tata Sky had made available. For many weeks now, Aakash's friend, former client and lawyer, Sparky Punj, had also been on television. He had become something of an expert on the case. I had seen him so many times from my stepfather's study in Alibaug that I almost didn't stop flicking channels when I saw him, all in white, with his handlebar moustache and his collapsible spectacles. He spoke in his usual self-assured way. 'Definitely a Maoist connection. Hundred per cent,' he said. 'Do you know that Jai used to drive a scooter in Delhi, which meant he was earning some thirteen to fourteen grand a month easily, right? Now, tell me, why would he give that up for two thousand, seven hundred a month at the Aggarwals' residence unless he was using their house to lie low in?'

The young reporter, in a white salwar kurta with a purple dupatta, said, 'But Sparky, sir, what do you ascribe as a motive?'

'Motive? What motive? The girl comes home late night, catches Jai and his associates drinking, plotting, getting up to God knows what. That's it, that's the motive. There might be a molestation angle, of course, but it could just be the straightforward rage of a young man.' Then by alluding to the curved Nepalese knife, he hinted at his views on the Nepalese. 'You know, a general tendency to settle a dispute with a khukri rather than with a discussion.'

The journalist was impressed.

The camera turned to a weeping woman. She was large, with warm brown skin, waxy hair and slightly jowly cheeks. I didn't know her immediately, in her sari and bindi, but when she took the mike from the reporter and I saw her nails with their white tips and tiger print I nearly shouted out loud. The Begum of Sectorpur! 'My son is innocent,' she cried. 'This is all the scheme of the girl's family to get their son off. They know they can target us because we're foreigners in this country.'

It was moving that even now, even when it would have been clear to her who had found her son his job with the Aggarwals, and who in all likelihood had now helped incriminate him, she didn't blame Aakash. The channel showed images of the day's headlines. The *Times of India*'s read: 'The Butler Did It, After All!'

'Shakti!' I yelled. 'Shakti!'

He came in a moment later.

'Please bring me the *Times of India*.'

He nodded moodily, disappeared and came back with the paper.

I stared for many moments at its front page. It always had a single colour picture in the top half. And there, at the centre of it, was the slim, dark man, with a Nepalese cast of face, seeming to me at once faceless and like a figure from fable. I looked closer. His skin was soft, with bronze lustre, his face, finely made and feminine, and his prominent lips curled into a smile as mean as an incision. There was something victorious about him. Even as Jhaatkebaal policemen manhandled him, his laughter seemed to ring out. Under his tattered denim jacket, he wore a purple shirt on which, like patriotic explosions on a night sky, were daubs of pink.

And seeing that face smile out at me from its rectangle of newsprint, I yelled once again to Shakti, this time to bring me some milky coffee, and after a year of paralysis and stagnation, of not knowing how I would digest India, I sat down to write of my arrival in Delhi, in those months before summer, the months of flowering trees, when in the icy-white cabin of a Jet Airways flight I had wept tears of fear and joy.

March–November 2008